B

Dear Reader,

If you are holding this book in your hand (and I'm going to be presumptuous and assume that you are), that means that the little girl who dreamed of becoming a writer has made it.

She didn't think she would make it when she sat down to write *Vicious* almost a decade ago. By then, I was no longer a girl. A young, tired mom, yes. One who was just crazy and sleep-deprived enough to think that maybe, somewhere, anywhere, someone shared her love for delicious, decadent, morally cinder alpha males who are unapologetically themselves.

Vicious, Jaime, Dean, Trent, and Roman grow on you like fungus. Slowly but steadily, and without you noticing until it is too late. Unlike fungus, though, they age quite well as the books progress and grow into the men they strive to be.

If I could go back to that girl who dreamed of writing books, who dared to imagine said books would be in bookstores, I would tell her not to worry. That she would turn out alright. Because that girl? She is me.

And to you, the reader, I say thank you. For giving her a chance. For making dreams come true. Most of all—for sharing her passion for a good, steamy romance novel with a lot of heart and (hopefully) just as much soul.

All my love, always,

L Shen
xoxo

ALSO BY L.J. SHEN

SCANDALOUS

L.J. SHEN

Bloom books

Published by Bloom Books, an imprint of Sourcebooks
P.O. Box 4410, Naperville, Illinois 60567-4410
(630) 961-3900
sourcebooks.com

Originally self-published in 2017 by L.J. Shen.

Cataloging-in-Publication Data is on file with the Library of Congress.

Printed and bound in the United States of America.
PAH 10 9 8 7 6 5 4 3 2

If he touched her, he couldn't talk to her.
If he loved her, he couldn't leave.
If he spoke, he couldn't listen.
If he fought, he couldn't win.

—*Arundhati Roy,* The God of Small Things

PLAYLIST

"Believer"—Imagine Dragons
"Girls and Boys"—Blur
"Just the Two of Us"—Grover Washington Jr.
"Pacific Coast Highway"—Kavinsky
"Sweater Weather"—The Neighborhood
"Lonely Boy"—The Black Keys
"Shape (of My Heart)"—Sugababes cover

NOTE

Seahorses prefer to swim in pairs with their tails linked together. They're one of the rare monogamous animals and engage in an eight-hour courtship dance that, among other things, includes swimming side by side and changing colors. They're romantic, elegant, and fragile.

Just like love.

They remind us that love is meant to be wild, just like the ocean.

PROLOGUE
EDIE

Gluttony.

Plural—gluttonies
1: excess in eating or drinking
2: greedy or excessive indulgence: "accused the
nation of energy gluttony"

The worst of the seven deadly sins. In my opinion, anyway. And my opinion was the one that mattered in that moment, under the unforgiving sun of SoCal on a May afternoon on Todos Santos's promenade, when I was in desperate need of some cash. Leaning against the white railing separating the bustling boardwalk from the shimmering ocean and dazzling yachts, I people-watched.

Fendi, Dior, Versace, Chanel, Burberry, Bulgari, Louboutin, Rolex.

Greed. Excess. Corruption. Vice. Fraud. Deception.

I judged them. The way they drank their ten-buck organic smoothies and glided on custom-made multicolored skateboards signed by Tony Hawk. I judged them, knowing full well they couldn't do the same to me. I was in hiding. Veiled beneath a thick black hoodie, my hands shoved deep inside my pockets. I wore black skinny jeans, an old pair of unlaced Dr. Martens, and a tattered JanSport backpack held together with safety pins.

I looked androgynous.

I moved like a ghost.

I *felt* like a hoax.

And today, I was about to do something that'd make living with myself harder.

As with any dangerous game, there were rules to abide by: no children, no elderly, no struggling average folk. I thrived on the rich, targeting the prototypes of my parents. The women with the Gucci bags and the men in the Brunello Cucinelli suits. The ladies with the poodles peeking out from their studded Michael Kors handbags and the gentlemen who looked like they were comfortable spending on a cigar what a normal person would put toward their monthly rent.

Spotting potential victims at the promenade was embarrassingly easy. Todos Santos was the richest town in California, and much to the old money's dismay, nouveau riches like my father had made this piece of land their home, armed with monstrous, Italian-imported vehicles and enough jewelry to sink a battleship.

I shook my head, staring at the explosion of colors, scents, and tanned half-clothed bodies. *Focus, Edie, focus.*

Prey. A good hunter could smell it from miles away.

My meal for the day had passed me briskly, unknowingly drawing attention to herself. She threw her head back, revealing a straight row of pearly whites. A middle-aged, Chanel-wearing trophy wife, wrapped head to toe in the latest season's garments. I wasn't big on fashion, but my father loved spoiling his beloved mistresses with luxurious garb and parading them around at social events, introducing them as his *very* personal assistants. My mother would buy these designer items herself in a desperate bid to resemble the younger women who entertained him. I knew wealth when I saw it. And this woman? She wasn't hungry. Not for food and not for love, the only two things that mattered.

Little did she know, her money was going to buy me love. Her soon-to-be-empty wallet was going to fill my heart to the brim.

"I've been dying for a duck salad at the Brasserie. Think we can go there tomorrow? Maybe Dar will tag along," she drawled, fluffing her chin-length platinum bob with her manicured hand.

Her back was already to me when I noticed her arm was linked with that of a tall, dark, and handsome type at least twenty years her junior. Built like Robocop and dressed like a dapper David Beckham. Was he her boy toy? Husband? Old friend? Son? It made little to no difference to me.

She was the perfect victim: distracted, disordered, and overbearing. Parting ways with her wallet would be merely an inconvenience for this lady. She probably had a PA or some other form of poor, unfortunate soul on her payroll to deal with the consequences. Someone who would order new credit cards and issue a new driver's license and unburden her from the nuisance of bureaucracy.

Someone like Camila.

Stealing was much like walking a tightrope. The secret was in your poise and ability to not look into the abyss or, in my case, the victim's eyes. I was lean, short, and nimble. I navigated through the throng of boisterous teenyboppers in bikinis and families licking ice cream, my eyes trained on the black-and-gold YSL bag dangling from her arm.

Sounds became muffled, bodies and food trucks vanished from my vision, and all I saw were that bag and my goal.

Recalling everything I'd learned from Bane, I inhaled deeply and lunged for the purse. I yanked it from her arm and made a beeline to one of the many alleyways slicing the shops and restaurants on the boardwalk. I didn't look back. I ran blindly, desperately, furiously.

Tap, tap, tap, tap. My Docs were heavy against the sizzling concrete beneath me, but the consequences of not coming up with the money I needed sat heavier on my heart. The thick sound of girls laughing on the promenade evaporated as I put more space between my target and me.

I could have been one of them. I still can. Why am I doing this? Why can't I just let it go?

One more corner to round and I'd be in my car, flipping the bag open and examining my treasure. Drunk on adrenaline and high on endorphins, a hysterical laugh bubbled from my throat. I hated mugging people. I hated the feeling that accompanied the act even more. But most of all—I hated myself. What had become of me? Yet the liberating feeling of doing something bad and being good at getting away with it shot an arrow of elation straight to my heart.

My stomach dropped in relief at the sight of my car. The old, black Audi TT my father had purchased from his business partner Baron Spencer was the only thing he'd given me in the past three years, but even this gift was loaded with expectation. Seeing less of me in his mansion was his goal in life. Most nights, he opted for not coming home. Problem solved.

I scooped my keys from my backpack, panting the rest of the way like a sick dog.

I was mere inches from the driver's door when my world spun in place and my knees gave out. It took me a few seconds to realize I hadn't stumbled on my own gaucherie. A firm, large hand twisted me by the shoulder, knocking the air out of my lungs. The hand grabbed my arm in a bruising grip and pulled me into the alleyway between a fast-food joint and a French boutique before I could open my mouth and do something. Shout, bite, or worse.

I dragged my boots in the opposite direction, desperately trying to wiggle free, but this guy was twice my size—and all muscle. I was too blinded by rage to take a good look at his face.

Chaos brewed in my gut, shot flames to my eyes, and momentarily blinded me. He slammed me against a building, and I hissed, feeling the impact from my neck to my tailbone. Instinctively, I sent my arms out, trying to claw at his face, kicking and screaming. My fear was a storm. Sailing through it was impossible. The stranger clutched my wrists and crashed them above my head, pinning them to the cool cement.

This is it, I thought. *This is where you end. Over a stupid purse, on a Saturday afternoon, on one of the most legendarily crowded beaches in California.*

Flinching, I waited for his fist to connect with my face, or worse—for his rotten breath to hover over my mouth, for his hand to yank my pants down.

Then the stranger chuckled.

I furrowed my brow, my eyes narrowing as I tried to regain focus and blink away the terror.

He came to me in pieces, like a painting in the works. His gray-blue eyes were the first to pop out from behind the fog of fear. They were sapphire and silver swirled together, the color of a moonstone. Next were his straight nose and symmetrical lips, his cheekbones sharp enough to cut diamonds. He was pungently masculine and intimidating in his looks, but that was not what made me recognize him immediately. It was what rolled off of him in dangerous quantities, the menace and the ruggedness. He was a dark knight made of coarse material. Cruel in his silence and punishing in his confidence. I'd only met him once, at a barbecue at Dean Cole's house a few weeks ago, and we hadn't spoken a word to each other.

He hadn't spoken a word to anyone.

Trent Rexroth.

We were barely acquaintances, but every piece of information I knew about the guy, I also held against him. He was a millionaire, single, and therefore probably a playboy. He was, in short, the younger version of my father, which meant that I was interested in getting to know him as much as I was in catching cholera.

"You have five seconds to explain why you were trying to mug my mother." His voice was bone-dry, but his eyes? Fuming. "*Five.*"

His *mother.* Crap. I really was in trouble. Though I couldn't find it in me to regret my decision, I'd been spot-on. She was a white, rich woman from suburbia who wouldn't miss the cash or the bag. But it was unfortunate that my father's business partner for the past six months was her son.

"Let go of my wrists," I hissed through still-clenched teeth, "before I knee you in the balls."

"Four." He ignored me completely, squeezing my wrists harder together, his eyes daring me to do something we both knew I was too much of a coward to even try. I winced. He wasn't really hurting me, and he knew it. He squeezed just enough to make me seriously uncomfortable and scare the bejesus out of me.

No one had ever hurt me physically before. It was the unwritten rule of the rich and noble. You could ignore your child, send them off to boarding school in Switzerland, and leave them with the nanny until they reached eighteen, but God forbid you lay a hand on them. I looked around for the YSL bag, confusion and panic churning in my gut. Rexroth caught up with my plan quickly enough because he kicked the bag between us. It bumped into my boots with a thud.

"Don't get too attached to it, sweetheart. Three."

"My father would kill you if he knew you touched me," I sputtered, trying to regain balance. "I'm—"

"Jordan Van Der Zee's daughter," he cut in matter-of-factly, saving me the introduction. "Hate to break it to you, but I don't give two shits."

My father was in business with Rexroth and held 49 percent of Fiscal Heights Holdings, the company Trent had incorporated with his high school friends. It made Jordan a threat to the man in front of me, even if he wasn't exactly Rexroth's boss. Trent's intense frown confirmed he really wasn't scared. But I knew my father would flip his shit if he knew Trent had touched me. Jordan Van Der Zee rarely spared me a look, but when he did, it was in order to assert power over me.

I wanted to taunt Rexroth back. I wasn't even entirely sure why. Maybe because he was humiliating me—though part of me acknowledged I deserved it.

His eyes shot daggers at me, burning the skin wherever they landed. My cheeks blossomed into crimson, and it hit me hard because he was nearly twice my age and outrageously off-limits. I was feeling juvenile enough getting caught red-handed without the side bonus of feeling my thighs clench as his fingers dug into my wrists like he wanted to split them open and pop my veins out.

"What are you going to do? Hit me?" I jerked my chin up, my eyes, voice, *and* stance defiant. His mother was white, so his dad must be either Black or biracial. Trent was tall, built, and tanned. His black hair was buzzed close to the scalp, Marine-style, and he wore charcoal slacks, a collared white shirt, and a vintage Rolex. *Gorgeous prick. Stunning, arrogant bastard.*

"Two."

"You've been counting down from five for ten minutes, smart-ass," I informed him, one eyebrow arching. He let loose a grin so devilish, I swear it looked like he had fangs, dropping my wrists like they were on fire. I immediately collected one into my palm and rubbed it in circles. He hovered over me like a shadow, completing the countdown with a growl. "*One.*"

We both stared at each other, me in horror and him in amusement. My pulse skyrocketed, and I wondered what it looked like from the inside. If the ventricles in my heart were bursting with blood and adrenaline. He raised his hand teasingly slowly and tugged my hoodie down, letting my mane of long, wavy blond hair cascade all the way to my waist. My nerves shredded into ribbons at how exposed I felt. His eyes explored me lazily, like I was an item he was debating whether to buy at the Dollar Tree. I was a good-looking girl—a fact that both pleased and upset my parents—but Trent was a man, and I was a senior in high school, at least for the next two weeks. I knew rich men loved their women young, but jailbait was rarely their jam.

After a stretched beat, I broke the silence. "What now?"

"Now I wait." He almost caressed my cheek—almost—making

my eyes flutter and my heart loop in a way that provoked me to feel both younger and older than my years.

"Wait?" I knitted my brows. "Wait for what?"

"Wait until this leverage on you becomes useful, Edie Van Der Zee."

He knew my name. My Christian name. It was surprising enough that he recognized me as Jordan's daughter just from seeing me across the lawn at his friend's barbecue weeks ago, but this… This was oddly exciting. Why would Trent Rexroth know my name unless he'd asked for it? My father wouldn't talk about me at work. That was a hard fact. He tried to ignore my existence whenever he could.

"What could you possibly need from me?" I scrunched my nose, skeptical. He was a powerful, thirty-something mogul and so completely out of my league we weren't even playing on the same field. I wasn't being hard on myself. It was by choice. I could be rich like him—correction, I was potentially fifty times richer. I had the world at my feet, but I chose to kick it aside instead of making it my oyster, much to my father's consternation.

But Trent Rexroth didn't know that. Trent Rexroth didn't know that at all.

Under his arms and scrutiny, I felt incredibly alive. Rexroth leaned in my direction, his lips, made for poetry and sin and pleasure, smiling into the skin between my throat and my ear, and whispered, "What I need is to keep your father on a short leash. Congratulations, you've just reduced yourself to potential sacrifice."

The only thing I could think of when he moved away and escorted me to my car, gripping the back of my neck from behind like I was a wild animal in desperate need of taming, was that my life had just gotten so much more complicated.

He tapped the roof of the Audi and smiled through the rolled-down window, tipping his Wayfarers down. "Drive safe."

"Fuck you." My hands shook, trying to pull down the hand brake.

"Not in a million years, kid. You're not worth the jail time."

I was already eighteen, but it hardly made any difference. I stopped seconds short of spitting in his face, when he rummaged in his mother's bag and threw something small and hard into my car. "For the road. Friendly advice: Stay away from people's pockets and bags. Not everyone's as agreeable as I am."

He wasn't agreeable. He was the very definition of a jerk. Before I could fashion a comeback, he turned around and walked away, leaving a trail of intoxicating scent and interested women. I looked down at what he'd tossed in my lap, still dazed and disturbed by his last comment.

A Snickers bar.

In other words, he'd ordered me to chill—treating me like I was a child. *A joke.*

I drove away from the promenade straight to Tobago Beach, getting a small loan from Bane to pay my way through the next month. I was too distracted to try to hit another mark for some fast cash.

But that day changed something and, somehow, twisted my life in a direction I never knew it could take.

It was the day when I realized I hated Trent Rexroth.

The day when I put him on my shit list, with no possibility for parole.

And the day I realized I could still feel alive under the right arms.

Too bad they were also so, so wrong.

CHAPTER ONE
TRENT

She's a maze with no escape.
An ethereal, steady pulse. She's there, but just barely.
I love her so much I sometimes hate her.
And it terrifies me, because deep down, I know what she is.
An unsolvable puzzle.
And I know who I am.
The idiot who would try to fix her.
At any cost.

"How did you feel when you wrote it?" Sonya held the whiskey-ringed paper like it was her fucking newborn, a curtain of tears glittering in her eyes. The drama levels were high this session. Her voice was gauzy, and I knew what she was after. A breakthrough. A *moment.* That pivotal scene in a Hollywood flick, after which everything changed. The strange girl shakes off her inhibitions, the dad realizes he is being a cold-ass prick, and they work through their emotions, blah blah pass the Kleenex blah.

I scrubbed my face, glancing at my Rolex. "I was drunk off my ass when I wrote it, so I probably felt like a burger to dilute the alcohol," I deadpanned. I didn't talk much—big fucking surprise—that's why they called me the Mute. When I did, it was with Sonya, who knew my boundaries, or Luna, who ignored them and me.

"Do you get drunk often?"

Chagrined. That was Sonya's expression. She mostly kept it schooled, but I saw through the thick layers of makeup and professionalism.

"Not that it's any of your business, but no."

Loud silence lingered in the room. I strummed my fingers against my cell-phone screen, trying to remember whether I'd sent out that contract to the Koreans. I should have been nicer, seeing as my four-year-old daughter was sitting right beside me, witnessing this exchange. I should have been a lot of things, but the only thing I was, the only thing I could be outside work, was angry and furious and—*Why, Luna? What the fuck have I done to you?*—confused. How I'd become a thirty-three-year-old single dad who didn't have the time or the patience for any female other than his kid.

"Seahorses. Let's talk about them." Sonya laced her fingers together, changing the topic. She did that whenever my patience was strung out and about to snap. Her smile was warm but neutral, just like her office. My eyes skimmed the pictures hung behind her, of young, laughing children—the kind of bullshit you buy at IKEA— and the soft-yellow wallpaper, the flowery, polite armchairs. Was she trying too hard, or was I not trying hard enough? It was difficult to tell at this point. I shifted my gaze to my daughter and offered her a smirk. She didn't return it. Couldn't blame her.

"Luna, do you want to tell Daddy why seahorses are your favorite?" Sonya chirped.

Luna grinned at her therapist conspiratorially. At four, she didn't talk. At all. Not a single word or a lonely syllable. There was no problem with her vocal cords. In fact, she screamed when she was hurting and coughed when she was congested and hummed absentmindedly when a Justin Bieber song played on the radio (which, some would say, was tragic in itself.)

Luna didn't talk because she didn't *want* to talk. It was a psychological issue, not physical, stemming from hell-knows-what. What

I *did* know was that my daughter was different, indifferent, and unusual. People said she was "special" as an excuse to treat her like a freak. I was no longer able to shield her from the peculiar looks and questioning arched eyebrows. In fact, it was becoming increasingly difficult to brush off her silence as introversion, and I was beginning to grow tired of hiding it anyway.

Luna was, *is*, always will be outrageously smart. She'd scored higher than average on all the tests she'd been put through, and there had been too many to count. She understood every single word spoken to her. She was mute by choice, but she was too young to make that choice. Trying to talk her out of it was both impossible and ironic. Which was why I dragged my ass to Sonya's office twice a week in the middle of a workday, desperately trying to coax my daughter to stop boycotting the world.

"Actually, I can tell you exactly why Luna loves seahorses." Sonya pursed her lips, plastering my drunken note to her desk. Luna would sometimes speak a word or two when she and her therapist were all alone, but never when I was in the room. Sonya told me Luna had a languid voice, like her eyes, and that it was soft and delicate and perfect. She had no impediment at all. *"She just sounds like a kid, Trent. One day, you'll hear it, too."*

I cocked a tired eyebrow, propping my head on my hand as I stared at the busty redhead. I had three deals I needed to attend to back at work—four if I'd forgotten to send the contract to the Koreans—and my time was too fucking precious for seahorse talk.

"Yeah?"

Sonya reached across her desk, cupping my big bronzed hand in her small white one. "Seahorses are Luna's favorite animal because the male seahorse is the only animal in nature to carry the baby, and not the mother. The male seahorse is the one to incubate the offspring. To fall pregnant. To nest. Isn't that beautiful?"

I blinked a couple of times, slicing my gaze to my daughter. I was grossly unequipped to deal with women my own age, so taking care of Luna always felt like shooting a goddamn arsenal of bullets in the dark, hoping something would find the target. I frowned, searching my brain for something—anything, any-fucking-thing—that would put a smile on my daughter's face.

It occurred to me that social services would scoop her ass up and take her away from me had they known what an emotionally stunted dumbass I was.

"I…" I began to say. Sonya cleared her throat, jumping to my rescue.

"Hey, Luna? Why don't you help Sydney hang up some of the summer camp decorations outside? You have a great touch with design."

Sydney was the secretary at Sonya's practice. My daughter had warmed up to her, seeing as we spent a lot of time sitting in the reception area, waiting for our appointments. Luna nodded and hopped down from her seat.

My daughter was beautiful. Her caramel skin and light-brown curls made her deep-blue eyes shine like a lighthouse. My daughter was beautiful, and the world was ugly, and I didn't know how to help her.

And it killed me like cancer. Slowly. Surely. Savagely.

The door closed with a soft thud before Sonya trained her eyes on me, her smile fading.

I glanced at my watch again. "Are you coming over to fuck tonight or what?"

"Jesus, Trent." She shook her head, clasping the back of her neck with her laced fingers. I let her have her meltdown. This was a reoccurring issue with Sonya. For a reason beyond my grasp, she thought she could tell me off because she sometimes had my dick in her mouth. The truth was, every ounce of power she had over me was because of Luna. My daughter worshipped the ground Sonya walked on and allowed herself to smile more in her therapist's presence.

"I'll take that as a no."

"Why don't you take it as a wake-up call? Luna's love for seahorses is a way to say 'Daddy, I appreciate you for taking care of me.' Your daughter needs you."

"My daughter has me," I gritted through clenched teeth. It was the truth. What more could I have given Luna that I hadn't already? I was her dad when she needed someone to open the pickle jar and her mom when she needed someone to tuck her undershirt into her black ballet tights.

Three years ago, Luna's mother, Val, had put Luna in her crib, grabbed her keys and two large suitcases, and disappeared from our lives. We hadn't been together, Val and I. Luna was the product of a coked-up bachelor party in Chicago that had spun out of control. She was made in the back room of a strip club with Val straddling me while another stripper climbed on top of my face. Looking back, screwing a stripper bareback ought to have awarded me with some kind of a Guinness record for stupidity. I had been twenty-eight— not a kid by any stretch of the imagination—and smart enough to know what I was doing was wrong.

But at twenty-eight, I had still been thinking with my dick and my wallet.

At thirty-three, I was thinking with my brain *and* my daughter's happiness in mind.

"When is this charade going to end?" I cut Sonya off, getting tired of running in circles around the real topic at hand. "Name your price and I'll pay it. What would it take for you to go private with us?"

Sonya had been working for a private institution partially funded by the state and partially funded by the likes of yours truly. She couldn't have made more than $80K a year, and I was being extremely fucking optimistic. I'd offered her $150K, the best health insurance on the market for her and her son, and the same amount of hours if she'd agree to come work with Luna exclusively. Sonya let out a long-suffering sigh, her azure eyes crinkling. "Don't you get it, Trent? You should be focusing on getting Luna to open up to *more* people, not allowing her to depend on me for communication. Besides, Luna is not the only child who needs me. I enjoy working with a wide range of clients."

"She loves you," I countered, plucking dark lint from my impeccable Gucci suit. Did she think I didn't want my daughter to speak to me? To my parents? To my friends? I'd tried everything. Luna wouldn't budge. The least I could do was make sure she wasn't terribly lonely in that head of hers.

"She loves you, too. It will just take more time for her to come out of her shell."

"Let's hope it happens before I find a way to break it." I rose to my feet, only half-joking. My daughter made me feel more helpless than any grown-ass person I'd ever dealt with.

"Trent," Sonya's voice pleaded when I was at the door. I stopped but didn't turn around. No. Fuck it. She didn't talk about her family much when she came over for a quick fuck after Luna and the nanny were already asleep, but I knew she was divorced with one kid. Fuck normal Sonya and fuck her normal son. They didn't understand Luna and me. On paper, maybe. But the real us? The broken, the tortured, the curiosities? Not a chance. Sonya was a good therapist. Unethical? Maybe, but even that was debatable. We had sex knowing there was nothing more to it. No emotions, no complications, no expectations. She was a good therapist, but, like the rest of the world, she was pretty bad at understanding what I was going through. What *we* were going through.

"Summer break has just started. Please, I urge you to make room for Luna. You work such long hours. She'd really benefit from being around you more."

I twisted in place, studying her face.

"What are you suggesting?"

"Maybe take a day off every week to spend time with her?"

A few slow blinks from my end were enough to tell her she was grossly overstepping. She backpedaled, but not without a fight. Her lips thinned, telling me she was growing tired of me, too.

"I get it. You're a big hotshot and don't want to take the time off. Promise me you'll take her to work with you once a week? Camila can watch over her. I know your office building offers a playroom and other amenities suitable for children." Camila was Luna's nanny. At sixty-two, with one grandchild and another on the way, her employment with us was on borrowed time. So whenever I heard her name, something inside me stirred uncomfortably.

I nodded. Sonya closed her eyes, letting out a breath. "Thank you."

In the lobby, I collected Luna's Cocomelon backpack and stuffed her toy seahorse into it. I offered her my hand, and she took it. We made the silent journey to the elevator.

"Spaghetti?" I asked, glutton for disappointment. I'd never get a response.

Nothing.

"How about Froyo?"

Nada.

The elevator pinged. We strode inside. Luna was wearing her black Chucks, a simple pair of jeans, and a white tee. The kind of stuff I could imagine the Van Der Zee girl wearing when she wasn't busy mugging innocent people. Luna looked nothing like Jaime's daughter, Daria, or the other girls in her class who preferred frills and dresses. Just as well, as she found zero interest in them, either.

"How about spaghetti *and* a Froyo?" I bargained. And I never bargained. Ever.

Her lax hold of my hand tightened a little. *Getting warmer.*

"We'll pour the Froyo on top of the spaghetti and eat it in front of *Stranger Things.* Two episodes. Break bedtime routine. You can go to bed at nine instead of eight." Fuck it. It was the weekend and my usual willing bodies could wait. Tonight, I was going to watch Netflix with my kid. Be a seahorse.

Luna squeezed my hand once in a silent agreement.

"No chocolate or cookies after dinner, though," I warned. I ran a tight ship when it came to food and routines in the house. Luna squeezed my hand again.

"Tell it to someone who cares, missy. I'm your dad, and I make the rules. No chocolate. Or boys—after dinner or otherwise."

A ghost of a smile passed on her face before she frowned again, clutching her bag with the stuffed seahorse to her chest. My own daughter had never smiled at me, not even once, not even by accident, not even at all.

Sonya was wrong. I wasn't a seahorse.

I was the ocean.

CHAPTER TWO
EDIE

Weightless.

The feeling never got old.

Floating on a fat wave, becoming one with the ocean. Curving it skillfully—knees bent, stomach tucked in, chin high, focusing on the only thing that really mattered in life—not falling.

My black wet suit clung to my skin, keeping my temperature warm even in the briny water at six in the morning. Bane was charging on another wave in my peripheral, riding it the same way he did his Harley—recklessly, aggressively, *ruthlessly.* The ocean was loud. It crashed against the white shore, deafening my negative thoughts and tuning out nagging hang-ups. It switched off my anxiety, and for an hour—just for one hour—there were no drama and no financial worries and no plans to be made or dreams to be shattered. There were no Jordan and Lydia Van Der Zee, no expectations and no threats dangling over my head.

Just me.

Just the water.

Just the sunrise.

Oh, and Bane.

"Water's fucking freezing," Bane growled from his wave, squatting down to prolong every moment of gliding on one of nature's most arduous forces. He was much taller and heavier than me but still good enough to go pro if he really put his mind to it. Whenever he rode a sick wave, he cleaved to it as if with bloody claws. Because surfing was like sex—it didn't matter how often you'd done it, every time was different. There was always something new to be learned, and each encounter was unique—wild with potential.

"Not a good day to hang eleven," I grunted, my abs flexing as I rounded the edge of a wave to keep the ride alive. Bane liked surfing naked. He liked it because I hated when he did it, and making me feel uncomfortable was his favorite pastime. Seeing his long dick flapping in the air, on the other hand, was distracting and annoying.

"You're going to eat it, Gidget," he said, rolling his ringed tongue over his pierced bottom lip. Gidget was a nickname for small female surfers, and Bane called me that only when he wanted to piss me off. His balance was already stuttering, and he'd barely hung on to his wave. If someone's board was going to snap, it was his.

"Dream on," I shouted over the ferocious waves.

"No, really. Your dad's here."

"My dad is…what?" I'd misheard him. I was sure of it. My father had never sought me out before, and he sure as hell wasn't going to make an exception at butt crack o'clock on a sandy beach that couldn't accommodate his expensive suit addiction. I squinted toward the coast, losing stability, and not just physically. The beach-front was lined with palm trees and bungalows in pink, green, yellow, and blue. Sure enough, amid the carnival of bars, hot dog stands, and folded yellow loungers, there was Jordan Van Der Zee. Standing on the beach, alone, the sun rising behind him like an inferno mounting straight from the gates of hell. He was wearing a three-piece Brooks Brothers ensemble and a disapproving glare, both of which he had refused to strip out of even after his working hours.

Even from afar, I could see his left eye twitching in annoyance.

Even from afar, I could feel his hot breath cascading down my face, no doubt with another demand.

Even from afar, despair clutched my throat in a death grip, like he was too close, too severe, too *much*.

I slipped on the board, my back slamming against the water. Pain shot from my spine to my head. Bane didn't know my father, but like everyone else in this town, he knew *of* him. Jordan owned half of downtown Todos Santos—the other half belonged to Baron Spencer—and had recently announced he was considering running for mayor. He smiled big for every camera in his vicinity, hugged local business owners, kissed babies, and had even attended some of my high school functions to show his support for the community.

He was either loved, feared, or hated by everyone. I stood with the latter group, knowing firsthand that his wrath was a double-edged sword that could slice you open. Deep.

The taste of salt attacked my tongue, and I spat, tugging the leash on my ankle to find my floating yellow board. I climbed on, flattened my stomach against it, and started paddling toward the shore, my movements quick.

"Let the prick wait," Bane's voice boomed behind me. I shot him a look. He was straddling his black surfboard, staring at me with fire in his eyes. His long blond hair was plastered to his forehead and cheeks, his forest-green eyes blazing with purpose. I watched him through the lens my father probably had. A dirty beach bum with tattoos covering the better half of his torso and entire neck. A Viking, a caveman, a Neanderthal who felt comfortable living on the outskirts of society.

A bad apple.

Van Der Zees always hang with the shiniest fruit in the basket, Edie.

Snapping my head back to the shore, I paddled faster.

"Fucking coward," Bane yelled loud enough for Jordan to hear.

I didn't answer, and not for lack of words. Bane didn't know the whole story. I needed to stay civilized with my father. He held my future in his callous hands. I wanted it back.

Bane had gotten his name for a reason. With zero filters, he was essentially a glorified bully. Only reason he was never kicked out of school was because his mother had a shit ton of connections with the city council. But Bane ruled us all. Every single damn kid in the school. The rich assholes. The corrupted footballers. The cheerleaders who made the other girls' existence a living hell.

Bane wasn't a good guy. He was a liar, a thief, and a drug dealer. *And my sometime boyfriend.*

So, while Bane was right—my father was indeed a world-class prick—Jordan was right about something else. I was obviously making dubious life choices.

"Jordan?" I asked, hoisting the board horizontally and tucking it under my arm as I strode toward him. The cool sand clung to my feet, numbing my skin. The rush of the surf still coursed through my veins, but I knew the adrenaline would die down soon and I'd freeze. I didn't wince, knowing my father would take small pleasure in watching my discomfort and deliberately lengthen the conversation.

He jerked his chin behind my shoulder, his eyes narrowed to slits. "That the Protsenko kid?"

I scrunched my nose, a nervous tic. Even though Jordan was a first-generation immigrant, he had a problem with me making friends with a Russian kid who'd come here with his mom from Russia.

"I told you to stay away from him."

"He's not the only person you've told me to stay away from." I sniffed, squinting to the horizon. "Guess we agree to disagree."

He thumbed the collar of his dress shirt, loosening it around his neck. "See, this is where you're wrong. I've never agreed to disagree with you, Edie. I simply choose my battles. It is called good parenting, and I try to execute it as much as possible." My father was a chameleon, interchangeable and adaptable to a fault. He masked his ruthlessness with concern and his bulldozing ways with enthusiasm and a type-A driven personality. His actions were what made him the monster he'd become in my eyes. From afar, though, he was just another law-abiding citizen. A poor Dutch boy who'd come to the States with his parents, fulfilled the American dream, and become a self-made millionaire through hard work and merciless wit.

He sounded concerned, and maybe he was, but not about my well-being.

"Father." I wiped my face with my arm, hating that I had to call him that just to please him. He hadn't earned the title. "You're not here to talk about 'the Protsenko kid.' How can I help you this morning?" I jammed the surfboard into the sand and leaned against it, and he reached to touch my face before remembering I was wet and withdrawing his hand back into his pocket. He looked so human in that moment. Almost like he didn't have a hidden agenda.

"Where did you hide your acceptance letters to Boston University and Columbia?" He parked his hands on his waist, and my jaw almost dropped to the sand. He was not supposed to know that—obviously. I'd been accepted to five universities: Harvard, Cornell, Columbia, Brown, and Yale. My GPA was 4.1, and my last name was Van Der Zee, meaning these people knew my father would donate a couple million dollars and a kidney to the fine institution that would unburden him of my presence. Unfortunately, I'd never had much interest in attending an out-of-state college. The obvious reason was my surfing. It was my oxygen and air. The sun and the open sky were food to my soul. But the main reason was that the only person I cared about in this world was in California, and I wasn't moving away. Not even to Stanford up north.

Jordan knew that damn well.

"I didn't hide them. I burned them." I stripped out of my wet suit, the latex slapping my flesh punishingly as I revealed my small purple bikini underneath. "I'm staying close to him."

"I see," he said, knowing we were not talking about Bane. The whole reason why my father had decided to have this conversation at the beach and not at home was because he couldn't chance my mother overhearing us. Lydia Van Der Zee was in a fragile state, her sanity constantly hanging by a thin thread. Shouting was a hard limit for her, and this topic was volatile enough to bloom into a massive fight.

"Just say it." I closed my eyes, a sigh rolling from my throat.

"Edie, I think I've failed you as a father, and for that, I apologize."

I was shuddering. The adrenaline from surfing had long subdued. I was standing practically naked and exposed, waiting for the stingy sun to come out and caress my skin.

"Apology accepted." I didn't buy it for one moment. "So what's your next scheme? Because I'm sure there is one. You didn't come here to check in on me."

"Since you are not going to go to college this year—and let us be clear that this does not mean you will not be attending next year—and since you've officially graduated from high school, I think you should come work for me."

For. Not with. The devil is in the small details.

"In an office? No, thank you," I said flatly. I taught kids how to surf three times a week. Now that it was summer break, I was trying to pick up more work. Yes, I was also mugging on the regular ever since my father had cut off my money stream. I tried to pay for my gas and insurance and clothes and life and *him* and wasn't going to apologize for stealing the cash. When I wasn't stealing, I was pawning stuff from my father's mansion. The one he'd purchased in Todos Santos the minute he'd shoved himself into the Three Comma Club. Jewelry. Electronics. Musical instruments. Hell, I'd pawn the family dog if we had one. I had very few limits when it came to keeping the dude I loved happy and content. And, yes, stealing wasn't a hard limit. Although I only stole from those who could sustain the financial hit. I made sure of that.

"It wasn't a request. It was an order," my father said, tugging at my elbow. I dug my heels deeper into the sand.

"And if I refuse?"

"Then *Theodore* has to go," my father enunciated, unblinking.

The ease with which he said his name broke my heart. "He's been a constant distraction in your life as it is. I sometimes wonder how much further you'd have gotten if I'd done it years ago."

Chaos brewed within me. I wanted to push him away, spit in his face, and yell, but I couldn't because he was right. Jordan did have power over me. And connections galore. If he wanted Theo out of the picture, he'd make it happen. No sweat.

"What's the job?" I bit the inside of my cheek until the metallic taste of blood rolled in my mouth.

"Whatever there is to do around the office. Mainly legwork. No filing or taking phone calls. You need a good dose of reality, Edie. Getting accepted to several Ivy League universities and turning them all down so you could spend your days surfing with a pothead? Those days are over. Time to apply yourself. You will come with me every morning at seven a.m. and open the office—and you will not leave until I tell you to, be it seven or eight at night. Understood?"

My father had never gone this far to try to punish me, and I was already well over eighteen, but that meant absolutely nothing. I still lived under his roof, I still ate his food, and most importantly—I was still at his mercy.

"Why are you doing this to me? Why here? Why now?" But the here part was pretty obvious. This was the only time he knew where I was.

His left eyelid twitched again, his jaw tensing. "Please, you brought this on yourself with your thoughtless lifestyle. It's time you lived up to your name. There's no need for these theatrics."

Then he turned around and stalked to the Range Rover waiting on the curb of the empty boardwalk. The engine was purring, his driver shifting his eyes between us and the time on his phone. A thin smile found his lips. My father had taken less than ten minutes to put me in my place.

I stood there, rooted to the ground, like an ice statue. I hated Jordan with the kind of passion people usually reserved for love. I hated him like hate was supposed to be felt—it tainted my soul and poisoned my mood.

"I've a feeling you're now regretting not taking my advice to tell him to piss off," Bane muttered beside me as he dug the sharp edge of his board into the sand and collected his wild blond hair into a man-bun.

I didn't answer.

"Sounds like your ass has been served." He elbowed me, plucking a Budweiser from his backpack lying on the sand because who cared that it was seven in the morning?

I clenched my seashell necklace and gritted, "You have no idea."

CHAPTER THREE
EDIE

Crazy.

The place was the very definition of madness.

I'd never been to my dad's office before, but I knew anarchy when it looked me in the eye. And on the fifteenth floor of the Oracle building in Beverly Hills in which Fiscal Heights Holdings was located, I met true chaos.

The only man whose madness could match Bane's.

Baron "Vicious" Spencer.

The whole place was buzzing with ringtones, women gossiping in St. John pencil skirts and men arguing in sharp suits. Ivory-colored granite and antique dark-brown leather adorned the reception lounge of FHH. Floor-to-ceiling windows offered the perfect view of ugly, beautiful, fake, real, raw Los Angeles in all its glory.

And there, in luxury, in indulgence, in power, I came face-to-face with the man who was a legend at All Saints High, so much so that even over a decade later, they'd named a bench after him—*Vicious*.

"If you are going to plagiarize a whole article about the stock exchange, at least don't steal it from the fucking *Financial Times*. Who hired your ass as head of PR? *Who?*" The man with the sleek raven hair and dark-indigo eyes threw a batch of documents in a horrified-looking young man's face. The papers rained down like hail, not confetti. Vicious's jaw clenched as he stabbed a finger into the guy's ironed shirt. "Fix this shit before you box up the two and a half pictures of your fucking family you probably brought here to domesticate your four-by-four-inch office, dickface. And do it by five because when I sit down for my six o'clock meeting, I want to act like it never happened. Am I clear?"

Although nearly every person on the floor had gathered in an open circle to watch the show, no one called Vicious out on his rotten behavior. Not even my father. Everybody seemed too scared of him, and while I felt really bad for the PR guy, who mumbled that his name was Russell, I didn't want to start off my employment by pissing more people off.

"Please, sir. You can't fire me." Russell nearly dropped to his knees. It was nothing short of torture to watch. I shrank into the sensible black-wool dress with a French designer tag I'd snatched from my mother's closet that morning—I usually never did that, but I had nothing else to wear to an office—and tried not to flinch.

"I can, and I am, and fuck, where is my coffee?" Vicious looked around, tapping his finger on his lip. He had a wedding band on his left hand. You'd think marriage would have made him mellow. You'd be wrong.

Suddenly, the commotion stopped. The throng of suits sliced in two, and in walked three men I recognized all too well from the financial magazines lying around my house.

Dean Cole, Jaime Followhill, and Trent Rexroth.

The first two were merely decoration, standing on either side of Trent, both a few inches shorter and leaner and generally less godlike. It was Trent who had the room, who stole the show. He wore a baby-blue button-down shirt and light-gray slacks. He looked like sex, he walked like sex, and I was obviously not the only one to think so because at least three women in my vicinity let out breathless giggles.

"Spencer." Trent regarded him coolly, clutching a Starbucks in his hand. "Is Aunt Flow in town? Tone this shit down. It's eight a.m. on a Monday."

"Yeah, what crawled up your ass, V?" Dean Cole chimed in, his wide smile making the room significantly warmer and less daunting.

"Language," my father boomed beside me, clutching my arm tighter. I'd forgotten he held me in place. He'd first started manhandling me at sixteen, when I'd showed up at his house with two rings in my left nostril, and had moved to bruising grips when I'd decorated my lower torso with a huge back cross. It was never too bad—as I said before, rich people don't hit their children—but we both knew he did it because I hated standing next to him. The fact that he'd sometimes leave bruises was probably a nice bonus in his eyes.

The cross wasn't about religion. It was a message, presented in bold, black ink.

Do. Not. Cross.

"Dudebro is fired. I want his laptop on my desk by noon. Not to mention all his passwords, company phone, and parking pass, which I will give to someone more worthy. Maybe the fucking kid who delivers us fruit baskets every morning." Vicious waved in Russell's general direction, snatching one of two coffee cups from Jaime's hands. My heart tightened.

Trent kicked what I assumed was his office door open silently. I probably shouldn't have felt sheer glee at how they'd all dismissed my father. "No one's getting fired today. Besides, we have bigger fish to fry. In my office."

"A—fuck your fish. And B—don't order me around." Vicious finished his coffee in two swallows and handed the cup to the person nearest to him. "C—coffee. I need more of it. Now."

"Vicious…" Jaime cleared his throat as the guy holding Vicious's cup quickly ran to the elevator to get him a second Starbucks.

"The man copied and pasted a *Financial Times* article to our site. We could have gotten sued or worse."

"P-please," Russell stuttered, tickling the blood sport inclinations in any predator in his vicinity with his overflowing weakness, mine included. "It was a mistake. I had no time to write the article. My daughter is two weeks old. She doesn't sleep well at night…"

I couldn't take it anymore.

"Give the man a break!" I blurted out. I wiggled my arm free, shaking my father off as my legs started working their way to the HotHoles. Or whatever people called them in this town. All four men snapped their gazes to me, and even though they all looked surprised, Trent was the only one who had that extra layer of abhorrence on his face. I ignored him, pointing at Russell.

"He said he was sorry. Why would he deliberately screw up? Come on, he's got a family to feed."

"I love this." Cole chuckled, slapping Spencer's back and shaking his head. "Bossed around by a teenager. *Cute*."

My cheeks turned scarlet. Vicious looked indifferent—barely acknowledging my existence and looking back to Russell, shooing him away and sparing him his redundancy, while Trent bared his teeth, turning his focus to me.

"Is this bring-your-kid-to-work day? Because I don't remember getting the email." His voice was laced with enough venom to kill a whale. I returned a stern stare, burrowing into faux confidence I wasn't feeling.

You're a potential sacrifice. His words swam in my head, drowning every positive thought I'd had about him and his good looks. He'd said it mere weeks ago, but I'd almost forgotten he'd be a complication in working here.

"Edie will be working here for a while." Jordan pulled me to his side again, not unlike a possession.

"Says who?" Trent asked.

"Says me."

"I haven't agreed to that. None of us have."

"Then it's a good thing I didn't ask." My father smiled politely, choking my arm with his thin, strong fingers. I ignored the pain.

Starting more beef with him could lead to me not going to see Theo on Saturday, and I couldn't risk that. Trent strode in our direction, every step he took sending a current to my body, like paddling into turbulent waters.

"With all due respect to white, upper-class nepotism and awarding your underqualified daughter with a job most deserving candidates would kill for, every major HR decision goes through the partners, correct?" He turned to his friends, who nodded solemnly, forgetting all about poor Russell. I was now the newest victim to mess with, spineless and helpless. A little mouse lured into a fat cat's den.

"For God's sake, Rexroth. She is going to be an assistant, not an account manager." Jordan's impatient wave did nothing to make matters better. His grip on my arm became so tight, my bones were ready to pop, sticking out of my skin.

"She is going to be on *this floor*, have access to our *things*. I don't care if her job is to peel bananas in the kitchen. This goes to a board meeting tomorrow morning. End of discussion," Trent growled.

All eyes were on him, the dark energy in the room buzzing with shock. The Mute had spoken. Not only a few words—but sentences. And it was because of me, no less.

I'd finally found him. The one man scarier than my father. Not that I was looking. Because while Vicious made a lot of noise, Trent Rexroth was the silent hunter who would circle you for hours, striking when you least expected it.

A desolate panther. Wild, quiet, and slick. His pale, cold eyes ran the length of my father like he was muck, coming to stop where his hand held my arm in a vise-like grip. I'd never seen anyone look at my father with such disdain. Jordan's fingers eased on my skin.

"You're really going to fight me over this?" My father scrubbed his smooth cheek with his knuckles, incredulous. Figured. He was so used to my mother and me bowing our heads to his every whim, I wasn't entirely sure I wasn't Team Rexroth. Sure, the Mute didn't want me around—but I didn't *want* to be around, either, so we were on the same wavelength. Trent stopped his stride inches from me, where I was able to breathe in his singular scent, of a clean man and a dirty fuck. He oozed sensuality, making me want messy, forbidden things. My reaction to him was almost sickening, and I made another mental note to stay away from him.

Trent tipped his head down to meet my father's eyes, whispering darkly, "I would fight you to the death over anything, Jordan, including the service provider for the coffee machine, if need be."

Bad blood. This place was like poison to the soul. Luckily, it looked like Rexroth hated me, and the HotHoles always had each other's back. That was the legend in All Saints High, and I very much doubted they'd break their tradition for little ol' *moi*.

"Fine," Jordan bit out. "We'll take it to the boardroom."

Trent's gaze cut to mine and stopped when his grays met my blues. The fading noise of Vicious barking at people to move along and my father finally letting go of my arm to move toward Jaime and Dean—probably trying to gain both allies and sympathy—died down.

"I don't like you," Rexroth whispered under his breath, his voice harsh.

"I never asked you to." I shrugged.

"You won't be working here." His arm brushed my shoulder, but I didn't think it was by accident. I let loose a sugary smile, scanning his face and torso for no reason other than to taunt him. "Good, you'll be doing me a favor. My father is the one forcing me to work here. He's pissed I turned down five Ivy League colleges. Remind me, Mr. Rexroth—which top-tier university did you attend for your degree?"

The low blow was supposed to retrieve some of my lost dignity, but bile burned my throat, shotgunned from my stomach. Trent Rexroth was known in Todos Santos as an exhilarating success story, rising from the gutters of San Diego. He had gone to a shitty state college that accepted even the illiterate, working as a janitor on campus after hours. Those were given facts he'd recited himself in an interview for *Forbes*.

Had I really just tried to make him feel less worthy because he wasn't born with a silver spoon in his mouth? It made me sicker than wearing my mother's designer garb.

Trent smiled, leaning into my body, into my *soul*. His smirk was more frightening than any scowl, frown, or grimace I'd ever seen. It threatened to tear me apart and sew me back together however he pleased.

"Edie." His lips were dangerously close to my ear. A delicious shiver moved down my spine. Something warm rolled inside me, begging to unknot and flower into an orgasm. What was happening, and why the hell *was* it happening? "If you know what's best for you, you will turn around and leave right now."

I elevated my head to meet his gaze and showed him my version of a grin. I was born and raised in a world of intimidating rich men, and I'd be damned if I went down like my mother—addicted to Xanax, Gucci, and a man who'd paraded her on his arm for a short, glorious decade before keeping her solely for public appearances.

"I think I'm going to go find my desk now. I'd wish you a good day, Mr. Rexroth, but I think that ship has sailed. You're a miserable man. Oh, and one for the road." I fished for a Nature Valley bar in my mother's purse and plastered it to his hard, muscled chest. My heart slammed into my neck, fluttering like a caged bird.

I hurried after my father as he glided down the vast, golden-hued hallway, not daring to look back. Knowing I'd started a war and arrived unequipped. But I also knew something else that gave me a surfer's rush—if I could slam the final nail in my employment coffin and make Rexroth vote against me, I'd be off the hook.

I had just the plan for it. All I had to do was act like a brat. *Game on.*

CHAPTER FOUR
TRENT

I ate lunch by myself.

Growing up as an only child because my parents couldn't afford to give me siblings (a decision I respected) had meant that dinners weren't a noisy event. Still, that had not made them silent.

I had met true loneliness the day Luna had stopped speaking. It had happened days after her second birthday and had deflated my already shaky confidence regarding parenthood. Up until then, being a single parent had been hard—but not impossible. I'd had the money and resources to hire the best nannies on the planet, my parents to rely on when I needed to get out of town, and my friends and their wives who were always accommodating and treated Luna as their own. Bonus points—I had been so used to being dealt every crappy card life had to offer, I had barely been surprised when Val had bailed on our asses.

I'd been robbed my whole life.

Robbed of my football scholarship when a douche named Toby Rowland had greased the floor under my locker, causing me to fall and break my ankle.

Robbed of my freedom when Val had broken the news about her pregnancy, though that had been on me just as much as it had been on her.

And, finally, robbed of a happy child when Val had fucked off and left Luna with me.

But this? This was the last straw. The silence. It ate me from the inside, and my normal, quiet self turned into a raging asshole of massive proportions who just needed a good excuse to unleash my wrath.

I was quiet and resentful and a fucking mess—because of my daughter.

After lunch, I walked into my office on the fifteenth, ready to tackle my mile-long to-do list, freezing on the spot when I spotted Edie Van Der Zee waiting on the other side of my desk.

Sitting in *my* chair.

Legs on top of *my* closed laptop.

Heels pointing at me teasingly.

Arms crossed over her chest.

Venus in a dress. Smart-ass. In need of fucking saving.

Not today, sweetheart. I've already got one girl to save, and she is keeping me hella busy.

I threw my briefcase on my desk, loosening my tie. "You have three seconds to take your feet off my laptop." *Before I spread them wide and eat you out for the whole fucking floor to hear,* I refrained from adding.

"I don't believe you." Her eyes clung to my face like they were trying to peel away a persistent layer of a facade to get to a truth. "Last time you counted down the seconds, nothing happened. I may be a thief, but you, Mr. Rexroth, are a liar."

Last time I'd let her off the hook because I'd needed to get home. I'd caught a quick lunch with my mother while my dad had watched Luna. Right now I had all the time in the world. Furthermore—I was her new boss until tomorrow morning, and she was begging to be disciplined.

I stepped over to the desk, grabbed her slim ankle, slid the heel off, and snapped the red Louboutin shoe, tearing the heel from the beige footwear. Her eyes darted to me in horror. I pocketed the heel like it was sexy underwear and nonchalantly slipped Cinderella's shoe back in place.

"Balance"—my voice was grave, and so was I—she needed this lesson—"is everything in life. I try not to be a dick unless absolutely necessary, but I've got a feeling you're here to test boundaries, aren't you, *kid*?"

Her cool evaporated like thin smoke, replaced with hot despair. She shot up from my seat and rounded the desk, hyperaware of her broken heel. Her hands were balled into fists.

"What. The. Hell!" Edie's eyes were dancing in their sockets. Her rage was pouring out in buckets, and I wanted to gargle with her sweet fucking wrath, drink from her well of sorrow. "What's your problem with me?"

"I don't have a problem with you. You're not even on my fucking radar. I walked into my office and found you here, all over my desk like a rash." I dumped my loosened tie onto my desk, rolling my uncuffed sleeves up to my elbows.

"Well, I came here to tell you that I don't want this job."

"Good. Because you don't deserve it," I shot.

"In that case, I'd appreciate you telling me you'll vote against me. I mean, I know you will, but hearing it from you would make me feel a lot better."

"I'm not here to make you feel better. What's so bad about working at Fiscal Heights Holdings, anyway?" I had no inclination to humor her, but she was still standing there, for a reason beyond my grasp, so I thought I'd throw her a bone. She scrunched her nose, something I'd seen her do before.

"I can't work here. I have things to do. Plans…different plans for my future. So can you just tell the others to vote against me, too?"

"Do I look like I'd take orders from you?" I blinked slowly, only slightly amused by her brazen approach.

"Please." Her voice was steady, her eyes afire on mine.

"Don't," I grunted, holding one hand in the air to stop her. I leaned a hip against my desk. "Never beg, Edie. Now, go make me a coffee."

She threw her head back and laughed. Rather hysterically, I noted. Teenage girls were typically full of emotions and bullshit, and I had to come to terms with that because Luna was going to hit puberty in less than ten years. Great.

"I'm not making you shit."

"I didn't ask for shit. I asked for coffee."

"I'm not your PA."

"True. You're lower than that. You're the office bitch," I retorted calmly, watching as Edie's eyes followed the veins on my forearms like her life depended on it. I'd chuckle if it didn't make me feel like a perv.

"I'm the *what*?" she hissed.

I nodded. "General assistant. That's your title. Your father just sent the contract to HR and cc'd all of us ahead of the board meeting tomorrow. GA is just diplomatic wording for an office bitch. I can ask you for anything within reason. So I'm asking you for coffee. No sugar. Black."

If nothing else, I was a fucking asshole for loving the look on her face. Like she'd been broken—but just for now. Just for this moment. Just for *me*. Realization washed over her, making her straighten her spine and slant her chin up.

She was going to do it. Take my orders, make my coffee, burn my time, and be a welcome distraction.

A maelstrom of emotions swam in Edie's eyes. If they could speak, they would scream. But they couldn't. So all I saw was an extremely irritated girl who'd recently grown a great pair of tits and had just discovered life was not a picnic.

"Chop, chop." I clapped my hands twice.

I wasn't the nicest person in the world. I liked to think I was good enough to at least warn her to take her shoes off before she walked away. But before I had a chance, Edie turned around and stormed toward the door, falling flat on her ass.

The only solace in her unfortunate scenario, as I leaned against my desk, watching her pull herself up on unsteady feet, was that I didn't laugh.

Then again, I didn't spare her the humiliation because I liked her. I hadn't moved to help her up for a different reason.

I was hard as a stone, and moving would have given that away.

"You failed your first lesson at balance. Big surprise."

"You're failing at life, Rexroth!" She galloped out of my office, her face red with humiliation.

I rearranged my package as soon as she left and shot a text message to Sonya.

Edie Van Der Zee had started to feel like an itch. Luckily, I was going to scratch her out of my life first thing tomorrow morning.

———

And then the morning arrived. It was the kind that reminded me why I fucking hated talking to people. One where everything was chaotic, everybody was loud, and everyone was on my ass, firing questions, begging for attention, and asking for shit.

"*Mr. Rexroth, you have the Duran-Dexter file on your desk. Can you sign it for me?*"

"*Trent, you have a conference call at three.*"

"*Can you go to a charity event in Palo Alto next week? Someone needs to, and Jaime is too busy with Mel and the new baby.*"

"*Trent—why is Luna here?*"

"*Rexroth—are we still on for drinks on Saturday?*"

"*Rexroth.*"

"*Hey, T-Rex!*"

"*Trent, darling…*"

I came to a stop in the middle of the hallway, ignoring the throng of colleagues, and squatted down to Luna's eye level, my voice rusty from lack of talking. She was clutching Camila's hand, a faraway look in her eyes. Dragging her into the office with me every Tuesday was a terrible idea, but Sonya seemed hell-bent on it, and I wasn't the fucking expert.

"How about tacos for lunch?" I brushed my thumb on her cheek and handed Camila some cash. "Take Luna to pick up some bagels and meet me in my office."

"Why? Where are you going now?" Camila's thick Spanish accent made a cameo, which meant she wasn't pleased with me.

I'm going to get an eighteen-year-old kid fired because I'm too selfish to trust myself not to fuck her raw in her father's office if she gets anywhere near me.

"Board meeting. Should be quick. Just voting on something and then I'll be out." I patted Luna's head and pressed a kiss to her forehead before rising up and gently squeezing Camila's shoulder.

Turning on my heel toward my office, I saw Jordan Van Der Zee appearing from the sliding-glass residential-elevator doors, his daughter shadowing his steps. He was holding her like she was a convicted criminal again, and I tried not to lose my shit over it—*again*. Today, Edie was wearing a navy sailor dress a size larger than her tiny frame. At knee length, it was conservative but still highlighted her killer calves. A little gymnast that could bend to a man's every need.

Whoa. Backtrack this shit, fast, Sir Perv-a-Lot.

She seemed to be a completely different person around her father. Away from him, she was confident, feisty, and a fucking headache. But now? Her eyes were on the floor, and her two nose rings were the only faint glimmer of her black, rebellious heart.

Badass, my ass.

Jordan nodded a hello, and I returned the gesture. We met at the custom-designed gold doors leading to the boardroom. I saw my three friends behind the fishbowl walls, hunched over the long, bronze table, discussing something among themselves.

"Reconsider." Jordan smoothed his Armani tie. A statement, not a request. Not a fucking chance. I didn't trust this man with a plastic spoon, let alone my company. In the six months since we'd been in business together, he'd killed four out of the five big deals I'd brought to Fiscal Heights Holdings. He'd slacked off on all of my big accounts—purposely—and blatantly tried to designate the greenest, least-experienced brokers for my clients. A week into our work together, I'd had my first unfortunate encounter with him. I'd overheard him talking on the phone on my way out from the office.

"No, not Rexroth. Let's send someone else to try to save the Drescher and Ferstein account," he'd said. An account I'd brought in, thank you very fucking much. I'd waited, loitering behind his office door like a *General Hospital* character and hating it. "He's too…you know what. Too hood. Too angry. Not very talkative. I don't want him anywhere near this account. Ask Dean to talk to them. He's the kind of pretty boy charmer their CEO, Helena, would appreciate."

And that was it. That was when I'd known Jordan Van Der Zee wasn't only a racist but wanted to push me out of the company. He had another thing coming, and it was going to boomerang straight into his face.

Vicious, Dean, and Jaime were already halfway out the corporate door, showing up to work three or four times a week and spending most of their time with their families. But me, I only had Luna. Though to be completely honest, even she seemed to prefer spending time with the nanny.

"This is where you part ways with Daughter Dearest." I tugged at my collar because Edie motherfucking Van Der Zee made the temperature in the room rise by at least ten degrees.

"Gladly." She plucked her phone from her purse and walked away.

Jordan entered the conference room, and I snapped my fingers, smiling. "I need to sign off on a contract for the D&D account. Be right back, Jordi-boy."

"I never saw this account." His brows dove down. He hated when I called him that.

"Exactly," I said, a bounce in my steps as I went to my office to fetch the contract. After signing it—taking pleasure in the fact I made Jordan wait in the boardroom for me like a little bitch—I walked over to the main reception area of the floor, where it split into two corridors with the huge boardroom in the middle. Deciding to make him wait a little longer, I took a sharp right into the break room to brew myself a coffee with the fancy machine I'd never tried before. Was it petty? Yes. Did inconveniencing Jordan make me smile? Hell yes.

I was about to push the glass door open when I stopped on my heel, watching the girls inside the kitchen.

Luna. Camila. Edie. Standing together. Looking…excited? What the…?

Edie threw her arms around Camila and hugged her, burrowing into her shoulder. Luna was standing beside them, observing the scene, doe-eyed. For the first time in a long time, she was interested in something that wasn't seahorses. Edie cupped Camila's cheeks before wiping her tears with the back of her hand. She wore her emotions like jewelry. Proud and unapologetic. It made me hate her a little less for trying to steal my mother's handbag a few weeks ago.

Then Edie did the unthinkable and yet what every girl her age would have done.

She crouched, ran her hand over Luna's curly piggy tails, and smiled.

Almost in slow motion, she pointed at Luna's fluffy blue seahorse, her mouth forming an O-shaped *wow*.

Luna's face broke into a timid grin. She never smiled at me like that. I blinked away my shock, trying to wrap my head around her reaction. Edie must've asked Luna something because Luna nodded.

Nodded. She never nodded. Nodding was one step away from vocalizing your needs, and Luna was all about keeping me in the dark.

My daughter looked alert and attentive and invested in that

moment, which was something I couldn't say about her 90 percent of the time. And I stood there, rooted to the floor, not wanting to step into the moment and pierce the fog of magic they were cocooned in.

"Yo, assface, is the weed eating at your memory? We're all waiting for you in the boardroom." Dean killed my trance by slapping my back from behind, chewing his gum deliberately noisily in my ear. "Come join us before Jordi hangs you by the balls and Vicious skins you and makes a new ottoman out of your flesh."

Reluctant, I followed his steps, moving toward the boardroom, my eyes still on the break room.

I took a seat at the conference table, sandwiched between Dean and Jaime. Jordan was sitting across from me, looking one argument away from a heart attack.

"Nice veins." I pointed at his forehead, fishing my cell phone out and dumping it onto the table.

"You're very funny, Rexroth. Your charm has brought you a long way, to Beverly Hills, to Todos Santos. But I see underneath it, and I'm less than impressed." A hiss slid between his thin lips.

I shrugged. "Thanks for the analysis, Dr. Strangelove. Now let's do this as quickly and as painlessly as possible so that Jordi can go back to admiring the reflection of himself on the four-grand mirror in his office. Shall we?"

"We shall." Jaime slapped the desk, dark circles framing his eyes. His wife, Mel, had just given birth to their second daughter, Bailey. He looked as happy as a pig in shit and as tired as the person hired to clean up the pigpen.

The poll had started off with Jordan, who obviously voted for keeping his daughter employed. Then came my turn, and I surprised everyone, including myself, with the answer.

"Yes."

"Yes?" Vicious blinked, giving me his what-the-fuck-is-your-game look. "Yes means you vote for her employment," he explained slowly, like I was an idiot.

"I know what *yes* means, dickbag."

Vicious, Jaime, and Dean exchanged puzzled looks. They were going to go with my plan, but now, I'd changed it. Jordan appeared out of sorts, looking among all of us, searching our faces, trying to make sense of it all.

Jaime was the first to recover, rubbing the dark bags under his eyes. "Whatever. I don't care."

Dean's turn. He tossed his tennis ball onto the table. "If Trent's fine with it, I don't give a damn if she works here."

Then Vicious. He looked up at me, shaking his head slightly in warning.

I don't want to fuck her, asshole. I mean, I do, but I won't.

Then again, I'd never had a serious girlfriend in my thirty-three years, and the one thing I did have was a runaway ex-stripper whom I'd knocked up in a dirty hookup and who'd left me with our kid. So maybe I did deserve that warning.

But even though Edie Van Der Zee was definitely trouble, Luna seemed to like her.

Maybe.

Probably.

Goddammit, hopefully.

I knew I was making zero sense. I didn't give a damn. Let them think I was crazy. More power to me. No one liked to mess with crazy. Ruthless? Why not. Powerful? Sure. But crazy was unpredictable, the worst attribute in human nature.

Vicious opened his lips, relishing the power of having the room. "It's a yes from me."

She was in.

My friends were my tribe, my custom-made, hand-selected family. Saying we had each other's backs was an understatement. Nearly twenty years and counting, we were still blindly loyal toward one another. When one of us jumped, the others gladly took the fall.

Dean stood up, collecting his shit from the table. "Now, if you'll excuse me, I need to call my wife. She had a doctor's appointment today. Mazel tov, Jordi."

Vicious and Jaime got up and started discussing a conference call with Japan they had tomorrow at the butt crack of dawn.

Van Der Zee and I found ourselves alone in the boardroom, surrounded by nothing but the white noise of the air conditioner. Jordan tapped his finger on his thin lips, his foot mimicking the irritated movement.

He was waiting for me to explain. Foolishly, I might add. Volunteering information to the enemy was a rookie mistake, one I'd learned not to make long before my rich, sheltered friends had learned how to wipe their own asses.

"Feeling indecisive today?" His long, bony, Voldemort-like face twisted in displeasure. He looked like a tsar and acted like a tyrant. Jordan thought he was intimidating, and maybe he was, but not to me. To me, he was all bark, zero bite.

I shrugged, resting my legs on the table, knowing it'd drive him nuts. "Nah, I was always okay with your daughter working here. Just wanted to make you sweat a little. Cardio is important at your age."

"How considerate of you. You're not one to waste time, and you just wasted plenty of ours, so I am guessing there's a plan behind your change of heart. Let me be clear—my daughter is completely off-limits for you. You will be wise to stay far away from her."

I couldn't get butthurt over his comment because no matter how wildly insane and sick it was, I did find his teenage daughter good enough to eat. At the same time, I knew better than to even think about it. She acted like a child. I had one at home. They weren't much fun and were ridiculously hard to tame.

"I expect the other guys won't be getting the same warning?" I tipped my chin down. Not that I was going to fuck little Edie, but he didn't have to know that. Pulling at his strings was my version of a hobby.

"Your colleagues are gentlemen."

My colleagues had fucked enough women between them to populate a medium-sized country, but I wasn't going to argue this point. Not with him, anyway. I stretched in my seat, yawning. I may have been the Mute—I was the one to never, ever talk. Not at meetings, not at company functions, and not to mingle with anyone—but when the situation called for it, like now, I was happy to fight for what I wanted.

"You know, Jordi, I sometimes feel inclined to pull the race card on you. You seem to approach me with a bag of prejudice that doesn't apply to my fair-skinned partners." My voice was breezy, and so was I. I really didn't care if Jordan was a racist as long as he stayed out of my way.

Van Der Zee snorted, shaking his head. "Don't even go there, Rexroth. You're practically white. You look like you're working on your tan."

"A simple 'I'm not a racist' would have been more sufficient," I pointed out.

"At any rate." He stood up. "Stay away from my daughter if you want to survive a year in this company." A year ago, Jordan had agreed to buy 49 percent of the shares in the company, with the four of us splitting the remaining shares. We had done it so we could all move to Todos Santos and live close to each other. But we hadn't known Jordan would be such a pain in the ass.

"Color me bored at your idle threat. Besides, I heard you the first time."

"Heard, yes. Acknowledged? No."

"I've got your acknowledgment right here, sir: Fuck. Off." I slid my hands out of my pockets and showed him my two middle fingers before getting up and grabbing my phone. I dialed Sonya's number to give her the good news about Luna nodding. She answered after the first ring. "Sonya, hold on one sec." I shot him a smirk, pressing the receiver to my chest. "Word to the wise, Van Der Zee—next time you get into business with someone, make sure they are a gentleman.

Because I sure as hell am not, and I don't care how many shares you have in my company. Let it be known—if you threaten me one more time, I will leave you to collect dust and a string of financial losses. We're done here, *partner*."

CHAPTER FIVE
EDIE

Two days.

Not a lifetime, but not a minute, either. Two days had passed since Trent Rexroth had broken my mother's precious Louboutins, and truth be told—I was still both disoriented and ridiculously aroused at what he'd done.

A delighted shudder seeped into me, bone-deep, from watching the lavish designer footwear snapping—seeing expensive things devalued was one of my favorite pastimes—but in the same breath, I was glad to put some distance between Broody O'Asshole and me.

I had no one to blame but myself. I mean—I'd asked him specifically not to hire me. Should have known it would only make him want to be petty and do it to spite me.

Work had left its mark on my body, soul, and mind. I had to wake up at half past four in the morning every day to make time for surfing. Then I usually did five hundred coffee runs for Vicious (cold and rude), Dean (fun and crude), and Jaime (polite and impersonal) before kicking off my shift as the secretaries' and PAs' bitch. Picking up clothes from the dry cleaner, holding ties for stockbrokers to choose from before meetings, helping maintenance when one of the faucets in the men's restroom was leaking—my father hadn't been joking. I'd been appointed to do the most mundane, mind-numbing tasks.

After our encounter, Rexroth steered clear of me, not even sparing me a glance as he glided through the hallways like a fire-breathing demon, darkness gleaming from his light eyes.

On my lunch breaks, when I sat alone outside the building and sucked on a ramen noodle from the sad pack I'd bought at the Dollar Tree to save some money, I found myself wondering whether my stunt on his desk had made an impact or if he thought I was a weirdo unworthy of his attention.

Didn't matter. What did matter was that now I was one of the many overworked, overstressed assistants to these privileged, rich, self-entitled men who in two short days had managed to make me want to commit serious crimes.

I hate this place, I hate these people, I hate this life…

I was standing in the break room, picking at a fancy fruit basket (those were delivered daily to the fifteenth floor of Fiscal Heights Holdings, accompanied with fresh pastries and cold-pressed organic juices) when the cute girl and Camila walked in.

"Show me what you want to eat for lunch." Camila handed the girl a tablet with pictures of food items. My old nanny looked up and saw me, and her face split into a grin. "My sweet Edie, we meet again!" Camila clasped me in a bear hug, and I embraced her back like she was an anchor. In many ways, she was. I firmly believed some people came into the world to make it bearable for others. Camila was one of them.

"Is it wrong to be jealous of a three-year-old because she has you?" I murmured into her delicate white hair, allowing myself some self-pity. Camila laughed and pulled away, running her fingers over my face, doing inventory, making sure that everything was in place. Physically, it was.

"She's four."

"Oh." I leaned against the counter, watching the pretty girl more closely. This was our second encounter, so I noticed things I hadn't in the first one. Such as she was dressed like a boy, as though trying to hide how lovely she was. It made me like her instantly. She regarded her beauty as a secret, and like any secret, she chose the people to confide in carefully. Which was probably why she was stingy with the smiles, too.

"You're not much of a talker," I observed, scrunching my nose at the kid. Years of being talked about when I was in the room had taught me that kids listened, discerned, and hated being treated like they were invisible.

"Guess you could say that." Camila cleared her throat and averted her stare to the fruit basket, grabbing a strawberry and popping it into her mouth. "She doesn't talk." She chewed instead of elaborating.

"Huh." I crouched, offering the girl a pecan. Did kids her age eat pecans? I wasn't sure, but she took it anyway, pocketing it. "I never asked what her name was," I said as an afterthought.

"Her name is Luna." Camila's voice cut above my head. She brushed the girl's soft brown curls. The kid was enchanting. A mixture of everything beautiful in the human species crammed into one person. Mocha skin and blue eyes. It reminded me of someone, but I couldn't remember who. Maybe a baby Adriana Lima.

"I'm Edie." I offered Luna my hand. She didn't take it. I wasn't embarrassed or annoyed by her rejection. "Fine." I withdrew my hand. "I don't need your germs all over me, anyway."

Luna swallowed down a snort.

"In fact, don't get anywhere near me, okay? You look like a nose picker."

I loved children. Not in the way most girls my age liked them. I liked the hardened and the disorderly. The ones who struggled to communicate their feelings and felt trapped inside their bodies. Maybe because I saw so much of me in them.

I walked over to the other side of the kitchenette, opening the fridge and grabbing a can of Coke. Luna followed me with her eyes, a taunting smirk on her full lips. I arched an eyebrow and cracked the can open.

"I bet they don't allow you to drink pop, huh?"

She shook her head. There was something hesitant about her movements. Like she wasn't entirely sure how to do them—or if she should be doing them at all.

"If I give you some, would you tell on me?"

"No, no, no, no," Camila interrupted, rushing toward us, her palms waving. "Her dad would kill both of us. Lord, no."

I said nothing because "no" meant "maybe" in Camila's world. It was a matter of how hard you pushed for something. Luna looked between us, trying to pick up on the nuance of our relationship.

"I need to go to the bathroom for a second. Can you watch her?" Camila smoothed her long skirt and blazer.

I nodded. "'Course."

"No soda." She wagged a finger from the door.

I nodded again. She knew better than to believe me but still felt it her duty to point the same threatening finger at Luna. "I mean it, Luna. Your dad will not be happy."

Needless to say, as soon as she left, Luna's lips united with her very first can of Coke. I held the can in my hand as I allowed her a small sip, squatting down to catch her every reaction when the fizz hit her taste buds.

"It's good, isn't it?"

Luna nodded solemnly in agreement. I took a long pull, staring into the little hole.

"Yup, so good. Wait till you taste beer." I snorted.

"No need, since that will never happen" came a steel voice from the entrance of the kitchenette, and I twisted my head, my jaw dropping in horror.

Shit.

Trent Rexroth walked in, looking fifty shades of pissed off and wearing one of the most sinfully sexy suits I'd seen on a human being. I wasn't even big on suits, mainly because Jordan liked them and I hated everything he loved by association, but the way the silky black fabric hugged Trent's ripped, tall frame made me wonder what he'd look like in a wet suit. *Or out of one.* Either way, he'd leave Bane and the other guys at Tobago Beach eating his dust. I wasn't sure what he did to maintain this kind of body, but it wasn't sitting on his ass from nine to five, writing angry emails and scowling at me and everyone else.

I drew the can away from Luna's lips, straightening up.

"Is she…" My gaze wandered around, looking for a distraction or a sharp object to defend myself with, should he decide to kill me.

"My daughter," he cut into my words. "She is. Where the hell is Camila?" He sounded like the prince from *Beauty and the Beast*. Low, gruff, and commanding. But I refused to shrink into a corner and let him intimidate me.

"What kind of four-year-old has never tasted Coke?" I accused, throwing my arms in the air.

"Excuse me?"

"You heard me." I put a hand on Luna's shoulder, hoping she wouldn't shake it off. She didn't. "Seriously, what is wrong with you? She shouldn't have it every day or even every week—agreed. But not, like, ever? Why? Soda is awesome. It's sweet, and it fizzles in your mouth, and it makes you feel happy. Right, Luna?" I nudged her.

She nodded vehemently, and now it was Trent's turn to stare at me, bewildered. He took a step forward, his eyes moving from me to his daughter.

Silence. And awkwardness. And what the hell was happening?

"What? What!" I lost my cool, looking between them.

"Do it again," he said, to both of us, I think.

"Do what?" I rubbed the back of my neck, still trying to read the situation.

"Make her nod again. *Please.*" The last word came out reluctantly, as if admitting defeat. I worried my lower lip, inspecting him like he'd just landed from space wearing a pineapple hat and a hula skirt.

"Okay…" I scrunched my nose, looking down at Luna. "Hey, dude, want another sip of Coke?"

Luna nodded and reached for the can. Trent laughed. God, he *laughed*. And not the way he'd laughed at me when he'd caught me trying to steal from his mother. He laughed like the world was ending and he didn't care. Like this office wasn't a hellhole and we didn't hate each other's guts. He laughed with a promise, with a melody, with a mellifluous sound that trickled bone-deep and changed the rhythm of my heartbeat. My knees felt as if they'd snapped like thin twigs, and I almost stumbled in shock.

He was such…a man.

Not that Vicious, Dean, and Jaime weren't men. They were—along with 80 percent of the people populating this floor. But only Trent Rexroth looked tortured and serious enough to cross all the bridges in the world and burn them shore to shore to get his way. Only Trent Rexroth looked capable of ruining your life if he put his mind to it. The fear he'd ingrained in me turned me on. And that worried me. A lot.

"I can do it again," I mumbled, half-desperate to hear the sound coming out of his mouth again, half-hoping it would make him look at me as more than a potential sacrifice.

He devilishly arched a thick eyebrow. "Let's see. But no Coke."

I squatted down to Luna and whispered something into her ear. She lowered her head and tried to stifle her laugh with her tiny fist. Triumphant, I looked up to examine Trent. This time, he wasn't smiling. His eyes were gleaming with something I wasn't entirely convinced he could even feel.

For a fleeting moment, something passed between us, but I didn't know what it was. He looked at me with an intensity I could feel on my shoulders. Like I had a superpower he wanted to get his hands on. I was almost relieved when Camila walked into the break room and he snapped his head toward her while I hurried to discard the Coke in the recycle bin.

"Mr. Rexroth! I'm s-so so sorry. I told her not to give Luna any soda. And I would never let Luna stay with a complete stranger." She was stuttering, her eyes moving frantically among the three of us as she cupped one of her cheeks with her hand. "Luna, come here, sweetie. Look, I was Edie's nanny for eight years. I know her very well. And I was just down the hallway, in the restroom…"

Wow. He must be a shithead for a boss. Although I didn't need Camila's reaction to know he was the take-no-prisoners type. Trent waved her off, losing interest in her speech.

"It's fine. Camila, can you take Luna to the playroom on the tenth floor? I'll be right down."

"Of course." Worry still marred every cell in my old nanny's face as she scooped Luna in her arms and rushed outside the spacious galley, her steps quickening as she glanced behind her shoulder at her dictator employer. Trent and I were left alone, and even though I felt disgusted with myself, my stomach flipped the way it usually did before a first kiss.

He got into my personal space with one stride. I gulped when I realized he was over ten inches taller than me.

"Is pissing me off your mission in life?" His tone was a flat line on a monitor, dead and grave.

I shrugged, not skipping a beat. "No, but it's a nice bonus."

He smiled. There was a threat in his smirk. His scent did stupid things to my head. Pulling at strings in my body I hadn't known could ache and tugging my reason in the wrong direction. I gulped, taking a step back. Trent seemed to disregard my plea for space and ate the distance between us again. My lower back hit the tawny, cool counter. Why was everything gold and corrupted here?

"There's a Funny Felix party on Saturday for Luna's kid camp. Tobago Beach. I want you to be there." His request was direct, callous. So was the big hand he put on the counter behind me, his body hovering next to mine. I shook my head.

"I… I can't."

"I don't think you understand, Edie. I'm not asking your under-age ass on a Chuck E. Cheese date. This is not optional. It's part of your job description. Look at your contract. Clause 4.4 requires you to put in some additional hours every month—weekends included. This is a business assignment. Nothing more."

"You don't understand." I gripped the counter behind me until my knuckles turned white, hyperaware of how his right hand was inches from mine. The idea of touching him was crazy and enticing. Sinful, even. "I don't do Saturdays. My Saturdays are mine, and I spend them out of town, in San Diego. I can work Sundays—no problem. But not Saturdays." I choked out every word. Trent's hardened face didn't flinch. His lips were so close to mine, I wasn't sure whether I was imagining it or if we really were molding into something else. I could feel his torso moving to the tempo of his breath without our bodies touching. The intimacy stripped me bare from the snark I usually carried like a cloak to keep the world at bay.

Please come closer. Please stay away.

"Why? What's on Saturdays?" His jaw was granite, his eyes titanium. If he didn't look so unattainable, I would caress his stubbled cheek the way I'd wanted.

I met his stare. "With all due respect, that's none of your concern."

"I'm hardly concerned. Just trying to figure out how reckless you are as I make plans around you and my daughter. For some reason, she seems to have taken a shine to you."

I hesitated, grimacing. "What makes you think I'm reckless?"

"Turning down Ivy League schools—and bragging about it—pickpocketing in the middle of a busy promenade, pissing off the most powerful men in the state on your first day at work, to name a few. Since we're hardly even acquaintances, I'm placing my bet on a lot more random shit coming my way if I dig any deeper." His words cut me like a knife as he unbuttoned the first two buttons of his shirt.

I'd noticed some things. Like how it was the second time he'd gotten rid of his tie or loosened his collar when I was around. Like maybe it meant he felt hotter when we were in the same close space.

I focused on the floor, trying to avert my thoughts from where he'd taken them the minute he'd loosened his collar. "Up until a week ago, I worked as a surfing instructor. I mean, yeah, I mug people. But only because…" I trailed off, looking for the right words without giving too much away. "Look, I have no choice, okay? Trust me, just because my father is loaded doesn't mean I see a dime of it. I'm not a kleptomaniac. And I only target certain people. The rich kind. The ones who don't need the money to pay for electricity or food," I added. Because to me, it made a difference.

"Bra-fucking-vo, Robin Hood. News flash—fifteen years ago, my mother *couldn't* have paid her electricity bill if you'd stolen her wallet. Stop making indolent assumptions. It's unbecoming."

"You should remind yourself of that—you just labeled me as reckless," I pointed out.

"Because you are. I don't think you'll be a good fit for Luna." But I wasn't sure I believed him, because he seemed keen to see me interact with her.

"I never auditioned for the job, so no harm done."

The speed with which he moved away from me was startling. Trent scanned me coldly, a sneer on his face. "You're coming to the party. Nonnegotiable, Van Der Zee."

"Don't," I said, grabbing my phone from the counter and angling my body toward the door. "I see what you're trying to do here. I like Luna, and I'm willing to be there for her—even after hours, no problem. But on my own terms. And ideally, without you around, either. Camila is great, but you and I don't get along."

He opened his mouth to say something, when Dean Cole waltzed in, grabbing a plate and loading enough fruit onto it to choke an elephant, his eyes impassive on the colorful basket.

"Hey, man." He stuck a toothpick into a piece of watermelon

and shoved it into his mouth, chomping. Trent spun to face him and offered him a wordless frown that screamed *fuck off*. Dean continued, undeterred, "As your best friend, I feel like I should give you a fair warning. Hitting on your business partner's daughter, who could practically be your own kid, is a bad move. We noticed you were in each other's faces from across the hall, and we all know hate turns into something else more often than not. So here's my two cents—keep your crotches to yourselves, kids. Right. Fucking. Now." Dean was still smiling cheerfully as he delivered the message. An onlooker from the other side of the glass would think he was discussing the weather or football. I looked between the two men. Trent's eyes flashed something Dean was obviously able to read, his lips remaining pursed.

"Gotcha, dude. Was just warning you." Dean lifted one palm up in mock defeat.

I excused myself, sneaking out of the kitchenette and leaving the two men locked in a stare-down. Before I managed to make my escape, Trent grabbed my arm—gently, not like my father—and whispered into my hair, "What did you tell Luna to make her laugh?"

I closed my eyes, leaning toward his neck, holding my breath so as to not inhale his scent and feed the growing addiction. "I told her that her dad is an uptight jerk."

I didn't look back to see who won the stare-down, Trent or Dean.

It didn't matter because I was the one who was losing.

My sanity, my logic, and my mind.

I was on the losing end, and I needed a fast win if I ever wanted to run away with Theo. Which I did. *A lot.*

CHAPTER SIX
TRENT

"Any news?" I let my shirt fall to the cathedral marble floor with a soft thud. Amanda stripped out of her dress mechanically, as she did most things, hanging the colorful number over the brown tufted wingback chair in my bedroom and watching the Todos Santos skyline from the floor-to-ceiling windows.

I realized that this was not a healthy way to conduct a relationship with the private investigator whom I'd hired to hunt down the woman who'd abandoned my child. I also realized that two-timing her and my child's therapist could go disastrously wrong. Yet I'd always liked messy, and mixing business and pleasure was a great idea—if you didn't mind the blowup and knew how to leverage the pleasure part to your own benefit.

Amanda worked extra hard for me. Sonya saw Luna twice as much as any other kid at her clinic.

And then there was another thing that kept me drawn to them: convenience.

As far as my family, parents, and friends were concerned, I hadn't touched a chick since Val fucked off to God knows where, and I wanted to keep it that way. I gave off strong not-over-Val vibes. I didn't want them to try to set me up with a woman, thinking I was in the market for one. Didn't want them to keep tabs and to tell me how goddamn wrong it was to be alone and how I needed to settle down.

Luckily, Amanda and Sonya didn't see me as more than a hot piece of ass who paid a healthy fraction of their salaries and fucked them so hard (with a condom—*lesson learned*) that they needed a whole week to recover. Amanda unclasped her white-lace bra from behind and it slid off of her arms. It looked like heaven against her chocolate skin.

"Still looking," she murmured, lighting a joint between her rosy lips.

"Where now?"

"Brazil. Trying to figure out if she's staying with her relatives there." Val's mother lived in Chicago. She'd run away from Val's abusive father in Rio when Valenciana was three years old. The chances of finding Luna's mother in Brazil were slim, but after three years and no news, I was okay with a wild goose chase. Money wasn't an issue these days, though it still felt weird spending it on such an abstract cause. Ever since Valenciana had decided to fuck off, I'd been searching for her relentlessly. It wasn't the leaving part I cared about; I'd given up on her acting like a mother long ago. I wanted to make it official. Wanted her to sign over custody rights to me. If Val decided to waltz into my life again—which wasn't that far-fetched, since she loved money and I had plenty—Luna not speaking at four years old would be something she could exploit in court to get her way. Because if Val took Luna, she would get enough child support to sustain her love for everything designer and expensive.

And if there was one thing I'd definitely never survive or allow, it was someone taking my kid away from me.

Amanda walked over to where I leaned on the window, still in her kitten heels, a Caribbean goddess who had no time for a husband or kids herself. She stopped by my wet bar (so nineties, but I'd been a poor kid back then and that had been my dream, and Old Trent had worked part-time on making Young Trent's dreams come true) and plucked a bottle of limited-edition Jameson. I wasn't much of a drinker, but after butting heads with a teenybopper today and having her scrawny ass refuse me, a little sip wouldn't hurt. Amanda sat on the bed and patted the velvety linen beside her, and I sat next to her, pressing my head against her bare tits as she poured the liquor into my mouth from above.

"I feel inclined to tell you, Rexroth, you're probably not going to find Val. No one cares if you cross the border into Mexico, never mind farther south. Val didn't even need burner phones, a darknet email address, and a fancy fake identity. She could likely skip to a beach town and stay there with a friend or pick up an odd job. She sold most of the things you'd purchased for her prior to her disappearance and had a healthy sum of child support, which could tide her over for a long time."

I felt the burn of the liquor slithering down my throat and wondered how the fuck Dean could have been an alcoholic in the past. Booze depressed me. Plus, I found myself doing stupid shit when I was drunk. Like writing notes about my daughter and showing them to her therapist. I plucked the joint from Amanda's lips and tucked it between mine, tilting my head back and puffing out a ribbon of sweet-scented smoke skyward. Amanda's coal-black hair engulfed my pecs as she leaned to kiss my bare shoulder, across the tattoo I'd gotten right before college when I had been sitting at home with a broken ankle and burning time was a priority.

"Fuck" was my sophisticated answer to her little speech. My dick was already hard and thick. She sucked on my neck, declaring her intentions by biting my shoulder. The air conditioner in the room hummed between us, and I listened closely for noise from the outside. Luna was fast asleep in the other wing of the penthouse, her room right next to Camila's. She would never meet Amanda. She would never know what her daddy did at night.

"Let go of her, Trent. Find a good woman who can take care of your kid. Literally every single woman on this continent with eyes and ovaries is a willing candidate. You're the whole package," she said.

Catching the joint between my teeth, I slid her matching white thong down her thighs and shoved three fingers into her at once, working my way up to her G-spot and rubbing it lazily. She didn't even have time to drop her ass back on the covers from giving me access to her pussy. Her sudden moan sliced the air when I pushed my thumb to her clit and started massaging, working her up.

"It's going to hurt today," I said.

"Why?" she purred, instantly warming up to the idea. "Who pissed you off this time?"

Her name sat at the tip of my tongue, but letting it loose was acknowledging Edie was on my mind. She was young. So goddamn young. And even if I didn't care about the age—which I did—her body was straddling the line between ripe and juvenile. It still hadn't reached its full potential and gotten all its defined curves. I cared about Fiscal Heights Holdings and had plans for it. Plans that didn't include Edie *or* her vindictive father. She was therefore a calamity, a downfall, and a sure-as-fuck distraction.

"No one." I licked my way to Amanda's throat, stopping to stare at her. Amanda didn't expect a kiss. No one did. "No one important."

It was a lie I wanted to believe in.

It was a lie I cultivated with my brain, my heart, and whatever was left of my soul.

It was a lie that would become truth. It had to.

EDIE

My phone alarm buzzed with enthusiasm we obviously didn't share at four a.m. sharp. Waking up in the ink dark wasn't my idea of fun, but surfing was, so I bit the bullet, convincing myself that it was temporary, even though I had no reason to think that.

Yawning, I stretched inside my twin bed, my eyes slowly

regaining focus. Pink walls. Two chandeliers. White antique furniture restored and imported from Italy. Everything in my room suggested I was a happy, cheerleader-type teenage girl. No one could suspect this room represented a cage, a persona I was supposed to perform. No one knew that I had to shove my surfing gear, wax, wet suits, and whatnot to the back of my garage, even though I used them every day, on the off chance someone would find out I wasn't an ice princess.

Surfing wasn't prestigious enough to be an approved-of activity for a Van Der Zee.

My surfboards were hidden under heavy brown canvas in one of the garages, where guests couldn't see them, even by accident, and all the family pictures I'd hung on my coral walls had been taken down the same day I'd put them there. The only evidence to the fact this room was once warm and mine was the naked nails hammered to the wall.

No one knew a thing about the real me because I wasn't perfect and the Van Der Zees were.

At least on the outside.

We were the Brady Bunch sans the gazillion kids. Blond and beautiful and with the biggest, whitest smiles in our zip code.

I slipped into an orange bikini, a matching wet suit, and a black hoodie and texted Bane. We didn't get to surf together now that I was working a dead-end job, but I still offered. It sucked to surf in the pitch black, not to mention it was exceedingly risky. But I didn't have much choice. I started work at seven in the morning and didn't get off until seven in the evening. And when I did, I had to check on my mom, cook for her, make sure she was okay. Someone had to, after all, and it sure as hell wasn't going to be Jordan.

I entered the kitchen for some coconut water and a granola bar. Blood-red granite countertops and stainless steel appliances shone from every corner. The kitchen was one of my favorite places in the mansion because my father rarely ever wandered there. He had his food delivered to his room by one of our housekeepers whenever he was home. When he did make an appearance, it was to make my mother some tea, which was the only thing that seemed to soothe her troubled mind.

"Mom?" I gasped when a frail, hunched back greeted me, wrapped in an off-white sateen robe. "What are you doing up?"

She was sitting at the marble dining table, staring at an article in a local newspaper. I walked over and pressed my lips to the crown of her blond head.

"Hey," I said softly. "Late night?"

"Who is April Lewenstein?" She pressed a thoroughly chewed fingernail onto an image of Dad hugging a young businesswoman, both smiling to the camera at one of FHH's functions. She dragged her finger across their picture, and ink smeared both their faces. I allowed myself an indulgent sigh, my shoulders loosening.

"April's in accounting, seventh floor. Married, five months pregnant. You have nothing to worry about. Go back to bed."

She whipped her head in my direction. Her lips were unnaturally plump, her skin too tight from endless injections, and her red-rimmed eyes told the story of another unbalanced cocktail of medication that we'd have to get replaced and prescribed.

"You would tell me if you knew he was cheating on me." She grabbed the fabric of my hoodie and balled it, pulling me in to her face.

I offered a noncommittal shrug. "Sure." *No chance in hell.* At this point, Lydia Van Der Zee couldn't deal with the simple fact that our pool was going to stay closed for the rest of the summer for maintenance. But I told her what she wanted to hear because white lies paved the path to living with her brand of instability in relative peace. For me, not her, of course.

"How's work for you, my darling girl?" She relaxed her grip on my hoodie. My eyes flicked to the clock above the fridge, knowing I owed her the company, if nothing else. I slid onto a chair next to her and unscrewed the coconut water's cap, bringing it to my lips. "It's fine. Jordan picked the biggest assholes in town to work with. I can't wait for him to find another pet project to spend all his time on."

Fiscal Heights Holdings was just another loop in my father's corporation belt. He had purchased and taken over so many companies before, I could hardly keep up with the count. He treated his businesses like needy lovers—giving them everything they needed in the first year and then dumping them to fend for themselves once he grew bored and found another exciting venture.

"I don't know about that," my mother mumbled, pulling at her fat lower lip. "He likes the idea of brushing shoulders with Baron Spencer and his ilk. They're big names in Todos Santos, and Jordan wants to run for mayor."

Fiscal Heights Holdings was based in Beverly Hills, in big LA, but we lived in the town of Todos Santos. And Todos Santos was small. Frighteningly so (see also: me trying to steal my boss's mother's purse by accident).

So Mom didn't have to remind me Trent Rexroth was a big deal. Recently, I'd found myself thinking about him obsessively, in and out of the office, which was why I made it a point to push him away whenever he was in my vicinity.

"Your dad's been acting weird. Cheating again, I'm sure. I think it's serious this time."

"Doubt it." I offered a consoling smile. I meant the serious part, not the cheating. He definitely cheated.

She rubbed at her cheek tiredly. "His business trips have never been this long or this often before."

"Maybe he is gearing up to become mayor. Meeting donors, yada yada." Though he hadn't talked about his political aspirations in a while and that meant they weren't on his mind. Jordan Van Der Zee had one true love, and that was the sound of his own voice.

The kitchen door made a soft noise, and I snapped my head around on an instinct, ready to yank a drawer open and chase a bastard with a steak knife. When I saw that it was the devil himself leaning on its frame, I exhaled but knew better than to relax.

"You're up, too? What's with you guys? It's half past four in the morning," I muttered, clutching my drink. The weekend was fast approaching, and I didn't want to piss off Jordan. I needed this visit on Saturday, so playing nice was crucial.

"Edie and I have something to discuss. Go back to bed, Lydia. I will make you some tea in a moment." Even though his disapproval was directed at my mother, it didn't make the burn less marring. She got up on defeated feet, walking out of the room not unlike a ghost. Every step she took screamed negligence, abandonment, and weakness. My mother was abused just enough to break her, but not enough for me to go to the police with it. *Balance*, Rexroth had said, *is everything*. And oh, how right he was.

I closed my eyes, taking a deep breath. *You will not lose your shit over this, Edie. Screw surfing and his little ego games and making a point. Look at the big picture.*

Jordan snatched the coconut water from my hand, slam-dunking the bottle into one of the two giant sinks in the kitchen island.

"I was drinking that." There was spite in lethal quantities in each of my innocent words.

"Not anymore. That and the surfing… It makes you look like a hippie. Van Der Zees drink coffee every morning. It keeps us sharp."

"You make Mom tea twice a day." I grinned.

"Your mother is not a Van Der Zee. Her claim to fame is marrying one."

There wasn't a way for me to acknowledge him that wouldn't start a third world war, so I kept my mouth shut.

"Edie, we need to talk."

"I thought that's what we were doing."

He leaned forward, his elbows on the table. The grave look on his face told me he was disappointed with me again, though hell if I knew why.

"I saw your exchange with Rexroth yesterday in the break room. The whole floor did."

My eyes darted to him, my mouth falling open before I could fashion a comeback. If my father suspected I was flirting with Rexroth, he would strip me out of everything I cared about and had left. I couldn't allow it.

"Listen—" I started, but he cut me off with a wave of a hand.

"No daughter of mine would be stupid enough to fall for his brute charm. I do know that, Edie." He started slipping on his tie, tying it without even having to look in the mirror. I sat back, folding my arms over my chest. "But I saw the way he looked at you and the way he leaned into you, both of which weren't appropriate considering your age difference and your recent employment with us. I'm not sure what Trent Rexroth has in mind, but he will not get his way, whatever that is. Now, you know your father well enough to understand the consequences of associating with Trent, correct?"

Was Jordan going to off Trent Rexroth? I wouldn't put it past him. He was positively certifiable when it came to protecting his family's honor, with *honor* being the operative word here. Love, feelings, and general well-being were disposable in his world. The realization that this conversation could go in so many different ways—all of them wrong—hit my stomach first and then rolled up to my chest, making my throat close up. My heart was littered with broken promises and half-baked happy moments. A wasteland of hopes and dreams that could never be fulfilled without Theo.

"Rexroth doesn't interest me, so don't waste your breath warning me off him," I said, flicking old sand from beneath my chipped fingernails. It was always there, no matter how much I picked at it. Truth be told—I loved it being there. The sand reminded me of the ocean, of surfing, of *freedom*.

"Would you like me to increase your hourly rate?" Father lurched forward like a heavy machine, taking my hand in his and clasping it robotically. His skin was cold and dry, a perfect metaphor to the man he was. I considered my words carefully, my gaze gliding over our hands, how unnatural they looked and felt.

"Well, you do only pay me minimum wage."

"And would you like for me to arrange it so that you could see Theodore on Saturdays *and* every other Wednesday evening?" he followed, his smile cunning. *Theodore.* Not Theo. Never Theo.

My fingers were shaking, itching to withdraw from my father's grasp. They trembled to touch Theo again. To feel his face between my hands. His laugh on my skin. His soul next to mine. At the same time, I knew Jordan well enough to recognize the carrot he was dangling in front of me was poisonous. My hand still stung from his touch, and I wanted to wash it with soap, scrub it until the first layer of skin peeled. He leaned closer, his breath full of minty toothpaste and venom.

"I need you to help me, Edie. There's a job to be done, and you're the perfect candidate."

"I'm listening," I said, wanting to see where he'd take it.

"Trent Rexroth. I want you to sniff around about him. Find out what his deal is."

"Why?" It didn't take a genius to know these two hated each other. Then again, my father collected enemies like one would stamps or Christmas cards. Dutifully and fondly. Every powerful person he came across was labeled, seen, and treated as a national threat. The term *egomaniac* was coined specifically for him. Jordan Van Der Zee had no problem being agreeable to people less worthy, rich, and important than he was. But the minute you became a competitor or an obstacle, he would run you over and then reverse back and forth just to double-check and be on the safe side.

"His silence is irking, and he always goes against me. He is up to something. I want to know what it is. I want to know all there is to know about what he does in his office behind closed doors. I want to know what days he takes his daughter to the therapist. I want to know his schedule. Where he keeps his safe and files and iPad. I. Want. To. Know. Everything."

Clearly, he thought Trent Rexroth was planning something shady behind his back. A hostile takeover or maybe a surprise ambush that would affect his beloved investments company.

Trent Rexroth definitely gave the impression of being a control freak. Maybe Jordan was right to be worried. It made no difference at all. Because as much as I hated turning down Wednesdays with Theo, I also didn't want to dig myself a deeper grave by letting my father play me like this. It was a damned if I do and damned if I don't situation. Either he was lying to me about giving me more time with the only guy I cared for or he was telling the truth but setting a precedent to a chain of blackmails now that he knew they would work. The double-edged sword cut my heart in two.

"No, thanks," I said slowly, flicking my thumb against the edge of the table. "Take your offer to someone who is interested in it."

"My dearest daughter." He grabbed my hand again, pulling at my arm on purpose. It didn't hurt, but it was far from feeling comfortable. "You *will* do it. The perks are just a little push in the right direction. You have no choice in this matter."

"I'm not going to spy on Trent Rexroth." My voice grew louder, steadier. "He hasn't done anything bad to me, and besides, you're barking up the wrong tree. Rexroth hates my guts." That was an understatement. At this point, I was sure he'd rather confide in a neo-Nazi than tell me all his secrets.

My father, of course, chose to disregard my growing resistance. "If you won't do it, Edie, I'll be sending Theodore to New York. You know I can pull the right strings and make it happen. His facility in San Diego is grossly overcrowded as it is. I'd be doing him a favor."

Back in familiar waters. This was more like it. The threats, I was used to. "Blackmailing someone *into* blackmail is an interesting method. I'd like to see you pull this off. Move Theodore to a lesser facility when you're trying to run for mayor. Someone you don't want anyone to know about in the first place," I said dryly, hating him and Rexroth and the whole world for standing between me and happiness. I didn't care about the money and the glitz or the broken Louboutins. I just wanted to surf and be next to Theo. The fact that those things felt impossible to achieve made me feel like a trapped butterfly in a glass bell jar. A tiny creature slamming against the barrier until I ran out of energy, breath, and hope.

"You're throwing the word *blackmail* around way too often and loudly for my liking, young lady. Consider it research," he suggested, releasing my hand again.

"You can call it research or blackmail or Uncle Joe. The answer would still be no."

It was already five in the morning, and I'd officially missed my surfing window. Screw it, I could come in at eight once a week. The chair beneath me scraped as I stood up.

Something hit the table with a heavy *slap*. I whipped my head around and looked at him once again.

A bag.

My mother's medication bag.

It shouldn't have sounded so heavy, but it did because it was. Because nowadays, my mother required three pills just to get her out of bed, and that was without her vitamins—which she was addicted to—and the gummies promising radiant skin, tough nails, and heavenly slumber, which she chewed on throughout the day. She also took another three to fall asleep at night.

"Reconsider. You have two people to think about. One of them—your mother—is a helpless child trapped in a woman's body. You've burned every bridge in order to save them, Edie. Every single one. From your education to your dream of becoming a surfer and getting away from here, from *me*. You've made all the sacrifices for your mother and Theodore. What's one more?"

I stood facing the hallway, an eternal scream making my body shudder. He had me exactly where he wanted me, and he knew it. He sauntered toward me, a cloud of his smugness hanging in the room like a stench.

"Make no mistake, Edie. I will sacrifice your mother and your locked-up obsession without a second thought. You signed up to be my little obedient marionette. You don't get to make the rules." The last sentence was spoken so close to me, I could feel his breath brushing my back.

I stormed out of the kitchen, feeling his eyes shooting daggers at my back.

I'd bleed to death before turning around and seeing his face. I knew how he felt.

Victorious.

CHAPTER SEVEN
TRENT

Funny Felix was a shit show.

Much to no one's surprise.

Actually, that wasn't entirely fair to the person dressed in a feline-looking teddy bear whatever-the-fuck costume standing in the center of a circle of screaming kids, dancing for them like a trained monkey.

I guess the party was okay for everyone who wasn't in my immediate circle. For all the parents who were smiling wide, holding hands—even the fucking divorcees were being civilized for the sake of their children—watching the fruit of their loins getting their faces painted and twirling with a bunch of clowns, aka Felix's Little Helpers. It was creepy, but when you thought about it—when you really, truly put some thought into it—a lot of what grown-ups found intimidating were kids' favorite things. Because kids, unlike their parents, watched the world sans the tainted lens of preconception and intolerance.

Kids were not racist.

Kids were not judgmental.

Kids didn't care that your car cost twice the annual salary of the average American.

Kids were fun.

Kids were pure.

But I'm not.

I was a biracial man in a white world, so I knew exactly how Luna was feeling. Just like Luna, I didn't physically stand out, not even in the WASP-y town of Todos Santos. I wasn't even dark-skinned. My mother was German, my dad African American. My skin color was diluted, watered-down. Still, it was there. It was there in my height and my soft lips and my curly hair (when I let it grow, which was fucking never). It was there when people made jokes about big dicks and basketball. It was there when I'd tried to apply for odd jobs while I was supporting myself in college. It was there, but others pretended that it wasn't.

There was something to be said about us biracial people. Society fucked us good in all holes and angles. I was too Black to be fully accepted in the white, rich town I'd gone to high school in (football prodigy) and too white to be accepted in the Black community in San Diego where I'd grown up.

It wasn't that I didn't have friends because I had many. It was the identity I'd been lacking. The tribe. That puzzle into which I'd fit.

Luna was both different from and similar to me in that sense.

She was beautiful and exotic, a rare diamond who was likely to suffer less from prejudice because times had changed. She drew people to her, and, fuck, she looked so normal, until she opened her mouth and nothing came out. Until an unsuspecting mother asked her name and my daughter looked away and tears prickled her eyes because she'd been spoken to by a stranger.

Until the mother's kid called Luna a freak.

"She doesn't speak English, Ma. She doesn't even speak Spanish. The freak doesn't speak at all."

What did I say? A shit show.

My mother was there to squeeze my shoulder, pleading with her eyes for me not to kick the kid's head to the ground and shove his face in the dirt and make him eat it. The party was on the beach, of all places, and the heat was slowly slaying the cupcakes, the face paint, and my nerves.

"What kind of fucked-up kid says something like that, anyway? They're *four*." I dragged a hand over my head. Luna was sitting with Sonya under a tree a few feet from us, trying to calm down from the incident. They were sharing an apple. Since Little Miss Busy on Saturdays was too important to accompany Luna and me, I figured I'd take an arsenal of people as moral support and to keep me company. My parents, Darius and Trisha, had tagged along, and Sonya had managed to stop by at the very last minute, even though she was supposed to watch her son in some sports competition I couldn't even remember.

"They're four, they're privileged, and they're blunt. You grew up with the nastiest kids in the country. Why this behavior still surprises you I have no idea." My mother ironed my shirt down with her hand. She'd come a long way from the Trish who'd worked at Walmart part-time, since I'd hit the corporate jackpot. Wearing designer everything and not apologizing for it, she now looked like the women she hadn't even had the honor of serving because they'd never set foot in that store. I loved that we were now part of a club that had never really accepted us. It was ironic in the Groucho Marx joke kind of way.

My dad was the only Black male member of the Todos Santos Country Club.

Luna went to school with the daughter of Toby Rowland, the rich bastard who'd broken my ankle in high school to grab the captain of the football team title from me.

We were blending, meshing, stealing everything that hadn't been offered to us.

And. I. Fucking. Thrived. On. It.

"Time to wrap this shit up. I've officially reached the end of my patience." I shook my head and let out a sigh when Luna refused to budge from under the tree and join the other kids in a dance, even when Sonya encouraged her, no doubt promising to never leave her side. Luna was especially trying in social events. I'd spent the first year after her mother disappeared at home with her before finally caving in to life. I wanted to share the world with her. She was mine. My blood, my DNA, my cells, my eyes, my fucking being. Still, I wished she'd be more accepting of the outside world and that it would be more accepting of her.

My parents exchanged worried looks, frowning. They'd been a tremendous help with raising Luna ever since I'd moved from Chicago, where I'd managed an FHH branch, back to Todos Santos, selling a healthy percentage of my stocks to Jordan Van Der Zee, along with a piece of my soul in the process.

"Why don't you go ahead and get some rest?" My mother rubbed my cheek, forcing a smile on her sweet face. "Dad and I will take Luna back to our place for a sleepover. She's been dying to help Dar build that spaceship for weeks."

The spaceship.

My dad was a dreamer. An inventor. He built shit that never worked. He wasn't really building a spacecraft, obviously. What he was building was a healthy relationship with my daughter, using empty batteries, cardboard boxes, superglue, and old matches that had gotten soaked in the rain and were no longer usable. He was building what I couldn't even set the fucking ground for: a healthy, fun relationship with my daughter.

Ignoring the awkward looks she was getting.

Helping to shoulder the burden that came with being different.

It bothered me because those differences were the things that people would blame me for if her mother ever came back into her life. Luna's differences were what Val would exploit. So, yeah, it made me resent them.

"You don't have to do it," I said, not really arguing with her. I could use the night off. I wasn't even going to call Sonya or Amanda. Straight to fucking bed for me. Maybe watch a stupid action movie and order greasy food I'd never allow myself to eat on a weekday. My six-times-a-week strength training didn't go well with junk food, but sometimes even grown-ass men allowed themselves a little pity party.

"Please." Mom jerked me into a hug. She was so much smaller than my six-foot-four body, it was funny to think I'd come out of her. It was also funny because Trish Rexroth was one of the most gracious people I knew and I was a Shithead with a capital S. "We love Luna and want to spend every chance we have making her happy. And anyway, I was planning on baking that apple pie, and your dad's sugar level is sky-high. She'll be doing him a favor eating the majority of it. Right, Dar?" She turned to my dad, who was arguing—legit quarreling—with a four-year-old boy over what the face paint they'd been using on the kids was made of.

I smirked. "Okay."

I said my goodbyes to Luna, my parents, and Sonya and climbed into my black Tesla. I called a Korean barbecue place on my way home, ordering every other dish on the menu, and drove in circles for a while, enjoying a different type of silence. Not loaded with words or tension but loneliness and selfishness, two things you learned to crave as a parent. If someone would ask me quietly, on their last breath, if I wanted to be a father, and I knew my admission would never leave their mouth, I'd say the truth. I'd say no. Because it was too hard, too heartbreaking, and too fucking all-consuming to be Luna Rexroth's dad.

And still.

And still. I loved my daughter hopelessly, desperately, urgently. Which only made my inability to help her all the more soul-crushing. The idea that she'd given up on people or—maybe even worse—on her *life* before it had even started infuriated me. I wanted to show her that the world was a beautiful, frightening place worth experiencing. That peasants could be crowned kings if they worked hard enough and how her daddy was living proof of that.

There was a wooded reservoir squashed between Orange County limits and Todos Santos I'd especially loved as a teenager. It was a little on the wild side. Large, remote, and a total money pit to local councils. No district wanted to deal with it, especially as it had been the city hall of Todos Santos before the latter had gotten all fancy and relocated to a downtown zip code with enough fountains and swans to be mistaken for Monaco. Since it was technically not a part of any city, it got neglected and forgotten. But only by the adults.

A lot of kids came to the reservoir to have sex, get drunk, and generally be assholes, which was most teenagers' favorite pastime. Back when we were in high school and Vicious's parents had been at home—which had been rare—we'd meet there for our weekly fights, in which we defied each other.

I decided to drive there on a whim, knowing the Korean place took a lifetime to get take-out orders made—especially one as large as mine. A trip down memory lane would remind me I hadn't always been this old, this bitter, this fucked-up.

I drove by the old benches, the lighthouse standing in the lake, sandwiched between the hiking trails. I rolled my window down, inhaling the perfume of nature. Freedom. Youth. Pure air. A small smile curved on my face, and I almost relished the feel of it.

Almost.

The person to wipe the smile off was the last one I was expecting to see, even though it made perfect sense for her to be there.

Edie Van Der Zee.

I heard her before I saw her, and even when I did see her, it was through bushes and fog, shadowed by the night. In fact, I only recognized her because her wild, wavy blond hair was cascading down her bare shoulders and because of that throaty, hoarse laugh. She was wearing a loose top, little shorts, and her unlaced Dr. Martens. She looked so much like a kid I wanted to punch myself in the balls for imagining her writhing under me while I'd pounded into Amanda the other night. Edie's legs were still curve-less, two straight toothpicks. Not very different from Luna's.

You're fucking disturbed.

She stood in front of two guys and a girl who were sharing a bench, sitting on the back of it because they were such fucking rebels. *Not.*

I only wanted to slow down so I could hear what they were laughing about but ended up stopping completely behind a wall of wild brush when I realized my black car blended perfectly with the night. This was the point when I should have probably acknowledged that I'd crossed a hard line of some sort. I was stalking my employee, *my teenage employee*, late in the evening. But I chose to dismiss the level of creepiness I was exhibiting by pointing out to myself that A—I hadn't actively sought her out, I'd happened to bump into her—and B—if she was in some kind of trouble and I turned my back on her, I'd never forgive myself.

Far-fucking-fetched, but I'll take it.

One of the guys, who was wearing a hoodie in the middle of the summer and deserved to die a slow death for this alone, stood up and sauntered over to one of the reservoir's most iconic symbols— the old town's city hall. It was deserted, decaying, and made out of sandstone. Big, boasting of empty rooms, and last time I was there fifteen years ago, every one of them had been occupied with a couple or a threesome getting lucky on dirty mattresses or sofas that had been dragged into the place and were probably contaminated. My teeth clenched as he threw his arm over Edie's shoulder, hooking her by the neck and jerking her toward him for a forehead kiss.

"C'mon, Gidget. We haven't fucked in forever, and all the new girls at the beach are too vanilla," the tool said as they zigzagged toward the entrance. *Gidget?* And why did his choice of words grate on my every nerve? I used the word *fuck* as a verb, adverb, noun, and simple decoration in every other sentence. If I could marry it, I most likely would. Yet I hated that it had left his mouth and hated it even more that it was directed at her. Mostly, I loathed that the tool was wearing a hoodie so I couldn't even see the goddamn face I was about to smash with my fist.

"Wait, let me get a blunt from Wade," Edie's husky voice murmured, and she jogged in the other direction, toward the losers on the bench. Was she really going to screw some asshole in an abandoned building? I wasn't buying it. Then again, what the hell did I know about this chick? Oh, right. She was a pickpocketing, self-centered liar who'd ditched my daughter's party to hang out with pot-smoking idiots. *And* she was a teenager. Of course, she was going to fuck him in an abandoned bastion. And, of course, she wasn't vanilla.

My dick stirred in my pants, and I did the unthinkable, cupping it with my fist and squeezing hard. My way of saying it was never going to happen. She wasn't even my type. Too small, too blond, too sweet-looking, though at this point, I knew she was nothing like her looks. Girl had some serious baggage.

In my desperate bid not to jerk off, I failed to remember my headlights were still on. Her friends on the bench craned their necks to see what—or who—was lurking behind the bushes. I needed to do something. That something was to get the fuck out of there.

Then again, I was always the bastard who did stupid shit, preferably with the most poisonous woman in his locale. Why stop now?

Instead of U-turning and leaving, I hit the accelerator, my car speeding silently—justifying its $170K price tag—and slammed the brakes when Edie's ass was directly in front of my window, mere feet from the doors to the old city hall.

"Van Der Zee," I roared. She whipped her head around so fast I thought her spine was going to snap. I leaned sideways and popped the passenger door open.

"Get in the car."

Her mouth fell open, and for a second, I wanted nothing more than to shove my tongue into it. Instead, I pushed the door open wider, growling.

"Now."

The tool she was about to spread her legs for was now directly in front of me. He had a neck tattoo, droopy green eyes, and a lip ring. He looked like a fucking Blink-182 reject. Only taller. And probably more muscular. Not as big as I was, but certainly the kind to pocket enough panties to open a Victoria's Secret store. *My kind.*

He waltzed over to my car and parked his elbows on my fucking window like he owned it. Ballsy. He was going to say goodbye to those balls if he wasn't careful.

"And may I ask who the fuck you are?" He lit a blunt coolly, puffing the stream of smoke directly into my face. He was playing the game I'd mastered when I was eighteen. The one where you pushed until something snapped. But I was thirty-three now and could crush his neck, and future, without blinking. I tried to remind myself that I didn't want to do any of those things to him. That he was just a hoodie-shelled teenager. A peacock trying to fart some extra pretty feathers to impress his lady friend.

"I'm her boss. Who the fuck are you?"

"Her steady dick." He cocked his head sideways, smirking. "And I don't like competition outside the ocean. So I suggest you take a hike." He tapped the blunt with his forefinger, sprinkling ashes into my car. Onto my leather seat.

Bad play.

I heard Edie's soft giggle behind him, and maybe it was because she'd bailed on Luna's party, and maybe it was simply because I was done restraining my inner asshole when it came to her, but I was already deep in ruthless mode, ready to kick it up a notch and become a total cunt. I threw the car into park, opened the door, and stormed outside, rounding the front of my vehicle before cupping her elbow.

"If you don't get in the car right now, you'll see exactly what happens when the countdown ends," I whispered into her hair, my lips accidentally brushing the shell of her ear. My cock jerked in my pants, and I groaned. She twisted her head to watch me, bewildered.

"Why in the world would I do anything for you outside of working hours, Rexroth?"

"Because you told me you had important business today and therefore couldn't attend my girl's party when you were, in fact, going to pork a goddamn meathead in a rat-ridden abandoned building. I swear, Edie. If you don't get in right this second, your father gets a Sunday visit from his business partner tomorrow morning, and I'll tell him all about your thieving ways and peculiar sexual escapades."

Threatening to rat out an eighteen-year-old to her parents was some sort of rock bottom, surely. At the same time, she didn't need this. Smoking pot and fucking in a public place. Make no mistake, I'd done exactly that at her age. Oh, well. I never said I was above being a fucking hypocrite.

"Hey, now, old man. Chill your calcium-deprived bones and stop treating her like crap, or I'll have to kick your ass." Blondie Dudebro got in my face, and I was going to end the night in a police station. I shoved him once before Edie thrust her body between us, pushing us both in opposite directions.

"Hey, hey, hey, stop it!"

"You don't need another Jordan, Gidget. Tell him to fuck off." The kid pointed at me, his lips twisting in disgust. She shook her head, her flat palms on his chest, walking him backward toward the bench. Her other friends were staring with their mouths open so wide you could practically see what they'd had for lunch. They stood up from the bench but didn't get any closer. Fucking cowards.

"It's not like that, Bane. Look, I'll explain later. See you tomorrow at the beach." She turned her back to me, pressing her lips to his. Their mouths brushed in a familiarity I'd never had with a woman because I'd never stuck with someone for longer than two weeks, and I watched, my teeth slamming into each other.

"Enough of this shit. Time to go." I practically threw Edie's ass to the passenger seat before rounding to my side of the car and buckling up. I started the engine, trying to wrap my head around my reaction to this surreal encounter and figuring out where in the fuck I was going to take her.

"Where do you live?" I threw the car into drive. She didn't answer, staring out the window, harboring unshed tears in her eyes. My car slid through the dirt road leading out of the reservoir, the noiseless electric engine making our silence particularly unbearable. I choked the steering wheel, feeling my nostrils flare.

She wasn't going to answer. Not before I explained my behavior.

"You're my business partner's daughter, Edie. I can't let you run around smoking pot and fucking tattooed boys. I can overlook it when I'm not around you, but if I bump into you in the middle of the night in a deserted place, I'm sure as hell gonna act on it."

"Please." She sniffed, clinging to her cool with everything she had in her. "Never bullshit a bullshitter. You can spare me your stupid explanation. You don't give a damn about Jordan Van Der Zee, and you sure don't care about his daughter. This was an act of power, Rexroth. You were pissed I didn't go to Luna's party, and you decided to retaliate. But know this—I *did* go somewhere today. Somewhere important. Just because I made it back in time to hang out with friends doesn't mean I ditched Luna."

Edie was partly right. I was pissed with her for choosing to hang out with her friends over spending time with my daughter. What was possibly worse was that the other reason I'd dragged her away from her weekend hangout was because I was infatuated with her ass. Or at least with the idea of tapping it. Of course, that would guarantee Jordan would somehow find a way to kick me off the board, out of the company, and essentially ruin my entire career. Not to mention I wouldn't be able to look at myself in the mirror after fucking a teenager, legal or not.

"Where do you live?" I repeated my question, ignoring the valid points she'd made. She huffed and dug inside the black backpack in her hand, reaching for her cell phone.

"Hey." I snatched the device from her hand, my eyes still on the road. "I'm talking to you."

"Yeah, well, that hardly means I'm listening," she muttered.

"The fuck is your problem, kid?" I asked.

"You're my problem. My father is my problem. The world is my problem. Let me out," she demanded, unhooking my fingers from her phone and retrieving it. The escalated tension in the vehicle made me lose focus on the road.

"In the middle of nowhere?" I chuckled. "Yeah, no."

"Trent."

I shook my head. I'd take her to my penthouse if need be. I had two guest rooms that were unused all year 'round. She could crash there, and I'd deliver her ass to her parents first thing in the morning. It was a complicated solution, but one where she was safe and not fucking Blondie Dudebro.

"Let me go."

I scrubbed my chin thoughtfully, ignoring her as I stared at the road.

Then she did it.

The crazy girl opened the door of my moving vehicle and jumped out into a bush.

I smashed the brake pedal, parked the car and bolted out, rushing toward her. She was lying inside a scrub, supine. Her arms were stretched like a snow angel, and she was laughing at the moon with tears in her eyes like the lost kid she was.

Not chuckling, not smiling, but full-blown laughing.

If it was a cry for help, I chose not to listen. I chose to ignore what she was obviously going through because we were all trying to stay afloat in this pond of misery and helping her out came with the price of sinking further down. I pulled her up by the waist, ignoring how intimate it felt. Disregarding how her body matched mine like two pieces of a puzzle, against all fucking odds. My hand was on her lower back again, my knee between her thighs, and she was firm and athletic everywhere, but her face was soft and tender, like an Edgar Degas painting.

Our eyes fought a silent war. Her baby blues glittered brighter under the full, fat moon. I knew that if we held this position for a few more seconds, I was likely to do something I'd regret. Make the kind of mistake that could ruin a lot of lives. So I leaned toward her face to whisper to her that I was sorry for tonight. For everything, really. For being a jackass and a hypocrite and an asshole.

I slid in her direction, only to realize that she'd parted her lips, waiting for…fuck, a kiss?

I'm in. I knew the feeling because I'd been in this position more times than I could count. She was giving me the green light, the okay, the consent to touch her. Her hips rolled toward my groin very lightly, and a low, leisured growl glided between my lips.

What an interesting turn of events. Edie Van Der Zee wants me to dick her hard.

Five years ago, I would have given her what she wanted, consequences be damned.

Tonight, though, I had too much to lose.

"Edie"—my lips moved on her temple—"is there a reason why you're humping my leg? Thought you were mad at me for clam-jamming your ass tonight."

She was no longer on the verge of crying, but now I had a much bigger problem to deal with, and it was pointed directly at her pussy, hard and swollen and ready to give her what she so obviously wanted.

"Why *did* you clam-jam me, Rexroth?" she breathed, almost into my lips, and she smelled of vanilla and woman. Not like a girl. It made standing like this, with her practically straddling one of my thighs, slightly less dreadful.

"You already know why."

"I'm starting to think I missed out on an important detail." Her hips rolled forward in a wavelike motion, hitting my erection once and slightly and so fucking teasingly, it was the last nail in the age-gap-debate coffin. This woman knew what she was doing. She knew how to work her body, work a man's body, and it killed me that fucking Bane—what kind of name was that? Was he a Vicious knockoff?—knew all the secrets to her silky, sun-kissed flesh and scarlet lips and probably very sweet pussy.

I stepped away from her, leaning on the still-running car with a smirk.

"I'm sorry, sweetheart. I don't do children."

She moved closer to me, her inner thigh pressing against the side of my leg. She smiled, her grin dazzling with white teeth—one of them crooked and slightly chipped and imperfectly sexy—and purred, "Don't make promises that will make you feel like a pervert when you break them."

"I won't break them," I deadpanned, but I still let her press her small, perky, braless—*shit, braless*—tits against my lower pecs. The notion that I could slam her against my hood and fuck her from behind was too much. Or maybe I could spread her and eat her out before I fucked her in the middle of the woods. She would let me, and that was the worst thing about our situation. Edie would let me do that to her, and not because she was a naive girl with daddy issues.

But because she'd come here to fuck, and I was a willing body to her. Nothing less, nothing more.

"Interesting," she said, bending her knees and grinding against me, clasping my whole thigh between her legs. Her bare skin scraped along my denim, her puckered, hard nipple brushing my forearm. I didn't move. Just stared at her like she was a fucking health hazard, hoping she would stop or take my dick in her mouth and put me out of my misery. "You know what my favorite word is?" she hissed, clenching my thigh, feeling warm and damp.

Fuck? I wanted to retort. *Because I'd gladly give you some synonyms, facts, and hard examples of how to do it.*

But I was too fascinated with the direction she was taking this—us—to interrupt her little speech. She had a point. That much was for sure. For the first time since we'd met, I let her express herself and speak her mind. Not only because she was rubbing her sleek pussy all over my thigh and I didn't want to break the spell but also because she needed it. Kid had jumped out of a moving car five minutes ago to make a point.

Not a kid, I reminded myself. *A woman, Trent. A woman.*

"Sonder." The word rolled between her luscious lips like an illicit proposition. She took my hand and pressed it against the swell of her ass, on the border between her thigh and cheek. Her warm flesh made the dull ache in the pit of my stomach disappear somehow, and the weirdest thing about it was that I hadn't even noticed that it was there before. I didn't squeeze or withdraw my palm. My mind was racing, knowing this shouldn't be happening, and again, I fired excuses at myself.

It was nothing.

We weren't actually doing shit.

We weren't kissing or making out or fucking or sucking each other off. We were barely touching, even though it felt heavier and dense, even more than being completely naked in a room with a woman who already had a condom ready in her mouth.

"Sonder is the realization that each passerby has a life as vivid and complex as your own. I have a feeling you think you're the only one to know hardship, Rexroth. It doesn't sit well with me. Not at all."

"Tough luck, sweetheart, because you're working under me, and that's the only thing you'll do in that compromising position." I dragged my hand from her ass to my pocket, making a teasing stop at her hipbone, brushing it with my thumb. She pushed into my touch, and I denied her, not only to stay in control of my hands but also because seeing her burning for me was a visual that could very likely set what few morals I had on fire.

"We've started on the wrong foot." She ignored the gesture, but her goose bumps gave away her reaction. Her nipples were so erect they looked sore, in need of relief. "I apologize for mugging your mother. Can you apologize for bullying me? We can put all of this behind us. Start fresh. I'd like that." Her voice was honest and soft, genuine.

But what Edie hadn't realized was that the day I would stop giving her shit would be the day we'd be indifferent toward one another because there was no way we could communicate appropriately on any level other than taunting. And hating. And despising one another.

Unfortunately for her, she was too much fun to loathe. I wasn't ready to part ways with what we were, even if the relationship we were developing looked and smelled and *felt* like an incurable disease.

So, instead of being a grown-up and accepting her truth, I stopped her little lap dance by spinning and plastering her against my car. My hand was on her throat, which bobbed with a swallow, telling me that she was feeling the rush, the excitement of being at my mercy.

Fuck, Edie. You have no idea how merciless I could be.

I put as much weight on her as possible, enough for it to be intimidating yet not painful. She could feel my erection, the ridges of my abs, my flexed pecs, and the way my sweat glued my shirt and skin together. I leaned toward her mouth, knowing how much she wanted to be kissed, knowing I would never, ever give it to her.

"The only thing I'd ever apologize for is not getting to you sooner tonight. If I ever catch you spreading these legs for that tool, here or anywhere else, it'd be the end. Of you, of him, of everyone involved. As long as you hang out with my daughter—and that is what I expect you to do every Tuesday when she arrives at work with me—you'll be celibate. You can grind yourself against the showerhead while you think about my cock inside you, and you can play with your clit wishing it was my mouth, but no more fucking *Bane*, understood?"

She laughed and slid away from my touch and into the car, slamming her door in my face.

I walked around and resumed our drive, watching as she programmed her address into my navigator without answering me.

That was fine. I didn't need her words. I needed her to understand.

Her jaw twitched, telling me that the message was received. Good.

CHAPTER EIGHT
EDIE

"What do you want me to find out about Trent Rexroth?" I dumped a pile of documents onto my father's desk the following Monday morning, wiping my forehead with the back of my hand. I'd spent my entire Sunday surfing, avoiding questions about Trent from Bane, and trying to convince my mother to get out of bed and have dinner with us. I'd made couscous (the microwaved kind) and lemon chicken (from Whole Foods) and even made a perfectly edible salad, all of which I had eaten alone, in front of the kitchen TV. I had been twenty minutes into watching a gruesome episode of a reality cop show before I'd realized I was chewing to the images of criminals throwing bottled piss at police officers.

Guess you could say I was distracted.

The nagging ache between my legs reminded me that Trent had played with my feelings, my sexuality, and my mind. Most of all, his notion that he could do this to me—control me the way my father did—made my vendetta against him almost mandatory. I wasn't a toy to be controlled and tossed from hand to hand. My father held a very particular power against me.

Trent didn't.

He was about to find out that I was no pushover, even as I, in fact, let Jordan Van Der Zee shove me around.

My father looked up from his laptop, rubbing his chin with

his finger pads. Today, he wore a pale-gray suit and a light-blue tie, both of which had been tailor-made and purchased during his brief business trip a week ago. Which gave away the fact someone had ordered it for him.

A mistress, no doubt.

He was hopping on a plane that afternoon, flying to Zurich for a week. It was the third time he'd visited there in three months, which led me to believe he had a new shiny toy to play with. Whether he was really going to Zurich, I didn't care. I was just happy he'd be gone for six days.

"Smart kid." He clucked his tongue in approval.

Screw you, I answered inwardly. He was right. I was his little shadow puppet, ready to entertain every time he sent a flicker of light my way.

My father collected the documents I gave him and tucked them into a drawer he locked, considering my answer.

"Let's start off by finding out whether he takes his laptop and iPad home with him or leaves them at the office. The floor is wired at the reception, outside the bathroom, and in front of the elevators. Having a camera in your office is a personal choice. Look for cameras on his ceilings or walls or embedded in his furniture. Also, I want to know how many electronic devices he has with email and internet connections. And how often he uses them. If you can get your hands on one of them—bring it here."

Wow, that was incredibly specific. And here I thought he'd give me the benefit of the doubt and wasn't sure if I'd cave. He obviously had a detailed plan.

For the millionth time, I silently swore that the minute I untangled myself from the messy business with my father, I would throw him out of my life and lock the door behind him for good measure. I didn't want to depend on anyone for my happiness. But my father had this ability to pull at strings and use his power and connections to hurt people who didn't see eye to eye with him.

Potential sacrifice, echoed the words in my head. *Oh, how the tables have turned.*

"Doable." I nodded. Trent's PA, Rina, had emailed me earlier that morning notifying me that I'd spend the majority of Tuesday with Luna and Camila. We were going to go to a local zoo and would catch lunch with Trent at the Vine. The idea of spending time with the girls—both of whom I liked—was nothing short of thrilling. But coming face-to-face with Trent after humping him, as he'd bluntly put it, was disconcerting.

Good news was, I was sure I'd have access to his office at some point tomorrow. "I want my visiting limitations dropped. I want to see Theo on Saturdays *and* every other Wednesday, and I want to spend my holidays with him." My voice held a bleeding edge. Jordan waved a hand, his head already buried in a contract he'd retrieved from the printer by his desk. "That's fine. Tell Max to sort it out." Max was my father's PA. My mother had demanded Jordan stop hiring women as assistants in the hopes it would get him to stop cheating with his employees. Yeah. Fat chance, judging from his erratic schedule and sparse visitations to our house.

I made my way outside my father's office, his voice halting me in place.

"And Edie?" I turned around slowly, examining him behind his titanium desk. He looked so smug. Like he owned the world. Like he was immortal. *Fool.*

"Just a friendly reminder as your father, your employer, and the man who holds your future in his hands—don't double-cross me. Trent Rexroth is a smart kid, but he is nothing compared to me."

I closed the door on him, keeping my twitching mouth from opening and spitting out the truth Father never wanted to hear: Trent Rexroth was more than smart. He was devilishly brilliant. But that wasn't going to help him in this battle because I made him weak.

Weak where it mattered.

Weak where he left me aching.

And in his weakness, I'd find power.

And use it.

Not because I was vengeful or angry, but because I wanted to save Theo and my mom.

Not because I was a bad person, but because I needed to be good to the ones who depended on me.

I stole his iPad.

The ease with which I did it was both exhilarating and baffling, considering he'd already caught me thieving.

I was sure he was surprised I'd joined them without a fight—I'd cornered Camila in the break room and casually told her I'd been invited by Mr. Rexroth and would be tagging along, which wasn't a complete lie—but true to his detached reputation, Trent had acted like I was his daughter's annoying friend. In other words, he'd completely ignored me.

All throughout lunch, he was busy lavishing Luna with attention, cutting her food, talking to her about their plans for the weekend. He was wearing sharp navy slacks and a crisp white shirt, his sleeves rolled up to elbow length. The snaking veins and strong muscles on his forearms were meant to slam a girl against a wall and make her praise the Lord like a born-again Christian. I wasn't a particularly sexual person. So it definitely caught me off guard when I had to excuse myself and go to the restroom, bracing against the sink in front of the mirror and shaking my head. I tried to make the idea of him crashing me against one of the cubicles, yanking my skirt and underwear down, and eating me out from behind dissolve before my body caught up with my dirty thoughts. I even went as far as convincing myself that wanting to have sex with Trent Rexroth was just a quiet protest against my father. *Those forearms, though.* I knew they'd haunt me at night, cut me open the next time my toes curled in pleasure. Imagining his strong arms grasping me would serve as a match to ignite the dormant desire sitting in the pit of my stomach. I washed my face with ice-cold water. *F-o-c-u-s.*

When I got back to the table, Luna pointed at Trent's cell phone before gesturing with her hands to demonstrate something bigger.

"You want the iPad," he said. I hated the way he spoke to her. Like he cared—like he truly cared—even though I knew he was just another Jordan. Maybe I was doing him a favor by getting him kicked out of FHH. He obviously needed the perspective and time to bond with his daughter. "It's in my office. Camila will give it to you when we're done. Finish your pasta."

Luna strummed her fingers on the table, her eyebrows wrinkled.

"Maybe she should learn sign language," I murmured, more to myself than to anyone else, sticking a fork inside a juicy piece of steak and dragging it along the mashed potatoes. I never went to restaurants anymore—I spent my money on important things like gas and Theo—so this, in truth, wasn't completely terrible. I hadn't had a meal this decadent in years.

Trent growled, his favorite form of communication. "She knows how to speak. She just needs to do it." He scrolled through his digital keypad, not even sparing me a look. Camila patted the corners of Luna's mouth with a napkin, filling the pregnant air with words like "washing hands is important" and "want dessert?"

"She obviously feels more comfortable communicating with her hands right now," I persisted, taking another bite of the steak. "Why make her life more difficult? You said yourself that she can speak. She will when she wants to. In the meantime, you can give her another way to express herself."

He raised his eyes to me, his gaze loaded like a gun, before returning to his phone.

"I'll ask Rina to find a sign language teacher," he surprised me by saying.

"You'll need to learn it, too," I pointed out. He didn't like that. I could tell by the way he put his phone down and regarded me with frosty eyes. He hadn't touched his chicken parmigiana, and I was almost tempted to ask if he would let me take it in a doggy bag.

"Are you done telling me how to raise my daughter?"

"Not really. And I'm not sure you talking to me—or anyone else, for that matter—like this is constructive for her."

That was the other thing that bothered me in the growing list of things that pissed me off about Trent Rexroth. He often acted like his daughter was not present in the room, even though Luna clearly understood everything he'd said. Her facial expressions molded and changed according to his words.

He stood up, disregarding me, and walked over to the hostess, paying the check. The hostess flirted with him, playing with her hair and laughing loud at what he'd said, even though Trent was the least funny guy I'd ever met in my entire life. If anything, he could bring me to tears just by looking at me if he really tried. He didn't flirt back, didn't smile, didn't look interested, but when she turned her head for one second to swipe his card, he rolled his eyes and sneered. If nothing else, I wasn't feeling so bad about my decision to steal his iPad now.

Walking back to the office on the busy sidewalk, Trent and I strode next to each other, with Luna and Camila trailing behind us.

"You seem to have a lot of criticism about my parenting style."

I laughed at his observation. "Oh, you have a parenting style? I hadn't noticed. You clearly kept your crappy attitude—the one you wear in the office like a badge—at the lunch table, too. You haven't spared Camila and me so much as a glance. Do you think your daughter can't tell that you're only civil to her?"

"*Edie*," he warned. His voice sent a tingle down my spine, and I tried not to let my mouth curve into a smile. We were at it again. The cat and the mouse. But I wasn't just a mouse. He was Tom and I was Jerry. He might win our battle eventually, but I'd managed to bruise him. I purpled and greened him all the time, leaving battle scars. Marks I loved to look at, in the form of his pissed-off face.

"*Trent.*"

"How's our little friend Bane doing?" He changed the subject.

I bit my lower lip in an attempt to suppress a laugh. The reluctance in his question was no less than thrilling. He shouldn't have cared. The fact he was the first to bring up that night felt like a victory.

"There's nothing little about him, and he is good. *So, so good.*"

"This sass is not worth the retribution, Edie. I promise you that."

"See, your assuming I care about your power trip is your first mistake. Drop it," I said easily, and that, right there, was what turned Trent on. I knew it because he stopped for a second, his throat bobbing on a swallow, and slanted his eyes sideways to see if Camila and Luna were watching him as he rearranged his impressive package inside his slacks. I stilled to allow him the time to do so—it was the epitome of provocation, after all. Then we resumed our walk.

"Are you keeping our arrangement?"

"What arrangement?" I bit out, prolonging the conversation. We stopped again, this time at a traffic light, and Luna huddled between him and me, watching the red light with interest. A pedestrian tried to push in front of us, forcing Luna to take a sidestep in my direction. I gathered her by the shoulder and squeezed her to my thigh. Trent caught it, his frown melting very slowly, his set jaw unclenching. The light turned green. We continued walking until we reached the revolving doors of the Oracle building.

At reception, Trent swiveled from the closed elevator doors and offered his daughter his business smile. The one he gave people who were important enough to be acknowledged on the fifteenth floor. All three of them.

"Camila, Luna, get us all some donuts for dessert." He plucked a bill from his wallet and shoved it in Camila's hand. She nodded, clasping Luna's hand and ambling out of the building. The elevator slid open. Trent and I walked in, along with two other suited businessmen who I think worked in accounting on the seventh floor.

The four of us stared at the red numbers above our heads with quiet urgency, the tension in the small space making the back of my neck dampen with sweat.

Then the two men filed out on their floor. The second they left the elevator and the doors closed, Trent spun in my direction and slammed my body into the silver wall, and not the way I'd imagined. He didn't even touch me. He pinned his arms on each side of my head, staring down at me. "Time to cut the bullshit. Did you fuck Bane this weekend?" His voice was an untamed snarl. I blinked innocently, wetting my lips with my tongue. Knowing it would drive him mad. Recognizing that the need was reciprocal. Whatever we were, we were toxic. A lullaby on a thoroughly scratched record that kept hiccupping again and again on the line that you hated.

This can't happen.

This can't happen.

This won't happen.

"What's it to you?" I jerked my chin.

"It's a yes-or-no question."

I scanned his face. The way he'd dismissed me on Saturday had left scars on my ego and blisters on my libido.

The way he'd shoved me in his car like he possessed me.

The way he'd undermined my plans like they were meaningless.

The way we'd played with each other's bodies like they weren't connected to our souls.

My eyes flicked to the digital numeral above the elevator doors. Fifteen. The doors slid open, and I slithered under his arm, making a beeline toward his office. I could feel him following me by the heat rolling from his body. We passed Vicious and Dean in the hallway. Normally, they didn't spend a ton of time here, so I concluded they were working on a big merger or something equally as boring. They were hunched together, frowning over a document.

"Everything good?" Trent inquired, maintaining his business-as-usual bravado. And maybe it really was nothing to him. What we were. But for me, it was everything. At least in the realm of the fifteenth floor of the Oracle building.

"Great, where the fuck do you two think you're going?" Dean was the first to snap his eyes up from the papers, biting his inner cheek to stifle a smile. Vicious ignored us, as he did the majority of the floor. The only time I'd seen him looking at someone—really looking *at* as opposed to *past*—was when his lavender-haired, boho-looking wife and cute son had visited the office last week. He'd looked at them with ferocious protectiveness. Like they made his soul both hungry and satisfied at the very same time. Everyone deserved to be looked at that way.

"Work." Trent sniffed.

Vicious chuckled, shaking his head, his eyes still on the page. "Oh, brother."

"And what the fuck is that supposed to mean?" Trent stopped, prompting me to do the same. The three men were staring at each other, and reading between the lines didn't take long. They all disliked my father and wanted Trent to stay as far away from me as possible. Rightly so. Jordan would burn down the whole floor and wipe the building off the earth if I messed with Rexroth the way I'd fantasized about not even an hour ago in the ladies' room. No daughter of his was going to be caught messing around with an older man. A biracial older man, at that. A biracial older man who despised him and was probably trying to dethrone him.

Trent was the only one out of the four of them who needed me. For Luna, not for work. That made me the others' problem by association, and I wouldn't be surprised to find out they wanted to eliminate me from the equation.

Trent tipped his chin up and cut his gaze to me. "Wait in my office."

I was going to argue, but then it occurred to me that he'd just given me the perfect opening. I bolted down the corridor, rounding corners, and threw his door open. I rushed over to his desk on shaky legs, stripping out of my scruples and good intentions with every step I took, like a snake shedding skin.

Like a snake. That's who I was in that moment. A true Van Der Zee.

I didn't remember how I got to his desk, but I did remember trying to rattle the first drawer open. Locked. The second one was locked, too. The realization the room might be wired crashed into me at once, and my head snapped up, my eyes searching for cameras. Abstract pictures hung on the walls, sparse furniture and a rug stared back at me, but no red flashing dots were anywhere to be found. Not that it meant they weren't there. My damp fingers left impressions on everything I touched, no matter how many times I wiped them on my skirt. Even if Trent had installed cameras around, it was too late to back out of what I was doing. Might as well take what I'd come there for. I resumed my search by reaching for a black-leather case under his desk, shoving my hand into it. A square, cool device met my skin. I fished it out, not taking my gaze off the closed door.

Jackpot.

His iPad was in my hand, nauseous euphoria washing over me. Jordan was in Switzerland. He wouldn't be able to attend to this until next week. I had to make a fast move.

Tucking the iPad into the waistband of my sensible skirt, I breezed out of the room, throwing polite smiles in my wake as I headed toward my father's office. I had the key to it, not because he trusted me but because he was expecting the delivery. Guilt spread inside me like angry cancer cells. My action had pointy teeth, and they ate away at my soul. But Theo was more important than Trent, and, yes, the need to protect him burned in me stronger than caring for Luna.

I slipped into my father's office, shoving the iPad into one of his drawers and nudging it shut. Quickly—so very quickly—I jogged back to the door, locking it behind me and turning the handle to make sure it was tamper-proof. My eyes were so focused on the key clutched in my unsteady grip, the voice behind me made me jump and squeal.

"This is not my office."

"Good God." I turned around, slapping a hand over my heart. "You scared the life out of me. I had to stop at Jordan's office to water his plants." The lie slipped so fast and easily out of my mouth, I wanted to throw up from what I'd become. True to his Dutch roots, my father was big on flowers and had an unreasonable number of plants in his office. Trent was going to hate me for real, very soon, when he realized how badly I'd screwed him over. I couldn't let his soul-sucking eyes and heartthrob body mess with my head.

"Jordan? Why the fuck are you not referring to your dad as Dad?"

Because he isn't. "European education," I explained, clearing my throat.

"European, my ass. Never bullshit a bullshitter, ring a bell?"

Trent glanced left and right, making sure we were alone, before grabbing my hand and dragging me to a narrow alcove that separated the restrooms and the break room. He pinned me to the wall again, crowding me. His scent hit me first, drugging my senses, and then the soft fabric of his shirt brushed against my shoulder. Every muscle in my body tensed as I tried hard not to shiver.

"I'm asking you this one last time. Have you or have you not fucked Bane since Saturday night?"

I was going to hell for what I was about to do. For the cruelty I was willingly pouring into this already toxic relationship. In my defense, I was certain he only cared because he was an egomaniacal asshole.

"I did," I lied, not daring to smile. Smiling was too much, but he needed to know he didn't own me. No one did. Not even Jordan. "As I said before, I don't take orders from you, Rexroth."

If I expected him to shout, slam a fist to the wall, or act crazy jealous, I was mistaken. Instead, Trent flashed me a dangerous smirk, turned around, and walked away, leaving me there to pant against the wall. My clenched, needy thighs felt like what we'd done was foreplay, but the hole in my chest suggested this was more than just physical.

Also, what the hell just happened?

CHAPTER NINE
TRENT

A thief and a liar.

She'd earned those titles through hard work and persistence.

The first time I had seen Edie Van Der Zee was at a barbecue when we were celebrating Knight's—Dean Cole's son—birthday. It had been mere weeks before she'd started working at Fiscal Heights Holdings, and she'd stolen the attention and limelight purely by standing there, looking like she did. Like a dirty grunge angel with big ocean eyes and hair like virginal sand.

The second time I'd seen her, her theft was literal—she was stealing from my mother.

The whatever-the-fuck time I saw her today, she was lying to my face about watering Jordan's plants (he hired a certified florist for that—she came in four times a week) without blinking an eye.

So why in the good fuck was I taken aback by the footage in front of me?

I was watching the security camera playing the same image of Edie trying to go through my locked drawers and slipping my iPad in her skirt. Over. And over. And over. Again.

Rewind. Pause. Squint. Repeat.

Finally, I leaned back in my chair, lacing my fingers together and assessing the shitstorm she'd so persistently brewed for me.

There was nothing on the iPad she could benefit from unless

she had the interests and hobbies of a four-year-old. The iPad belonged to Luna. The only repugnant evidence Edie had access to were pictures of animals and food items and some kiddie apps.

But why would Edie need my iPad in the first place?

The girl wasn't swimming in materialistic things. That was not an assumption but a fact. The way she'd eaten at the restaurant, like she was tasting food for the very first time, was a dead giveaway to her situation. Then there were the small things not many people would have noticed, but someone who used to be poor would. Her shoes—not the ones she'd borrowed from her mother—were tattered and worn-out. Her backpack was stitched, held by safety pins, and not because it looked cool. Her car needed an urgent date with the shop. She never ate out or ordered takeout with the rest of the floor.

She needed money.

She saved every penny.

Fuck if I knew why.

Fuck if I knew what for.

I wanted to believe that she'd stolen Luna's iPad so she could sell it. Unfortunately (or fortunately, depending on how I looked at it), I'd grown up among enough thieves to know that jewelry and cash were the only things they were actually interested in. Shit you could pawn or burn. Anything else was…well, pointless.

Which left me with the inevitable conclusion—Jordan Van Der Zee.

She hated her father, but that really didn't mean shit. At the end of the day, life was not a game of chess. Life was fucking Jenga. You tried winging through it, hoping it wouldn't fall down in spectacular fashion and bury you. I was the first to acknowledge that sometimes you had to do stuff you weren't completely okay with for the greater good. There was always a bigger game to be played, and Edie's father had clearly cut the umbilical cord to her money stream.

She had a secret. A dark lie that had thrown her off her golden path. Everyone harbored a clandestine secret or two. No exceptions.

I'd never been interested in knowing what they were before. Part of me was thankful that Vicious, Jaime, and Dean allowed me to stew in my silence. They didn't push me to talk about shit, which was a blessing.

But with Edie, I wanted to know. I wanted to pull the secrets out of her like a magician. To wrench this endless handkerchief from her mouth and know everything there was to know.

Why does she need so much money? Why did her dad cut her off? What lies behind her agenda against the wealthy? Why does she call her father Jordan? Why do I get the feeling that she hates him almost as much as I do? Who the fuck is Bane, and how can I make him disappear without any grave consequences?

Really, the iPad was the least of my worries.

Edie Van Der Zee consumed me in ways only my daughter ever had, and that should be enough for me to demote her ass to another floor or, better yet, get her fired. Acting on my craving for her was impossible. But I couldn't get rid of her, either, because Luna loved her. Fuck, Edie had *hugged* her today at the traffic light. That was huge. Maybe not for Edie, but definitely for me. So I decided to go against my instincts, rules, and basic principles and let the iPad incident slide. I was going to keep an eye on Edie's ass from now on, and not in the way I'd been checking her out, but allowing her the benefit of the doubt. For now.

For now.

The following Saturday, Camila asked if she could take Luna to the zoo and I jumped on the opportunity to have some time for myself. Even though my parents took a huge chunk of the parenting load and Camila did some of the heavy lifting, I was the one who had to tackle the real emergencies. Like when I had to take Luna to the pediatrician when a rash had broken out all over her body or when she'd gotten stung by a bee or when she'd had a fucking breakdown in the middle of Target and cried on the floor for twenty minutes straight because some douchebag had smacked his dog in front of her in the parking lot and her heart had broken along with the dog's back leg.

I spent my morning weight training with the guys. All their wives had decided to take the kids for ice cream. I was half-relieved Luna was with Camila because I knew Emilia would ask to take her with them and Luna didn't like hanging out with my friends' kids very much. Knight protected her furiously every time someone made fun of her—he was a year younger but acted like an older brother every time they were together—but Daria regarded her with caution and confusion.

"So are you growing a hymen on your dick, or how does it work?" Dean grunted, curling his biceps with a forty-pound dumbbell in each hand in front of the mirror in my building's gym. Every single one of these bastards had their own personal gym at home, but they always ended up crashing here because they enjoyed the music, the company, and making fun of the local meatheads.

Jaime slapped the back of Dean's neck. "Time to shut up. Let the man live his life the way he pleases. You've never had to deal with something like this."

"That's right." Dean gritted his teeth, shooting Jaime a dirty look. "I don't have to deal with any bad shit. Right, man?"

Vicious was close to rolling his eyes, and the fucker never showed exasperation, even at the toughest times. He finished his set of chin-ups, jumped down from the bar, and walked over to us, squeezing his water bottle all over his face and opening his mouth to drink some of it.

"This conversation is as pointless as a tit-less chick. Fucker probably sees more pussy than your wife's OB-GYN." Vicious pointed at Jaime with his bottle, his black hair dripping sweat and water. "And even if he stayed celibate for a while—which I don't buy for a second—he is about to fuck Little Miss Jailbait."

"Edie Van Der Zee," Jaime supplied, moving over to his bench and reaching for his protein shake. "No chance in hell. Up until she started working for us, I used to see her every morning while I was jogging on the beach. She was surfing with her blond, very naked, very tattooed boyfriend. She had hearts in her eyes when he handed her beers at seven in the morning and cupped her ass like it was his beloved firstborn. Apparently, that's what the cool kids do these days. Drunk surf." He laughed, shaking his head. I stared at him blankly, not answering, because the only comeback I could think of was going to be my fist. "Bane" sounded fucking fitting. He was quickly becoming the bane of my existence. I wasn't even sure why I cared. I wasn't jealous. No way. She was a teenager, for fuck's sake. Maybe that's what looking after someone felt like. Bane looked like trouble, while she simply looked troubled. There was a difference. A huge one.

Troubled could be forsaken, forgiven, and redeemed.

Trouble was the arms in which Troubled died an unhurried, raw death.

He gave her drugs. He gave her booze. He wanted to have un-vanilla sex with her. In short, he did exactly what I would have done had I been eighteen again.

"You're shaking," Dean noted dully, moving over to me and taking away the two dumbbells I used for my shoulder press. They hung in the air for long seconds while I contemplated all the ways I could break Jaime's teeth so he wouldn't tell me shit like that again.

"Anyway, so, yeah, are you seeing anyone or what, Trent?" Jaime asked, finishing his protein shake with a gulp.

I shook my head.

"Why not?" Dean asked.

"Because it's complicated. Because I don't think there's a woman out there who can really understand Luna's situation. Because I'm busy with work."

Because the furthest I'd ever gone with a woman emotionally or otherwise was with Val, with whom I made a kid, and she fucked off, and I'm trying to find her, and it's becoming increasingly difficult not to sink under the weight of pity and expectation. And sometimes at night when I lie awake, tossing and turning in my bed, I tell myself that Luna's turmoil, problems, lack of words, are all Val's fault and hope she is dead.

"Luna seems to have taken a shine to Edie. I keep seeing them hanging out together." Dean walked over to the bench next to me, and now we were all either standing or sitting in a circle, sweaty and spent and ready to tackle the day. I plucked the towel off my bench and rubbed it on my face.

"So?"

"So is that why you're keeping her? Jesus, dude, pulling words out of you is like performing dental extraction on a hippo. Spill it."

They all chuckled and stared at me, waiting for an answer. I shrugged, getting up. "Guess so. She is harmless. Just a kid. And Luna likes her. Don't ask me why. So I let them hang out when Camila is watching."

"Maybe she can babysit Luna while you go out on dates. She seems to be strapped for cash for some reason," Dean—always too fucking perceptive—suggested.

"Maybe. If I were dating. Which I'm not."

"Which you will," Jaime amended, burping loudly. "Mel has a friend from her dance studio. She teaches ballet. Beautiful, smart, divorced with one kid."

Here we go again. Ever since I became a single dad, people tried throwing divorcees with kids at me like beads at Mardi Gras.

"Single parents are not a fucking cult," I gritted through my teeth, adding, "and it's a no."

"I don't think Mel asked for your permission, bro. She is just waiting for Katie to get back to her about her class schedule to see when she's available."

An ambush. Perfect.

The last thing I told them before I went back up to my penthouse for a shower and a long afternoon of watching shitty movies and flipping through the pages of all the useless reports Amanda had given me over the years was "I'm not interested in dating."

But, of course, my friends' wives were much more stubborn than them.

And so much more determined than me.

CHAPTER TEN
EDIE

"You know how much I want to see you, but not on Saturday. I wish you'd let me come see you at your house. Your mom can't be that bad, and I miss…us," I told Bane on the phone at work. He was the only person to listen to me. The only person to care. Mom was too out of it lately to do much more than lie in bed watching television.

"Just say you miss my dick and we'll call it a day. And a date." I could hear the waves crashing on the shore behind Bane. He was teaching at the surf club again. Jealousy prickled the back of my neck.

"I didn't mean it like that." I rolled my eyes. "I meant as a friend."

"Yeah. Whatever. I'm here if you need me. Be strong against Daddy Delirious."

My father had come back from Switzerland all smiles, which meant this particular mistress was a keeper. He didn't even seem too bothered by the fact that the iPad I'd stolen from Trent wasn't connected to any of his accounts and was utterly useless. He'd just given me another assignment, firing orders and not taking one goddamn moment to ask me how my meeting with Theo had gone that Saturday. Or how Mom was doing. Or if I'd taken her to the doctor because her meds were messing her up again.

Bane scoffed. "Fuck Jordan. You keep doing this thing, Edie, where you're trying to hold the entire universe on your shoulders and sprint with it to the nearest safe haven. You can't. It's too heavy. You'll collapse. Ever tried to see what'll happen if you let go?"

"No." I rubbed my face tiredly. "I'll never let go."

"Well, then you'll never be free. Not this year, not next year, not fucking ever."

The truth hit me in a sensitive place, right between my gut and my heart. Bane was right. My situation was hopeless.

The previous night, I'd cried into my pillow until the imprint of my face had settled into it. Not gonna lie—it had felt good. I'd tried to remind myself that breaking was necessary in order to rebuild yourself. Only problem was, I had no idea where to start and how to get out of this pickle.

"Talk later, Gidget."

"Okay."

He hung up first. Bane didn't need to see my tears to know that I was tangled in suffocating wires of distress, but he hadn't invited me out to initiate sex. He should have. I would have slept with him solely for the purpose of pissing off Rexroth, even if only in my twisted head.

And now I was in the office, on the fifteenth floor, at eight o'clock in the evening, about to do something I'd always considered a very hard limit.

Trespassing and burglary. I was looking at jail time if I ever got caught.

Everyone was long gone. It was Monday, one of those summer evenings where the whole world caved into happiness, vacationing or downing drinks at the beach. I relished the quiet and the fact the next day was a Tuesday and Tuesdays meant time with my precious Camila and Luna. The fact I got to skip all the dirty work I normally had to do around the office didn't hurt.

Standing in front of Trent's door was like facing a firing squad aimed straight at my conscience. I was running out of ways to justify my behavior, even to myself.

I tried to reason with myself that I wasn't actually ruining Trent's life. Not actively, anyway. What was the worst thing that could happen? My father might manage to kick him off the board of Fiscal Heights Holdings. Rexroth would still hold shares in the company. He would still be a millionaire and have his precious, precious money. He would likely be courted by other companies. So I'd be doing him a favor. He obviously had his priorities all wrong. He'd get to spend more time with Luna. He should fight for her, not with his money and nannies and a team of experts but with his love.

I tugged at my stupid, out-of-place hoodie, inhaling.

Retrieve the flash drive. I can do that.

Someone was vacuuming the carpeted boardroom while talking on the phone loudly in a foreign language. He was the only person on the floor, and he would never notice me. I was too far. Too hidden. Too careful.

Trent's office was never locked. Paranoia and anxiety didn't drive him like they did my father. But that didn't mean the reception desk in front of his office wasn't wired like the freaking Pentagon. I'd changed into my black hoodie and a pair of jeans in the bathroom, knowing he could easily spot me on the security camera and also knowing I was going to deny everything he'd accuse me of. For all everyone on the floor knew, I had come in that day in a powder-blue DKNY dress. Trent could say whatever he wanted—the security footage would show someone who looked nothing like me.

Head ducked down, hoodie covering my hair and face, I pushed the door to his office open in one go, ready to bolt to his desk.

Then froze, heart hammering in my throat.

The sound came to me before the visual. The dry jingle of bracelets hitting one another and skin slapping skin.

Then came the sight that melted my knees into jelly.

A woman, bent over on Trent's desk, her scarlet hair spilled across her shoulders like fire, one cheek pressed against a stout stack of documents. He was standing behind her, fully clothed, pounding into her while squeezing the back of her neck like he'd done to me the day he escorted me to my car after he'd caught me pickpocketing. *Like an animal.*

I wanted to move. Knew that I needed to, fast. But I was overwhelmed by everything—my being caught, them being caught, and the realization that I was about to catch on fire with jealousy. I was glued to my spot, unable to tear my eyes away from the scene in front of me. I didn't have to make myself known. I was standing right in front of them, choking the doorknob with my grip, mouth comically agape. My heart parachuted, making my stomach roil in both agony and thrill.

Trent's eyes locked onto mine, his hips rolling forward as he showed me how he fucked. Thrusting, moving, demanding. He twisted the tresses of her burgundy hair between his strong, long fingers. And he watched me. Watched as if it was me bending for him, taking him in. I returned his gaze.

"Van Der Zee, you're here just in time for the eight o'clock show." His indifferent tone was a contrast to the wild act he was performing for his audience. *Me.* "I know what you're looking for, and it is in my pocket. Word to the wise—this game is played by two. If I finish before you make yourself scarce, I will chase you. And I *will* catch you. Which means that you will sing for me, Edie. You will tell me exactly what your father's fixation is with me. So *leave.*"

This was the part where any sane girl would run for her life. Take his advice, turn around, and make an escape. But I was coming to terms with the fact that maybe I wasn't completely sane and that I was undeniably not a smart girl where Trent Rexroth was involved. I dropped my eyes, scanning the woman. Her wide eyes told me getting caught wasn't her kink, and yet she kept grinding against him. Horror and embarrassment leaked from her features. She looked back at me like she knew me. Like she recognized me. But that couldn't be true. The redhead looked to be older than Trent, which put a thorn in my gut, twisting painfully. If seasoned was his favorite flavor, he had nothing to look for in me.

Not that I want him, anyway.

My gaze snapped back to Trent. His eyes fed me lies I was tempted to believe, even from him. They told me I was the seed from which everything beautiful grew in this world. That I was air and water and art. That I was the woman he wanted to sleep with. They were naked of everything life had tainted him with and sent raw goose bumps down my skin.

The jealousy. The unbearable green monster felt like it was sucking the logic out of me. I needed to react, even if I had no way of explaining what I was doing there in the first place.

"You wanted me to catch you," I said quietly, my voice barely quivering. He was still going at it, one of his hands digging into the flesh of her waist as he thrust so hard into the woman, the heavy oak desk moved and scraped along the granite floor. She closed her eyes and moaned. He didn't acknowledge me with an answer.

"You're twisting our game," I added, my hold on the door relaxing. I was still on guard, but my make-believe nonchalance leaked into me, giving me courage.

"I'm making it interesting."

"You're cheating," I said. I didn't know why. Maybe because it stupidly felt like it. Like he was mine somehow, even though I had no reason to believe that.

"You cheated first."

"How?"

"With Blondie."

"Blondie is just a friend."

"Yeah, well, Sonya is just a fuck."

I swallowed, my eyes darting to the woman on the desk. She looked too lust-crazed to care about the exchange anymore, and I briefly wondered if this was what being a "proper" adult felt like. My father was indifferent. Trent was indifferent. His friends were. Everyone on this floor was. And the only person who did care about love—my mother—had lost her mind in the process.

Trent's lover's cleavage was exposed, the top half of her conservative navy dress unbuttoned, and she was moaning so loudly, her eyes rolling in their sockets, there was no doubt the objectification was mutual with these two.

I hate you, I mouthed, feeling my sweaty hand slipping from the handle. It was directed at both of them. I wasn't counting on Trent to understand me. It was more of a private declaration. Then again, I forgot that Trent lived with a person who made him scrape for words and beg for sounds.

"Good." He smirked, jerking his chin up. "Because the feeling is mutual. You're going down, sweetheart. On your knees, and otherwise."

"That's no way to talk to a child, Rexroth," I taunted, flashing him a grin to match his own. I turned around and walked away, not bothering to close the door behind me. I believed him when he'd said he knew what I came there for. I also knew that Sonya was his answer to me telling him I'd slept with Bane. She was not a part of our equation. In his mind, he was evening the score.

I got to my car in the parking lot, expecting him to follow me, spin me, stop me. That was what the only constant man in my life was known for. Tugging at my arms and making sure I listened and obeyed and complied. But Trent was the antithesis of Jordan. He enjoyed pushing me, but he never really let me fall. I started my coughing piece of old metal, looking around the dark parking lot, swallowing down my erratic pulse and the scent of burned rubber and fuel. Nothing happened. I was alone.

Driving home, my mind was not on the road. Somehow, I made it back in one piece and cooked my mom some dinner. She was always watching her weight, so I opted for quinoa with veggies and a tofu burger I pulled from the pack and threw into the oven. I brought it to her bed on a tray and sat at the edge, offering her my idea of a smile, considering my crazy evening. Her eyes were sunken, and so were her cheeks. My mom had been a Miss America contestant at one point. She was still beautiful, but in a sad, wilting way. A flower in sand, without water, air, or roots. She'd never asked Jordan for anything but to love her.

But he couldn't even do that.

"Did you have dinner, darling?" She sniffed around the food like I would poison her or something.

"Yes," I lied. Maybe it wasn't such a lie. I'd just had a big slice of humble pie, served by my very own dark knight. He'd shown me what he could do to a woman's body, and I'd wanted to continue watching even though it made me sick. A tight knot squeezed my throat at the memory of Trent having sex with a woman who wasn't me. It not only felt bad, it also felt awkwardly good.

Anything that could drive you mad couldn't be all bad, right?

Even jealousy. Even hate. Even Trent Rexroth.

"That's good. Hear from Daddy?" Her tired smile failed to light her face. My father asked me about Rexroth, my mom asked me about my father, and no one asked me about me. Or Theo. Or surfing. I pushed my lower lip out, ironing her linen with my open palm.

"You know how he gets with the time difference and everything."

I had no idea where my father was, but I wasn't protecting him. I was protecting my mother. Though I really wished she would divorce him and spare me from taking part in this charade. According to the laws in California, she was eligible for 50 percent of everything he had. She didn't even need 5 percent of it to maintain a luxurious lifestyle. I was going to convince her to do it one day, to just get rid of him. But she needed to get better first, and I wasn't entirely sure she wanted to.

A part of me suspected that her helplessness was a trap. My father couldn't discard my mother like he did his mistresses when she was in such a fragile state. It would be the kiss of death to his career for two reasons: It made him grossly unrelatable—which he was—and it made her a ticking time bomb who could dish out all his dirty secrets.

Mom sprawled in her bed and blinked at the flat TV in front of her. She was watching a soap opera without really paying attention. The show played on mute, and it made me think about the Rexroths.

"I think we should all go on vacation when he comes back," she declared, tugging at her blond locks like she wanted to get rid of them. I raised a hand and stopped her from pulling her hair, afraid she was going to yank it out.

"Sure, Mom. Sure."

The last time the three of us had gone on a vacation was eight years before. Jordan had snuck out one of the nights to sleep with one of the hula girls. Mom had had a claustrophobia attack in the sauna—probably as a result of his disappearance—and had been rushed to the hospital. Needless to say, it hardly left me craving more family time.

"Is there anything on your mind, Edie? You seem quiet." Mom paused the TV and cupped my cheek, frowning. Her room was huge and white. It suffocated me, pregnant with still air from her sitting in it all day and stale with her Chanel perfume. I wished I could tell her. About Trent. About Theo. About Bane. About Sonya. I wished I could tell her about Jordan and what he'd blackmailed me to do. I wished I could be the daughter in our relationship, just for once, and break down. Instead, I rolled my eyes, patting her blanketed knee.

"I'm fine. Totally okay. Hey, we need to get you to the doctor tomorrow at nine thirty. Will you be ready, or do you need me to wake you up? I was thinking of catching some waves beforehand."

"Definitely. I'll be ready. Dr. Fox, right?"

"No." I scrunched my nose, giving her a funny look. Dr. Fox was her plastic surgeon. "Dr. Knaus." She thought she was getting Botox? And that I would take a day off work to get her there?

"Oh, *him*." She pursed her lips, rolling her eyes to the ceiling. "I think I should just go cold turkey on the pills, to be honest. I've read an article, Edie. It says that they really mess with your head. Those psychiatric pills make you feel like there's a weight lifted off of your shoulders and you get addicted to it, and to them, and it never stops. A vicious cycle. I don't need them."

But you certainly do.

"Listen, Mom…"

"Yes, *Mom*. I'm your mother," she reminded me, pulling at her hair again, like it was a nervous tic. "The responsible adult in this situation. And I don't want to take the pills anymore."

"But…"

"No but."

"You need them, Mom. I'm not saying forever, but you have to get yourself checked and take care of this, eh, situation. Please, let's go to Dr. Knaus. He's been dealing with issues like yours for years. He'll know what to do."

"Is that why he gave me the wrong meds?"

"It's all trial and error with these things. It's difficult to find the right balance, but once he does—"

"Edie Van Der Zee." Her voice turned to steel in a second, her tone like whiplash on my skin. My shoulders sagged. *Unreachable.* She always lived behind a screen I didn't know how to peel back. "Enough with that. I understand that you are desperate to go surfing and taking me to the doctor is the perfect excuse to ditch work for a few hours, but you need to respect my decision on this. It is my body. I have plans to make, and I want to go on a family vacation, which I intend to start planning for first thing tomorrow morning. The pills are making me gain weight. It's a proven side effect. They make me tired all the time. I have a bladder infection because of them. Again. I'm telling you, I'm better off doing yoga and drinking that herbal tea your daddy makes me every night when he's at home."

For a moment, I just blinked. She thought I was mad because I wanted to go surfing tomorrow. Thought she was a tool, a pawn, a small chunk of a bigger plan. Clearly, she'd lived with my father far too long. I got up from her bed, running my fingers through my long, untamed hair.

"If you need anything, you know where to find me," I murmured.

She gave me a slight nod, pressing the play button on the remote, her eyes shifting to her soap opera. "Same goes to you, darling."

I walked out of her room trying to think of the last time Mom had helped me with anything and couldn't come up with one.

An odd feeling coated me. Like everything was going to shit and I had no way of stopping it. I'd caught Trent having sex with another woman—a *woman*, God, she'd looked to be in her late thirties—and my mother was starting to deteriorate, slipping further away from sanity right before my eyes.

I stuffed my cell phone into my JanSport, grabbed my keys and surfboard, and went to the beach in the middle of the night, not caring how stupid and dangerous it was.

Everything felt pointless.

Everything but the ocean.

CHAPTER ELEVEN
TRENT

Cardio. I needed to work on it.

At least that's what I tried to tell myself when I found my pathetic ass in running shorts, a Dri-FIT gray shirt, and my Prada sneakers. I'd been doing too much weight lifting recently. It was time to do some aerobics.

I almost believed myself but for the fact that I was standing on a sandy beach at six a.m. staring at the young surfers paddling their boards into the ocean, looking for a blond mane.

You're fucking mental, and you're taking this way too far.

I started jogging, throwing a look over my shoulder to the troubled waters every once in a while. She wasn't there. I replayed last night in my head, trying to see it from her eyes. Sonya had come over with sign language brochures. She'd praised me for making the effort to try to communicate with Luna and gone through all the classes near us and what they had to offer. We were strictly in business mode. In fact, I hadn't fucked her in quite a while. Preoccupied with work and shit. Then Sonya had said that she was thirsty, and Rina was no longer at the office, so I'd gone to make us some coffee. In the hallway, I'd spotted Edie. She was leaning against a wall, her back to me, talking on the phone. I'd slowed down, not stopping—I wasn't a fucking creep, no matter how much I felt like one around her—and her conversation had leaked to my ears.

"No, Bane. I can't. I know you mean well, but…no."

I'd hoped he was offering her his dick. I'd hoped she turned him down. I'd hoped that was the end of them as a couple.

"You know how much I want to see you, but not on Saturday. I wish you'd let me come see you at your house. Your mom can't be that bad, and I miss…us."

She missed him.

She fucking missed *them*.

I'd turned around in the other direction, not bothering to hear the rest.

The coffee I'd given Sonya was horrible.

"Are you sure you put two spoonfuls of sugar?" She'd twisted her lips in disapproval, her eyes still on the brochures she'd been sorting through.

I hadn't answered her. I'd simply raised one leg under the desk and pressed the tip of my shoe between her thighs, separating them. She'd looked up for a second, her frown turning into a grin. My office was the only one without glass walls—I had one floor-to-ceiling window and it was dark outside and the blinds were shut. I was the only one out of my friends to not like an audience. Ironic, seeing as I was the guy to draw most of the attention.

"Bend over my desk," I'd said, my eyes and tone laconic.

"We still haven't agreed on a sign language course." She'd pointed at the brochures littering my desk on an excited smile. "By the way, I am so happy you've decided to initiate something like this. It's absolutely…"

I'd tuned her out. I hadn't initiated shit. It was Edie's idea, and it was a good one, so I'd taken it. Now she'd given me a bad idea—fucking someone else to make her disappear from my mind—and I was going to do that, too.

"I choose this one." I'd picked a random brochure and tossed it into Sonya's hands, sitting back and dragging my foot to her groin, rubbing at her center. Her navy dress had flipped up, accommodating my derby shoe. "Now bend over."

She'd tucked the brochure into her shoulder bag on the floor and got up, sauntering over to me. She'd parked her ass on my knee and knotted her arms around my neck, leaning down for a kiss. But kissing was defeating the purpose. Besides, I'd never been too big on kissing. I fucked. Dirty, hard, raw—always. Painful—sometimes. Kissing was giving away something personal. And that was a courtesy I couldn't afford.

"Nah-ah, no one ever said anything about first base. You come to me, you know what's on the menu. What are you in the mood for today?" Sonya liked my filthy mouth, though she often pleaded with me to stop using it when my daughter was around. I knew I wasn't hurting her feelings. We were in the same place in life. The place where we didn't have time or anything else to offer to a partner. We just wanted to concentrate on our careers, our kids, and surviving this shitstorm called life. I'd never asked her anything about her son or Roman's father. I didn't care.

"I'll take the dirty fuck, please." She'd smiled, rising to her feet. I'd stood up after her. Flipped her skirt.

Scratch that itch.

Scratch it with fingernails.

Until it bleeds.

I'd slammed into her, and she was soaked and ready and *wrong*. The condom slid in and out effortlessly. My mind had drifted. I'd squeezed the back of her neck and watched her ruby-red hair on her shoulders.

Not the right hair.

Not the right woman.

Not the right anything.

Then Edie had walked in, looking torn and guilty. Looking like she was going to try to fuck me over again. If I'd had any doubt in my mind what she'd been there for, it evaporated as soon as her eyes locked with mine when Sonya's ass was in the air, with me spanking it, making her slam harder into my desk.

I grunted, squeezing my eyes shut. When I opened them, I was at the beach again. I ran the five miles from Tobago Beach to the Morello reef. I didn't even pant.

I made a U-turn and jogged all the way back to my apartment building, not skipping a heartbeat.

Turned out I didn't need cardio.

I needed to scratch that itch until I bled to fucking death.

For the most part, I liked my friends' wives. They were nice, classy ladies. Vicious's Emilia—Millie to everyone who knew her—was the one I liked best because she never shoved her nose too deep into my shit. Rosie, her sister and Dean's wife, was pretty great, too. She *did* shove her nose into my shit—she was just the type of extrovert who always needed to know and talk about everything and everyone—but she always respected my decisions. Jaime's Mel was another story.

Because Mel had ideas.

Her most recent one, ever since we'd all moved back to Todos Santos, was finding me a wife. Fuck knew where she got the notion I needed one. As I said before, at thirty-three, I'd never even had a girlfriend. Not even a month-long fling. I'd grown up in a poor home with parents who had a rich love. The kind of love that flipped the fingers on prejudice and social expectations. I'd never met a woman who made me as fucking crazy as Trish Schmidt made Darius Rexroth. I'd never wanted to work three jobs just so I could buy someone an engagement ring. Never wanted to ask someone to marry me on a boat trip even though I had seasickness tendencies because that was her dream.

People thought children who were the product of a divorce had fucked-up relationships. They were wrong. People who were the product of broken homes tried really fucking hard not to repeat their parents' mistakes because they knew the misery of a loveless house.

People like me, people who saw their parents sneaking kisses in the park and laughing under the sun when they didn't even know how to pay for their next electricity bill or my textbooks for next year, were the bastards. I had high expectations, and so far, I hadn't met a woman who was a candidate to meet them.

Problem was, I didn't need someone to meet them. At this point, with my baggage, I needed someone to *smash* them.

Which was why I knew Katie and I were going to fail on our date tonight.

I'd agreed to go out with Katie for selfish reasons. I thought by going and not speaking a word to Katie and being a complete asshole, Mel would finally give up on trying to fix me up with her friends. Katie was the first date I'd agreed to, and if things went according to my plan, she was also going to be my last.

Camila had Friday nights off. It was nonnegotiable. Those were her nights with her grandson. So I needed a babysitter.

Which was the only reason why I stopped at her desk first thing in the morning.

Edie's head was bent, and she was typing something on her laptop, frowning. Her teeth rolled a pencil back and forth in her mouth, and I tried not to pay attention. I set my Starbucks down on her desk and snapped my fingers in front of her face. She looked up slowly, arching an eyebrow questioningly.

"Hey," I said. *Hey*. I never greeted anyone like this. Not a coworker, anyway. I usually dove straight to the point. She didn't answer, but at least she looked calm. I wasn't sure why I was expecting her not to be. So what if she wanted to fuck me? She was a teenage girl. She'd want to fuck any tall, dark, handsome type who didn't smell like puke. And let's not forget she was not exactly in a position to give me shit. I knew why she'd come into my office. My flash drive held all the files and spreadsheets to my connections and companies. I had big plans for my career, and her father wasn't part of them. How he'd gotten her to help him I wasn't sure, but what I knew was that Edie Van Der Zee was not Team Rexroth and therefore should be regarded with suspicion.

"Are you going to say what you came here for or just wait until your friends fetch you from this spot for lunch?" she inquired, folding her arms over her chest.

"I need a babysitter for tonight." I ignored her snark. It was beneath me.

"What for?"

"I'm going out."

"Who with?"

"None of your goddamn business."

"Au contraire, Mr. Rexroth. If you feel comfortable enough telling me who I should and shouldn't sleep with, I think you at least owe me this."

I slammed my hand on her desk and leaned down, baring my teeth. "First of all, lower your voice before I really flip my shit. Spoiler alert: It ain't gonna be pretty. Second of all, wrong again. I never told you who you *shouldn't* sleep with. I told you you *can't* sleep with anyone. Pay attention, sweetheart. That's the second lesson you're failing."

She threw her head back and laughed, showing me her white, crooked-at-the-front teeth. They were beautiful. So was she, and there was no point denying it. I straightened my posture, ignoring my clenching jaw.

"I love your double standards. Especially after yesterday. Has anyone ever told you you're funny?"

"No," I grumbled.

"That's because you aren't. What you are is seriously annoying."

This was getting out of control, and fast. I let loose a thin smile, smoothing my crisp white shirt. "In my office, Van Der Zee. You have ten seconds to follow me."

She huffed, but I heard her shoes clicking behind me. We got into my office. I closed the door. The floor was busy, and I knew people were going to start asking questions soon. I was the only one out of the four original founders who'd spared her a minute of his day. And she was in my office. All the time.

"I expect you to be there at seven." I fell into my seat behind my desk and jotted down my address on a Post-it Note.

She stood by the door, letting the handle dig into her back, and stared at me with murder in her eyes. "I'm not coming until you tell me where you're going."

"I'm going on a date."

"You don't date," she retorted, no emotion to her voice.

Finally, I looked up. "And why the fuck would you say that?"

She wasn't wrong, but she was stating something I didn't exactly advertise. She worried her lower lip, staring at the ceiling like she hated herself for volunteering this piece of information. That she knew this. That she cared enough to look into my love life—or rather lack of—in the first place.

"I heard Vicious scolding Jaime the other day. He told him to get Mel off your back when it comes to dating because you're going to die alone and single. He said you hate people."

"He said that?" I brushed a finger over my lip, contemplating this. It wasn't necessarily untrue. Though I was more indifferent than hostile.

"You do. You hate me."

I don't hate you. Not even close. Not even if I try really fucking hard. And I have.

She sighed, looking over my shoulder to the LA skyline. "Don't go on the date, Trent. I know what happened yesterday. That woman… She was your Bane. She was your pastime. But dating is different from sex."

"Seven at my place," I repeated, jerking my chin toward the note on my desk. "Don't be late."

"What makes you think I'll do it?"

"I'll pay you well."

"How well?"

"How well do you need to get paid for you to stop sniffing around my fucking business for your dad?" I laced my fingers together, propping my elbows on my desk. If she was taken aback by my candor, she didn't let it show. Her forehead was still smooth of a frown, her full Cupid's lips still smeared in a smirk.

"Twelve thousand dollars a month," she said, unblinking. I hadn't expected a specific number. I hadn't even expected her to take my question seriously.

I laughed. "That's a lot of babysitting hours."

"Well, I have a feeling you'll need a lot of dates before you find someone who is willing to put up with your behavior," she retorted nonchalantly.

I like you, you little diehard hustler.

I like how you act like you're equal to me, even though you aren't.

I like that you try to be a badass when all you want to do is make my kid smile.

I like your bark and your bite and everything in between when we fight.

"Seven," I repeated for the third time, realizing that only Edie Van Der Zee managed to pull so many words out of my mouth—sometimes the exact same ones, and I made it a point to never repeat myself. "I'll pay you fifty bucks an hour, which is far more than you're getting paid for working here. I will add a generous bonus if you manage not to shove soda or sugar or fucking alcohol down Luna's throat while I'm gone."

"Don't go," she said again. I wanted to know why she was pushing it, but asking her was admitting I cared. And I shouldn't have. I was in a fragile position at work with only 12 percent shares in the whole company. Jordan held 49 percent. My career, my life, my hard work could all go down in flames because of this, because of her, if I wasn't careful.

"I'll tell Luna she'll see you tonight." I ignored her.

She sighed.

I was a bastard, but I was saving both our asses.

CHAPTER TWELVE
EDIE

It wasn't a good idea.

The realization smacked me in the face when he opened the door to his penthouse in his ridiculously glitzy building that kissed Tobago Beach. One of the only skyscrapers in the city, and a new one at that, the building was two years old, max, and still had that fresh paint smell, with every fountain and plant looking like it was out of a catalog.

Trent wore a white V-neck shirt that clung to his bulging biceps, dark jeans, and outrageously expensive-looking sneakers. He looked like an Armani ad. So ridiculously proportioned, symmetrical, and tanned. Soft lips and hard jaw and chin. His eyes scanned me briefly before he took a step back, letting me in. Rather than greeting me, he called, "Hey, Luna, look who's here for a playdate."

Playdate. I loathed that he'd said that, even though I had no reason to. It was just banter, right? I walked in, taking in his living space for the very first time: industrial shelves, a monstrous home theater system, one wall that looked like someone had thrown dark paint at it haphazardly, one exposed-brick wall, dark-wood floors, and pipe lamps, making the place look like a luxurious crack lab. Trent Rexroth might've been quiet, but his place definitely spoke volumes about who he was. Rough around the edges. Unconventional. Dangerous, even.

Luna padded barefoot from her room, already wearing a yellow pajama set. Her hair was braided sloppily—probably by her dad—and I loved that he'd tried, even as I made a mental note to redo it. I squatted down and smiled, poking her belly button.

"Hey, Germs."

She grinned, rolling her eyes at me.

"Germs?" Trent asked from behind.

"Yeah. Your daughter is a germ farm. And she likes to pick her nose, so I asked her not to shake my hand."

Luna's eyes widened in horror. You could tell that no one ever tried to be silly with her. People were always serious when it came to her, and why wouldn't they be? They wanted her to get better. But what they didn't realize was that for someone to get better, they needed to feel better. My mom, case in point.

People need something to fight for.

I was going to give Luna a reason to laugh until our journey together ended—knowing it would end badly.

"I'm not going to explore this subject any further because I see Luna is finding it amusing." Trent picked up his keys and wallet from the black island in his open-space kitchen, and I remembered why I'd come. So he could go on a date. My skin prickled. "Luna's bedtime is eight o'clock. She didn't have supper yet. I'm letting her splurge because I won't be here tonight. There's spaghetti, and Froyo in the freezer."

"Wait." I dumped my backpack on his floor and kicked off my Docs. "Spaghetti and Froyo are supposed to be treats?"

He stared at me, dead in the eye, not flinching. "Yes. Don't give her too much of it."

"Wow, are you, like, on C-R-A-C-K," I spelled, walking over to the island to stand next to him, "or are you simply a product of the Soviet regime? This is not splurging. I wanna order pizza."

He shrugged into his blazer. "You're not. And by the way, she knows how to spell."

I stood there, wondering why I'd humored and indulged him in the first place. He was terrible to me. Rude, arrogant, and cold beyond words. And I was awful to him, too. Stealing, spying, and constantly snooping around him. But the answers were there, plain and simple. I needed the money, and I enjoyed hanging out with Luna.

"It's five past seven." He glanced at his Rolex. "My number is on the fridge if you need me. Underneath it, you'll find Camila's number, my mom's number, and Sonya's—her therapist. Luna needs to brush her teeth before she goes to bed, there's a small lamp that always stays on at night in her room, and she gets a bedtime story, which she chooses from the library next to her room. Any other questions?"

Sonya? I had one question, but it wasn't related to Luna. It was *Holy shit, are you actually screwing your kid's therapist?*

"Are you sure you're going?" The underlining question was—do you really not want me? Stupid. Pathetic. Thoughtless. Why would Trent Rexroth want me, and why would it make any difference? I was a high school graduate with a hole in my heart and problems bigger than my existence, and he was…the opposite of what I needed right now.

"Give me one good reason not to," he deadpanned, tucking his wallet and cell phone into his back pocket, his eyes still on his watch.

"Because you don't want to."

"You don't know what I want."

"Do *you?*"

He looked up, assessing me, before smirking. "By the way, I have more nanny cams in this place than your porking buddy Bane has tats, piercings, and STDs combined, so stay out of my shit." He hissed it low so his daughter couldn't possibly hear it. He walked over to Luna, kissed her crown, told her he loved her, and waltzed out the door.

Leaving me to stand there, my jaw on the floor, drowning in the delicious, dark energy he'd left behind.

I ordered pizza.

Small, meaningless protests were my stock-in-trade. I often felt like a citizen of occupied Europe in World War II. Someone who wasn't brave enough to join the resistance, but couldn't completely bow their head to evil. I paid for the pizza myself, even though Trent had left a few bills on the counter, just in case. And I let Luna have soda.

Because it made her smile.

And when we blew bubbles into the soda, she even snorted.

And when I told her I was so full I could throw up but the pizza was so good I would probably eat whatever I'd puke out, her eyes lit up along with her smile.

After dinner, I poured half a cup of sugar into the organic, sugar-free Froyo and took it to the living room, where we watched *Girl Meets World*. I was 99 percent sure that it was out of her age bracket, but it kept both of us entertained. Eight o'clock came and went. Rules were bent because Trent had been the first to break them. He'd broken them the day he'd broken my mother's expensive Louboutins. The day he'd agreed to hire me. He'd broken them when he'd bossed me around to get into his car when I was with friends and forbade me to have sex with Bane and way more other times than I cared to count.

After watching the show and slowly recovering from the food coma and sugar rush, Luna, who was sitting next to me on the dark-brown leather sofa, turned her head in my direction and grinned, staring at my rib cage.

"What is it, Germs?" I frowned. She pointed at my neck, and I looked down. "This?" I fingered the seashell on my necklace, made out of a black shoelace and dark cerith shell. It looked like a dagger, and it felt like one, too. Luna nodded, her hand tapping her thigh. She wanted to touch it. I removed it from my neck, placing it in her hand. "Watch out, though. It's sharp."

She pressed her fingertip to the end, sucking in a breath.

"I was running on the sand one day—it was really hot, and I left my flip-flops in my car because I like walking barefoot—when I stumbled over something. It cut my heel so deep I could see my tendon. I picked the prickly thing up. I couldn't believe something so pretty could hurt me so badly. So I decided to keep it. Because sometimes, our favorite things are the ones that make us cry." I chuckled at the skeptical look on this girl's face. "Have you ever swum in the ocean?" I asked. I had a feeling I knew the answer to that one. She hesitated for a moment before shrugging.

"I'll take that as a no."

It was definitely a no.

"Would you like to?"

Luna shrugged again, but in a totally different way. Her first shrug was disappointed, resentful. Her shoulders sagging down. Her second shrug was more wistful. Maybe I was reading too much into her movements, but I clung to nuances like they were my lifeline. After all, sometimes they were the only thing I could squeeze out of Theo.

"Would you? If I took you? If I…taught you?" I probed, my skin catching flames at her intense stare.

She nodded, her head snapping up, as if she remembered something. She put her little hand on my forearm, telling me to wait, and jumped from the sofa, padding down the hallway. This girl was living directly in front of the ocean, yet all she was ever allowed to do was go to Funny Felix parties on the dry, boring sand without dipping a toe. Her dad seemed like such a self-centered prick. I wondered if she was able to share any of her likes and dislikes with him. I sat on their couch, gawking at the walls around me. The feature wall was decorated like some big-shot artist had thrown dark paint on it on purpose. Grays and blacks and deep purples. It was half-graffitied and looked exactly like something you would find in a bachelor pad. But Trent wasn't a bachelor anymore, no matter how emotionally unavailable and single he was. He had a daughter.

This place looked like him.

Dark. Brooding. Moody.

It didn't look like Luna.

Hesitant. Curious. Gentle.

Luna came back with a big children's book, square, thin, and flat. She dumped it on my legs, climbed on the sofa, and started flipping through it until she found what she was looking for. She stabbed her finger to the image.

"Seahorse?" I asked, furrowing my brow. She nodded, staring at me expectantly. "Oh, you want to know if I ever see any seahorses when I surf? No. They're hard to find. They're shy creatures, I think. They live in reefs and sheltered places."

The disappointment on her face made my heart twist. I rubbed the back of my neck and looked around. Trent's laptop sat on the dining table across the room. I knew it wasn't an afterthought. He'd wanted me to see it. Wanted me to touch it. It was a test, and I was about to fail it—jeopardizing my father's plan—to try to pacify Luna.

"Hey, why don't we read more about seahorses on Wikipedia? Maybe there's a good documentary on them on YouTube."

Her eyes lit up like Christmas, and it was worth all the shit he was going to give me when he found out.

"I'm kind of bending the rules for you. Are you going to tell on me?"

She scrunched her nose, shaking her head like the mere idea was insulting. And that gesture—the nose wrinkling—it was so *me*.

For the next forty minutes, Luna and I learned everything there was to know about seahorses. We watched a male seahorse giving birth to a gazillion baby seahorses and laughed. She laughed because there were so many. I did because it looked like a man shooting his load after watching the filthiest porn ever recorded.

Then before we knew it, it was ten o'clock and bedtime became nonnegotiable because I was pretty sure Trent would dangle me from his balcony if he found us still hanging out in the living room when he got home. Luna didn't put up a fight, which I thought was strange because Theo always had. He would yell and plead and bargain and try to manipulate me, just like his father.

I tucked Luna in, sitting at the edge of her black-wood bed. The whole room was blue and full of posters of seahorses, seashells clinging to the walls. It had her personality, and suddenly, the need to cry slammed into me. Because it wasn't my first rodeo tucking someone into bed, and it wasn't the first time I knew I'd have to say goodbye to them eventually.

I wanted to hug her, but I didn't. Couldn't.

Every bone in my body ached, burned, and yearned for it. Which was exactly why I needed to stay away. I couldn't bulldoze into her life, knowing I couldn't stay. It was like planting myself in, watering the seed, letting the sun kiss it and allow it to grow only to yank it from its roots. Luna was like me—attached to an unstable man who could tear her away from me tomorrow morning if he wanted. And who knew what Trent Rexroth really wanted? He was an eternal riddle enfolded in a delicious suit.

"Hey, Germs, do you know what?"

Luna shook her head, letting me "burrito" her by tucking the edges of her blanket under her body so she was positively cocooned. That was what I'd used to do to Theo, the rare times he'd let me.

"I had a lot of fun tonight. And I hope you did, too."

She nodded, and I smiled, and maybe it was too dark for her to see it because the next thing she did shocked me.

"Me, too."

Throaty. Small. Breathy, like wind caressing waves at dawn.

Floored, I blinked away my surprise. Luna had spoken. To me! I wondered if she did it with Trent and Camila, too, every now and again, but I doubted it—he'd made too big of a deal about her not talking. I wanted to jump up and call him but had to play it cool. Fretting about it would only serve as a reminder that she was different.

"You're just saying that because I fed you pizza and Coke and broke every single one of your dad's rules." I smirked. She laughed. I stood up awkwardly, moving away. Not kissing. Not touching. Not caressing.

"Good night, Germs."

A little nod in the dark. I turned on the *Frozen* lamp by the door and smiled. *I'll take it.*

CHAPTER THIRTEEN
TRENT

Katie DeJong made me think about teenage Trent.

One thing about him was he didn't believe he'd be sitting here today, eating a lobster (he hated lobster), drinking imported wine even though he lived in California (he hated wine), and discussing the pros and cons of college rankings (he didn't give a shit).

This was exactly why I'd never dated. It was boring. The endgame—marriage and kids—didn't interest me, and the short-term touchdown—sex—was available without the inconvenience of wining and dining someone.

I didn't say more than sixteen sentences the whole date, but I wasn't rude, either. And I walked Katie to her car and smiled at her and didn't promise I'd call, but when she leaned forward for a kiss, the kind I'd never give a steady fuck, I smoothly diverted it to a peck on the cheek.

Then I drove the fuck out of there, realizing, when I parked my car in the underground lot, that I couldn't even remember what she'd worn or what color her hair was.

The weird sense of urgency grasped me by the balls in the elevator. The notion that I had fucking gone and put my kid in the hands of someone I barely knew suddenly made very little sense. All I knew about Edie Van Der Zee was that she was a liar, a thief, and a girl in trouble. Why I'd have her anywhere near my kid unsupervised was a mystery. I was worked up even before I shoved my key in the door. By the time I opened the door and saw what was going on, I was on the verge of flipping my shit.

A pizza box was sitting on the island, making the whole living room and kitchen area smell like oily bread and fucking mushrooms. Two cans of Coke on the counter—of course, she hadn't even bothered throwing them in the trash—and that was before I walked into the living room and found Edie sleeping on the couch with my laptop in front of her. Spying, no doubt, and not giving a single fuck about hiding it.

I walked over to her, tucking my hands in my pockets, watching her. The way her chest rose and fell. The blond hairs of her eyebrows. Her full, pink lips and golden hair. The tan lines on her shoulders. Her freckles.

"Wake up," I commanded, my voice dripping ice all over her stirring body.

Her eyelids fluttered, at first slowly, and she didn't sit up until I took another step forward, nudging her arm with my knee.

"Hey." Her voice was hoarse. "How was it?"

"You ordered pizza." I ignored her. "My daughter doesn't eat fucking pizza."

It wasn't about the pizza. It was about the laptop. Not that there was anything on it—I kept everything on the flash drive—but it drove me nuts that I'd trusted her with my own daughter and she, in return, had spent the time in here trying to fuck me over. *Again.* Had she ignored Luna the whole time to play hacker?

This thing between us had long since left fucked-up territory and was now deeply in batshit-crazy-ville.

"I paid for it, and she only had one slice. I also made her eat the bell peppers and mushrooms, if that makes a difference." Edie yawned, rubbing her eye sockets with the base of her hands before standing up. She stretched, her long limbs on full display. She was barefoot, and a purple tank top and cutoff denim shorts clung to her body.

"And Coke? Really? Again?" I growled, getting in her face. I was angry. So fucking angry. At Mel and Katie and Edie and Luna and Val and life and, fuck, women were such complicated creatures. I tried goddamned hard to stay away from them as much as I could, but they seemed to be everywhere.

"Jesus, Trent, she brushed her teeth. It was a one-off, so I thought we could splurge. And I mean really splurge. What the hell!" She bolted to the other side of the room, sitting on the floor and putting on her shoes. I wanted her to get the fuck out. At least, I thought I did.

"Last but not least—the computer? Really? No fucking class whatsoever."

"We were watching YouTube videos!" she exclaimed, snagging her backpack and getting up in a hurry. "Geez!"

"YouTube videos. Right." I let loose a chuckle, pulling out my wallet from my back pocket and plucking out the money to pay her. "Wasn't it you who told me to never bullshit a bullshitter?"

"I'm not bullshitting you!"

I shoved the banded stack of money to her chest and growled into her face, "Just go."

"Hey, wait…" She hurried after me as I pivoted toward Luna's room. The money dropped to the floor. She didn't bother to pick it up. "Luna talked."

I spun in place, my eyebrows dropping down.

"Edie…" I warned. If she was lying again, there were going to be consequences. She fidgeted with the hem of her shirt, tugging at it, but her eyes were determined and brave. She didn't look away.

"She did! When I tucked her into bed. I told her I had fun tonight, and she said, 'Me, too,' and it was small, but I heard it, Trent. All I wanted, all I ever wanted was to make her feel not like a robot or a charity case. We ate junk food and watched TV past her bedtime. We broke the rules, and she survived. Not only that, but I'm pretty sure she had fun. Maybe it'll help her through another week of therapy sessions and you acting like she is in some kind of dire situation."

I rubbed my forehead. Shit. She was doing this again. Confusing me. And the worst part was that I believed her. I shouldn't have, but I clung to each of her words and let them settle in my stomach and revive me. Luna had spoken. This was a huge breakthrough, but daring to believe it and hoping for more could break me—and I didn't know if I could trust Edie as far as I could throw her.

We stared at each other for a long beat, from a safe distance.

"She talked," I repeated, finally. It felt monumental. As if she was going to wake up tomorrow and start blabbing about the weather. It wasn't the case, but Edie was only the second person Luna had spoken to.

She nodded. "Her voice is so sweet and soft. Like velvet on cool skin."

Who the fuck talked like that? Edie. Edie talked like that. "I've never heard her."

"You should. It's really great."

I believed her.

She swallowed. "Let me take her to the beach on Sunday. She's never been in the water. I want to...show her things."

I looked down, wanting to say no. I was scared for Luna. I didn't trust Edie with Luna outside the apartment building. But I also couldn't just hang out with them because that wasn't appropriate or beneficial for the raging obsession I was beginning to develop toward this girl.

"You know what your problem is, Trent?" She was panting, breathing fire, and I was too selfish to cool her down. I liked her hot. I liked her messy. I liked her all over the place because that was how she made me feel. Deprived. There was some poetic justice in it.

"No, but I'm sure you're about to tell me."

"You fight the tide. You fling your arms, kicking your legs, trying to escape it, overpower it. The secret is to go with the flow. The secret is to ride the wave. Don't be afraid to get wet."

I was wet, though. I was fucking dripping. Shit, half the time it felt like I was drowning. Maybe that was her point. Edie was a lot of things. Stupid wasn't one of them.

"Don't forget your money." I pointed at the floor, clearing my throat and averting my gaze. I was uncomfortable to say the least, and that was a fucking first. She walked over and picked it up, flipping through and pulling four fifties off the top.

"There." She tried to hand me the rest. "I think it was, like, four hours."

"It's yours." I shook my head, curling her fingers around the wad of cash. "All of it."

"What?" She blinked, thumbing through them. The Benjamins were fanning each other like in the movies. "That's a lot of money."

"Twelve thousand dollars."

"What?"

I shrugged, staring at the pizza box on the island to keep myself from doing something stupid. "You said you needed the money. I'm not going to ask you why. But I am going to be a responsible adult and strongly advise you to get this situation sorted quickly because it's not an easy sum to come up with on a monthly basis."

"I appreciate the tip and the money, but I can't take this." She shoved it to my chest.

"You can, and you goddamn will."

"No." She took a step back, the money falling between us again. We were both too engrossed to even look at it. It wasn't the fucking point of all this.

"Give me one reason why not."

She started counting with her fingers. "One—it's a lot of money I didn't earn, two—it would make me owe you, and three—because we're not friends. We're enemies."

I used the same finger method. "One—it might be a lot of money, but not for me. Two—I don't expect shit from you, and three—it's cute how you think you're my enemy. You're not on my level."

Her stare told me she didn't care that I'd undermined her. And for a good reason. The girl had managed to get her way and steal my shit several times. She might have been the underdog, but she sure as hell knew how to put up a fight.

I expected her to argue over this, as she had with any subject matter, but she surprised me by tucking the money into her bag. She swallowed roughly—her pride, most likely—flung her backpack over her shoulder, and silently made her way to the door. Watching her made me feel like shit, so again I looked the other way.

"Thank you, Trent."

"It's fine."

"No, I mean it."

I meant it, too. I didn't know what the fuck was happening with her or *to* her, but I knew the idea of her being in deep shit made me queasy.

The door was beginning to slide shut in my peripherals as I braced myself against the counter, and I couldn't resist showing her that not only was I getting wet, but we were both about to get soaked if we weren't careful.

"You still there?" I asked.

She didn't answer, but I didn't hear the *click* of the automatic lock.

"The date. It sucked."

I heard the smile in her voice when she said, "I didn't have sex with Bane after you found me at the reservoir."

Click.

I didn't go after her. But I was still screwed because I knew that next time—I would.

CHAPTER FOURTEEN
EDIE

Love is merciless.
Love is cruel.
Love is not a feeling, it is a weapon.
Love destroys.
Love destroys.
Love destroys.

I couldn't stop reading that line on my way back from Theo. My car had stopped working two days before and was at the shop. I didn't want to splurge on a taxi or an Uber, so I took two buses each way. It gave me the time to read an old paperback I'd found in our library. An autobiography of a French poet who'd ended up committing suicide after his fiancée had left him for a man she'd treated as a nurse in the army. The other man was a hero, so French Poet Dude's unrequited love had been swept under the carpet.

Love destroys. These weren't just words for me. They had weight and a scent and a tainted color that never faded. Every single person I'd loved had hurt me.

I still had to find a way to get my hands on Trent's flash drive. I knew he carried it with him everywhere he went—he'd told me it was in his pocket while he'd had sex with someone else—and also knew he was too smart to leave any of the things my father wanted to get his hands on in any of his devices. That made my task impossibly hard, but at least I was beginning to find the patterns of his everyday life, which Jordan had also asked for.

I put the book down, watching the Pacific Ocean from the window.

"It gets better," someone in my vicinity said, and I wasn't sure whether they were talking on the phone or to me, but it didn't matter because I didn't believe it. Not for a moment. I fished my phone out of my backpack and checked my messages.

Bane: Are you coming to surf tomorrow?
Unknown: If she comes with you tomorrow, I want her grand-
mother to be there.

Trent.

The idea that he'd taken the time to open a message and write to me—spent this time on me—was pitifully thrilling. What was it about this man that made me want to break all my rules? No getting attached, no complicating things, and absolutely no poking the tiger—Jordan Van Der Zee—giving him a reason to pounce on Theo.

I tried to tell myself that this was innocent. I was taking Luna to the beach. Trent was not going to be there. It was reasonable enough. And Luna could really use a one-on-one with the ocean. I opened the first text message, to Bane:

No can do. I'm taking my boss's daughter to the beach to
collect seashells. Next week. x

Then I opened another one, writing, deleting, amending, correcting, deleting again, before finally pressing the send button.

8am/Tobago Beach/by the surfing club.

I walked into the house to find my father sitting at the dining table, which meant he was about to initiate a conversation. One that I most likely didn't want to have. I slowed my steps, watching him pushing out the chair opposite him with his foot, silently ordering me to take a seat.

Reluctantly, I did.

My life was not seamless. It was made out of patches. There was the surfing and Bane patch. The mentally ill mother patch. The controlling father patch. The Theo patch. And even though they were stitched together, there was never an overlay. Each square stood as its own island. And if there was one thing I hated, it was bathing in the softness and cleanness of the Theo patch before jumping to the rough, worn-out Jordan patch. Which was what was happening right now.

"How is Theodore doing?" he surprised me by asking, but predictably he did so while he checked the stock market on his laptop on the table. His eyes were glued to the screen, and I tucked my hands between my thighs, trying not to gulp.

"He's been better."

"Oh?"

You don't care, you cold-hearted bastard. So don't "oh" me. "There's this special program where they let you visit your family at their house and monitor you throughout. Two nights. He wanted to go." This time I did swallow the lump in my throat because how could I not? It sounded too much like a plea, and hearing a "no" would crush me.

"That's wonderful for the families, Edie. Any news on Rexroth?" He shot me a look, and I faltered.

For the families.

As in *not ours.* I didn't have a family.

Talking to Mom about this would get us into an argument again. She'd tell me that she needed to run this by my father and that she was feeling pressured. And Jordan...he took pleasure in ripping us apart. Besides, he'd just said no in his own way.

"Edie?"

I looked up, blinking. He gave me a tight, warning smile, shutting his laptop screen and pushing it aside, folding his arms on his chest. "Rexroth's flash drive?"

"Still working on it."

"Why is it taking you so long?"

"I only ever have time with him on Tuesdays," I said, conveniently leaving out the fact that I'd babysat for him on Friday. If my father cared at all about my whereabouts—which he didn't—he might've thought to ask. Telling Trent not to say anything was pointless. We both knew how dangerous it was—especially after he'd given me so much money.

If he'd felt like a secret before, now he was covert sin.

"And he carries the flash drive with him everywhere. That's the only place where he keeps everything important."

"Huh." Jordan stroked his chin, looking out the window. The sun was beginning to set, and a bluish glow filtered through the curtains. It was time to show him what I'd managed to retrieve from Trent's apartment when I'd gone there on Friday. I wasn't proud of stealing it, but that was before he'd given me the money. The fact that he'd barked at me, degraded me, practically thrown me out of his place only helped a little to soothe my burning guilt. I stood up and walked to my backpack, taking out a paid invoice I'd found on his counter, tucked under a bunch of other invoices that were neatly stacked, waiting to be filed, no doubt.

"What am I looking at?" My father frowned at the invoice.

I tapped the upper-left side of it. "Amanda Campbell, PI. She is a private investigator. He is using her for something."

"Where did you find this?" Jordan asked.

The lie slipped from my mouth without a blink. "His office."

"What do you think this is about?"

"I don't know him very well, but I'd be surprised to find out it's about you." Trent never spoke about my father. Not to me or anyone else at the company. He seemed to disregard him completely. But then what did I really know about the guy? Other than he didn't like me one bit.

"I know who it is."

"Oh, yeah?" I cleared my throat, trying not to sound too eager.

"His child's mother."

His child's mother. After I'd found out Trent was Luna's dad, I'd snooped around with Camila, finding out that her name was Val, she was from Brazil, and they'd never been together. Not in a relationship, anyway.

I watched Jordan's face carefully. Watched how it morphed from boredom and disdain to interest. He really was fascinated with this guy, and it irked me. He folded the paper, pocketing it.

"More," he said. "And soon."

Deflated, I pushed some hair from my eyes, groaning. "Can I please fill out the papers to have Theo visit me sometime this summer? Just for the weekend."

Me.

Visit me.

Be with me.

Heal me.

"Absolutely not." Jordan got up from his chair, making a show of preparing my mother a cup of tea like he was Husband of the Year. For him, this conversation was over. For me, it had only just begun. He took the steaming cup and sauntered out of the kitchen. I jogged after him down the hallway, the sleek marble, the beautiful arches, the ugly truth beneath these walls. Tempted to yank the sleeve of his Prada suit, I decided against it when I considered the consequences.

"Please," I said.

"Parading him around for a weekend is going against our agreement, Edie."

"Jordan…"

"*Father.* Focus on your Rexroth task and forget about this. You need purpose. This is it. Helping your family."

"Theo is my family!"

My father stopped in front of the closed door to the bedroom and spun in place. The expression he wore told me I'd crossed the line.

"If you don't deliver—I will make sure Theo is thrown out. I want everything there is to know about Rexroth. Everything. And I do not negotiate with children."

"You won't do this to me." My voice trembled. What if I couldn't find more dirt on Trent? What if finding this dirt made it so difficult for me to look in the mirror I'd want to throw up on myself?

"I will. You know I will."

"You're breaking my heart." The admission felt sour on my tongue, like defeat.

"It's all broken anyway. There's nothing left to be ruined." He meant Theodore, I knew.

I opened my mouth to answer when he slammed the door in my face.

My father had given me two choices—take Trent down to save the person I loved or compromise the person I loved to keep an innocent man safe.

I knew what option I was going to choose.

It just made me sick to my stomach.

CHAPTER FIFTEEN
TRENT

I watched Tobago Beach from the comfort of my terrace, smoking a fat blunt in my designer briefs, my Bling H2O water still at room temperature despite the unforgivable heat thanks to my housekeeper, who kept sliding one ice cube into it every ten minutes. I tipped my Wayfarers down, staring at the black dots spread around the golden beach. I didn't fucking know why anyone would buy water at forty bucks a bottle, but I still did it because I could. I did it because, once upon a time, I'd been so poor that the soles of my old shoes were too thin and I'd had to smear superglue on them and let them dry in the sun so my feet wouldn't burn against the concrete.

I was fascinated with my bank account, as all poor boys who grew up to be rich men were. Flaunting my money was almost mandatory—a flaw I wasn't proud of—and money made Edie Van Der Zee sick. It was easy to see why we disliked each other.

Anyway...

I tapped the ashes into the ashtray beside my lounge chair, smoke rising in lazy spirals from my mouth. When I looked back down, my eyes focused on my targets, the ones who'd poured out of my building moments ago. They were walking closely next to each other. My mother, Luna, and Edie.

They were moving almost in slow motion, and I couldn't see who was who. Other than Luna. She was the smaller dot. One of the women set a red towel on the beach—my mom, probably—the color barely recognizable from the distance. The two other figures ran to the ocean together maybe even hand in hand. My heart stuttered in my chest as I put the water to my lips, my eyes chasing them before they slowed down close to the wave breaking on the shore. They were just dipping their toes. Nothing more.

Calm the fuck down. Luna is fine.

I needed a distraction. I took out my laptop and started working, glancing down every now and again, trying to guess which dots were the girls I cared about. And Edie. Half an hour later, my phone began to vibrate, and I snatched it. It was my mother, calling through a video chat. I slid my finger across the screen. My mom appeared, blurry but happy, smiling to her phone camera and waving. "Hey!"

"Mom." I couldn't help but smile. For all the shitty things I had to say about growing up poor, I wouldn't trade places with any of my friends. My parents were the bomb, which no one else in my group could say.

"This girl." She turned her head to the ocean before whipping it back and laughing. "She's amazing! You have no idea how much fun she is having with Luna. She's been teaching her how to surf." My eyes must've bulged out of their fucking sockets because she was quick to add, "On the sand. She just put Luna flat on her stomach on a surfboard and showed her what to do. They're collecting seashells now. Edie said she will surf out to the deep part and get the real special ones. Luna... She's never looked so happy, Trent."

I swallowed, standing up and taking my phone with me as I slid open the screen door and entered my living room, dragging my hand over my face.

"Show me." I nearly choked on the request. "Show them to me."

Mom's phone danced in her hand as she tried to zoom the camera to the two girls sitting by the ocean. I saw Luna in her little black bathing suit (no pink for this girl), on her knees, watching carefully as Edie examined a pile of seashells. Both their heads were down, their tongues poking out from the corners of their mouths, like they were concentrating hard. Edie was wearing red bikini bottoms and a long surfer's elastic top—red, too—and her long, wavy hair was partly tied into a bun at the top of her head, with the rest cascading down her shoulders.

"Closer." My throat bobbed with a swallow.

The camera wobbled as Mom stood up and walked over to them. The more I saw, the less I felt like I was in control over the Van Der Zee situation. Luna was fucking glowing. There was no mistaking the grin stamped on her face.

"What do you think about this one, Germs?" Edie plucked one seashell from the pile and wrinkled her nose. Luna rolled her eyes and shook her head. "Yeah, it's meh, right? I thought so, too," Edie said. She was about to throw it to the ocean—watching them for a couple of minutes, I'd noticed the shells that were deemed unworthy were thrown back to where they'd come from.

At the last moment, Luna stopped Edie, jumping up to her feet and holding Edie's fist, shaking her head. Edie opened her hand, allowing Luna to take the shell from her hand.

"What is it?" she asked. They were so busy sorting through their shells, they hadn't even noticed my mom was documenting the whole thing. Luna pointed at the shell and then arched one eyebrow. "It's broken," Edie said. Luna nodded again. I wasn't following. "You want to keep it because it's broken." A smile spread across the blond teenager's face.

Luna shrugged.

"That's beautiful of you, Germs." Edie rubbed Luna's arm before realizing what she was doing. She withdrew her hand quickly. I didn't know why, but I made a mental note to tell Edie she can always touch Luna. If there was one thing I was good at, it was hugging the shit out of my daughter. She wasn't scared of affection when it was given by the right person.

"Hey, I have an idea. Can you give it to me? I promise I'll keep it safe and give it back," Edie said. Luna hesitated but dropped the shell in Edie's palm.

They shared a smile. I collapsed on my couch, watching as history unfolded. The camera spun, my mother appearing again, this time with the hugest grin.

"Edie is the best thing to ever happen to this family, Trent."

My mother was wrong, but I didn't have the heart to tell her who Edie really was.

The end of her son.

Luna came back home full of stories she couldn't tell. My mother suggested she put her in the bath and make dinner for her, and I jumped on the opportunity to get out of the house and sort through the jumbled mess that was my thoughts.

"Edie is still there, surfing, bless her heart." Trish frowned, twisting her David Yurman watch. If only she knew that was the same girl who'd grabbed her bag all those weeks ago. "Actually, I think she might be leaving right about now. The sun is beginning to set."

Without thinking much about what I was doing, I slid into my sports gear and went downstairs. I told myself I was going to jog on the beach again, but that was total bullshit.

I was going there to find her.

I was going there to catch her.

And once I had…what the fuck would I do with her?

Spotting her was easy. She was the only person left on the beach. The promenade was still bustling with people, rich and colorful like a festival, but all the surfers and tanning ladies were long gone now. She was lying face up to the sunset, her head resting on her black backpack, with nothing on but her bikini. Her surfer top was discarded along with her sunglasses, the cool sand pressed against her skin. Her eyes were closed, and she was mouthing the words to whatever song she was listening to in her earbuds. Her yellow-ish surfboard was there beside her, like a loyal companion. A living entity. Like a pet.

I closed the distance between us, simply watching her. Standing over her. Fuck, I was one step away from a restraining order, but it was hard not to look. She revived something in me, just as she had with Luna. I didn't know what it was, but I relished the unsolic-ited warmth that came with it. What was really shitty, though, was that both Luna and I were fucked because this girl had her heart somewhere else.

And that might compromise my daughter and me in the process.

"Holy shit!" Her voice pitched high, and she was up in a second, yanking her earbuds out and slamming them against her backpack. "You have to stop sneaking up on me like Pervy McCreepson, dude. What are you doing here?"

I don't fucking know, but you need to make me leave.

Everything about her felt ripe. She was alluring, more than just physically. Like an old song with a sweet memory stapled to it. Or like a first. First beer. First joint. First kiss. I knew she was going to haunt me to my grave if I didn't do something about it—and would do worse to me if I acted on it.

I watched her tits rising and falling, the way she sucked in a desperate breath when I stepped toward her with confidence I wasn't entirely feeling for the first time in years. She backed away slowly. The beach was deserted. The sun had already set. I was cornering her, probably scaring the shit out of her, and I was too fucked to care. I wanted to get wet and let the tide wash over me without dipping a toe in the ocean.

I wanted what was forbidden and wrong and fucking crazy.

I wanted my partner's daughter, who was nearly half my age.

The tango stopped when her back crashed against the blue-painted lifeguard station. Her spine hit the wooden rails, and she had nowhere to go. I got in her face, inhaling her. The sea, fresh sweat, and her singular sweet scent drove me up the wall. I wanted to bury my nose in her wind-tossed hair and never come up for air. And I wanted to kiss her, which was insane because I never wanted to kiss anyone.

I cupped her cheek in my palm, and it was cold. Her whole body was shivering. I was wearing a long Dri-FIT shirt, but she was still in a bikini. I looked down like the fucking asshole I was. Her nipples were puckered and hard, pointing at me. My hand moved from her cheek slowly to her neck. She didn't withdraw or look away. I caressed her soft skin, moving down to her collarbone and then flicked one of her nipples through the fabric of her bikini. I stared at her silently, too hot to feel the shame accompanying messing around with a teenager.

She looked up, fear and lust swimming in her pupils, their bottomless depth luring me to jump in.

"Again," she breathed, her pulse quickening under my palm. I felt her body moving against mine, even though we didn't touch, and fuck, this wasn't good news for my cock.

Defrosting. She was getting warmer.

Not breaking eye contact, I brushed my thumb against her nipple again. She groaned, lifting her arms to touch me. I took a step back and *tsked.*

"It's not fair that you're the only one to have fun," she groaned in frustration, her body still tilted toward mine.

I arched an eyebrow. "You think it's going to be fun to go back home with blue balls?"

"They don't have to be blue."

"Unfortunately for me, they do."

"Your funeral."

"The things I want to do to you…" I trailed off, exhaling my hot breath on her cold skin. "Will undo you."

She closed her eyes, shaking her head. "Again."

I was going to hell for this, but I flicked my thumb against her right nipple for the third time, watching her hips roll to chase something that wasn't there. I wasn't close enough for her to rub against me, and not because I didn't want to be. If we got close, I'd lose control. I couldn't. I wouldn't. Not when so much was at stake.

"Again," she moaned.

I did it again.

"Again…and again and again and again."

I used my thumb and forefinger to rub her right nipple through her bikini, watching her throw her head back, her mouth falling open in pleasure. I leaned against her without meaning to, just an inch. Then another inch, when her hard nipple got so tight and sensitive, I found myself twisting it a little to amplify her pleasure. I wanted to get her off so bad, but somehow, taking her in both hands and claiming her felt too final. A point of no return.

"How can it feel *this* good?" she nearly protested, reaching with her hand to touch me again. I moved away quickly, still playing with her tit.

"Because it's different when you're in the hands of a man."

"Show me."

I didn't answer.

"Please," she purred, and this time she managed to glide her bikinied groin over my training shorts. Fuck, I wasn't sure if it was the ocean or her, but something there was damp.

That was when I lost it.

I closed the distance between us, allowing her to grind on me freely, like I was a fucking stripper pole, while playing with both her tits, watching her as my dick grew impossibly hard. Already, the strain in my balls felt like too much. I wasn't much of a foreplay guy, but here I was getting hot slowly and steadily, being led by the fucking cock to something that wouldn't materialize.

"I want to come," she said, her legs clenching around my thigh. My cock poked at her inner thigh, and she knew it because she goddamn rubbed against it even more, the friction making a little pre-cum leak. It made my crown stick to my briefs, and this really was getting out of control.

"Tell me why you need twelve thousand dollars a month, and I will let you," I hissed in her face, careful to leave enough space for her not to try to kiss me. She whimpered, riding my thigh like a fucking rodeo, rubbing her clit on my quad, her eyes shut. She was inside the moment, in a bubble, and didn't want me to burst it. "Answer me, now."

"Trent…"

"Who is giving you trouble?" *Who the fuck am I going to need to end?* "Why do you need to come up with this kind of money?"

Nothing.

She was getting close. Her thighs were quivering, and now I knew it wasn't the fucking ocean. It was her. "Spit it out."

"No."

"Edie."

"No."

I withdrew from her in a hot second, leaving her to fall to the sand, panting and aroused. Her hair was all over her face, her bikini bottoms had a small spot of arousal, and her nipples were so hard she could probably cut me to a bleeding point with them.

I frowned. "One last chance, Edie."

But she knew as well as I did that the moment was gone. I couldn't touch her after this. After breaking that drunken spell. My cock was still pointing at her furiously, demanding her attention, but my mind was starting to catch up with reality.

"Fuck you," she said, again, just as she had when I'd caught her stealing.

"Not happening," I said, again.

"Maybe next time." She laughed, getting up from the sand and walking over to her backpack, retrieving her earbuds, hoodie, and shorts.

I smirked, turning my back on her, making sure I was loud and clear. "Cling to the memory of dry-humping me, Van Der Zee, because that's where it ends."

CHAPTER SIXTEEN
EDIE

There was something in that morning that had felt rotten even before I opened my eyes. My intuition proved to be right as I walked into the kitchen to find my mother crawling on the floor, gathering bits and pieces of…what? What in the world was she holding? It fell between her fingers, like molten gold.

Hair.

It was her hair. My eyes darted from the floor to her.

My mother had cut it all off.

Every inch of wispy blond hair was gone. The lonely patches of yellow hung from her skull reluctantly, uneven in shape and length. Her eyes were red. And the blond beautiful hair she took pride in… it was everywhere.

"I need it back." She snapped her head up to look at me. "Oh, God, Edie. What have I done? Now he'll never want me. I just… I need to fix this."

I made her tea. Shoved her pills down her throat. Told her I would get it all fixed, even though we both knew there was nothing I could do. Then it was time for me to face the music and her husband.

I stood at the front door, my father outside, his monstrous Range Rover already purring. He stuck his head through his window, obviously annoyed at how his driver had called in sick that morning and now he had to do the journey from Todos Santos to

Los Angeles using his precious hands and holy feet. My car was still at the shop, so it made sense to carpool, even though the idea of spending time with him in a confined space sent uncomfortable shivers up my spine.

"Come on, Edie. It's time to go," he barked.

"Mom," I said, gripping at the doorframe and feeling myself losing balance, "do you need me to stay with you today? Please be honest because I will. I totally will." She was getting worse. So much worse. But not as bad as she'd been when she'd been hospitalized for a year because she'd completely lost it and tried to slit her wrists. She hadn't cut too deeply, fortunately, which meant I wasn't orphaned at the age of twelve. But I still remember what my father had told her two months after she'd gotten back home from the rehabilitation center.

"Can't even end your own life properly, can you, Lydia?" he'd huffed, shaking his head as he'd zipped up his suitcase, no doubt on his way to another mistress. "Next time let me know if you need any assistance."

I wasn't sure when exactly my father had started despising my mom, but I knew it had to do with the fact that he couldn't leave her, in her current mental state, if he ever wanted to get into politics. What was even more confusing to me was the love my mother still felt for him. Though I wasn't sure whether it was love, a habit, or simply a crippling fear of being alone.

Back in reality, my mother huffed, her chin resting on her shoulder, her back to me.

"No, I don't need you, Edie."

"Are you sure?" I pressed. I knew she'd ignore my existence altogether if I stayed without permission.

"Edie! We're going to be late. I have a meeting at ten. Drag your butt over here before I let you walk all the way," my father boomed behind me. I ignored him.

"Positive. Your dad wants you to go. Just go."

I didn't even ask her what had happened to planning a vacation and getting better. She probably didn't swallow the meds I gave her and was now on a nasty downward spiral, spinning out of control all the way to rock bottom.

"Okay. I'll keep my phone on." I waved the device in the air.

"Thank you, sweetie. When you come home, can you... Can you help me with my hair?"

I nodded. "Of course."

"Keep an eye on your dad."

There was no need to elaborate. I knew what she meant.

"I love you, Mom."

"I love you, darling girl."

And I believed her because Lydia Van Der Zee wasn't a bad person.

She was just a bad mom.

To-do list: attain flash drive.

I couldn't let Jordan send Theo off somewhere on the East Coast. I couldn't.

And that was the thought that drove me on that Monday when I fetched people their coffee, made dry-cleaning runs, did other people's children's summer school homework, held a whiteboard up for twenty minutes straight while the maintenance guy tried figuring out why it had fallen from a wall in one of the meeting rooms, and grabbed Jordan's mail.

The mail room was my favorite place in the building.

It was situated on the fourteenth floor and was deserted of people. The PAs picked up mail every day at four p.m. Any other time, it was just the envelopes and me. And even though I could see the cameras wired all over the place (Fiscal Heights Holdings dealt with sensitive contracts and packages), I still felt alone there.

It wasn't the ocean, but it was good enough.

I leaned against an industrial printer, exchanging text messages with Bane and burning time. No one needed me for another hour or so, and I couldn't stand all the suits and pencil skirts roaming the fifteenth floor. They thought what they were doing was so important. I called bullshit. They didn't save lives. They didn't teach kids how to read. They didn't build houses, fix broken cars, or produce food, electricity, clean water, *life*. They just made rich people richer, or less rich if they were doing a terrible job. They made corporate companies stronger or weaker. It was the adult version of Toyland, and it bored me to death.

> Bane: So when the fuck are you going to drag your ass to the beach?
> Me: Things are busy right now. Just trying to keep afloat tbh.
> Bane: That's the point of surfing, smart-ass.
> Me: What's up with you?
> Bane: I'm buying a houseboat.
> Me: GTFO
> Bane: ¯_(ツ)_/¯
> Me: Does that mean that you'll finally let people come over to your place? I've never been to your house. You're always so secretive.
> Bane: Yeah, that means I can ride you somewhere private from now on. The perks of being a boat owner.

About that.

I should have probably told Bane we weren't going to have sex anytime soon or maybe ever again. It wasn't because of what Trent had told me. No. I'd really meant it when I'd said that I wasn't going to take any orders from him. Unfortunately, that didn't mean that I could sleep with Bane anymore.

Trent was on my mind. He invaded my brain, occupying more

and more space there, nudging aside all the things that used to inhabit me, to the point of madness. I thumbed the neckline of the black dress I'd borrowed from my mother's closet, getting ready to text Bane back, when the sound of a closing door made me snap to attention. I twisted my head and saw Trent standing there, his shoulder leaning against one wall.

Hands in pockets. Dark-navy suit. The eyes of a predator. *Delicious.*

Our encounter yesterday had left me aching for more, but it also buggered my mind that he'd gone that far. It made me wonder how much more I could get him to do with me. I clutched my phone, arching an eyebrow.

"Are you stalking me, Mr. Rexroth?"

"Are you complaining, Miss Van Der Zee?"

Never. But I'm not sure I'll get out of this alive once you find out just how bad I am going to hurt you.

"Undecided yet. Depends on whether you're in the mood to be a jackass today." I pretended to examine my nails. My heart drummed so fast and hard, it threatened to shatter my rib cage. He looked, walked, talked, and moved like a flawless demon. It both scared and thrilled me at the same time. Trent stopped when his body was next to mine. When everything ceased to exist but us and we were alone in the world. My breathing was ragged, and it became painfully difficult to look at him without closing my eyes and giving in to his powerful scent.

"I love the color black on you." He raised his hand, seemingly to brush a lock of hair away from my face. I wondered if he knew what he'd said because it sure as hell was obvious that he had meant it.

"What are you doing here? Rina gets your mail every day," I said quietly, staring at his pecs, not his eyes.

"I saw you on the CCTV."

"And?"

"And I wanted you alone."

"Why?" I licked my lips. Why did he want me alone? He was nothing but rude and arrogant toward me unless Luna was involved. I reached for my seashell necklace and clutched it like it was expensive pearls. His gaze followed my hand. He unwrapped my fingers from it and took it in his hand, examining the shell. "Why did you want me alone? You say you can't touch me, but you almost do. All the time. Last night, you lost control. Tomorrow, you will do it again because we can't stop this. Whatever it is, it is happening. You tell me I can't sleep with other people, but you don't give me what I need. Give it to me, Trent, or I will find it elsewhere." I couldn't believe those words left my mouth, but at the same time, I was relieved they had. His thigh pressed against mine, and my back was firmly pressed against the printer. Now his hand moved away from the necklace, his thumb brushing my collarbone.

"I should warn you, Edie. I'm not the prince in this fairy tale. I'm the villain. The poisonous apple, the flame-breathing monster."

"Good. I always enjoyed the broken in the fairy tales better. The apple always looked shinier because I knew it could destroy me. The villain was just damaged and misunderstood, and the monster..." I leaned on my tiptoes, biting the tip of his ear, just barely reaching his impossible height. "I always kept the door to my closet a little ajar as a kid to make sure it could come out in case it wanted to play."

His breath skated on my neck, hot and wanting and deliriously fresh. "The monster wants to play."

"And I'm not scared of the dark," I retorted. "So what are we waiting for?"

"Frankly, for you to be legal," he deadpanned.

"I turned eighteen in January."

Pause. Tick of an overhead clock. A loud swallow—I wasn't even sure if it was him or me. And then...

"There will be rules," Trent informed me, pulling away to cup my cheek and look into my eyes. "And if you break them, the consequences will be grave. Do you understand?"

My eyes dared him to continue. I wasn't going to give him the pleasure of answering him. He moved away, walking out of the room. He left me there for several minutes—standing, waiting, hoping, begging. I looked up, watching the cameras in the room die off, one by one, the red dots disappearing. Then the door creaked again, Trent reappeared—was the security panel even on this floor?—and walked back over to me.

"I don't kiss. I fucking hate it. I don't do relationships—my life does not allow for it right now. And I don't like when people try to stab me in the back."

A thin smile found my lips when he reclaimed his position, almost on top of me. "Gotcha. *Pretty Woman*. No kissing. No flowers. No stabbing. I have rules, too," I said.

"Of course you do," he humored me, his hand skimming to my neck. "Let's hear them."

I hooked my leg over his thigh and leaned back on the printer, feeling his erection digging into my stomach, and moaned my answer. "Rule one—it's just sex, nothing more, so you don't get to boss me around about what I do separate from this. Rule two—no Saturdays. It's nonnegotiable. I have somewhere to be on Saturdays. Rule three…" With this one, I got a little creative. I'd only had two in mind, but it gave me an excuse to demand what I'd silently prayed for. "I want you to go with Luna to those sign language classes."

"Already booked us a private lesson for tomorrow evening." He hoisted my leg against him, his self-control hanging by a thread. "There's a fourth rule," he informed me.

"Fine, but it's the last one." I grinned as his palm dragged up under my dress.

"I'm going to give you the twelve thousand dollars a month, no questions asked, and in return, you will stop stealing shit from me and sniffing around my business."

I froze. He knew about the iPad. About my little mission. Why hadn't he said anything until now? Even now, he was just implying. I wanted to keep it that way. The less I knew, the more I could shrug off later when it came to bite me in the ass. And I did absolutely need to keep giving Jordan dirt on Trent. It wasn't personal against the handsome devil in front of me. It was about saving the only person who'd ever really loved me.

"You're not going to pay for the..." I started, but Trent slammed his groin into mine in one thrust, causing my back to arch and my legs to spread and curl around him, clinging to his waist like poison ivy. I was dripping and ready for him to finally claim me.

"Shut up, Edie. I said no arguing. This is one of the rules."

"I'm not going to stop." I swallowed hard, refusing to look him in the eye. "You should know now, Trent. I'm always going to do whatever Jordan tells me to do. Not because I like him. Not because I'm scared of him. But because he has something I need. I will always obey him, Trent. Always."

For a moment, it looked like he was going to pull away. Everything about his posture said it. His hand stopped sliding up my thigh, invading my flesh, riding up my dress, and his body pulled away, the heat from him subsiding.

"You do know what it means, right?" I cleared my throat. I may have been a thief and a liar, but I wasn't a jerk. I needed him to know. To acknowledge what we were. His hand resumed its journey to my inner thigh, his swollen cock pressing against me.

"It means"—his teeth dragged along my neck—"that what we are to each other is potential sacrifice. As long as you know I will throw you under the train if you mess with my plans, I'm good."

I swallowed. "I'm good, too."

"Let's have some fun then."

And that was all the preparation he gave me before shoving his hand inside my panties. His strong, warm fingers stroked my folds gently, as if soothing them, preparing for whatever he was going to give me.

"One last warning," he said, his hot tongue making its first appearance, licking a trail of tantalizing desire up the side of my neck, making me shiver violently. "I fuck rough." He shoved one finger into me, and I arched my back, gasping from the sudden penetration. "Deep-throating is a requirement, not an option"—he shoved a second finger into me—"and I'm about to fucking ruin you for any other man. So when the time comes and no one else can compare to me, just remember—you asked for it."

Third finger.

Fourth finger.

Jesus Christ, this man had four fingers inside me, and he thrust them in and out. His thumb rubbed my clit—which he found in record time—while he played with me with little regard to the fact this was the first time we'd properly touched each other and we hadn't even kissed. I hooked one arm around his neck and ground my core against his hand, moan after moan escaping from my mouth. My lips felt naked, in contrast with the fullness between my legs. I was riding his hand shamelessly, our eyes locked. My core tightened, and the buildup to orgasm was quicker than I'd ever felt it. I wanted to cup him in his pants but knew he would never let me.

"Oh my God, I'm going to come," I panted, knowing I sounded like a cheap porn star but not really caring. This was…what the hell was it? I'd never had a man enter me so roughly and boldly, and we weren't even having sex. He acted like he already knew my body, like he owned it. Worst part was, I couldn't argue with that notion. I usually took a long time to get off with a partner. Trent had managed to get me soaked, moaning, and chasing his touch after less than two minutes.

He smirked. "Check you out, wet as a fucking lake."

He withdrew one finger…two. What the hell was he doing? The sense of loss was immediate, but that was before I realized he wasn't slowing down. He was setting me on fire.

"Hello, Edie's G-spot," he murmured into my ear, rubbing the spot furiously. I think I had a mini-orgasm just having him do that to me. I groaned loudly when his fingers curled inside me, rubbing at the sensitive place. "I've a feeling you and I are going to see a shit ton of each other."

"Ohhh." I arched and slithered to bite his exposed neck, tasting the bitterness of his fragrance on my tongue and teeth. "This is insane."

"Why does he call you Gidget?" Trent asked, strumming on every nerve in my body like a violinist. A hot wave of pleasure was brewing in me, ready to crash. My toes curled.

"Huh?"

"Bane. He calls you Gidget. Why?"

"Why are we talking about Bane?" My annoyance almost caught up with my tone. Almost. I knew Trent. He was a stubborn jerk. He wasn't going to back off. If anything, he was going to deny me another orgasm, and this time I was going to kill him for it. No one in the world other than Jesus Christ himself was going to deny me this orgasm. Especially not some rich jackass in a suit—someone I'd promised myself I'd never be associated with in the first place.

"Gidget is a term for a small female surfer," I bit out, as his fingers started slamming into my G-spot brutally. He was relentless. True, Trent didn't kiss me, but his whole body did. It was glued to mine, and I felt him everywhere. The orgasm claimed me like a storm, starting from the bottom and working its way up until every hair on my arms stood on end. I clutched his broad, muscular shoulders and squeezed his waist between my thighs, the intensity of my climax momentarily blinding me.

But he wasn't done.

Trent grabbed the back of my knees and raised me flat on the printer, my back against a warm stack of papers. He spread my legs wide, throwing them over his shoulders and nudged my panties aside, not even bothering to remove them.

"What are you doing?" I murmured, horrified. I was still coming down from the high. It was difficult to find my footing when every organ and system in my body was still busy recovering from what might have been the most brutal orgasm I'd ever experienced.

He didn't answer me. Just stared intently at my bare pussy, slowly pushing his forefinger into me. He then pulled it away, coated with my lust and wetness, and sucked on it hungrily, his eyes still dead on my pussy.

"I ask myself the same fucking question every time I touch you," he muttered to himself.

He didn't look horny. Or delighted. Or turned on. But disturbed.

My already cherry cheeks reddened further. He'd shoved his whole hand into me less than five minutes ago after blatantly breaking the company rules by shutting down the security system on one of the most sensitive floors in the building, and he was bothered by this?

"You just fingered a teenager to orgasm." I licked my lips, taking control and nudging his hand away from my pussy. I yanked my underwear back in place and jumped down from the printer. My panties were soaked and uncomfortable.

He matched my steps easily as we walked to the door. Before we got out, he switched the cameras back on and punched his phone screen a few times. "Joe? Yeah, Trent Rexroth. I think the CCTV system shut down on the fourteenth. Need you to check it. I just passed by the security monitor and saw that it was blank."

Oh, God. He was such a sociopath. And I was in so much trouble.

We walked to the elevator together.

"You go first." He shoved his phone into his front pocket, his cool tone and fuck-everyone attitude on full display now.

"Where are you going?" I asked, walking into the open elevator.

As the doors started sliding shut, he said, "I'm going to jerk off until my dick falls off. With you in my mind, on my fingers and my lips, Edie. Teenager or not, you're about to do a lot of grown-up stuff with me."

CHAPTER SEVENTEEN
EDIE

Seven days had passed since the mail room incident. A whole week without Trent's hands on my waist, spreading my legs, twisting my hair, claiming my body in ways I hadn't known were even possible. After that Monday, I'd spent all Tuesday with Camila and Luna. Jordan seemed content with this arrangement, immediately reading between the lines and wanting in on the conspiracy. We girls went shopping for clothes for Luna, and even though Camila cringed at the girl's tomboy tendencies, I was actually pretty impressed with Luna's individualism and encouraged her to try on the silver Converse she eyed with a smile or those little black jeans that were ripped at the knees. Trent couldn't meet us, not even for lunch, because he was in meetings all day out of the office. The thought of waltzing into his office after I came back from my time with Camila and Luna occurred to me, but I dropped the idea, knowing for a fact now that he had cameras around the place. And it wasn't just that—it was also the guilt. The nagging, awful guilt that told me there should be a separation between when I hung out with his beautiful daughter and when I let him finger me until I reached ecstasy…to when I stole from him, handing my findings to my father.

The week had dragged. Trent hadn't said a word to me—not even good morning when he passed me in the hallway. He ignored me completely, making it a point to act like I wasn't there.

Mom hadn't left her bed more than twice, including over the weekend. I'd had to cook her meals and bring them to her upstairs. We hadn't had a cook for years because Mom had once accused one of trying to poison her. And from there onward, we'd decided there was no point. Jordan ate out, Mom was usually in bed all day—and barely ate—and I wasn't a picky eater. I'd tried to get her to see Dr. Knaus, but she'd rejected the idea again and again until I'd had to call my father and beg him to reason with her. He'd barked at me that he didn't have time for her dramatics and that he was on his way to LAX, catching another flight, this time to London.

My car was still in the shop. The mechanic said I needed to replace a bad cylinder, and when I asked him for the price, I almost fainted. I couldn't pay it, not that month, so I just asked if he could keep the car until I got my paycheck. All the money Trent had given me had gone to where it was supposed to, after all. And I never took anything from my parents—not their money, not their cars, not their love, mostly because those things were never offered.

On the flip side, my father wasn't around, so I could come to work at nine a.m. like a sane person, which gave me surfing time again.

I was lying flat with my back on my surfboard, still water around me, watching the sky growing brighter with every passing second. The orange and pink gave way to the white and blue. I was floating, staring, dreaming, the taste of the ocean on my lips. From the day I was born, I knew I had a salty soul. I knew I loved differently. More violently. Everything I'd ever loved. That's what had gotten me into so much trouble in the first place. The sheer obsession I had with everything I cared about.

"Are you coming out, Gidget? I've got beer," Bane said beside me.

Close, but not close enough to break my spell with nature. I blinked once at the rising sun.

"I'm good," I said.

The sound of water moving filled my ears before he appeared

next to me on his black surfboard. He was straddling it, both feet slung in the water.

"So. You and Rexroth." There was no particular tone to his voice. He didn't sound mad or annoyed or even surprised. I refused to look at him, still enjoying the intimate moment with the rising sun.

"How do you know his name?" I murmured.

"How do I know Trent Rexroth's name? Did you go to your own high school in the last four years before graduating? He was quarterback legend douchebag schmuck blah blah fucking football captain blah. As soon as I saw his face that Saturday I knew who he was. Do *you* know what he *is*?"

I had a feeling Bane wasn't waiting for my permission to spit it out.

"Old. Fucking ancient, more like. Are you guys bumping uglies?"

A little smile found my lips. "No."

The half-truth came naturally to me. Like swimming. The thought of telling Bane the full truth never even occurred to me. We were done, with me having little time for surfing and for him and with him getting a boat and living the single life, no doubt. We had never been in love. We were barely even in like. We were just… bored. And sexually compatible, I think.

He sighed. "Look, it's your life, and not only are you old enough to make your choices, you're also one hell of a strong girl. So let me just leave it at this, and you'll never hear me saying shit about it ever again—Trent Rexroth is trouble. He will chew you up and spit you out if he needs to. Make sure he doesn't need to because the whole town knows him and his friends and there's a reason why they keep to themselves. No one else is willing to get close enough to burn."

Bane left shortly after that. I stayed longer, smiling when my mother's words echoed in my skull. *Stop staying outside so much. Your freckles are coming out. Your skin will get old. What man would want to marry a twenty-five-year-old with a forty-five-year-old's complexion?*

I didn't want to get married.

I didn't want to stay away from the sun.

I simply wanted to...*be*.

When I got out of the water, my surfboard tucked under my armpit, I walked straight to my backpack. Not bothering to change or dry off, my feet still bare and coated with sand, I walked up to the promenade where I was going to take Bane's car back home for a quick shower and then work. Bane liked to park his 2008 Ford Ranger on a little dune uphill where no one could slap him with a parking ticket for not feeding the meter. He lived by the beach so could walk home whenever I needed to borrow his car. I rummaged in my bag for the spare keys he'd given me when a heavy hand found my shoulder. I spun around, wet and frightened, to see who it was, but the person slammed my stomach into Bane's car and glued their body to mine. Strong, tall, muscular, terrifying. Then his scent crawled into my nostrils, making my thighs quiver.

"I thought we'd agreed on no more Bane," he hissed into my ear, his hand snaking down my waist and to my inner thigh. The dune was far away from civilization, and the need to spread my legs for him was urgent and wild.

"Not that it's your business, but we aren't having sex. He is just lending me his ride until mine gets fixed."

"Fuck no. You'll be taking my spare car." He squeezed my inner thigh, licking the salt from my neck.

"No, thank you, Mr. Sugar Daddy. I've seen that movie. I watch it every goddamn day. I'm not going to become my mother, and I'm not going to depend on you for rides and money."

This made him laugh and withdraw his hand from my thigh, spinning me in place. Upon the first gaze at him, my breath got knocked out of my lungs. Not only was he breathtakingly gorgeous, shirtless, and wearing running shorts, but his eyes told me he was going to kill someone if his orders weren't followed.

His six-pack was the kind of glorious that needed a Times Square billboard to celebrate it.

"Is that what you think this is?" One side of his mouth pulled into half a smirk as he *tsked*. "Oh, I'm not your boyfriend, sweetheart."

"Then what are you?" I gulped.

He leaned closer to me, whispering to the crook of my neck, "Your undoing."

Then, before I knew what was happening, the door to Bane's back seat popped open, and I was thrown onto it, on my back, with him climbing on top of me. He filled the space, leaving no room for anything else but lust and desire and sin. He ground himself against me, and I felt his huge erection. I accommodated it by spreading my legs as far as I could in the small space, cupping his ass cheeks and bringing him to me.

I moaned, scraping at his bare, sweaty back as his cock speared my stomach, making me go crazy, slinking and sliding uncomfortably just to get more of his touch. He was dry-fucking me in my ex-boyfriend's car, and it wasn't by accident. This was how he operated. He claimed his toy, played with it, and after a while—destroyed it.

"Why are you doing this?" I asked, feeling the friction between us heating my skin. My body was begging for the barriers between us to disappear. I needed him inside me.

"Why am I doing what?"

"Why are you making this stupid point in Bane's car? You clearly followed me here. Have you done this every morning this week?"

"Yes," he said honestly, rising up on his forearms to pull my bikini bottoms down. He stared at my slit again, like he'd missed it. At my black cross tattoo across my hipbone, rubbing his thumb on it absentmindedly. "But the time wasn't right. We can't get caught."

"I know. We won't," I said. We both had too much to lose. Me more than him, but he didn't have to know that. I loved how Trent made me feel, but I wouldn't trust him with my hair straightener, let alone my secret. I didn't want him to have any more leverage on me.

He lifted both my legs to rest against his shoulders and leaned forward, making my hamstrings stretch and my legs spread wide as he moved his tongue from my ass all the way up my folds. I trembled, my eyes widening in shock and pleasure. No one had ever touched that part of me. The back-door part. And Trent… He hadn't even asked for permission.

"So fucking sweet," he growled into my soft skin, sucking on my clit. I whimpered, clutching his head in both my hands and raising my hips to his lips to get more of this heady feeling. "So fucking mine."

"Sweet? Maybe. Yours? No," I panted, rubbing myself against his face shamelessly as he took his sweet time sucking my clit leisurely, his fingers brushing against my slit but never really penetrating. He was just playing with my arousal at this point, rubbing it against my entrance like he was building for something more.

"Care to test that theory?" He bit at the flesh of my folds, and my fingers squeezed his temples as I rolled my head back, my eyes shut, feeling drool pooling in my mouth. What the hell was happening?

"Sure," I managed. Barely.

His wet finger traveled along my pussy and toward my ass, and I instantly clenched there but didn't want to be the chicken to pull away before he tried anything. Plus, his mouth devouring me was the best thing to ever happen to my body since surfing.

"Ever tried anal?" he asked. His finger prodded at my hole, drawing lazy circles around it. It felt…funny but not bad. It tickled and was oddly teasing. I swallowed, shaking my head, my eyes still shut.

"You will by the time I'm done with you. Got your pussy slapped?" His finger pushed into my puckered hole, just an inch, but he plunged into my pussy with his tongue at the same time, making me roar in desire and lust and causing my legs to quiver.

"No," I admitted.

"Yeah, that's gonna happen, too. How about ice cubes?"

"Y-yes!" I breathed out, as he thrust his tongue in and out of me, penetrating me in a way that felt rougher than actual sex. I was drenched, and not from the ocean. I shoved his head deeper between my thighs, not caring about the consequences, and he, in return, pushed his entire finger inside me and curled it upward, his smile against my hot, warm skin making me burn like a bonfire. My climax gripped every bone of my body, shaking me in slow, intense waves and making my teeth chatter. Oh my God. Oh my God. I didn't know this could feel so powerful. So crazy. I was...*full*.

"Of course, you tried ice," he murmured into my pussy, laughing evilly. "I bet that's why Bane said you weren't vanilla. You're not only vanilla, you're vanilla and gluten-free. Repeat after me: safe, sane, and consensual, Edie," he ordered.

The orgasm was slamming into me like whiplash. Again and again. It took me a few moments to realize I was experiencing multiple orgasms for the first time in my life. They were all equally intense, and I was beginning to wonder what it was about Trent that made me feel like I was burning from the inside out. Bane was good in bed. He was great, actually.

But he didn't set me ablaze only to turn his back on me once the tongues of fire consumed me.

He didn't ignite in me the need to do and say crazy things.

"Say it." Trent raised his head, staring at me intently with his livid eyes, his mouth glistening with my juices. My eyes traveled down from his face to his veiny, muscular forearm, his arm disappearing between my legs as his finger was still shoved inside my ass.

"Safe, sane, and consensual, Edie," I repeated cheekily.

"This," he said, hovering over me, his lips almost touching mine. All of a sudden, he was close, too close. Close to my face. Close to my body. Close to my heart. His finger slid out of me slowly and teasingly, and a final tremor washed over my relaxed limbs. "This is why I know that you're mine, Edie. Your body is already mine. Your pussy belongs to me, your ass is halfway there, and the rest..." He smirked, the lust churning in his irises making him look devilishly sinister. "The rest I don't fucking care about."

His eyes dropped to my lips, which were sealed and closed and not open for business. He may have been great in bed, but he was right. Kissing wasn't a part of the package. Not because of some Hollywood movie bullshit, but because there was nothing intimate in what we were. In fact, when it came to our hearts and minds, we kept as much distance as we could from one another.

Trent's mouth parted, and for a minute I thought he was going to say something more. Worse, I thought he *was* going to kiss me. His plush lips almost touched mine before he got up and slid out of the vehicle, turning his back to me and giving me time to slide my bikini bottoms back on.

Outside, he grabbed the surfboard leaning against the vehicle.

"I'll take you home."

"What?" I snort-laughed, catching up with his step. "You can't be seen with me."

"I have tinted windows. Plus, your father is out of town. If you don't strap your board on the roof, we're good. We need to talk."

We walked over to his building. He carried my surfboard all the way there and then tucked it into his car, and I had to remind myself that he wasn't a gentleman. In the car, he had one hand on my bare thigh, squeezing it while his eyes were on the road. I loved being there with him. Everything smelled like him. Clean, expensive, with a bite of forbidden. Of something dirty and sexy. Luna's booster behind us was the only reminder that he was a dad. Everything else about him felt like a reckless single man. A single man who wanted to destroy me.

"So what's with Luna's mom?" I probed. It wasn't even about him. I knew he was very much on the market. I just tried to wrap my head around leaving your kid and never looking back.

"That's not what I want to talk about." His voice was steel.

"Tough luck, Rexroth, because you don't control every aspect of this relationship," I said, pretending to look out my window at the beach town we lived in when really all I wanted was to catch him in my peripheral vision.

"Luna's mom bailed on our asses when my daughter was a year old. I've been looking for her since." His tone was direct and business-like. I enjoyed this side of him. The side that gave me something without feeling wounded or annoyed from his ego.

"Why?"

"Why what?"

"Why are you looking for her? She obviously doesn't want to be found."

He shook his head, one hand on the steering wheel, the other still kneading my thigh. It was difficult to concentrate with him touching me. I was barely able to decipher his words while he was simply there, all man and muscle and cocky attitude, never mind when he was touching me. But I was too turned on to make him stop.

"It's complicated."

"Why?" I persisted.

"Because everyone needs a mom."

"Depends on the mom," I said vacantly.

"Not really," he said.

"Trust me on that one." I chuckled, looking away, this time for real.

After a stretched beat, he began to talk again. "Tell me why you need so much money, Edie. Tell me why your dad makes sure you're broke. Why you hate wealth like it wronged you."

How could I tell him without somehow trying to justify my still living with my parents? I should've moved long ago considering my toxic relationship with both of them. I didn't want to live on the streets, and I didn't know anyone who was crazy enough to piss off Jordan Van Der Zee and allow me to live with them. Well, other than Trent Rexroth. The truth meant admitting that I was completely bent and owned by my father.

"That's not what I want to talk about," I said, echoing his rejection from earlier.

"Tough luck, Van Der Zee, because you don't control every aspect of our relationship." A bitter smile found my lips. His hand traveled up between my thighs, now covered by short shorts, and he started rubbing my sensitive spot, making me clench and groan.

"Okay." I sucked in a shaky breath, still delirious from my previous orgasms this morning. "In short, Jordan has something on me. Something that gives him a lot of power over my life."

"Is it something you've done?" he asked.

I thought about it objectively. "No."

"Can it be changed?"

"In theory, yes. But in practice, he has too much power to ever lose that kind of legal battle. And besides, I have some stuff going on at home. My mom…" I didn't know why I was confiding in Trent, but maybe it was because I had no one else to talk to. "She's suffering from mental health issues. Cutting ties with Jordan would mean cutting ties with her by association. She is too weak. And she needs me."

"So you're raising one parent and trying not to get destroyed by another," he clarified, his tone dry and emotionless. I inwardly winced at the way he put it, but luckily, his hand between my thighs made it a lot less depressing than it really was.

"Accurate."

He pulled into a gas station and yanked his wallet from the center console.

"I'm getting coffee. Want some?"

I shook my head. "Coconut water would be great, though."

He snorted, rolling his eyes. "Fucking rich hippie."

The moment he was gone, his hand no longer on my clit, my mind kicked into overdrive. What was I doing, talking to him about personal things? And what was I doing, getting closer to him when I should be using him?

Dazed and confused, I jerked open the glove compartment that looked almost bionic in the Tesla, knowing I had to bring my father something for next week, *anything*. The flash drive required more time, but I could still show him I'd done my due diligence.

I yanked an old cell phone—the kind of Nokia people used to play Snake on—and a stack of business cards I didn't even bother reading. Some of them ought to be useful for Jordan. I shoved the treasures into my backpack, feeling the back of my neck get sweaty as shame overflowed in my gut. I was going to hell for doing this. But I would take a million hells to spend this lifetime with Theo.

Trent came back with one coffee and one bottle of coconut water, handing me my drink. He buckled his seat belt and backed out of his parking space, looking casual and untroubled. I couldn't look at him the rest of the way, and he must have sensed the shift in the mood because he didn't touch me anymore.

When he parked in front of my house, he turned to face me. Staring into his eyes felt like playing Russian roulette with five bullets in the chamber.

"From this day on, you spend time with Luna and Camila on Tuesdays *and* your Sundays are mine."

"What about Luna?"

"She's a package deal. We'll spend the day with her, and when it's her bedtime, it will be ours, too."

I caught my lower lip between my upper teeth, dragging it slowly as I watched him. I was getting entangled in him. I knew I should stop.

"Okay." Stupid Edie. Stupid mouth. Stupid lust.

"Today, in the office, I am going to install the Uber app on your phone through my credit card. This will be your mode of transportation until your car gets fixed. No more fucking Bane and no more *fucking* Bane."

"No, I…" I started again, but he grabbed my jaw in his hand, tilting my head so our noses almost brushed we were so close.

"Was there a question mark in my sentence? I don't think so. Save me the bullshit about your mom and dad, Edie. You're not them. And you're not driving some unreliable piece of junk. You'll be taking an Uber. End of story."

I smiled, knowing he wasn't going to get his way. Not that day, and not ever. I was no pushover. Not when it wasn't about Theo. I opened the passenger door, stepping out and leaning against his window, like I had in the reservoir. His Wayfarers were already on.

"Hey, Trent?"

"What?" he nearly growled.

"About Sundays. I get to decide what we do with Luna."

"Absolutely not. We can't be seen together, Edie."

"I'll make sure we're discreet."

"No."

"Was there a question mark at the end of my sentence?" I played our game again, where we threw each other's words at one another like boomerangs. "I get to decide what we do."

He sighed, kicking the car into drive. "Such a fucking headache," he said.

"Drive safe, sane, and consensual." I tapped on his car's roof, grabbed my surfboard and walked away. I thought I heard him laughing behind me, but I didn't turn around to check.

Instead, I closed my eyes and imagined that his voice was a wave.

I rode it all the way to a smile.

CHAPTER EIGHTEEN
TRENT

"Is anything wrong?" Sonya asked.

Same old sweet, warm office, but now all I got was a cold shoulder. My fingers were laced together on her desk, my don't-fuck-with-me face on full display. Luna was outside, playing with Sydney. Sonya had sent her away, and I knew exactly why. Luna and I had gone through the motions of another futile session—but that was to be expected—and I'd even told Sonya about the sign language class we'd gone to and how we'd learned practical signals, like *I'm hungry, I want to go home,* and *I'm uncomfortable,* which Luna had already used a few times and I was able to read—albeit fucking slowly.

The only thing that didn't sit right with Sonya was the fact I hadn't called her in a couple of weeks. My sexual appetite wasn't satisfied. Not by a fucking long shot. In fact, I'd never suffered from such an extreme case of blue balls. But what could I possibly tell my child's therapist? That I didn't want to tap her ass anymore because I was too busy eating and fingering someone almost half my age, who'd recently added to her collection of stolen items my ancient cell phone, my iPad, and every piece of crap document I'd kept in my glove compartment?

"Nothing's wrong," I hissed.

"I don't believe you."

"Luna has responded pretty well to the sign language class,

and she is spending more time with the work chick." Sonya knew about Edie. Knew that the girl who'd caught us fucking was making friends with Luna. Sonya was cautiously in favor of the relationship, liking the idea of Luna enjoying the company of someone else, but worried that Edie wouldn't understand the consequences of suddenly pulling away and ignoring Luna when she went off to college, got a new boyfriend, or fuck knows what. Fortunately, I'd blocked the boyfriend issue. She wasn't going to date anytime soon.

Sonya leaned back in her chair and pursed her lips, oozing bad vibes. "You haven't invited me over in a while."

She could file this complaint alongside Amanda, who hadn't had a phone call recently, either. As with everything I did, it wasn't personal. It was just that there was only one person I wanted to roll between my sheets right now.

"Things have changed." I snapped my gum, my gaze hard and bored.

"How so?"

"I'm seeing someone." Blunt lie, but hey, lies were what kept this world running. I wasn't seeing Edie. I was merely watching her lust-drunk face as I ate her out and fingered her sweet, tight ass. At the same time, I no longer needed Sonya, and I had to let her go. Our no-strings-attached relationship had reached its expiration date. It was time to move on.

"Oh." The therapist perked up in her seat, her eyebrows shooting so high up her hairline, they almost disappeared. "Do I know her?"

"Why would you?" I bit out. Fine. Maybe I was a little defensive because Edie was barely legal and the idea of being a cradle snatcher rubbed me the wrong way. I bit the inside of my cheek thinking about how illicit we were, felt, *looked*. The ripped man and the petite teenager.

"Come on, Trent. You hardly get out of the house. And I bet you anything in my savings account you don't have the Tinder app. How did you meet?"

"Work."

"She's in finance?"

Not even close. I cocked my head sideways. "Something like that. I trust this doesn't change your commitment to Luna?" I tried to sound courteous and keep the edge off my voice.

Sonya frowned at this, reaching across her cluttered desk to tap my hand. "Absolutely not. I am one hundred percent committed to your daughter and about eighty percent happy for you."

"Eighty?" I quirked a brow.

"The other twenty is mostly jealous and bitter." She laughed. I almost smiled at that.

After the session, I put Luna in her car seat and drove aimlessly for a while. It was too early to go back home and start our bedtime routine, and Luna liked small places, where she could watch but not be seen. I didn't know what it was about Edie that infuriated me. Maybe it was the fact that our introduction had started off with her trying to steal from my mother. Maybe because her dad was a racist and I thought—hoped, even, because that would make things so much easier—that perhaps she was one, too. Or was it the fact that I knew she was after me—after my shit, after my secrets, after my neck?

Well, things had gotten out of hand.

And I hadn't stopped them.

I should have, but I hadn't.

She was eighteen. That was good. She was legal.

That was also bad. She was still too young to understand what all this meant.

If my daughter met a man twice her age and decided to be with him, I'd be losing my shit and going Gran Torino on his ass without so much as a blink.

Luckily for me, Edie didn't have a loving father. She had Jordan Van Der Zee.

Luna kicked my seat, and I snapped my eyes to the rearview mirror, frowning.

"What's up?"

She pointed at something outside the window. I shifted my gaze to see what she wanted. "Ice cream shop? Yeah, not happening."

Two kicks. Then one more for the road.

"No junk food, kid. You know the drill."

I was good at the technical stuff. I fed her a nutritious, well-balanced diet, made sure she got plenty of sleep, and gave her the appropriate kind of intellectual stimulation. It was the personal stuff I was hopeless with.

Luna waved her tiny hands like she was screaming, making her point, and it occurred to me that she'd never tried to communicate with me like this before. *Actively.* A bullet of thrill shot to my stomach. It may not have looked like a breakthrough, but it felt like one. I found myself tapping my fingers on my steering wheel, trying to contain my excitement. The smile I was biting down was slipping out.

"Are you hungry or just in the mood for something sweet?" I asked, my eyes glued to the rearview mirror. She huffed and threw one hand in the air, looking at me like I was an idiot.

"Sweet tooth, then. If you were hungry, you'd have kicked until you broke my back."

Her smile was slight, but it was there. It was intoxicating.

I wanted to write her something. Something good. Something that would make Sonya proud.

> *Luna, Luna, Luna.*
> *My tangled maze.*
> *Show me the way to your beginning and your end.*
> *To the exit point.*
> *To your pure little soul.*

"I'm going to make a suggestion, if I may." I sniffed, rubbing my face with my hand to hide my stupid grin.

She shook her head, smirking. This time, I couldn't help it. I laughed. My daughter had a fucking sense of humor, and it was lit.

"Little brat. It was a figure of speech. I wasn't really asking. There's a churro stand by our building. They also sell cinnamon pretzels. You've never had a churro, have you?"

She shook her head again.

"Well, we need to rectify that before social services takes you away from me for denying you everything good in this world. But—if you have a churro today, you don't get any junk food until next week. That includes Sunday with Edie, and I don't know what she's got planned for us."

Her eyes. Her fucking eyes. They looked like mine, and they ignited like fireflies at night. They looked like the eyes of any four-year-old kid. Hopeful. She kicked steady, fast, eager kicks to my seat.

"Is this about the churro or about Edie?"

One kick.

"Kick once if it's the churro, two if it's Edie."

Kick, kick. I sat back, brushing the steering wheel, feeling calm for the first time in years.

"Yeah, she's going to come over on Sunday and spend some time with us. Hey, why does she call you Germs?"

I knew why but wanted to try to get her to talk to me.

Luna looked perplexed. I'd stopped asking her questions that required her to talk or elaborate long ago. My mother said I was killing her with kindness by letting her not speak. I usually retorted that she had enough shit getting asked and poked by other people for me to nag her, too. I saw the wheels in Luna's head turning. She was trying to figure out how to communicate with me. Usually she'd ignore me and move on. But for the first time ever, she *wanted* to tell me. Someone honked their horn behind us. I'd been too deep in the moment and had missed the green light. I didn't give a fuck. The car lurched forward and swerved around us just as Luna opened her palms and waved them around.

"You…danced?"

She shook her head, looking annoyed. She put her hands near her face and made a disgusted sound.

"You're dirty?" I tried, pretending like Edie hadn't told me the night she'd babysat.

Talk, Luna. Talk. I'll take anything, not just words. Not just gestures. Any. Fucking. Thing. Then maybe we both wouldn't be so fucking lonely in that big penthouse.

"You met her when you were dirty? You had something on your hands? She helped you get it cleaned?"

She shook her head violently, her eyebrows diving down. She pointed at her open palm and then pinched her nose in a bad-smell gesture, her wide eyes begging me to get it.

Say it.

"She stinks? You stink? You had something on your hand? She gave you something smelly?"

The worst part of my week was the moment I saw Luna giving up on our conversation. Her shoulders slumped and she sighed, crossing her arms and looking out the window. Ignoring me.

We didn't communicate for the rest of the drive until we got home and I asked her if she still wanted that churro. She ignored me for the millionth time that day, just as she did every day.

Nothing had changed.

Sunday couldn't come fast enough.

———

Edie Van Der Zee was probably the whitest person I'd ever met. Fact.

I pondered this thought as she sat beside me, cooing over a dog who licked his balls while we were having a picnic in an Anaheim park, which was the last place anyone we knew would be. It was also where Disneyland was, where we'd taken Luna.

Luna was wearing Minnie Mouse ears that were too big and

eating the sandwich Edie had made before we got out of the house. Peanut butter, jelly, and a slice of cheddar cheese in between.

"Are you enjoying the view with your meal?" I snarled, sitting at the edge of our picnic table and not touching any of the food. I wasn't particularly hungry, and not only because Miss Van Der Zee had invented the grossest sandwich known to man. I was also being a jealous asshole because Edie had managed to squeeze reactions and facial expressions I hadn't known existed out of my daughter.

The girls ignored me, their huddled heads almost touching as Edie explained to Luna something about how the crust of the bread is obscenely underrated and how she likes to toast it and nibble on it like a breadstick.

"Trent, are you a crust eater?" Edie asked me, snapping her head up. I scratched at my stubbled jaw, avoiding a gross sexual innuendo in front of my daughter. Edie had behaved like the perfect nanny all through Disneyland. She'd basically ignored my ass, held Luna's hand the whole time, and not even blinked when two young mothers had hit on me while I'd bought us slushies.

"I don't eat bread."

"Why?"

"Don't like it."

"Who doesn't like bread?"

"Someone who likes their six-pack." Spoken like the true conceited bastard I was. Luna's eyes flew to Edie in alarm, and she put her hand on my daughter's shoulder.

"It's okay, Luna. We don't need a six-pack. Life is too short to deny yourself a peanut butter, jelly, and cheddar cheese party."

It was one thing to be a jerk to Edie—an outsider—but I couldn't do it to Luna. I bent down, tapping Luna's Minnie Mouse ears. "Hey. Care to give your old man a bite?" The apology to her was in my voice.

She handed me her sandwich, and I took a small bite, watching her face melt into a smile. *So fucking worth it.*

By the time we got home, it was six. By the time Luna was bathed and fed and I'd read her a story—Edie had taken the opportunity to gingerly make a beeline to one of the bathrooms and take a shower—it was after eight.

Then it was just us. Edie, me, and our sinister thoughts.

I figured walking into the bathroom while she showered was too creepy, especially considering I'd already indulged my stalking tendencies to borderline restraining order territory when it came to her.

Reluctantly, I waited for her on the couch, staring at an action movie without really watching it, wondering what the fuck I was doing.

I knew she was still coming after me.

Yet I couldn't. Fucking. Stop.

Did I have feelings toward her? I didn't think so. But I liked having her around. Liked how she put a smile on my daughter's face. How her fuckable ass and lean surfer's body felt against mine. How she responded to my touch the same way you responded to your first kiss. With uncontained rawness. She was clay. I could do whatever the fuck I wanted with her. And I wanted to do everything. Down to the last sordid fantasy that sat dormant in my head.

To validate my point, Edie padded out to the living room barefoot, her long yellow hair still wet and in knots. She was back in the clothes she'd worn to Disneyland—a pair of turquoise shorts and a rainbow-colored Rip Curl tank top. She looked like a gift waiting to be unwrapped, and I forgave myself for not confronting her about the stolen phone, trying to remind myself it shouldn't matter. The only thing with compromising information on Jordan was my flash drive, and she would never get her hands on that. It was currently in my safe, locked away from her sticky fingers.

She could only get her hands on useless things, and we were just messing around, so no harm done. Neither of us had lied about our intentions. It wasn't as though she'd backstabbed me.

Sprawled on the sofa, I tapped my thigh, dropping my head to the heap of fluffy pillows behind me. "C'mere."

She peered from under her wet lashes, looking shy for the briefest moment. I wondered if it was because of what we were going to do or what she *thought* was going to happen. Bane had said she wasn't vanilla, but what he really meant was she wasn't vanilla for *him*. Me, I was different. A dark, depraved animal lived inside me. Whenever I let it out—and I always let it out in bed—it bloomed.

I couldn't lose control with Edie. Not with her.

Edie walked over and straddled me like she was a stripper on her first day and wasn't sure what to do. It was awkward because we weren't a couple. We weren't intimate. We weren't even friendly. I didn't comment on this because familiarity was off the fucking table with everyone but with her specifically.

Instead, I dragged my hands up her thighs to the curve of her ass, and we both watched, her fair skin under the dusk of mine. Lust didn't have color. But it did have a face, and it looked at me, blinking rapidly to the rhythm of her hammering heart.

"I like Luna," she said quietly, wrapping her arms around my neck, her fingers trying to grasp at my very short hair. For a second there, I wanted to kiss her, just for saying that.

Instead, I squeezed her ass, slamming her body into my erection, my denim and her shorts brushing together.

"She likes you, too," I retorted.

"Yet I don't like you," she continued, grinding against my cock deliberately, and since when was I doing third base on a regular basis? I'd had multiple chances to fuck Edie, but I couldn't bring myself to do it. To take this girl—so different from my usual mature, curvy type—and do grown-up things to her.

I wanted to bite her lip and watch her bleed on me.

Instead, instead, *in-fucking-stead*, I locked my jaw, feeling my Adam's apple bobbing with a swallow. One hand still on her ass, I reached with the other one to the coffee table by the couch, opening the childproof drawer and retrieving a joint. I tucked it between my lips and cupped the tip with my hand, lighting it.

"I don't like you, too," I answered casually, clicking shut my Zippo and placing it back on the stainless-steel table.

"But I like how you make me feel." She rode me through our clothes. The aching need for her escalated torturously slowly, reminding me why sex as a teenager was so much more fun than it was in your thirties. The anticipation made my dick twitch. "You make me feel wild. Fearless. Like I'm someone. Someone strong." Her lips dragged along my neck, hot and soft.

I exhaled a ribbon of smoke upward, leaning and sweeping my lips against the side of her neck. "What's your fascination with power?" I ran my hand up her arm, thumbing the hem of her shirt. I wanted it gone. Her nipples were erect under her top, begging to be licked and sucked and bitten. Her tits were so small—so fucking tiny—the idea of kneading them in my big hands made my balls tighten, knowing there wasn't enough of them, that I'd be left hungry for more of *her*.

"It's less of a power thing, more of a strength issue. Why wouldn't I want to be strong? Isn't that what everyone's after?" She tilted her head, slipping her fingers to clasp my joint and take a hit. I let her. I let the eighteen-year-old on my lap, rubbing her wet pussy all over my Diesel denim, smoke with me. It'd been years since I'd given a woman the time of day, and I'd never, ever done anything illegal with a chick who straddled the line between barely legal and hot as shit and worth the self-loathing.

But Edie wasn't a chick.

Edie was the fucking end of me.

She exhaled the smoke straight into my face, and I took the opportunity to pluck the joint from her hand and place it in an ashtray. I yanked her top off and threw it on the floor, admiring her bare tits for the very first time. Her nipples were two pink coins. She shuddered with pleasure when I cupped one of them, rolling the plump skin beneath my fingers and staring at her like a hungry hound.

"If you want to be strong, be," I hissed.

"Easy for you to say." She thrust her tits into my face, losing every ounce of control over her self-restraint. I held her back, my fingers feathering, skimming her ribs as I took one of her nipples into my mouth, sucking on it ravenously before biting the tip and feeling her pull her breasts away but grind into my dick harder. I stopped when I felt the goose bumps around her nipple and sucked the pain away, and she moaned louder.

That's it, baby. Pain and pleasure. Playing together, but not nicely.

"Oh yeah, I'm a lucky bastard," I snorted, brushing my thumb over her blushing nipple. "Going to high school with the richest kids in the state when I couldn't even afford football gear. Working two fucking jobs after school just so I could buy supplies for my next school year. Being the playboy, the good, casual fuck no one would ever date seriously in this town—because I'm half Black, because I'm poor, because I'm the stereotype people want as a friend but never as family. You're right. I don't know hardship." I slapped her tit, not too hard, but not softly, either. She winced and grabbed my head, pulling me into her. We melted into each other, and it was dangerous, doing whatever the fuck we were doing in the living room, where Luna could easily walk in. I took one last pull of the joint before putting it out and then tucking both it and the lighter into my pocket to kill every evidence that it was ever there. I grabbed Edie by the ass and carried her to my room, my lips and teeth on her other nipple. Kissing, caressing, licking, making her skin blossom. I didn't bite her. Not when she was expecting it. Half the fun was not expecting the spank and the bite. She was going to learn. I was going to teach her.

My cock was so hard I thought I was going to shoot my load in my pants like a goddamn teenager.

"Mine," I said, my lips running from her tits to her rib cage, all the way up to her neck. Everything was soft and tanned and baked by the sun. I kicked the door to my bedroom open and laid her on the dark-oak platform king-size bed. Her legs spread for me willingly, but her heart wouldn't, and maybe that was why she was the girl to make my dick extra hard and forget about all the others.

"Every inch of you is mine. Your breath is mine." I squeezed her throat, sliding on top of her, my tongue exploring the space between her breasts, just above her lungs. My mouth moved like a straight arrow down to her belly button. "Your mind is mine." I tugged at her hair without even looking up from her flat stomach, hearing her moan. She used both hands to push my head down, her poise snapping like the flying buttons of a ripped shirt.

"Your body is *definitely* mine." I shoved my hand into her panties and squeezed her pussy hard. "Admit it, Edie. You're drowning in me, fast. You're way past wet." I let the word roll on my tongue as I slipped two fingers into her, playing with her arousal, and she was so soaking, and I was so fucking her tonight—yes—even if it meant it would put me straight on God's shit list. "You're mine, and you hate it. You're mine, and I'm not a wave you can ride. I'm the fucking ocean. And every single day when you pull shit like stealing my iPad or my old phone or the fucking trash I keep in my glove compartment, you're falling deeper. Tell me, Van Der Zee, do I make it hard for you to breathe?"

My mouth was near her panties. Her shorts were on my floor. I looked up at her, and she looked like she wanted to cry. How beautiful would that be? Her tears running down her perfect porcelain face. A broken doll. *My* broken doll.

"You do." She inhaled sharply, watching me slide her underwear down her thighs. My heart stuttered unevenly at seeing her naked—completely naked—for the first time. Not in a compromising position against the printer or in someone's back seat with her top still on, but completely bare. I was still fully dressed, but somehow it didn't make me feel less exposed. It made me uncomfortable, but not enough to stop what we were doing. "I can't breathe when I think about the things I want to do to you, and I breathe too fast when I think about the things I want you to do to *me*," Edie admitted.

"Tell me," I whispered into the crook between her thigh and pussy, watching her whole body quiver under me before I'd even touched her. "What do you want me to do to you?"

"Everything," she whispered. "I want you to do everything to me."

I licked her inner thighs, her pussy, inside and out—every drop of her lust for me—then got up and reached for my nightstand, pulling out a condom. She peeled my shirt off in a hurry while I worked my jeans, the condom between my teeth.

"One thing, Edie. Whatever we do, we take this to our graves."

"To our graves," she echoed. "My father will take everything I care about if he finds out."

Same goes for me, I thought bitterly. Only difference was, I was going to fight the motherfucker to the ground. She couldn't. Or wouldn't. Same difference.

I rolled the condom on, feeling the familiar appreciative twitch of my cock. I kneeled between her legs and then slapped and stroked my sheathed cock while fingering her. She moaned, watching me.

"I liked it when you bit my nipple hard," she said. I ignored her, pulling my fingers out and coating her pussy with her arousal. "You make me feel deranged with need," she whimpered, just as I slapped her pussy for the first time. It made her body stutter and stir, and she let out a little yelp I stifled by shoving my wet fingers into her mouth.

"Shhh," I said. "You said you like it. Show me how much."

She sucked my fingers clean, and I cupped the back of her head, pulling her closer as I slid into her without warning. No different from any other woman I'd slept with before. Just the same, I convinced myself. Just the fucking same.

So fucking wet.

I thrust once, twice, three times, without asking whether it felt okay or any consideration, like I'd done with other women.

But hell if she felt like any other woman.

Edie moved underneath me, slow at the beginning, catching up with my pace. She grunted every time I entered her, scratching my back as I slid one of her calves against my shoulder and slammed deeper into her. She was tight and small, but the smile she gave showed me she enjoyed this agony the way I did.

Every time I felt this surge in my chest, I thrust harder, faster, more violently, trying to shake off the feeling that accompanied my tingling balls and tight muscles. She, in return, scratched harder, drawing blood from me, screaming my name into a pillow she flung over her face.

I rode her.

But she rode me, too.

"I'm close, I'm close, I'm close," she chanted, and this was my cue to flip her onto her stomach, enter her from behind, and press her head against the pillow.

"I want to hurt you," I said, because that was what I always said, because that was what I always *felt*. But I didn't feel it now. I was on autopilot. Like when people said they were hungry at noon sharp just to get the fuck out of the office and take their lunch break.

"Then do," she moaned into the pillow, completely pliable, and she fucking came, clutching my dick and shuddering like she was having a seizure. "Hurt me, Trent. I love your wrath on my skin."

I wrapped her long hair around my fist and pulled hard, making her arch her back when she was on all fours. Her ass was round and white against her obvious tan lines. I slapped it.

At first cautiously, getting the feel of it, and when she moaned and clenched around me, barely making it possible for me to slide out and then back in, I slapped harder.

But I wasn't feeling it. The need to inflict pain on her.

"Harder," she groaned.

I slapped her ass harder, and the *thwack!* hung in the air. A red mark formed around her right cheek. I hated it. Inflicting pain on her. But I also undoubtedly couldn't deny her. Her wish was my command, consequences be damned. What the fuck was wrong with me?

"Harder," she yelped.

And I did, hating that my dick was so swollen and ready to explode to the pained sounds she was making. She confused me. I'd never felt guilty about the things I wanted. I did now.

"Harder."

"No."

"Trent."

"No."

"I need it."

"You've had enough for one day, Edie. Your cum is all over my dick. I can eat you out if you want another orgasm." Was I bargaining with her mid-fuck? That was a first. And a last. This chick wasn't running the show, no matter how hard I wanted her tight pink pussy to milk my cock.

"If you won't, *Bane* will." I heard the smile in her voice but couldn't see it. Fuck it. She'd asked for it.

Thwack!

We came together like a storm. Her grip on my cock tightened as my thrusts became erratic, jerking before I found my release. I swear I came enough to fill up a bucket in that condom. Shit, it felt good.

I pulled out immediately, rolling off of her and sauntering to the bathroom to dispose of the condom. I didn't look back to see her when I washed the cum from my dick, watching it shrinking tiredly above the sink. I let her have my back, knowing if she caught my expression through the bathroom mirror, she'd flash a victory grin.

I made a note to never take the flash drive from my safe.

She was starting to feel a lot like an addiction. Couple more fucks like this, and I didn't trust my fucked-up self not to hand it over willingly.

CHAPTER NINETEEN
EDIE

I was six when I first realized there was something seriously wrong with my father. Way before the whole thing with Theo happened. It was a rare fall afternoon when Jordan had come home on time and my mother was "cooking" dinner in the kitchen. Or that was what she'd called downing a bottle of wine while staring at the circling plate in the microwave warming up our meal.

Everything felt eerie, askew, and dangerous. Breaking routine scared me, but the idea of living with a man I barely knew and was too terrified to ask to tuck me into bed was scarier, so I'd obediently sat next to him on the couch as he'd mindlessly watched a finance show on CNN and flipped through his mail. A commercial appeared on the screen advertising a nonprofit organization for abused and neglected animals. In the commercial, they showed sad puppy faces and disfigured kittens staring at the cameras, begging to be helped. One of the dogs was lying in a pool of mud. A fleabag made of bones and skin. Both its eyes were missing, and it looked like it didn't have any teeth left. I'd gasped in horror, clutching the fabric of the expensive sofa in my tiny fingers.

"Edie, stop doing that. It's suede. It's a very gentle fabric." He'd slapped my wrist, but not forcefully. Never forcefully.

I'd immediately let go, curling my spine, turning to face him. "Can we donate?"

"I donate enough at work."

"Really? To shelters?" I'd perked up, desperate to cling to a positive thing about him. Building a character of the people we knew was a psychological mechanism I would later learn can also bite you in the ass—because I'd wanted badly to believe my father was a good man and that my mother was okay. In my mind, he was caring and generous. Not calculated and indifferent. He'd given me a sideways glance, most of his attention still divided between the screen and the thick pile of letters.

"No. I donate to whoever needs my help in our community."

"The commercial makes me feel funny, Dad. Funny...sad," I'd admitted, looking away from the screen as the narrator explained all the horrific things these animals had been through. Back then, I'd still called him that. *Dad.*

"It's life, Edie."

"I can't look." My head moved back and forth, my knees tucked under my chin as I'd held myself together. "It's too sad."

"Life's sad, so you better get used to it."

I'd known very little about the world back then, which was probably why I'd still clung to my optimism. What I had known was that he'd made me feel uncomfortable. Because, for the first time since I could remember, a smirk had formed on his thin, hard lips as he'd continued flipping the letters.

I'd thought, *Why here, why now, why so happy?*

The next day, he'd picked me up from school. I'd been shocked to say the least. We usually had a driver who helped me get around from place to place. School, afternoon activities, and playdates. Never my parents. I'd felt flattered and anxious as I'd climbed into the back of Jordan's car, trying to be on my best behavior. I'd wondered where we were going, since he'd driven in the opposite direction from our house, but hadn't wanted to sound ungrateful or suspicious. It was only when I'd started seeing the woods and Saint Angelo Lake, past the city limits, that my mouth fell open.

"Where are we going?"

He'd just grinned in the rearview mirror like a predator, flicking the signal and taking a sharp right. I later realized why.

It was an animal shelter. My feet had dragged, and going past the rusty gate leading to the kennels had felt a lot like handing my soul to someone I didn't trust.

"Sometimes, Edie, you need to look cruelty in the eye and not do anything about it. In order to succeed in life, you need to let logic and rationality dictate your behavior, not your feelings. Now, you know that you're allergic to dogs and cats, right?"

I remember nodding, my mind still a nervous fog. I could never have a dog or a cat—that was a given—but I'd never asked for one. All I'd wanted was to donate some money to that nonprofit organization on TV. They'd needed it so badly, and we had so much of it. The shrill sound of frantic barking had filled my ears, and I'd wanted to turn around and run. The only reason I hadn't was because I knew he wouldn't chase me. He'd let me get lost in the woods without so much as a blink.

"So you know we can't adopt any of those animals. Now, I need you to see them, look them in the eye, and walk away from them. Can you do that for me, Edie?" Jordan had squatted to my eye level, smiling. Behind him there'd been a volunteer wearing a green shirt with the name of the shelter and a peculiar, too-wide smile.

No.

"Y-yes."

We'd spent nearly an hour and a half strolling through the kennels staring at begging, pleading, distressed dogs and cats. I'd had to look each of them in the eye before I moved to the next crate. The volunteer who'd joined us on the tour had thought it was odd, my father never specifying what he was looking for in a pet. She'd been oblivious to the thing that was made crystal clear to me that day: He wasn't looking to adopt, but he definitely did want a pet. He wanted to make me his tamed, trained puppet.

And what killed me now was that to some extent, he'd succeeded.

That day had broken me, and every day since, he'd made the crack in my heart a little bigger.

I was not allowed to give money or food to homeless people down the street. *Don't encourage them, Edie. Life's about choices. They obviously made the wrong ones.*

I wasn't allowed to talk to strangers, not even small talk with responsible adults around me. *Van Der Zees do not enjoy small talk. We are far too busy for that.* I was expected to conduct myself as the perfect ice princess. And at the beginning, I'd rebelled. But then Theo happened, and my father became more than the breadwinner. He became the master who pulled at the invisible strings of his shadow puppet. Me.

Twelve years after Jordan showed me cruelty by breaking my routine, he did it again.

I was at home, cutting open packages with potential wigs for Mom that I'd ordered when he walked into my room. Jordan didn't bother knocking, and I didn't bother asking why he was at home. He never was—and he sure as hell never entered my room—but I treaded carefully around him. His peculiar, self-centered behavior seemed to have deteriorated further in recent weeks.

"Can I help you?" I asked, arranging the blond human-hair wigs on my bed and brushing them, trying to decide which one Mom would like best.

Jordan propped one shoulder against my doorframe, staring at me with disdain. I wondered if he could feel it. That I was different. Because sleeping with Trent Rexroth had definitely changed me, much more than the evidence on my body. The cracked nipples, sore and red, and the pink welts on my ass and inner thighs were just an external decoration. But when he'd come inside me, he'd left something behind. Some of his strength.

"Sit down, Edie."

"Give me one good reason to," I blurted, picking up a wig and running the bamboo brush through it. I wasn't in the mood for a lecture, and if it was the flash drive he was after, he needed to give me more time. Trent wasn't only on my tail. He had it wrapped around his little finger now.

"Because I'm your father and you do not talk back to me if you want a peaceful, calm life. Now sit." He stepped into the room, his stern blue eyes leaking scorn. I sat on the edge of the bed unhurriedly, looking up to meet his gaze. My silence spoke volumes. I hoped he was able to hear all the words it dripped.

"Edie, I'm afraid things are going to change quite soon in this household, and it's my duty to break it first to you, since you're the responsible adult of you and your mother." Ignoring the dig at Mom—he was hardly a respectable candidate for the Todos Santos Parent of the Year award himself—I folded my arms over my chest, waiting for more. "I'm leaving." He said it simply, as if the words didn't slap me across the face. As though black dots weren't swimming in my vision.

"Why?" I asked. I didn't care about him leaving. If anything, the term *good riddance* sprang to my mind. I hated him. But Mom didn't. Mom depended on him, and I was tired of collecting the broken fragments of her that he left behind, trying to piece them back together.

It wasn't the cleaning up after him part that killed me. It was the sharp edges that dug into my skin when I picked her up. Because whenever he shattered Mom, both of us bled.

"Let's admit it. Your mother has not been well for a very long time now, and she's been refusing to seek the help she obviously needs. Not all creatures can be helped. I can't be saddled with her situation if she doesn't make more of an effort, and sadly, I cannot see myself sitting around waiting for that to happen."

She's unwell because of you. She doesn't want to go into rehab because she is scared you'll run off with someone else. Which you probably will. The words swirled in my head and pushed their way to my tongue, but I bit down my upper lip. He was the one who'd said that Van Der Zees should always be calculated and shrewd. I dropped the wig on the bed beside me, turning my face up to the ceiling on a sigh.

"Won't this kill your political aspirations?" I rubbed my palms across my cheeks.

"It would." He shrugged, stepping deeper into the room and closing the door behind him so that my mother wouldn't hear. Not that she was big on leaving her room these days. "I'm not running for mayor. I went down to the city hall yesterday and withdrew my candidacy. The campaign is off."

My rapid blink gave away my surprise. I straightened on my bed, using one hand to knead my aching skull. Everything hurt. And I do mean everything. My thighs, my ass, my core were all still sore from having spent the night with Trent Rexroth. My head was spinning at Father's recent revelation, and my heart was drowning in sorrow and self-pity at what this meant for me.

Jordan Van Der Zee was a careful planner. He knew where he wanted to be five years from now and worked toward it quietly and with determination. So hearing this more than threw me off-balance.

He shook his head, reaching for one of the wigs, fingering the human hair with a scowl. "I'm going to focus on expanding Fiscal Heights Holdings, kick Rexroth off the board, and live my life peace-fully," he confirmed, withdrawing his hand like the wig was made of cold fire. "And I am not going to stay with your mother. You have your future to concentrate on. Here is my advice, Edie—enroll in a good college, far away from this place, and make something out of yourself. Stop smoking dope. Stop socializing with losers, and stop giving your mother the time of day when she clearly doesn't do the same for you."

And do you? Do you give me the time of day? But again, I had so much to lose. Trent's words were like a faint echo inside my head. *If you want to be strong, be.*

"You can't do this right now. She needs to get better first." I shook my head.

Jordan looked up to my ceiling and fingered the golden chandelier, smiling to himself at the memory of who I was supposed to be. "She'll never get better. I'm going to do it, and soon."

"I need more time," I argued, feeling completely out of control.

"I don't owe you a thing."

"When are you going to tell her?" I stood up, toe to toe with him. He looked like the cold, white man who went to Pocahontas's village. The destroyer. He looked like a Harry Potter character that could suck your soul away.

"This week. Maybe next. It doesn't matter. When is a good time for something like this?"

"Considering you vowed to love her forever, in sickness and in health, *never* is a good time. She needs you," I insisted, narrowing my eyes.

"It is not up for discussion." He pointed at the wigs on my bed. "This is not healthy or constructive for someone your age. You should be focused on your studies and on making a future for yourself."

"My future is taking care of my family," I answered, jutting my chin out. "My future is spending every morning surfing."

My father looked around the coral room with dead eyes, like it represented all the dreams and hopes I'd shattered along the years by being myself. By choosing Doc Martens over Louboutins. By choosing the beach over chess. By choosing guys like Bane over the preppy boys of All Saints High.

He shrugged. "Your funeral."

Teeth chattering, fists clenched, eyes bleeding hatred. "What about him?"

"Theodore?"

No. The pope. "Yes."

"Our deal still stands. You will get to keep him around as long as you provide the information I need on Rexroth. Now that my plans have changed, staying on top of things at Fiscal Heights Holdings is vital," he said dryly, running a hand over the vanity I'd never used, a sheet of dust coating his palm.

"And if I fail?" I hoped he didn't pick up on that gulp.

"You won't fail. Failure would mean Theodore moving away to an East Coast facility. I know of an excellent one near the New York branch of Fiscal Heights Holdings."

"It's difficult to find dirt on Trent. He is not a stupid man." I choked on my words, stomping my feet. I hated that I'd stomped my feet. I wasn't that kind of girl. I wasn't *a* girl.

"He's smart, but I trust you're smarter. You came from me, after all."

Barf. How could I react to this without sounding hateful? I changed the subject. "Do you have someone else? Are you leaving Mom for a mistress?" The words felt dirty in my mouth. I wanted to take a shower and bury myself under the duvet, but most of all, I wanted not to feel so impossibly tired of fighting this cold war that never ceased. This was exactly how my mother had started off her rocky affair with prescription drugs and depression.

Not leaving the bed.

Day in and day out.

Jordan examined me emotionlessly. He took a step back, indicating he was done with the conversation, and wiped his dusty hand on my black hoodie, resting on the back of my chair. "Don't be childish, Edie."

"I got to meet quite a few of your lovers over the years. I'm wondering if one of them has finally managed to do what the others couldn't. Is it Tracey? Holly? Maybe Cadence?" I pouted, knowing full well I was losing control and not caring anymore. I was vindictive and full of red wrath. A wrecking ball of fire. I was hungry for that power he took from me whenever he was in the room.

He shook his head. "Mental like your mother."

I took a step toward him, watching as his face twisted in

confusion. I never invaded his personal space. But now my nose was dangerously close to his, and I saw everything swimming in his light-blue eyes. I saw myself in his features, in his clenched jawline, in the little curve of our noses, in the pastiness of our skin—mine diluted by my tan and freckles and youth—his still stern white. And for the first time, I realized that maybe I was him. A product of something horrible that was going to give birth to more awful things.

"I don't care if you leave her for someone else. I know I can't convince you to stay, and even if I could—half the time I think she's still like this because of you. But I will tell you this—if you decide to parade your new toy around town and humiliate my mother, there will be consequences. As for Theo—*not* Theodore, Theo—and Trent Rexroth, I am sick and tired of asking you how high every time you tell me to jump. I will get you the goddamn flash drive, *Daddy Dearest*, but in return, you will sign all the legal documentation I have stashed in the drawer of that useless vanity you bought me when I was twelve and set Theo and me free. Agree to this right now, Jordan, or we don't have a deal. And please, before you say anything, never underestimate a broken person. We're unpredictable because once you're broken—what's one more crack?"

The words left my body like a hurricane, and after I was done, I was left panting. I felt the disloyalty for Luna and the unfaithfulness to Trent in my bones. I was sick to my stomach, knowing how it was going to affect Camila, but things were getting too complicated. I needed to run away with Theo and disappear. SoCal wasn't the only place in the world with good beaches. We could live somewhere else. Build a life. We could sit on a porch I hadn't even seen yet, watching the sunset, eating pistachio ice cream, laughing. Making good memories and bottling them in our minds. We could.

"Edie," my father said. I looked straight at him and then past him. He knew that I'd meant it. Besides, something told me that he was done with me, anyway. With me, with my mom, with Theo. Getting the flash drive and cutting me out of his life was a two birds, one stone situation. Of course he'd say yes. "Get me that flash drive"—he leaned close to me, his cheek pressing against mine—"and you will get your future with Theodore."

"Keep your lovers in the dark, where sin should be hidden," I reminded him. This time it was I who held his wrist. I couldn't wrap my fingers around his cold flesh—like a snake's dead skin—but I'd hit home this time. The tightness of his jaw told me so.

"True Van Der Zee," he muttered, shaking me off like I was a wet stray cat in the pouring rain.

Because at that moment, I was the kid who'd stared at the dying dog and hadn't blinked.

At that moment, I was ruthless.

At that moment, I was the Van Der Zee I never thought I'd become.

I hated that person. But that person hated Jordan much more than she feared him.

My stomach growled for the eighteenth time that morning, loudly enough to be heard even through the sound of the crashing Pacific waves.

"God, Gidget, what the fuck? Eat a goddamn energy bar." Bane rummaged in his bag and threw a protein bar at me, scowling. His sullen expression didn't melt one bit when I walked over and tucked the bar back into his backpack, sliding into my flip-flops and hoisting my board up to balance on my head the rest of the way to the promenade. I didn't not eat to spite him. I couldn't eat. The nausea ate at my stomach, making acid dance on the back of my tongue. Ever since I'd told my father I was going to retrieve that flash drive with God knows what on it, I'd felt sick. Not just physically but mentally. I wasn't entirely sure what I was feeling for Trent, but I was more than certain no one in the world deserved what I was about to serve him.

Bane snatched his radio from the sand, "Pacific Coast Highway" by Kavinsky blasting from the speakers. He grabbed my board and tucked it under his arm, carrying both our surfboards up to the board-walk. I followed him on failing legs, the bile still fresh and sour in my throat. When we got to the walkway, he greeted homeless people living in makeshift cardboard homes on the grassy hills by the shops. He knew everyone on this beach. Every failing artist who shoved their CD into people's hands and every new salesperson in the weed, surfing, and bike shops. Bane was still shirtless and barefoot when he walked me over to my car. A not-so-secret donor had paid my pending invoice at the shop, and they'd finally released my Audi, new cylinder and all. Bane turned around and leaned against my passenger door when we got to my car, folding his arms over the angry dragon on his chest. His lethargic jade eyes scanned me with amused disinterest, and he tilted his head, like I was a weird mystical creature he couldn't figure out.

"Come over to meet my mom," he said out of nowhere.

The laughter bubbled from my sore throat. It wasn't happiness but embarrassment diluted with anxiety. I rubbed my hands together to warm up from the water, slapping my palms over my face to keep him oblivious to my blushing cheeks. "Aw, I didn't know we were getting serious. And this after you refused to take me to prom when we were actually dating."

He rolled his eyes before shooting me a serious look. "Prom is lame, and we were never really together. We were fucking exclusively until your daddy issues came out in full force. Anyway, I think my mom could help you."

"Help me with what?" I nearly snorted. I was beyond help. I was about to fuck over two people to save one I loved.

"With your family situation." Bane didn't know everything, but he knew enough. Getting assistance from an outsider was tempting, but I'd never met Bane's mother before, and even though I knew she was a hotshot with all kinds of connections, I didn't trust adults. *Real* adults. The ones who ran the world I lived in.

"I appreciate the offer, but I've got it covered." I walked over to the driver's side of my car and swung the door open, sliding into the Audi. I could still smell the scent of Vicious—the previous owner—in my car, and he reminded me of Trent. Of his sharp posture and formidable frown. Bane appeared by my window and tapped the roof of my car, smirking.

"Is that why you forgot to tie your board to your roof? Look, you should at least think about it, Gidget. For what it's worth, I think you don't have it covered, and if you need a helping hand, you know mine is good for more than fingering."

"Disgusting, but thank you."

I tied my surfboard and drove away, not even bothering to make a stop at home to take a shower and change. I needed to think about what I was going to do with my mother. I needed to come up with a plan for that flash drive. But most of all—I needed to stop thinking about Trent like he wasn't the enemy.

CHAPTER TWENTY
TRENT

Atlanta fucking Georgia.

"Are you sure?" I tap-tap-tapped my fingers on my desk, one hand cupping my cheekbone. I stared at Amanda like she was delivering me a roadkill and not the fucking news I'd been waiting for for years. In a way, she was. This information was useless, futile, dead weight. She sat across from me, looking every inch the professional private investigator—dressed smart but not too sophisticated in a white blouse and a pair of black cigar pants—and nodded, sliding a manila file across my desk.

"Positive. She lives in a nice apartment building in Buckhead, an upscale area in Atlanta. She has a Chihuahua. No husband. No children. As far as I am aware, she doesn't work. Not sure where the money comes from. I can look deeper into it, of course, but that would entail flying out to Atlanta. You will need to cover the ticket and hotel plus the hourly rate. Or I could connect you with a colleague who works there. He could find out all the data that you need."

If there was a fucking guideline as to what to feel, about the Val thing and in general, I'd buy the shit out of it and order extra copies. For the first time in years, it looked like things were picking up. My parents and I took Luna to her weekly sign language classes. We all made an effort, and she'd actually started communicating with us. Luna had Camila, whom she liked, and Sonya, whom she absolutely adored. And, somewhere in between, Edie Van Der Zee had managed to make my daughter smile, laugh, shop for clothes, and go to Disneyland. It seemed like I was on the brink of a break-through, and rocking the boat felt like a wild Vegas bet. When I'd started my hunt after Val, the situation had been different. I had been sitting alone in Chicago with a one-year-old baby in my arms. I still remembered the moment I'd decided to pick up my phone and call my best friend Dean, asking if his lawyer dad knew of a good PI I could trust. I'd been staring at the city from my penthouse, Luna chewing my arm with her new pointy teeth between pleading cries for her mother.

I had been angry.

I had been frantic.

I had been desperate.

I had been vengeful.

And I realized that now I was no longer any of those things.

Or perhaps I was, but not enough to screw up everything I'd achieved in the last few months. Luna came first, and it didn't look like her mother was interested in claiming her. If anything, it seemed like Val had found a new fat wallet to leech off.

"Leave it," I said, waving my hand. I stood up and stepped to my floor-to-ceiling window, frowning at Los Angeles. The city was like lust. Ugly and raw and filthy yet somehow utterly irresistible. She lacked all the things people love. Structure, sophistication, beauty. Yet she attracted everyone and everything. Sucking in and spitting out people with pockets full of dreams and money. That's why I'd decided to stay in Todos Santos, even though a single biracial man was not the best candidate to live in ultra-white, obnoxiously high-class Todos Santos. I didn't want Luna to know ugliness. She deserved more than life had given her so far.

"Are you sure?" Amanda asked, her Jamaican accent slightly thicker than before. It happened to her when she was thrown off-balance. My answer was definitely surprising. I nodded, turning around, my hands clasped behind my back.

"Luna's in a good place right now. I don't wanna throw her off-kilter. I'd rather focus on making her better." *Making her speak.* "Then if all goes according to plan, I can contact Val discreetly and have her sign her rights over."

Amanda bobbed her head, already clasping her purse. It was the end of an era. I'd worked with Amanda for too long, fucked her for months, and now it was all over. She stood up, and I walked over, feeling the need to do something civilized. I wasn't a shithead. Not most of the time, anyway. And definitely not to people who weren't shitheads to me.

"Thank you." I squeezed her upper arm. "For everything. For helping me with the Val situation, for everything on that flash drive…"

"If you ever need anything else"—she returned my embrace, getting closer now—"you know where to find me." Her lips brushed my ear, and I moved away, capturing her chin, dragging my thumb over her lower lip as I shook my head.

"Not anymore," I said softly.

"Lucky girl." She raised one eyebrow.

"Not at all. Trust me."

She moved away from me, all business now, one hand on her hip. "Should I proceed with the Jordan Van Der Zee case or close everything and send it to you?"

I didn't need time to think. "Continue relentlessly, and don't stop until I have the bastard's head speared."

EDIE

Monday, Tuesday, Wednesday, Thursday seemed unbearably long and boring. The only notable things were that my father was blissfully out of the office, probably taking a long vacation with one of his mistresses or planning the next step of his world domination, and I couldn't stomach eating or looking at my mother. The latter was still oblivious to her husband planning to leave her. She was spending her days staring at her bathroom mirror, waiting for her locks to miraculously grow ten inches longer. I made food for her. She ate it without complaining. There was no Trent, and no Trent meant no hope. I was walking the hallways of the fifteenth floor with my heart in my stomach, veins, chest, legs, everywhere. It was swollen, diseased, infected. On Tuesday, I spent the day helping Luna find pictures of seahorses online and paint them with watercolors. I gave her the necklace I'd made for her, of a seashell, one that looked exactly like mine but also different.

Hers was chipped, broken, imperfect.

I'd used the second black lace in the pack to make it, so I guess it was like one of those friendship bracelets. I'd never made one for anyone else. When I told her this, puzzled delight shone from her eyes. She didn't understand me.

Neither could I.

I hovered and loitered everywhere on the floor, desperate to catch a glimpse of Trent. I needed that flash drive.

And on Friday, my wishes finally came true.

I was at my desk outside my father's office. It was a smaller, sadder version of his assistant Max's oak L-shaped desk. My head was between the pages of a surfing magazine I'd brought from home, and I was just about to flip a page when someone threw something at it. Two somethings. A Snickers bar and a Nature Valley. My head snapped up. I arched an eyebrow. Trent stood in front of me. Tall, dapper, and irresistible. He was silent, as I expected him to be, so I picked one of the bars without even examining the label, tearing the wrapper open and taking a bite. The hunger of the week slammed into me all at once, like I'd been waiting to see his face to know that it was okay to consume food.

"We haven't played this game in a while," I commented.

He shrugged. "I found better games to play with you." Only he could say it so quietly no one would hear. My soul was a balloon losing air, and fast. I'd yearned for him, but for him it was just another spontaneous encounter. Maybe screwing him over was a blessing in disguise. There'd be nothing left to hold us together once I blew us apart. My mind drifted from my original goal when he was around. He obviously didn't share the sentiment. "In my office." He cocked his head in the direction of the hallway. "In twenty minutes, so it doesn't look suspicious."

The fact we hadn't been caught so far just went to show that people were really, mostly, self-centered pricks. Because I didn't hide my interest very well. Sure, we hadn't spoken, hung out, or made out with each other in the hallways. But my eyes didn't leave any room for doubt. When I saw him—they were hungry.

He disappeared down the corridor, giving me some much needed time to collect my thoughts and hair into a messy bun, and then I walked over and knocked on his door.

"Come in."

I closed the door behind me, leaning against it with my hands tucked behind my back. I gravitated toward him like he was the sun. A beautiful pleasure conceived by nature that could very well kill you if you got too close. He looked at me like I was the moon. Pale and lonely and so far away.

"Why do they call you the Mute?" I asked. Finally. I'd been meaning to do it ages ago, but it had never felt right. Trent looked to be in a good mood today. I was going to capitalize on that while we were still on speaking terms.

"Isn't it obvious?" He leaned back in his chair, looking powerful and stern. "I hardly fucking talk, Edie."

He had no problem talking to me. "Yes, but have you always been like this, or is that something that—"

"Happened after Luna's mother ran away? Nope, I was always quiet."

"Any reason for that?"

"I don't enjoy small talk or gossip or anything in between. I talk for a purpose. Tell me, Edie, is there a point to this conversation, or are you done wasting my time?"

I frowned. "Why did you tell me to come in here? You're obviously in one of your moods."

"I was thinking more along the lines of something dirty and wrong, but I have a proposition. Sit down." He motioned with his chin toward the chair across from him. I stared at it before finally walking over and taking a seat. My hands were on my lap, and I held them together to keep from biting my nails. "Let me start by saying that I know and respect that your Saturdays are yours. Trust me, you made that point very clear. But I have a favor to ask. Vicious is throwing his annual summer barbecue—actually, his wife, Emilia, is in charge—and Luna and I have to go. Luna absolutely fucking despises these kinds of gatherings and the kids who try to talk and play with her. I'd take my parents to keep her company when I have to help around the kitchen and grill, but they'll be out of town. I wouldn't ask unless I had to. You know that, right?"

I was so used to his stern demeanor, it took me a moment to decipher his request.

Saturday.

Barbecue.

Theo.

No.

I swallowed hard. "Listen…"

"Breaking point. Everyone has one. These kinds of situations are my daughter's, Edie." He shot me a look I tried to decode. It wasn't exactly wrecked—but it sure as hell wasn't his usual put-together self. "I don't know your story, but I do know that you're not a stranger to feeling like Luna. She is going to stand there alone because I won't be able to be with her every single second. She is going to get approached by kids. She is going to be uncomfortable and scared and stressed. I don't want that for her, but I can't fucking decline every single invitation I am given and lock us in my penthouse forever, which is what I'm forced to do half the fucking time."

It stung. His speech hit me somewhere deep because he was right. The outcast. I knew it. It lived in me, even if I didn't look or talk like one. I shook my head, feeling tears pricking my eyes. No matter what I'd choose, I'd walk away from this room with a heavy heart. Ever since Theo had entered his facility, I'd always visited him, every Saturday, not skipping even once. Not even when I was sick. Was I really going to break the tradition for Trent and Luna?

How much longer would I even be in Luna's life? The thought of saying goodbye to the beautiful, silent little girl who reminded me of myself tugged the words from me. "Just this once," I heard myself saying. "Please, don't ask me again and make me say no to Luna. Because I'd hate myself for turning her down and you for asking again. My Saturdays are *mine*," I insisted. He gave me a curt nod, trying to conceal his obvious glee.

His tense shoulders released. "First and last time. I don't know who he is, but he is lucky to have you," he said. The paranoia in me perked up and made my body shoot up.

"How do you know it's a he?"

"Mainly because I'm not an idiot. Is he in jail? Are you planning to be with him when he gets out? Setting up a nest egg, paying off his debts?"

It was almost laughable if it wasn't so tragic. How right and wrong he was. I walked over to the door, grabbed the bronze handle, and stared at it, deflating with an exhale. Behind me, I could feel Trent's stare on my back as he waited for an answer. Outside, I could hear the sound of a buzzing office. "I'll see you on Saturday."

"You don't get to walk away before you answer me."

"Says who?"

"Says your boss."

I turned around. "You didn't act like my boss when you gave me weed and dick."

To this, he said nothing. His eyes slid a needle of pain into my neck, reminding me of the power he had over me.

"First and last time I do this for you," I stressed. "I mean it."

"*Edie*," he scolded. Why? I was just some girl he'd used to get off and get his daughter to communicate with the world. And I was stupid enough to let him use me because I loved Camila and Luna and enjoyed his hands on my body. Even though, frankly, I also had a dog in this fight. His flash drive. My key to freedom.

"Thank you for paying the shop, by the way. For fixing my car. I appreciate it, but I don't need a sugar daddy."

"Good, because if you call me a sugar daddy one more time, I'll smash it back to the piece-of-crap state it was in before. This is not what we are, Edie. You use me as much as I use you."

I wanted to believe him, but I knew what I felt.

The flash drive wouldn't make us even. Not even close.

I opened the door and walked out, not bothering to close it behind me. There was no point in trying to conceal myself from him.

He'd find me. He always did.

CHAPTER TWENTY-ONE
EDIE

Later that day, I slurped my ramen noodles in an alleyway sandwiched between the Oracle building and a large concrete parking lot. The place had the uncomfortable scent of stale piss, but it was so deserted, cold, and quiet, I simply couldn't resist. Which was ironic because it was exactly how I'd describe Trent. Sans the piss, obviously.

I sucked the last noodle between my lips and threw the plastic bowl into the bin behind me, my stomach full but my heart empty, when I turned around and slammed right into a concrete-strong body too hot to be a wall.

Trent.

"What?" I bit out. I wasn't in the mood for his games. Though clearly, it wasn't just about Saturday and Theo and his questions. I simply didn't want to be around the guy who had so much power over me without holding anything hostage, unlike Jordan. Trent cornered me until my spine pressed against the cool metal of the back elevator leading to Oracle building. Reaching into his pocket, he plucked out a key card and swiped it behind my head, making the elevator *ping* in delight. The door slid open, and I stumbled in, my knees weak. He pushed me the rest of the way until my back was against the wall. The door slid shut. He turned around to punch a floor and then twisted his head to face me again.

"What's going on, Trent? I've given you what you want. Why

are you here?" I pursed my lips. His face was serious as a heart attack.

"It's easier that way," he said, rolling my hair around his fist and tugging it, arching my back. My neck was long and exposed, and he dragged his hot lips across it, making my thighs quiver with anticipation.

"What's easier?"

"Not to talk. That's why I'm the Mute. When you don't talk, people assume you don't listen. They stop asking you for shit. They start caring less. People love the sound of voices. Theirs and others. That's why they love music. I don't. I don't like music, and I don't like people. So I don't say shit. But I never thought it would be like this with Luna."

The candid revelation caught me off guard. That was why I barely noticed that his hand was already working the buttons of my gray pants. Trent was like a spice. I tasted him everywhere, even though our lips had never touched. Never would, probably. But he still made my mouth water and my eyes burn.

"I need to fuck you," he groaned into my neck, crowding me to the wall. "That's all I can fucking think about, Edie. Your pussy clenching around my cock. I need to fuck you, and it's fucking with me. With my mind. With my priorities."

"Then do it," I moaned, pushing a hand into his slacks and cupping his junk. It was huge, and he was so hard, I actually whimpered. I needed him inside me, too. I needed him to fill me and make me forget. Forget about Mom and Jordan leaving and what I had to do to Trent to protect Theo. Forget that life was mostly a chain of disappointments linking tragedies together.

Trent turned around and pushed a button that made the elevator come to a violent stop. He then scooped me up by the backs of my knees, making me wrap my legs around him. He kissed my face for the very first time. *Really* kissed, not just skimmed. Not my lips. My neck and jaw and closed eyes. His straight teeth dragging over my skin teasingly, his tongue darting out for a first taste. I wanted to die in his arms and never come back. I started rubbing him through his briefs, feeling him harden even more against my palm. My panties were so damp, the skin of my sex clung to the fabric.

"Please," I hissed.

"Please what?"

"Please fuck me," I choked. I never begged. Never had to. I'd had very few partners in my eighteen years, but they were all more than willing to get rid of our clothes before I'd even uttered a word. Not Trent. With him, there was always a push. Then a pull. Then an explosion in between when we finally happened.

"I don't have a condom," he said, just as he tugged my pants awkwardly down between us. My legs were still spread, and he started rubbing me through my panties. His cock in my hand, my pussy beneath his fingers, it wasn't enough. I wanted more. I wanted *everything*.

"I need you inside me," I moaned.

"That could be arranged." He smirked, taking a step back and letting me slide down to the floor. My bare knees hit the rough surface, just as his cock sprang out of his tight white Armani briefs. It was thick, hard, and swollen. He fisted my hair and brought my face to his monstrous dick. I hooked my fingers in the loops of his slacks with one hand and wrapped my fingers around his base with the other, kissing the tip.

"And you said that we're not allowed to kiss," I deadpanned. His chuckle vibrated through his strong, muscular body. My hunger for him was so carnal, it wasn't even dipped in the usual shame of what I wanted to do. I took as much as I could of him, first coating his cock with my saliva before I sucked it like a lollipop, making sounds I knew were driving him mad while pumping his base with my fist.

"Fuck," he whispered, tugging at my hair harder. I still had my back to the wall, while he stood in the middle of the elevator thrusting himself into my mouth. He stumbled a little, propping one hand against the wall. "Why do I keep coming back for more of you? What makes you so goddamn irresistible?"

I pumped him faster, sucking him off harder. Then I pressed the tip of my tongue to his slit, feeling the salty taste of his pre-cum and nearly blacking out in pleasure. I wasn't going to answer him.

"Finger yourself," he commanded, seemingly frustrated with my lack of response. I complied, interested to know where this was going to lead.

Three thuds came from above our heads, like someone had punched the elevator.

"Hey! Is anyone there? This is Clint from maintenance."

"Fucking Clint from maintenance…" Trent muttered, grabbing onto the back of my head and starting to fuck my mouth mercilessly. Tears stung my eyes, threatening to run down as my gag reflex was assaulted with his cock again and again. "Shove three fingers into yourself. Let go of my dick. Play with yourself. I'm close."

I did as I was told, hearing him moan above me and feeling a little shiver running through my body. We could get caught. We would. Clint would be obligated to file a report. I knew that because I spent my days printing and filing forms filled out by maintenance people in the building. And what he would say would ruin us.

"Fuck, Edie, fuck. Don't stop."

I didn't. Tears were now running down my cheeks as I took all of him in my mouth—in and out, in and out—and I felt him jerking on my flattened tongue.

"I'm coming in your mouth." Statement, not a request. I nodded.

"Anyone there?" Clint echoed above us, and Trent smashed his fist into the wall.

"Trent Rexroth and Edie Van Der Zee from the fifteenth. Would you mind sending fucking help instead of slamming the door?" he roared. There was a brief silence. I didn't know if Clint was going to get help or try to fix the problem himself.

"Edie," Trent said, cupping my cheek. "I'm fucking coming."

In seconds, my mouth was full of warm, thick liquid. All salt and man. I'd done this before, and I always, always swallowed it down before I let the tang assault my taste buds. Not this time. This time I drank him. He was fine wine, and I was addicted. I continued touching myself.

"Holy mother of blow jobs," he moaned, yanking my hair to make me stand up. I got it. We were running out of time. But I still wanted to finish. My hand was still between my legs when I got up on shaky feet. He pushed me against the wall again.

"I want your ass," he whispered into my ear. "Tell me I can have it this Sunday, and I'll make you come before fucking Clint arrives."

"No." My voice was gruff from lack of talking. "I'm not even close. Now that I know Clint is coming…"

"Clint is not coming, sweetheart," Trent cut me off, cupping my pussy over my hand and squeezing hard. "You're coming. If you give me your word I can ride your sweet ass this weekend."

"I've never done anal."

"I want every hole in your body, Van Der Zee. Hell, I want to create new ones in the process of fucking you."

I nearly chuckled, but then he placed his fingers on mine and directed me, making me finger myself. I spread my legs as wide as I could, feeling his middle finger caressing my tight hole as he helped me work myself up again.

"You're quiet today," he said, his breath hitching once again.

"Thought you'd appreciate it. You don't like talking to people, right?" I propped one of my legs against his waist, and he pushed his middle finger into me—touching my own fingers inside myself— stoking my arousal before slowly pushing the finger up my ass instead.

"I hate it when people talk. I like it when you do. You're not like the rest. You always have something interesting to say. You hate this shit as much as I do. The fake rich stuff."

"You love the fake rich stuff," I huffed, feeling my lower stomach tickling with an orgasm.

"Nope. Just playing the game, my Little Tide."

"Did you just give me a nickname?" I smirked, feeling the muscles of my tight hole clenching around his finger. It hurt a little but mostly felt weird. Not weird bad, either. But the kind you needed to get used to in order to enjoy. The way he worked his fingers over mine…that was the real treat.

"Better than Gidget." He bit my chin.

"I like Gidget."

"You like Little Tide more."

"No, I don't."

"You're about to." He slammed his finger deeper into my ass, and I yelped, clinging to his broad shoulders. His lips met my ear, and he bit my earlobe, smiling.

I exploded on our fingers. Shattering like never before, in a way that made me doubt I'd ever be able to piece myself back together. The shivers were so violent and profound, I thought I was going to break into pieces. Knocks sounded from outside.

"Hey! Hey! Mr. Rexroth? It's Clint. I'm here with the elevator technician, Steve. We're coming to get you. Stay calm."

Trent looked down at me, smiling. My cheeks were flushed—I could feel them burning and making the tight space hotter—and our fingers were completely soaked with my juices. He eased his finger out of me, and I noticed how my muscles were no longer tight and tense.

"Are you calm now?" Trent's voice caressed the crown of my head.

"Physically, yes. But we're entering danger territory. I've never been in waters so deep." I squeezed my eyes shut, suddenly afraid of being so frank.

"Neither have I, but I'm a good swimmer. And Edie? You're an excellent surfer."

CHAPTER TWENTY-TWO
TRENT

"Jesus Christ, you slept with her." Dean closed his eyes, throwing his head back and rubbing his face tiredly. We were all standing by the grill Vicious was manning. He was flipping steaks and burgers, wearing a scowl and semi-casual clothes while Jaime was unwrapping baked potatoes and dumping enough coleslaw to choke a fucking giraffe into them for the kids. I placed the burgers in their buns methodically on a long porcelain island in Vicious's six-thousand-square-foot garden, ignoring them.

They couldn't know that.

Not from one fucking glance I'd thrown her way while I'd thought no one was looking.

"Spit it out, bastard. We want to know." Jaime laughed, taking a swig of his Bud Light. Behind him, Daria, his six-year-old, was playing with Vaughn and Knight, Vicious's and Dean's kids. Lev and Bailey, the infants, were in baby swings at the far end of the garden, with Rosie and Mel watching over them and sharing iced tea. Emilia, Vicious's wife, was in the kitchen getting everything ready.

And Luna and Edie were in their own little world, lying on the grass, staring at the sky, their arms tucked under their heads. Edie was talking, and Luna smiled a little and nodded a lot, listening. I was dying to be with them, to get closer, to ask them what they were talking about, but sharing this moment with the two of them was exactly the kind of deep waters Edie was talking about.

"Well?" Dean elbowed my ribs, passing by me with a bowl full of potatoes. "Did you or did you not stick your dick in a teenager?"

I looked up from the buns and the burgers, blinking slowly. Sometimes, it was beneficial to be called the Mute.

"I know you want us to fuck off, but come on, we gotta know. We're your best friends," Jaime reminded me, stretching the point by plucking a joint out of his pocket. Dean rolled his eyes, and everybody stopped what they were doing.

"Give it here, you little shit. I haven't had a smoke in a lifetime." Figured. Dean's wife had a lung disease. He made countless sacrifices for his family, which made me respect him even more than I had in the past. Rosie looked fine. Normal. Pretty. But still sick. So every time he could get away with smoking pot, we were reminded of how not so normal his life was. The fucker had a big heart. He willingly wedded what I bitterly accepted—a situation where we had to take care of someone else.

Dean lit the joint and braced the island, passing it on to me. "Come on, now," he said, smoke crawling from his lips. "Talk."

They weren't going to let it go, so I threw them a bone for no other reason than to shut them the fuck up.

"We have something going on," I said quietly, not meeting any of their gazes. I took a long hit and passed it on to Vicious, who stared at me questioningly before bringing the joint to his lips. "It's nothing. She hangs out with Luna a lot, but she's got her own shit to take care of at home, and I have my stuff to deal with. It's just casual. For both of us."

What a fucking understatement that was. Edie wasn't casual. She never had been. But admitting to anything else was goddamn crazy.

"Should I be the one to point out that Jordan Van Der Zee is our partner and that you're the only person he has a beef with?"

Jaime asked, taking the joint from Vicious. Dean plucked another beer from a bucket full of ice.

"Fuck knows why. Trent is the only person who actually works hard out of us four." He laughed. Everyone nodded.

"Maybe he really *is* racist." Jaime's voice was depressed.

"Nah. If he were, he'd try to hide it." Vicious shrugged. "It goes deeper than that. All I know is that Jordan wants to kick you off the board, Trent. I see the way he looks at you. Whatever he has on you, it's big. He wants you out of Fiscal Heights, and he wants you out of his life. His daughter is the perfect excuse."

"No one is going to know," I gritted out, snatching the joint from Jaime. "We're careful."

But even that wasn't true. Two days ago, I'd had my finger in her ass in the elevator, minutes after she'd nearly swallowed my cock. We needed to be more cautious, and I needed to stop being drawn to the most dangerous pussy in my vicinity. She was untrustworthy. She wanted to hand her dad all the information he needed on me. Edie Van Der Zee was starting to look a lot like the death of me, and yet here I was, coming back for more and more of her poison. Addicted like a crackhead.

"Are you sleeping with her to get back at her father for trying to get rid of you?" Jaime asked.

I scoffed. "Fuck no."

"Do you have feelings for her?" Dean added.

I rolled my eyes, turning to Vicious. "Can you shut them up for me?"

Vicious shrugged. "Do I look like your errand boy? You seem to know how to take care of yourself pretty well."

I was about to open my mouth and tell them that, in the very near future, Jordan wasn't going to be a problem for me anymore. Then I heard a shriek coming from behind Dean's back. I dropped the joint to the grass, hurrying toward the sound I recognized because I'd studied it too fucking obsessively.

Luna yelping.

"I didn't do anything to her! I swear!" Daria's voice screeched. She was running around the lush, carefully cut grass with her blond ponytails in little pink bows, wearing the ballet uniform she wore constantly. This one made her ex-ballerina mother extra proud. But she was starting to look and feel and talk like a mean girl.

"Oh, no! Luna, sweetie, what's wrong?" Mel hurried toward the scene at the same time I did. Edie was on one knee, pulling Luna into a hug. Luna buried her face into Edie's shoulder, and Edie was shooting an ice-cold look I'd never seen before at Daria.

"That was not cool, dude. At all. Did it make you feel good? Hurting her?"

Hurting her? It was the first time I suspected I wasn't above screaming at a child. I wanted to yell at Daria until every vocal cord in my throat tore apart.

"What the hell is happening here?" I stopped at the same time Mel did. She looked at me helplessly. We hadn't spoken to each other since I'd shit all over the date she'd sent me on. She hadn't mentioned introducing me to anyone since. I considered that a victory.

"I went to get us some lemonade," Edie was quick to explain, not waiting for guilt-ridden Daria to speak up, "and as I walked back, I noticed Luna's seahorse was in Daria's hand. She tore it apart and took out the fluff." Edie tightened her grip on Luna, who cried harder. Edie stood up, and Luna was wrapped around her like she was her child.

And it broke me.

And made me happy.

And sad.

And so, so fucked.

I turned to Daria. Mel did the same. She was fuming, too, and it took some of the edge off because at least I knew she was taking this shit seriously.

"Why, Daria? Why did you do that?" Mel crouched in front of her daughter, holding her shoulders. Her voice was soft, but her imploring eyes were urgent. This wasn't the first time Daria had been mean to Luna.

Daria hitched one shoulder, staring at the ground with a pout.

"Luna is so nice to you all the time," Mel stressed. No one asked Luna anything because all of us knew we weren't going to get an answer. She was still in Edie's arms when Daria lifted her gaze slowly and pointed at the far end of the yard. We all followed the line of vision and saw Knight and Vaughn sitting at a picnic table, munching on the burgers I'd made for them.

"*What?*" Mel asked again, seemingly irritated. Shit. Her kid was boy crazy at the age of six. Jaime was in for a long fifteen years or so.

"Knight always picks her side."

"There is no side. Luna is not against you," Mel said, her flowery skirt flipping in the wind. I had to calm my rage by averting my gaze to my girls again. Edie pressed Luna's head to her shoulder and shook her head, still shaken by Luna's reaction.

"How do you mean, sweetie?" Mel asked Daria.

And had I just thought "my girls"? Shit, I had. I'd called Edie my girl, even though she wasn't, even though she never would be. But she fucking felt like it right there and then. Like someone who belonged to me, not because I wanted to tap her ass—even though I did—but because she was made. For. Me.

"Knight always wants to play with her, even when Vaughn and I play a different game. And Luna doesn't even play. It's ridiculous. She just stands there being stupid."

I took a step forward, but it wasn't necessary. Edie was next to Daria in a heartbeat, and the look on her face…fucking priceless. She had the potential to be as daunting as her father. She just didn't want to be.

"That's enough, Daria. What you're feeling right now is jealousy. It's okay, we all do sometimes. But what's not okay is how you chose to act on that jealousy by taking it out on Luna and her favorite toy. I think you owe her an apology, don't you?"

There was silence for a moment. Daria twisted her fingers together, looking horrified and embarrassed, pulling at her pink tutu dress. Luna was watching her with big, beautiful eyes full of sorrow.

"It's true." Melody sighed, staring at me in an I-don't-know-what-to-do-with-her expression. I shrugged. Not my problem.

Emilia walked out of the kitchen for the first time since we'd gotten there, holding a bowl of fruit salad. She put it on the table and rushed to us, wiping her purple hair from her face.

"Hey, what's going on?"

Melody filled her in. Daria apologized, and Luna finally consented to let go of Edie and go with Emilia to wash her face.

Mel, Edie, and I stood in a small circle afterward. The sun made everything more heated, and between my anger and Melody's obvious embarrassment, I knew we could explode pretty quickly.

"I think I'm going to go have that lemonade now," Edie said, turning around and walking into the house. Mel stared at me skeptically, and for the millionth time that year, I thanked God I was the fucking Mute and she didn't expect an actual answer.

I walked into the house looking for Luna and Emilia. I trusted Vicious's wife. She and Rosie had this thing about them. They made you feel at home, even when you clearly weren't.

I passed by the two empty bathrooms on the first floor, about to walk up the stairs to the bedrooms when I stopped by the stairway. Edie was in Vaughn's playroom, which was full of toys. Trucks and soldiers and whatnot. She was standing by a slide coming out of a giant castle, fingering something small in her hand. I squinted, trying to see what it was. It was a toy soldier.

She looked…sad. For the first time, I actually saw it on her. The wariness. The despair. She looked wrecked, and I'd always been too busy to notice because this wrecked soul happened to have an amazing ass and a gorgeous pair of tits and a father I loathed. *Fuck.*

There was no excuse for what I was doing. For me walking into that room and closing the door behind us. For me striding over to her with chaos dancing in my chest, watching her as she lifted her eyes from the toy, reading everything that was in mine.

I could say it was because she'd protected my daughter, but that wouldn't be true.

I could say it was because I saw her layers as she held that toy soldier in her small hand, but that would be bullshit, too.

I did it because I had to. Because fuck the consequences and Jordan Van Der Zee and everything standing between us. For the first time in five years, I put my lips on another person's and kissed her. Hard.

My mouth coming down on hers was like riding a bike. It came to me instinctively but at the same time felt so fucking different I almost choked on that kiss. My hand cupped her cheek and drew her close, and my tongue darted out to open her mouth. She moaned into our kiss and clung to my face as if she'd wanted to do this since the day we'd met. I held both her cheeks and deepened our kiss, letting the strange, strange notion of my tongue dancing with another's sink in. It was so fucking wet and intimate. I wanted to eat her.

"Tide," I breathed, sinking my teeth into her lower lip and closing them until I heard the familiar whimper of joy. "You're such a fucking tide."

"Seahorse," she retorted.

"I wish."

"You are."

"Maybe," I said, sounding unsure for the first time in a long time.

"I'm not your tide, Trent." Sorrow laced her words, and I knew she was right. She wanted my neck. Bad.

"No. You're my Delilah, Edie, and I'm your Samson. You want to ruin me, destroy me, strip me of my power, and betray me. I should stay away from you, but I want you too fucking much. And when it's all over, when all that's left of us is sweaty flesh and shattered minds and torn hearts, you will remember me as the man who made you cry, and I'll remember you as the girl I had to break to stay afloat."

We stared at each other, almost smiling. What a fucking way to break my rules, with a girl who both was at my mercy and tasted of betrayal. Brushing my thumbs over her cheeks, I crashed my lips into hers, kissing her with abandon and passion and regret. I kissed her with everything I had that was worth taking. We nibbled and bit and made this kiss our fucking bitch, knowing there probably wouldn't be another one. Doing what I'd been wanting to do since I'd seen her across Dean's lawn standing next to her father, sneering at the world like she was ready to declare war on it.

I was opening up to someone who wasn't my parents or my three friends, feeling the walls of something disastrous closing down on me.

Our lips were swollen and our eyes were hooded when we were caught, in the middle of the colorful playroom, propped against a plastic castle with a slide. The door swung open and Vicious leaned against the doorframe, hands in his pockets, examining us with boredom. Knight and Vaughn were standing next to him, each of them hugging one of his thighs, watching us without really understanding what they were looking at. "You said you were careful. No chance at getting caught." My friend threw my words back at me mockingly.

My urge to deny everything was crushed by the impulse to claim her. I dropped my hands from her face, but only so I could tilt my body toward his.

"You need to leave."

"You need to come up with a good plan before her father kills you," Vicious retorted calmly.

"What I *need*"—I looked down, trying not to curse in front of the kids—"is your cooperation. Before I snap."

That made Vicious take a step back. Before he closed the door, I heard him say, "I think it's time to make some popcorn, kids. These two are going to give us the best show this town has to offer."

CHAPTER TWENTY-THREE
EDIE

I liked Rosie the best.

They were all nice, but Rosie was the one who truly got me. She was wearing a Queens of the Stone Age shirt and ripped jeans, cradling her son, Lev, in her arms and nodding at me.

"Yup. That sounds like our Daria."

"I don't mean to be rude, but hell, the kid is cruel. I'm not sure where to find an identical seahorse for Luna." I plucked a grape from a fruit bowl in the middle of the table.

Rosie took a deep breath, her lungs straining for it, like her airway was blocked. After Vicious had caught Trent and me making out in his son's playroom, he'd asked us to try not to hump each other on his property as soon as we evacuated said room. Trent hadn't gone down without a fight, telling Vicious everything there was to say with a look that could kill. We'd walked out of the room together. For a second, it had looked like our hands were going to meet.

But they didn't.

The buzz from that kiss still gripped every part of my body. I felt it on my swollen, stung lips. They throbbed, hummed, became alive. Almost like an entity separate from my body.

Rosie leaned across the table toward me when she spotted Emilia and Melody walking in our direction with bottles of wine. I knew I wouldn't be offered a glass, and that alone made me remember just how inferior I was to those people solely because of my age. "What's going on with you and Trent? He always struck me as mysterious and quiet but also kind of dangerous." Rosie waggled her brows.

"Does Emilia know him well?" I asked, partly to evade the question, but mostly because I was eager to find out more about him. Rosie shook her head, shooting me a look that told me that I was not off the hook.

"I doubt anyone knows him well, his best friends included."

"Knows who?" Emilia sat next to me, squeezing my shoulder and smiling at me. "Thank you for joining us today, Edie. Luna really loves you, and I enjoy seeing her shine."

God, she was perfect, even in her vintage baby-blue *Alice in Wonderland* dress and yellow cardigan. No wonder Vicious was so infatuated with her.

"We were talking about Trent. Surprising, right?" Rosie kissed her son's blond head, and he stirred awake, immediately reaching for her breasts. "Like father, like son." Rosie rolled her eyes, popping one boob out by lifting most of her shirt. I looked the other way, knowing it was perfectly normal—a mother feeding her infant like nature intended—but I still felt like a stupid, immature teenager.

"What about Trent?" Mel chimed in, sitting at the table with us. Luna was on the other side of the garden with him, and suddenly, this felt a lot like suburbia's answer to *Sex and the City*. Mel cracked open a bottle of wine and poured two glasses, one for her and one for Millie.

"Bitch, you're breastfeeding." Rosie frowned, and when Millie arched an eyebrow, she added, "What? Lev doesn't understand a word yet. I'll get rid of my bad mouth by the time he hits one."

"As if." Mel rolled her eyes, taking a generous sip of wine. She, too, had little Bailey, who was even younger than Lev. "I'm pumping and throwing it away. Bailey is mostly on formula. The nurse said she doesn't know how to latch well, which is weird considering her daddy has no problem in that department."

"Thanks, Gross Central." Rosie smirked.

"So what about Trent?" Mel repeated. "I tried to fix him up with a friend of mine. He is hopeless. He screwed the date up on purpose."

Flutters. Butterflies. Smile fighting to sneak in. *I knew it.*

"He didn't want to go on that date," Emilia said in his defense. "I think it's because of Val. He's never been in a relationship before, and I think what happened with her made him give up on the idea. Which is sad."

Mel arched an eyebrow, topping off her glass of wine and shrugging. "She could always come back."

"Fat chance," Rosie snorted.

"I hope she does. Luna needs a mother," Emilia muttered.

"If she does, I bet he will never let her go. He should have given her a fair chance when she told him she was pregnant. Jaime said he still beats himself up about it sometimes. While he's always been a good dad, Trent never gave Val a chance to be more than Luna's mother. I'm not saying I understand her or sympathize with what she did, but if she does come back, I think he might actually try to make it work with her. Does that make sense?" Melody explained in her no-nonsense, approachable tone.

"No," Rosie deadpanned, rearranging Lev's head on her arms as he sucked on her tit hungrily.

"I second that, my sister." Emilia took a small sip of wine. "Trent is rightfully angry."

"And hurt," Rosie added.

"More reason to wait for the woman who rocked his world to come back and collect the pieces with her." Mel poured herself a third glass of wine.

I tried to tell myself that she was drunk and wrong and absolutely out of line. But deep down, she touched on my biggest fears. She had been his teacher in high school. She knew him. Probably more than anyone at that table, myself included.

I spent the rest of my time wishing I was far away, with Theo, where boys were never an issue. My lips were still burning with my and Trent's kiss, so I picked an ice cube from my virgin lemonade and pressed it against them, trying to think clearly.

Trent Rexroth wasn't a crush. He was the very thing that'd end up crushing me if I wasn't careful.

People often had flairs for dramatics. That's why I never believed it when someone told me they knew something bad was about to happen even before it did. I stood corrected the minute I opened the door to my house on Saturday night because the bad feeling gripped me by the bones. Calamity, as it turned out, had a scent. It smelled of faint, expensive alcohol, a stale cigarette, and Chanel No. 5.

I watched the floor like I was walking death row. Every step I took toward the kitchen filled me with more dread, and I didn't understand why. Everything looked the same. The walls were still the same contemporary shade of light gray, the French furniture was still fair and heavy, the silk crème couches were still a hundred grand apiece, and the paintings on the walls still cost more than anyone could ever dream of having in their bank account.

A gurgling sound came from the kitchen, and I tensed up.

It's nothing. You heard nothing. Move on.

Another step and then another. I wanted to be a coward. I wanted to go up to my room and not deal with it. Not again. It *could not* happen again. How bad was it that I suspected my mother's life was in danger and all I wanted to do was bury my face in a pillow and replay the last day, especially the part where Trent had broken all of his rules and sucked my mouth like I was the most delicious thing on the menu? I knew the answer to that one. It was very bad. Inexcusable, actually.

"Khhstttt, ehhss, pppfff…" The gurgling continued. This was not a drill. It was not my sick imagination. I threw my backpack down and ran to the kitchen. My hair covered my face, as if to protect me, and I blew it away, chanting breathlessly, *"No, no, no."*

My mother was lying on the floor—why did she always do it in the kitchen? Why not in her bathroom? Why did she always need an audience?—foam trickling from her mouth. On the table above her were dozens of empty pill bottles with a rainbow assortment of pills scattered like sad blown dandelion fluff. A pile of divorce papers sat atop the table, already signed by my father. "Shit." I sucked in a breath, running over toward her.

Jesus Christ, he was here. He told her.

I rolled her onto her side and cupped her cheeks, staring into her vacant eyes.

"How many did you take?"

She shook her head, not answering. I was pretty sure the main reason for her lack of response was that she was halfway gone. I plucked my phone from my back pocket, my hands shaking.

I forgot about the cute girl who'd handed me her heart and her dad who'd rewarded me with hidden kisses. I forgot about laughing with Rosie and Emilia and scowling at a drunken albeit harmless Mel. This, right here, was my real life, and I shouldn't have allowed myself to forget it even for a moment.

My mother lurched forward, retching. The only thing to come out of her mouth was more foam.

"Throw it up, throw it up, throw it up," I repeated sullenly. Last time I'd stuck a finger down her throat, I was only twelve. I had really been hoping to keep that incident a one-time thing. My mother's eyes rolled in their sockets. I hated the world once again. I pushed my mother onto her knees with the phone pressed between my ear and shoulder and shoved a finger down her throat, but nothing came out.

"How long ago?" I asked, even though it was futile. She couldn't answer. She wasn't even all the way conscious. Not like last time. *Jesus, Mom.*

"Please, Mom, please. Just…throw it all up. *Please.*" I didn't know what shook harder, my voice or my hands. Both were out of control, and I felt myself slipping beyond. Beyond the control I'd held over myself.

Did she not love me?

Did she not care?

I pushed and shoved, but she just quivered like a leaf, going through some kind of seizure. Finally, the call went live.

"Nine-one-one, what's the emergency?"

I broke down in tears, giving her our address. The operator took our details and sent help, sounding bored out of her mind. Even nine-one-freaking-one couldn't wait to get rid of her.

CHAPTER TWENTY-FOUR
TRENT

"My mom tried to kill herself."

The words haunted me as I sped through the streets of Todos Santos toward Saint John's hospital. I wasn't an idiot. I knew exactly what I was doing by rushing to her side. Her dad was probably there—*he fucking better be*—I thought angrily. I was the first person she'd called, and I wasn't going to put a time limit on my stay there. The minute I'd received the call, I dropped Luna at Camila's—I didn't want them in the penthouse in case Edie wanted to crash there—and told her I'd need at least a few hours to sort through some personal shit and let her know when I'd be back.

Poor Edie.

Poor, poor Edie.

While my child's mother was avoiding responsibilities at all costs, Edie tried to take care of everyone in her world while watching her youth slip between her fingers. I loathed myself for having assumed the worst about her. That she was a spoiled-ass kid who tried to steal money for the thrill of it or just to be a cunt. Edie wasn't a brat. She was dealing with a very ill mother and, apparently, was being blackmailed by her father, too.

I parked in a hurry and called Edie's cell. She picked up on the third ring, making my fucking heart almost detonate inside my chest. And it was ironic, the way I'd thrived on her weaknesses when we first met and now how desperately I wanted for her to cling on to her strength to survive this.

"Fourth floor, I'll be inside room 412," she whispered, like she didn't want to disturb anyone. The journey to her was the longest I'd ever taken. The pale-blue walls and tired, reassuring eyes of the hospital staff haunted me, slamming me with memories I'd wanted to forget.

"Your leg is broken. Your college scholarship is, well, not going to materialize, Trent."

"Congratulations. It's a girl. The mother will sign the birth certificate shortly. Here's hoping she'll give the kid your last name, eh?"

"She is fine. There is nothing wrong with her voice. She is just... well, anyway, I have the name of a really good child psychologist."

I stopped by door 412, pressing my palm onto the cool wood and closing my eyes. I was past caring about Jordan at this stage. If he was there, asking questions, like why the fuck Edie had called me, I'd be frank. I rapped on the door three times as softly as I could, turned around, and paced the hallway.

Ten seconds later, Edie walked out. She was still wearing the same flowery #SunChaser tank top and tiny burgundy shorts that had made all the men at the party salivate. Only she no longer looked like Edie. She looked like someone ten years her senior. Ironically, someone I wouldn't feel so horrified about sleeping with.

"Hey." My voice came out soft, and I wasn't sure what to do with my hands, my face, my fucking being, so I approached her for an awkward hug, which she—thank fuck—returned. We stood there in a loose embrace outside her mother's hospital room. I stared at the plain door; she stared at some banal painting behind me probably donated to the hospital by some rich asshole. Her shoulders were frail, and so was her mind, I was sure. Time seemed to stand still just like we did, for a while, before she disconnected from me and looked down.

"Is she okay?" I asked. Was it wrong that I didn't truly care?

The only person I was interested in at that moment was Edie, and I wasn't entirely sure if her mother's recovery would be a good or a bad thing for her. Edie blew a lock of hair from her face, her eyes cutting to the mostly empty corridor behind us. A nurse was leaning lazily along an oval reception desk. Phones were ringing. A doctor was scribbling something on a whiteboard.

Edie was waiting for someone. For her fucking father, most likely.

"I don't know. She is stable now, but..." She rubbed her face wearily, shaking her head. I wanted to suck her pain away and make it my own. "But she's in a coma, Trent. Her vital organs are working, but she's not conscious." Her chin was quivering, and tears glimmered in her eyes. "I don't know what to do. I don't know whether I should tell him..."

"You haven't told your father yet?" I asked, caving in to the urge to touch her. I stroked her arm, putting some reassuring weight on her body and encouraging her to lean into me. She shook her head, throwing another glance at the corridor. Edie sniffed.

"Let's talk somewhere else. I have a long night ahead, and I probably need to recharge."

"Coffee?" I asked.

"Coconut water." She almost smiled.

We walked to the cafeteria on the same floor. I got her a coconut water and got myself some coffee. We sat in front of a window overlooking our small, sinful town. Edie stirred her drink with a straw, staring at it.

"I told my father, but I hardly needed to. It's all his fault. When we were at the barbecue, he arrived home without any notice and decided to break it to her that he wants a divorce. Mom... It's not the first time she's tried to kill herself... Anyway, so, my father. I texted him. He still hasn't answered, but I'm not holding my breath. I was the only person to sit there beside her eight years ago when she first tried to slit her wrists, and I'm definitely not expecting anything to change now that he's left her."

Fucking Van Der Zee. It was so fucking like him to pull shit like this. Leave a woman who was so obviously ill, and his own daughter, who was in need of help, to pick up the pieces. I swallowed, my Adam's apple bobbing, and tapped my fingers over my knee. "I'm sorry."

"It's fine." She scrunched her nose. "Really. I'm not even disappointed at this point. Not at him, anyway. But it would have been nice if she at least gave me a call before trying to do this. My mom is not a bad person. She is just troubled. But I still need her. Everybody needs a mom."

My face must've contorted in agony because she sucked on her lower lip and slapped the base of her palm to her forehead. "God, what a stupid thing to say. Sorry."

"No need. You're right. Everybody does need a mom. Even my daughter. Maybe especially her." But it wasn't Luna I wanted to talk about. A sudden urge to touch Edie coursed through me, and I slid my hand from my thigh to her knee, squeezing it softly. Not to seduce, but to comfort.

"When you said you didn't know whether to tell him...you didn't mean Jordan, Edie."

She cautiously turned my palm upward, lacing our fingers together. We both watched our hands like they were magic. My dark fingers wrapped around her tiny snowy ones. The light outside was dying, and so was my will to keep this thing between us casual.

It wasn't casual.

It had never been casual.

It was a fucking disaster, and I needed to end it before it ended me, but how could I, when her mother was in a coma and she was holding my hand like I was her friend, like I was her boyfriend, like I was her *lover*?

I looked up, and she was no longer crying. Her face was jeweled by hatred, her jaw cut.

"Theo," she said.

"Theo?" I echoed. I had a feeling I'd heard that name before, but I wasn't sure when or where. Obviously, there were a shit ton of Theos. But there was a nagging itch inside me insisting that the Theo *she* was talking about, I knew. Or at least knew of.

"Yeah. My brother. He was born when I was six. He is twelve now. But…there were some complications at his birth. Mom was induced twice. The umbilical cord wrapped around his neck, but she was already deep into labor, and they couldn't perform a C-section. He was deprived of oxygen for…a long time." She cleared her throat, looking up and furrowing her brow, reminiscing.

"I remember asking my mother why he was so funny looking, even before we found out about all his problems. My father freaked out. He was a senior executive in this fancy-ass company and was working hard on his image. He didn't want this to taint his precious career and his perfect family. He got an offer to open a branch in Holland and took it, but it was mostly to hide Theo. He has autism, epilepsy, and cerebral palsy. He is…different. Very different." She chuckled, but her eyes were softening. As if talking about him soothed her. "But he is also smart. And kind. And so, so brave. He is patient and accepting and always smiles at me when I visit him like I'm the best thing in the world. He doesn't complain about my parents never visiting. He doesn't cry about being dealt this hand of cards, this kind of life. So I'm rooting for him. I root for him all the time."

My hand felt sweaty in hers, but I didn't want to pull away. I wanted to know more.

"So where is Theo now?"

"A special group home in San Diego. It's actually an amazing facility, but it costs a ton. My father wanted him sent away, somewhere on the East Coast, so that he wouldn't have to deal with his proximity. The staff really encourage families to visit consistently and participate, and Jordan doesn't like it. I don't think he's visited him in years. My mom goes every Christmas to say hi and bring a gift. But, in order to keep him there, my father and I agreed I'd pay half of the monthly fee. Otherwise he'd take him away from me."

I scoffed. "That's got to be a ton."

"Twelve thousand dollars." She nodded.

"Why? He's got enough money to start a war with Canada. And win, probably."

"To see me squirm. To watch me fail. You name it. Ever since Jordan realized I wasn't going to give up on my brother and actually continued seeing him every week and made him a part of our family, he's been bitter toward me. He fails to see why I insist on staying here and not going to a good college."

"And your mom?"

"Too weak to handle Jordan, too fragile to deal with Theo and his needs. The first time she tried to take her own life…" Edie hesitated, placing her elbows on her knees and burying her head between her hands. "It was right after my father put him in this institution. She wanted him close. She wanted to take care of him. But doing so was taking a toll on her. She wanted to be a good mother but couldn't."

I wondered, briefly, if that was the case with Val, too. If she'd wanted to be better for Luna but couldn't, so she'd decided to fuck off instead. I brought our hands to my lips, pressing a kiss against her soft skin. She closed her eyes and gave in to the moment.

I was broken, but she was breaking, and that hurt more.

"So that's why you're after me? Your dad threatens you with sending Theo away?"

Edie nodded again and retrieved her hand. The tears made a comeback. Again, she didn't let them fall. I admired that.

"He said if I don't get my hands on your flash drive, Theo will be sent to New York."

"I can give you my flash drive sans the information he is looking for," I offered without thinking it through. Why the fuck would I care if Jordan had his hands on a bunch of contracts and contact lists he already had access to? It made zero difference to me. And most of my flash drive had just that. A bunch of shit you could find in the company's records if you did a general search in our database. There was just the one file, leading to a few other files, with information he actually wanted…

"He knows, Trent. Whatever you're planning, he is not stupid. He's already figured out that whatever you have on him is on your flash drive, and he expects it to be there."

Good point. Especially as I knew how and why he'd found out about it. I stood up and paced in front of her.

"The thing is…they only let me see Theo on Saturdays. Which is why Saturdays are sacred to me. If I try to go tomorrow, they won't let me in. I think my father is bribing someone there or something."

"That's why you hate rich people so much." I rubbed the back of my head, staring at the floor as I paced. It was simple, when you thought about it. Her father chose his career and money over his family, and so she hated money and her father—the two things that had ruined her life.

"Yeah." Her hands dropped to her thighs, her head hanging down. "Money makes people do stupid things. It eats at your morals and makes you lose sight of what's really important."

"Not always," I argued. I didn't feel that way. Maybe because I didn't come from money, I knew you could, and should, survive without it. But I loved my life as a rich man. I just didn't love it enough to give up the things that kept me alive. My daughter, parents, and friends. I'd spend every dollar I had, give it up in a heartbeat if I could get Luna's voice back.

She looked up, shooting me a tired smile. "You're a good man, Trent."

I didn't know about that, but the notion I should be good, even if just for her, gripped me hard.

We hung out there for another half hour, and then I went out to grab us some sandwiches from a nearby joint. We sat on the damp, dewed benches outside the hospital before returning to the reception area of the fourth floor. Edie was chewing on the collar of her top like a kid, looking out the window. She'd tried to call her father twice since I'd arrived. He never picked up the phone.

"You should probably leave. It's getting really late, and Luna will be worried. Plus, it doesn't look like I'll get out of here anytime soon, so…"

"I'm staying." I brushed off her nervousness. Not because it was the humane thing to do—because fuck humane—but because she was there alone and I selfishly wanted her with me. No matter how. Even like this.

"You really shouldn't." She let go of the damp collar of her shirt, biting her lip now.

Our eyes met. "I know."

Edie rested her head against my shoulder and wept, and I let her. Even when she fell asleep on me and I couldn't move, I waited until her soft snores drifted into my ears.

Then I carried her quietly to her mother's room, tucking her on a sofa next to the hospital bed. The light was still on. My gaze traveled between them, and they looked so similar and yet so different.

That night, I watched Edie for far too long.

That night, I'd changed.

That night, I didn't take anything from Edie Van Der Zee. For the first time in years—I gave something of myself. Worst part? I'd never be able to retrieve it.

It was hers.

Forever.

CHAPTER TWENTY-FIVE
EDIE

A Great Big World has this song, "Say Something." It's supposed to be a love song, but for me, it would always be the song I cried to when I got on a bus from San Diego to Todos Santos, with my headphones plugged securely into my ears to silence the rest of the world after Theo had thrown a punch at me.

He hadn't meant it. I knew that. It must be horrific, being caged in that head of his. Things that came so easily to me were foreign and strange to him. But giving up on him just because he couldn't *say* it, the things he was feeling, was out of the question.

And I couldn't give up now.

Sunday did not go as Trent and I had planned.

After he'd spent the night sleeping in the waiting room while I went in and out of my mother's hospital room, he drove home to take a shower and pick up Luna from Camila's and drop her off with his parents, who'd gotten back into town from Vegas.

I'd used the opportunity to head home for a shower and a snack. My mother had come to in the middle of the night. She was awake but hardly coherent. We'd spoken while Trent waited outside. She told me how my father had walked in late Saturday afternoon and broken the news to her like he was delivering an obituary for a long-distance relative. How he hadn't even cared when the divorce papers he'd placed on the table in front of her were so wet with her tears, you couldn't read a sentence of them.

I took a long, scorching-hot shower, slipped into a loose yellow summer dress, and then ate a quiet, lonely breakfast at the kitchen table. Granola, yogurt, and coconut water.

Our house was part of a gated community in an exclusive Todos Santos neighborhood called La Vista. In order to get in, you needed a code or to know the sleepy guards at the gate. That was why, at first, I didn't pay attention to the honking outside my house. I assumed it was a friend of the teenage boy across the road and cursed them inwardly for being so loud on a Sunday morning.

Beep, beep. Beeeeeeep.

I hated teenagers. I didn't even care that I was technically one of them. I dumped the bowl of yogurt into the sink, not feeling like washing it, but then thought better of it. I could leave it for the housekeepers, but I was never that person. No matter how much my parents took them for granted. I started washing the bowl, feeling my body sagging with the weight of the world.

Beep, beeeeeeep, beeeeeeeeeeeep.

Where the hell was Adrian, the guy who lived across the street? Usually, he all but jumped out of his second-story window to go out with his friends. I sulked quietly as I dried the bowl and the glass I'd used, moving toward the door.

Beep, beep, beep, beep, beeeeeeeeeep, beeeeeeeeeeeeeeeeeep.

Reaching the end of my nerves, I flung the door open, my eyes already squeezed shut and the shriek leaving my mouth. "This is a quiet neighborhood on a Sunday morning! Keep it down, will you?"

"Not a fucking chance. I have a reputation to live up to."

I popped my eyes open, staring at Trent in his black Tesla, wearing a plain white T-shirt and a beanie that didn't look stupid at six o'clock in the morning, when the desert chill was still gripping. God, he was gorgeous.

"What are you doing here?" I blinked.

He threw his car into park, got out, and walked over to me, taking my hand. It looked foreign and dangerous, having him do that. So natural but also so reckless. My father could still drop by to get something from the house. Not to mention my neighbors had big mouths and he'd probably gotten everyone's attention with his honking. If Trent was feeling like breaking our rules, he needed to talk to me about it first. Because I still had everything to lose.

I took a step back. "No. What's happening?" I frowned. "You shouldn't be here."

"I second that statement, and yet I am. Come with me."

"I don't think that's a good idea. I need to go be with my mom."

"It's a brilliant idea," he retorted. "Your mom is stable, and she'll be sleeping for the majority of the morning, probably. I have a surprise."

A surprise. It made my heart lift and twinge with guilt. He was trying to be nice to me, and I'd pretty much admitted I'd screw him over the minute he'd let me. I really was his Delilah. But the worst part was that in the end, it was Samson who had won. Not her. Because sneaky, shady people always ended up losing the battle, even if they did win the small fights.

Too bad Samson died in the fucking process.

"Trent…"

"I got you a visitation permit for Theo," he cut in, hope sneaking into his hardened face. I blinked at him, perplexed. I'd never seen him look like this. Like a buoyant kid.

"H-how?"

"Your father is not the only person in the world with connections."

"You will need to elaborate."

"Sonya."

Sonya. I immediately gave him a funny look, taking a step back. He rolled his eyes and grabbed me by the arm, ushering me to his car. I was lucky to have my Dr. Martens on, or else he'd probably have taken me barefoot.

"Calm your tits, Tide. She is Luna's therapist. She knows people who know people who make things happen. And she has a very big heart."

"And big tits to match," I couldn't help but bite out.

"That's true." He chuckled, hurling me into the passenger seat like he loved doing so much. He slammed the door and rounded the car, starting it.

He drove out of Todos Santos toward San Diego, meaning he was going to accompany me on my visit to Theo. I didn't even have my purse with me. Just my phone. The town flashed by, and neither of us said a word for a while before I finally caved in.

"Are you still seeing her?" I asked.

He stared at the road, smirking to himself, like he took pleasure in watching me squirm. After a purposeful beat, he said, "What's it to you?"

"You asked me not to have sex with Bane anymore. I'm trying to figure out how much of a hypocrite you are," I answered honestly.

"I'm the mother of all hypocrites, Edie. If I wanted to fuck other people while I was fucking you, I would." It felt like a punch straight to my heart, even when he added, "But I don't. I haven't. You're the only one I want right now, and you keep me goddamn busy, so don't worry your pretty little head about that."

"That was the most backhanded compliment I've ever received." I blew out air.

"We both know you don't deserve more than that."

It was true. I was after him.

We spent the rest of the drive in the silence I deserved and he loved so much to give.

———

"You really don't have to come with me," I mumbled as Trent and I walked into the reception building of Big Heart Village. It looked warm, woody, cabin-like, only five hundred times bigger. The receptionist, Samantha, was a meaty woman in her early fifties with jazzy red curls and feline reading glasses with a jungle pattern. Her clothes were out-of-control weird like colorful tents. I loved it.

"Edie!" she exclaimed, standing up from her station and hugging me across the counter. I returned the hug, feeling my shoulders melting into relaxation. Trent was behind me. He still hadn't responded about staying at the reception desk while I visited Theo, but I was hoping he'd join us. I wasn't ashamed of my brother. Come to think of it, he was the only member of my immediate family I was actually proud of.

"What happened yesterday?" Samantha pushed her glasses up her nose, silently opening a bag of chips and offering me some. I shook my head, inhaling deeply before I answered.

"My friend here"—I pointed at Trent, who slid off his beanie and looked around nonchalantly—"had this barbecue thing, and his kid needed a babysitter, and so…" I was stumbling over my words, making it painfully awkward again. Samantha ran her eyes over Trent, assessing him. She saw what I saw. What every woman in the world did.

"Your friend looks like trouble." The corner of her lip twitched upward.

"Trust me." He took a step forward, dumping his designer beanie onto the reception desk with a smirk. "You have no idea. My acquaintance Sonya said we could visit Theodore real quick? Seeing as Edie wasn't able to yesterday." He tilted his body toward her, and his muscular arm brushed mine. It sent a current of warmth to my lower belly and made me grin despite my best efforts.

"Yes. We have written instructions from Mr. Van Der Zee that Theodore is not to be visited on any other day than Saturday, but considering his file hasn't been updated in two years, and seeing as Mr. Van Der Zee has failed to visit his son in this period of time, social services has decided to open a case on this minor at Sonya's request. I am actually quite grateful, Mr.…?"

"Rexroth," he provided, flashing her a cool, good-enough-for-porn grin.

"Yes. The only person who seems to care about this kid is his sister. Big Heart Village firmly believes that the mental and physical health of its residents comes first. I'm familiar with Sonya and was glad to hear she was able to pull a few strings. You will have to see him with a caretaker present, but thank the Lord, it is possible. Now, you take a seat. Gustav will be right here and take you to see Theo."

We both walked over to the couches with the scratchy yellow fabric and sat down. Trent was messing around on his phone, while I was trying hard not to cry at what he'd done for me. How could a person be so cruel and so compassionate at the same time?

"Thank you."

He was still staring hard at his phone. "You've been there for Luna. It's only fair I'd be there for Theo."

"Yes, but you don't have to physically stay with me. This is not your mess."

"That's where you're wrong."

"Wrong how?" I cleared my throat.

This time he looked up from his phone, something rather than ice and wrath swimming in his eyes. "I wish you weren't my mess, Van Der Zee. I really wish you were just a dirty little fuck."

"Edie?" a voice called from above our heads. It was Gustav, the nice Swedish caretaker who was assigned to Theo. He was waving at me, standing on the other end of the reception—not the entrance, the exit to the picnic area, with the door open. "He is waiting for you. Come on."

The one thing I was worried about was that Trent wouldn't be able to understand Theo. His speech was slurred and slow, so you really had to pay attention to know what he was saying, but Trent and Theo clicked immediately.

Trent behaved as if Theo was just a normal twelve-year-old boy. We were sitting at a picnic table under the sun, with Gustav pretending like he wasn't watching the exchange and coloring a Harry Potter coloring book with a frown. Theo was wearing a Chicago Bears ball cap, a Ren and Stimpy T-shirt, and a smile.

"No, man, no. You can't root for the Chicago Bears living in California. That's just not acceptable." Trent shook his head, leaning across the picnic table, talking animatedly to my brother.

"Y-y-yes, I can. M-m-mike G-g-glennon is God." Theo slammed the table with his open palm a little too roughly. Gustav and I were used to it and knew better than to flinch, but the great thing was that Trent wasn't fazed by it, either. Trent waved his hand around impatiently, rolling his eyes and not doing the polite, whatever-you-say fake shit people usually did in front of Theo.

"Jesus. No. Where is this coming from? Next thing, you'll tell me you like Tom Brady."

Theo laughed. For all the love that we'd shared, I couldn't talk to him about boy stuff to save my life. And he didn't care about surfing because he hardly ever saw the ocean, living in a group home for so long. The simple fact that Trent related to him had his face glowing.

"I, I, I like T-t-tom B-brady!" he exclaimed, ecstatic.

"Yeah, well, I think it's time for me to barf. Where's the bathroom around here?" Trent made a show of looking around, using his hand as a visor from the sun. He made it a point not to wear his Wayfarers while he was talking to my brother. He gave him eye contact. That was amazing.

Gustav pointed behind him, to one of the small cabins circling the picnic area. There were many families sitting at the tables with food and soda, talking and laughing. For the first time in years, we looked like one of those families. It wasn't just Theo and me. There was someone else, too. And it both killed and revived me.

When Trent left, Theo's smile widened.

"Wh-who is *he*?"

I gave him a mean side-eye. Special or not, Theo was still my little brother, which meant he could still be a huge pain in the butt.

"He works with Jordan. I babysit his daughter sometimes. She's really cool. How are you doing, dude?"

Theo shrugged. "G-g-good. Y-you d-didn't come yesterday."

Guilt choked me. I was ashamed to tell him the truth, but then some people you couldn't lie to. He deserved better than the half-lies I spat on autopilot to my father.

"Trent asked me to help him with Luna. She doesn't really talk, so sometimes she needs reassuring company when she goes places."

"A-a-always saving p-people." My younger brother grinned, his blond hair and blue eyes reminding me of my mother's ice-queen features. I wondered how she could turn her back on someone who looked like a carbon copy of her. Theo was a little heavy from lack of activity—he really hated physical therapy—but other than that, he looked like Lydia Van Der Zee's mini-me.

Trent got back to the table ten minutes later, dumping what looked like a whole junk food aisle from Safeway onto the table.

"They only had sandwiches and soda in the cafeteria, and no offense, Theo, but the food here looks like some sort of a medieval punishment, and I'm hungry."

"Yeah, I could eat just about anything right now," I said. Trent gave Gustav, Theo, and me our sandwiches and opened all of the bags of chips.

After lunch, they bickered more about football, and then Trent and Theo arm-wrestled. Trent let him win once, and for that, I wanted to kiss him openly and wildly. Theo had a small meltdown when Gustav hinted at us having to leave, but once he settled and we said our goodbyes, we were out the door and walking to Trent's car. I felt emotionally drained but also recharged and full at the same time.

We didn't speak until he reached the traffic light onto a road leading to downtown San Diego. His Wayfarers were on, and he looked cool as a cucumber.

"Saint John's?" he inquired, confirming the hospital was our next destination. I didn't get it. Why was he doing it? Standing by my side, like he could get something out of it.

"Yes, please. But before…can we stop somewhere else?"

"Where?" he asked.

"Anywhere." I scrunched my nose, my gaze dropping to my thighs. The only excuse for what I had in mind was that I was still a teenager and Trent was still the hottest man I'd ever seen. His face was casual, his posture blasé. One of his arms was draped against the steering wheel, and he looked a lot like a James Dean picture come to life.

"Why?" The laughter in his voice annoyed me but also made me hotter for him.

I rubbed my bare thighs under the summer dress, feeling my cotton panties already damp just from thinking about it. "You know why."

"You need to refresh my memory. I'm old, and I don't take all my omega-3."

I laughed, wetting my lips as I tilted my body to face him. "Sunday, we were supposed to, um…" I laughed, thinking about how ridiculous it looked and felt.

"That's not a sentence, Van Der Zee. You will need to finish that."

Oh my God. He was going to make me say it. Fine. Whatever. "You were supposed to take me from behind." I blushed.

The car stopped with a comic screech.

Where were we? I looked outside. A vineyard between Big Heart Village and San Diego. Other than the birds chirping and golden mountains, there was nothing but fat grapes and thin, wiry trees. I wish I could say I wanted him to take me from behind as a reward for how he'd been with my brother. But the truth was, I wanted him desperately. Like water in the desert, in desolate sands.

"What are you doing?" I asked.

"Fucking up a hundred-grand car, probably." He glanced over

his shoulder, reversing his car, his arm slung behind my seat, before driving straight into the vineyard. On the sand and dust and everything else a Tesla shouldn't be on.

The car jerked to a stop a few inches from a tree, and he got out, pulling me along with him.

"Where to?" I asked breathlessly, following his footsteps. I could see what he saw in the distance, and sweat dripped down my neck. No way was I going to do this. There was a cabin at the end of the vineyard. Empty, most likely, since the windows were shattered and the door was wide open. It belonged to someone, and that someone wasn't us. I pulled him toward the car, but instead of fighting, he picked me up and slung me across his shoulder, sauntering confidently toward the hut.

"You're insane. Someone could be in there. Someone could catch us." My hair was in my face, and my panties were completely exposed, as one of his arms was pressed on my thighs, making my dress ride up. He bit the soft flesh of my ass in warning, his breath hot, his pulse quick under my leg.

"I meant we should do it sometime today, not right this second." I giggled.

"Your panties say right this second. They're fucking soaked, and you're rubbing against my shoulder like you've never had a cock in your pussy before. But we both know that's not true, right, Edie?"

"Right," I lamented, raking my fingernails down his back, feeling his goose bumps even through his shirt. "Bane fucked me, too," I teased.

To that, he responded as I wanted him to. With a loud smack to my ass. I moaned, feeling the familiar rush only Trent had ever given me, and spread my legs slightly while he continued making his journey to the cabin.

"He never fucked you like I do, and we both know that."

No truer words were ever spoken, and as he dumped me onto a stack of straw like a rag doll, towering over me, I inwardly prayed he would kiss me again, the way he had at Vicious's. Like there was no one else in the world but us. Reminding me that we were alive and beautiful.

"Kiss me," I breathed, blinking. *Please*, my eyes begged. *Now*, they demanded.

It was stunning, watching the way he undressed from his anger for me, still fully clothed. How he bent his knee in front of me, leaned forward, clasped the back of my head, and brought me to his face, pressing his lips sweetly onto mine. Like what we were doing made some sort of sense. Like this wasn't going to blow up in our faces as soon as he declared war on my father or my father found out I'd slept with him.

He opened his lips, his tongue pushing in to open my mouth. I tilted my head, giving him access, holding his stubbled cheekbones in my palms, feeling how alive he was under my fingertips. I kissed him deeper, hotter, leaving a piece of soul behind, making sure that it'd seep deeper into him so he'd never forget me.

He circled his fingers around my sweaty neck, catching some stray locks of blond hair that stuck to my skin, and squeezed softly as his tongue flicked against mine. He sucked my tongue hungrily. My eyes rolled back, and I clenched from the inside.

"I should get rid of your ass, Van Der Zee. Already we're treading past the point of no return."

"Go ahead. I'm not going to come begging." I swallowed against the pressure of his hand, my eyes locked on his, but I could see him releasing his cock. I knew we would do it the way we both liked. Like animals. With our clothes still on, the dry hay sticking to our sweat, hard slaps of skin against skin reminding us there was nothing pretty or elegant in how we wanted one another. We would have sex the way nature intended us to. With no dignity or pride or shame. We wouldn't make love. We'd battle this down like everything else we did with each other.

"You won't beg," he repeated, a growing smirk decorating his face. He taunted me, holding his cock in his hand and pressing it against my sex, still clothed with underwear. He drew delicious circles around my lips with his tip, teasing the hell out of me. Again, I found myself gulping down my lust for him.

"I won't beg."

"You won't beg," he repeated, pushing his whole cock past my panties, penetrating me. The fabric of my underwear stretched along my inner thighs painfully, and I threw my head back, wincing.

I wanted more.

I wanted it harder.

I wanted *everything*.

I moaned, slipping my fingers into his denim and underwear and clutching his ass as I opened my legs wider for him. "What are we doing?"

"Exactly what I promised myself I'd never do again. Fucking without a condom."

He chuckled, kissing my lips, then my cheek, then my forehead. His lips met my ear and whispered what I knew would be his last words for a long time: "Remember, Edie, don't beg."

Then he flipped me over, my stomach pressed against the hay, my ass in the air. It was so quick, I didn't have time to fathom the fact that he'd torn my panties off of my body. They ripped at the seam on one side, and I cried out at the sudden discomfort, clutching the stack of hay, trying to whip my head around and see what he was doing. He quickly grabbed my jaw and turned it so I faced the floor.

Then he shoved one, two…three fingers into my pussy, one after the other. He curled his middle finger, immediately hitting my G-spot. He thrust cruelly, making me squirm, every bone in my body screaming at me to get away.

Don't beg. Don't ask for more. I already wanted too much.

My spine was a candlewick, burning slowly and hotly. My first climax felt wild, unnatural. Like I was bursting at the seams, my body like a too-tight corset. *Pop, pop, pop*, muscles tensing, belly clenching, toes curling, every organ in my body—his. The warmth was unbearable. Too much and not enough. I was going to explode into little atoms, into minuscule cells, and the worst part was that with Trent, I knew he wouldn't put me back together afterward.

Shaking like my body wasn't mine anymore, I came on his fingers, feeling myself dripping. He pulled out his hand, wiping all of my arousal on his cock, which he fisted in his palm.

With one flexed movement, he pulled me up on all fours, guiding his cock to my rectum. I flinched before it even got there.

"You're making me crazy," he said.

"You're making me unhinged." I grinned, my cheek pressed against the hay. I felt his bare tip poking at my backside and clenched on instinct. He brushed his finger against my puckered hole softly. "You're filthy."

"Relax for me, Edie."

I tried, feeling the head of his cock again. It was completely lubricated with my arousal. He coated it by stroking himself up and down. At first, it was just the tip. Then the pressure shot up to my lower back, but I bit down on my lip and waited for the good part.

"You've ruined me," I muttered, when another inch and then another rolled into my burning hole. I didn't enjoy it. It felt horrible. Like he was going to rip me apart.

"You've fucked me up pretty good, too," he retorted, pushing all the way in. He settled there, and I bit into the hay, feeling its bitterness bite back. My fingers clutched the dirt.

He kissed my ear, my cheek, licking a lone tear of pain away. "Next time you make a joke about someone else fucking you, just remember I own every single hole in your body, including the one I'll leave in your heart when I'm done."

When he moved inside me at first, I thought he was pouring gasoline into my ass and lighting a match. But after six or seven thrusts, I relaxed, getting used to his big cock inside me. That was when he snaked his hand around me, pinching my clit softly, borrowing some of my wetness from my pussy and playing with it.

"Ahh." I closed my eyes, getting lost in his touch against my sweet spot.

He kicked my legs farther apart, making me open up as a result. He pounded into me, paying close attention to my clit now. My elbows were shaking. God, yes. It felt so much fuller and more intimate and crazier than what I'd ever experienced.

"Shit, you're tight. I'm gonna come."

It felt oddly comforting to have him filling me from behind. Especially as he had one of his hands all over my pussy—filling me from both ends—and how he clutched my waist, squeezing it extra hard every time my legs quivered so badly I was about to fall down.

"Fuck, fuck, fuck."

"Jesus," I moaned, feeling a smile on my lips.

He yanked my hair, making me arch. My shoulders met his clothed torso, and he bit at the tip of my ear. "I knew you'd beg. You're so weak for me, Edie. So fucking gone."

"Do it," I hissed.

He came inside me, and I came on his hand.

The drive to the hospital was littered with silence and my moving around to try to soothe my sore butt. No more words were spoken. In fact, the only gesture he'd made before I'd poured out of his car was squeezing my thigh with a hand that still smelled very much like me.

Trent nodded to me in assurance, and I scrunched my nose—because that was my thing.

"We need to stop," I said.

"So stop." He shrugged.

"I will," I lied, getting out of his car. I couldn't miss his laughter. It rang in the air long after he drove off.

CHAPTER TWENTY-SIX
TRENT

A WEEK LATER

"Yeah. Palm Springs. I know. A driver will be waiting for them downstairs." I jammed my finger into my temple, rolling my eyes and pretending to shoot myself. Dean, sitting in the chair opposite to me, was chuckling, playing with a joint between his fingers. No fucking way. I was not smoking downstairs with him. Not on my office patio, either. I had too much shit to do.

I paused again, listening to the person on the other side before responding.

"It's a one-month program, and for all I care you can chain her to the fucking bed and let her piss and shit into a bowl. She's not running away this time. This woman needs to get well."

So that Edie will be happy, I didn't add.

I hung up, taking a long breath and loosening my tie. Dean cocked his head, placing the joint above his ear. Dudebro move, but then again, every single thing in the world had the potential to piss me off these days. I wanted to put the Jordan Van Der Zee shit on lockdown because it was starting to become evident I couldn't, for the life of me, stop seeing his daughter. And it was ironic how I was trying to get her mom off drugs when Edie became my very own addiction.

"Luna started young. I don't think my kids will touch drugs before ten," Dean commented on my phone conversation.

"Hey, dickface, here, you dropped your sense of humor." I groaned, scratching my cheek. "The rehab is for Lydia Van Der Zee. Since her husband is too busy to help her and I can't really ask Rina to do it for me because that'd lead to questions," I explained.

"Questions to which their answers are *yes, I am fucking his daughter, why, I'm glad you asked, yes, we did it in the office, too, and of course, I want a bullet to my head. That's why I did it in the first place.*" He tapped his chin, like he was waiting for me to throw a fist in his smug face.

I got up and sauntered over to the bar by the window, grabbing two bottles of water for him and me. "I'm glad you're in a good mood," I noted coolly.

"I'm in the best mood. You finally have a girlfriend."

"Incorrect. And even if it wasn't, don't repeat that outside these walls," I shot back quickly, chugging the majority of my drink.

"If you're not her boyfriend, then why the fuck are you admitting her mother into a rehab facility? You taking a side job as Mother Teresa?"

Glancing at my watch, I asked myself whether today would be the day she'd finally show up in the fucking office and spare me the agony of walking these hallways without seeing her perky ass in another ill-fitting number she'd stolen from her mom. Even if I never looked at her when she was noticing, I *did* look. She was my fuel for the rest of the day. She was what kept me going.

"Mmm?" I hummed at Dean, still not committing to answering him. He leaned forward, stroking the J he plucked from behind his ear in long motions.

"What is she to you, man? Why are you helping her so much?"

"Because she needs help and because her dad will never give it to her."

Jordan hadn't missed a day of work in the week Lydia had been in the hospital. He even stayed late most evenings to catch up on work. The relationship between us had escalated to the point where I no longer pretended like he didn't make me sick and he no longer acted like he was indifferent toward me. We openly hated each other, and it dripped from every glance and encounter we shared.

I locked my office every single day. The unattended, full trash bin had already started smelling like leftover protein shakes and stale coffee, but at least the fucker didn't have access to my shit when I wasn't there.

"Speaking of Jordan…" Dean got up from his seat, walking over to the door, his bespoke blue suit so full of swagger you'd think he was Harry Styles. "Thought you should know, he is sniffing to buy one of us out, and he is offering big bucks. He wants you gone, bro. Do you think he knows about you and Edie?"

Who the fuck knew? But the thing was, Jordan had wanted to get rid of me long before I'd drilled my cock into his daughter's mouth, ass, and pussy. I tucked my hands into my pockets. "Probably not. He wouldn't miss a chance to make a scene or taunt his daughter."

Dean gripped the door handle, swiveling to face me. "Well, watch your back."

"When have I ever not?"

The rest of the afternoon was spent smoldering in my own wrath. I knew, logically, that my friends would never sell Jordan shit, which meant he was desperate, and I wondered—why? What the fuck had I done to deserve his hatred?

That day, I wasn't the Mute. I was the Asshole, and I was holding that torch for dear fucking life. Even Vicious couldn't take it from me. I yelled at Rina for bringing me the wrong sandwich for lunch—she'd been working with me for six months, what the fuck was so difficult to remember?—and fired an intern who'd accidentally sent a contract to the wrong client to sign. I fired her on the spot without a hearing or even time to collect her things from her desk. I then proceeded to patrol the hallways, shooting ridiculous orders at random people, but it did nothing to soothe my anger.

Edie was still with her mother at the hospital. She said she might drop in to work, just to see me, but she didn't.

At first, I thought it sucked. But then I looked at the bright side—with her gone, I could finally confront her piece-of-shit dad.

I knew I needed to play my cards right. I couldn't saunter into his office and tear him another melon-sized asshole. So I waited.

At five o'clock, all the administrative staff tucked their things into their bags and left.

At six, the brokers followed suit.

At six thirty, Jaime, Vicious, and Dean met at the hallway where our offices faced one another.

Vicious knocked on my open door twice, poking his head in. "Shitface, are you coming or what?"

"I'm going to catch up on some crap." I nodded toward my unlit computer. He couldn't see it from his position, but he could still smell bullshit from miles away.

He flicked one eyebrow in acknowledgment. "If you're going to murder Van Der Zee, please note that I don't practice criminal law and will not be able to help you legally. But if you need someone to help hide the body, I'm your guy."

"How precious," I commented dryly.

He shrugged, slapping the oak of the door, already spinning on his heel. "Well, you're most fucking welcome, Rexroth."

Six thirty.

Six thirty-five.

Six forty-five.

At seven, the cleaning staff walked in, talking among themselves. I lurked behind my computer—what the fuck was it about the Van Der Zees that brought out the stalker in me?—and when I saw the maintenance people heading over to the other side of the floor, I stood up and strolled assertively toward the corner office next to mine. To the biggest, most luxurious room in the building. To where the man who'd hurt Edie and her brother tremendously, and was trying to do the same to me, was working. I expected him to be sitting at his computer and typing away as he always was, but the place was empty. It made no sense. Jordan rarely left the office before eight p.m. Working—making money—was his entire life. I whipped my head and caught a glimpse of him entering the elevator.

And that was how I knew he was already one step ahead of me.

He'd realized I would corner him and had walked away before I could confront him. But he had another thing coming.

Quickly, I made my way to the emergency stairway and started down to the parking lot. I took the stairs two at a time, knowing I'd arrive before him. The elevator stopped on every fucking floor on its way down because people in accounting and HR stayed way later than the fuckers on our floor.

When I arrived, I was covered in a thin layer of sweat. Calmly—so fucking calmly—I made my way to his black Range Rover. My heart didn't beat as fast as it should have. I leaned on the driver's side of his vehicle, hands in pockets, and waited.

When the elevator pinged and glided open, the frown on his face twisted into a gape, and he clamped it before I could laugh.

"Are you playing hard to get, Jordi? Because it's not your ass I'm after." I flashed him a winning smile. He stepped backward, his arm already moving to the button panel, before I *tsked*, shaking my head and holding his gaze with mine.

"Come on, Van Der Zee. Ignoring me won't make me go away, but it will make me very fucking pissed."

Reluctantly, he loosened his red-silk tie, taking a step forward. The elevator slid shut behind him, almost taunting him, and we were alone. We stood maybe twenty feet from each other, but it didn't make the situation any less suffocating. For him, at least.

"What are you going to do? Beat me? Kill me?" He raised his head, his eyes spewing hatred at me. Fear was an old enemy. I didn't allow room for it in my life. Everyone on the floor other than my three friends practically shook whenever Jordan addressed them. I was mildly amused with his self-importance. I scoffed.

"Just because I'm not the same sickly white color you are doesn't mean I'm a thug."

"You've made some questionable mistakes in your life, leading me to believe self-restraint is not your strong suit," he retorted, walking over to me. We were now standing dangerously close to each other for him to say shit like that.

"What on earth are you talking about?"

"Your daughter situation," he said.

I cupped my mouth to hide my laugh. "I've never conducted myself less than one hundred percent professionally in my career. Whatever happens in my personal life is my business, not yours."

"The way a person behaves outside the office is a direct reflection of who he is as a professional." Jordan stiffened, his spine pencil-straight.

I pushed off his vehicle. "Let's not open this shit, Jordi. You're hardly a saint, and your sins aren't limited to fucking the wrong person at the wrong time."

I left it at that, refusing to let him know Edie had confided in me—I'd never compromise her secrets—but at the same time, I made sure he realized that while he'd been doing his due diligence on me, I'd done the same.

"What's your beef with me, huh?" I asked straight up. Our eyes never broke contact, engaged in a bloody battle of wills. "Why do you want *me* out so fucking bad?"

Jordan surprised me by taking a final step toward me, erasing all space between us. We were now toe to toe, nose to nose, closer than I'd ever been to any of my friends.

A wicked grin bloomed on his wilted face. "You'll find out soon enough. Tell me, Trent, do you have a plan for how to get rid of me?"

I didn't answer. Didn't need to. He knew the answer. Otherwise, he wouldn't want my flash drive so fucking much. The fact that he knew about it in the first place was not an accident. I always told people I didn't trust the secrets I wanted to be passed along. Max, his personal assistant, had been the perfect target. We'd had drinks after work at some HR woman's birthday party when I'd leaned in and mentioned the flash drive, knowing it would send a message to Jordan—watch your back because you're not the only one with tricks up his sleeve.

"Because let me tell you, Rexroth, I definitely have a plan to get rid of you, and it is going to hurt you in all the right places. In all the places you hurt *me*."

"What the fuck does that mean?"

"You'll know soon enough."

I gave him a sure grin, ignoring his stupid comment. Next thing he was going to vague-post about me like a hormonal twelve-year-old girl. He obviously had a problem with me. But instead of coming out and saying it, he chose to dance around the subject like a little pussy.

"The gloves are off, old man." I smirked, opening the door for him. Confused, he climbed into his vehicle, staring at me suspiciously as I played the dutiful valet. I tapped his window and winked. "May the best man win."

"What is it that you think you have on me, Rexroth, that makes you so bloody confident?"

"That's not how this game works, Van Der Zee. The surprise is half the fun. Drive safe." I gave him the words I'd spewed at his daughter on our first encounter. Only with him, I didn't mean them. I strolled to the elevator, punched the button, and walked in.

That evening, I called Edie, asking if she was going to come in for work. She said yes.

The next morning, I placed my flash drive on my desk, in plain sight, left the door open, and walked out.

"I'll be taking the rest of the day off," I told Rina, dropping some paperwork on her desk on my way out. "My office is open. Miss Van Der Zee, Dean, Vicious, and Jaime are allowed in. Everyone else must stay out."

It was bait, and I hoped to shit my prey wouldn't take it.

It was bait, but what I really did was compromise my life to save hers.

I didn't know why I was doing it. Putting my daughter's future and my own on the line for this teenage girl. But, for all intents and purposes, my decision was already made. She needed the flash drive, so I gave it to her.

That night, Edie came over after she'd finished work. She made Luna spaghetti and hot dogs—and I let them have their junk. At night, Edie and I fucked hard. In the morning, we fucked soft.

I didn't mention my encounter with her father or leaving the flash drive on my desk, and she didn't, either.

We took separate cars to work, and of course, I got there first because she took hour-long showers.

I walked into my office with my heart in my throat, only to swallow it down.

The flash drive was gone.

CHAPTER TWENTY-SEVEN
EDIE

The first thing I did when Trent left his apartment, taking Luna and Camila with him since it was Office Tuesday, was run into his bathroom and vomit.

My head was swimming, white dots blurring my vision. Bracing myself with the seat, I slowly got up and limped my way to the sink like an old dog. I washed my hands and face, avoiding the mirror in front of me at all costs. I couldn't look at myself without throwing up again.

Traitor. Impostor. Judas. Backstabber. Bitch.

Stumbling down the hallway, I leaned against the walls for support. Super dramatic, but I couldn't help the way I felt. Like the world was collapsing directly on my body, crushing me to dust. How I'd managed to live through the last twenty-four hours, I wasn't sure.

Yesterday, when I'd arrived at his apartment, Camila hadn't been there. Trent had sent her home, telling her she wasn't needed that night. I'd cooked Luna's food for her on autopilot, burning myself on the stove twice and making frequent trips to the bathroom to wash my face and take deep breaths.

Dinner had been fine. I'd filled in the voids telling Luna more about surfing and things I'd read about seahorses. I told her about my brother, how I hoped one day I could take him to the beach. She'd seemed to understand. She looked like she had, anyway.

At night, I'd crawled into his bed, stealing what I no longer deserved. His kisses, his caresses, his body brushing against mine. I stole his heat and the strokes of his tongue and the thrusts of his cock. I stole his lust, for it was no longer mine. I enjoyed the pain I earned and the pleasure I didn't. And in the morning, I asked for another round, knowing full well that this afternoon—when I'd give the flash drive to my father—it'd all be over for us.

"This time, I want us to go slow." I'd writhed beneath him, under my dark knight with chipped armor, who'd let me crawl into the broken cracks of his shell and settle in even though he'd known who I was. The Trojan horse.

"Why slow?"

"So I can remember."

"Why would you forget?"

Silence. He'd kissed away my tears, knowing exactly what I wasn't saying but not wanting to believe it. He'd made this sacrifice for me—that much was sure. He'd let me break him, and I had. Without blinking or hesitating or even stopping to think about it.

He moved on top of me like I was a wave, filling my body, my core, and my soul. Stroking my cheeks, kissing my eyes. "My girl, my obsession, my Tide."

It sounded like a goodbye, which only made me cry harder, clutching him like an anchor. Trent knew, and at six in the morning, half an hour before Luna woke up, we'd done the closest thing to making love, knowing that by the end of the day, that love would turn into hate.

———

My father's office door was open.

It made everything so much more final. If I passed by, he'd call me in. He'd ask about the flash drive. I would have to give it to him, and then everything would be over.

Luna.

Trent.

Seahorses.

Tide.

The ocean was stormy that day. Bane had left me a message at half past six in the morning when Trent was in the shower.

Don't even bother coming down. Black flag.

He hadn't known I could literally see the flag waving from my spot, at Trent's window, in his bedroom, butt naked, my hand pressed against the glass. The waves crashed, and the wind wailed. It was the weirdest weather for August in California, but as a surfer, I wasn't surprised.

The ocean knew.

In the office, I'd loitered by reception, prolonging walking over to my desk by my father's door and taking a seat. By eleven o'clock, I couldn't postpone the inevitable. I was making the twelfth pot of coffee that day—for whom, no one knew—when Max walked in and leaned his arm against the door. He looked like a weasel in a suit, reeking of a pine-scented disinfectant. He always smelled like he bathed in aftershave.

"Your dad wants to see you," he announced in his signature chilly tone before walking away. The flash drive burned inside my pocket. I made my way out of the break room, leaving the coffee I never planned on drinking behind me. I passed by Trent's office. The door was open. I knew he knew. Knew that among other things, this was a test. Knew that I'd failed. I stopped in front of him, briefly. His head was bowed down, and he was signing some papers. I cleared my throat, feeling like my whole body was foreign and strange and not mine.

"Is this a trick?" I croaked. I hoped, prayed, willed for it to be part of a bigger plan that we could both share. Trent's eyes were still on the papers. Like he hadn't held me in his arms hours ago and breathed life into me.

Not shaking his head—not even moving—he said, "Nope."

"So all the information is th…" I started before he shot his head up and stared at me, his face blank. Chiseled out of titanium. Godlike and angry.

"Everything is there, Edie. Every single file and plan and contract. You made your choice. If you want to be strong, then be strong. Now, leave."

I wanted to argue with him. Wanted this to turn into a loud, ugly, angry, *real* argument after which I would be convinced there was another way to save Theo. But I also acknowledged that all those things would just serve to show that I was still an indecisive teenager and he was the older man who'd seduced me. And we weren't those things. We were so much more.

My legs took me to my father's office, and I didn't remember how I got there, but I did remember the door clicking shut behind me. The sound it made was concluding and grave.

There was an ocean of space and unspoken words between us, every inch a toxic drop of bitterness. I wanted to keep it that way. With Jordan Van Der Zee, I preferred to stay dry and guarded.

"Well?" he asked, sitting back in his leather chair and arching one skeptical eyebrow. Not once had he asked me how my mother was while I was sleeping, eating, and living in the hospital by her side. This, combined with what he'd made me do, with what my life looked like, triggered my anger to overflow. My mouth was paper-dry, and every muscle in my body was taut with the need to launch at him.

I wasn't sure where the next words came from, but I was certain I couldn't stop them from pouring out even if I tried. "Can I ask you something?"

He huffed, leaning back in his chair. He rolled one hand in a go-on motion.

"Now that you know what happened to Mom, do you wish you would have waited? Maybe not pushed her to doing what she did?"

A part of me realized I was being irrational—perhaps even pathetic—trying to reason with him. Looking to find a person with a heart. Because if he was a monster, then I could become one, too. But if there was a sliver of humanity inside him, maybe I could bargain with him and save Trent. Jordan flicked his gaze to his watch, sighed like my very presence was an inconvenience, and rubbed the tip of his chin.

"I didn't push your mother, Edie. We're all responsible for our own lives. Dumping the blame on someone else is for the weak."

Again with the power games. My father didn't care. What's more, I was starting to suspect he actually took pleasure from this screwed-up situation. I was the one to coax Mom off the ledge time and time again, while he was the one to push and watch her fall, all the while waiting for me to let her go. This was where we danced. On the edge of her sanity. I needed to break this cycle—smash his foot in—to make sure he wasn't going to hurt her.

I sucked in a breath, swallowing down a juicy curse. My mind was made up. "I have the flash drive." I changed the subject, looking straight ahead at him.

His face was smeared with delight, confirming how cocky and self-assured he was. "Well, are you waiting for a royal invitation? Give it to me."

"Not until you tell me why you hate him."

"It really is none of your business, Edie." He rolled his Cartier pen between his fingers.

And then…and then…

If you want to be strong, then be strong.

I folded my arms over my chest. "Actually, it is, seeing as I'm in love with him."

The silence in the room was dense and heavy and real. Jordan's eyes widened, his nostrils flared, and his mouth twisted into a scowl

I'd never seen before. It's like he'd invented a new pissed-off expression just for me. But I couldn't take my words back now and didn't want to anyway.

I stepped deeper into the office, knowing what I was doing. Risking everything. My relationship with Theo. My relationship with Trent. With Luna. With my mother. But I was tired and weary of tiptoeing around this man. I'd lose everyone else, but maybe I'd finally find *myself*.

And if I had to press the self-destruct button to sever the ties between this man and me, so be it. I wanted to feel like I could take a lungful of oxygen without fearing the world would collapse.

"I'm in love with Trent Rexroth so blindly, Jordan, I'm not even sure I see anything other than him when he's around. I will die for this man, not to mention protect him at all costs. He is a wonderful, broken human being, who is trying hard to do what you've failed so miserably at. To be a dad. A parent. Someone to lean on. He is making the right choices, time after time, at any cost. He is taking care of the fragile, even though he is callous as hell. And he does everything with integrity and without running anyone else over. So tell me, Jordan, why in the hell do you hate *my boyfriend* so much?"

He stood up from his chair, his face blood-red. I thought a vein was going to pop out of his temple. Maybe I even hoped that would happen. His fists were clenched at his sides, his body quivering to the rhythm of his own uncontained rage.

"Give me the flash drive."

"No." I stood taller. "What has he done to you?"

"He stole something of mine."

"What was it?"

"It was *everything*. Now give me the flash drive before you regret it." He reached his open palm across his desk, expecting me to obey. He was sorely mistaken. I took a wide step back, feeling like the flash drive was ten times heavier than its feather-weight.

"Never."

He pounced on me before I could react, lunging across his desk to take what he wanted without asking. It shouldn't have surprised me. All the times he'd manhandled me had proven he had no respect for me. I moved away, clawing at his face instinctively.

"Jesus Christ, you little bitch!" He palmed the scratch I'd left on his face, stumbling backward. For all his height, my father was grossly unequipped to fight anyone. Even me. He'd spent his whole life tucked in an office like a hamster in a cage.

"Don't you dare touch me ever again!" My voice shook, but I didn't. It gave me strength.

"Pack a bag and leave your mother's house." He pointed at the door, panting, gasping, seething. "You're eighteen, so opinionated and mighty. You have it all figured out, don't you, you little slut?" The last word slapped me in the face and knocked the breath out of my lungs. "I'm sure Trent will happily take you in. But then he is a walking, talking STD, just like the rest of his friends. I am no longer obligated to put a roof over your head. Pack a bag, Edie, and while you are at it, make sure you take whatever you have here with you as well because you're fired."

Instead of doing all the things I thought I would—crying, begging, fearing for what was to come, I turned around and made my way to the door. My back was to him when my father put the last nail in our relationship's coffin.

"It's a shame you won't have time to say goodbye to your brother. I am going to transfer him this week."

I turned around, smiling for once, because I knew something he didn't. "You can't do that."

"And why is that, little slut?" he spat, as if he wanted to remind me that was who I was to him right now. His precious little girl who'd opened her legs to the big bad wolf.

"Because social services are looking into Theo's situation. Besides, you can't transfer a minor from one group house to another so quickly. I checked. You think you're so powerful, Father, you forget there are other forces around you equally as strong. Even the biggest wave crashes. You're about to hit the sand. I hope you like the taste of dust."

CHAPTER TWENTY-EIGHT
EDIE

I spent the rest of the day on the beach, alone. I didn't have time to tell Trent what had happened, and I wanted to have that conversation face-to-face. I was buzzing with adrenaline and high on the danger of what I'd done. So, after calling the rehab facility where Mom had been checked in the day before, I went to the beach to spend some time with the violent ocean. We understood one another. I sat in front of the setting sun, my toes in the sand, hugging my knees and listening to the sounds of seagulls and waves crashing ashore.

I didn't want to think about the fact that it was probably Trent's doing. That he called the rehab center. That he made it all happen.

I didn't even notice when it got chilly, staying put until about eight in the evening, when I knew for certain Trent and Luna would be home. Showing up at his doorstep unannounced was something I'd never dreamt of doing before, but this wasn't the type of conversation to have over the phone.

As I made my way to his building, I tried to convince myself that there was nothing to be worried about. After all, I had turned my father down in the end. I hadn't gone through with it. I couldn't give up Trent's secrets.

I thanked God there was no doorman at Trent's building because if there was, he'd have had to call him through the switchboard and announce my arrival. I couldn't face it if Trent had said he didn't want to see me. But I certainly felt like things could still go wrong as I took the elevator up to his penthouse.

My feet felt impossibly heavy on the marble floor. Step after step after step.

My ocean. My secret. My weakness.

I rapped the door three times, listening carefully. Behind it, there was the soft sound of Luna's chuckle. It wasn't exactly a laugh— Luna never laughed—but it was the sound she made when she was pleased. It put a smile on my face before the door swung open.

But when it did…

Camila shot a confused smile when she saw me. Behind her was a woman I didn't know but I recognized. She had tan skin, long raven hair, and light eyes. She looked like a supermodel—like Adriana Lima—and she wore a tight pink dress that highlighted how curvy she was.

She was crouching, her butt parked on the back of her Prada heels, admiring the stuffed seahorse Luna held in her hands. An identical seahorse to the one Daria had ruined.

Luna's mother. She was beautiful and right, and she belonged.

I felt nausea washing over my body and stumbled backward, feeling my throat closing up. A bitter lump twisted inside it. *Don't cry.*

"What are you doing here, Edie?" Camila's face was etched with surprise.

"Is this another nanny? Gosh, Carmella, is it? Don't let her stand there. Invite her in." The woman stood up, adjusting her tiny dress and strutting her way to the door. She wore a smile that told me she'd already won. It was carved with allure and dripped intention.

She'd been gone for years. It was some kind of sign from the universe to show me Trent and Luna were better off without me. That they had someone better than my father's daughter. The one who'd tried to get Trent kicked off the board. I didn't deserve them.

She was Luna's mother.

I couldn't compete with her.

I didn't even want to.

"Why are you here? Are you in trouble?" Camila pressed, just when Val stopped by her side, putting her hand on Camila's shoulder.

Camila, not Carmella, you idiot.

"It's fine if she wants to babysit the kid. Trent and I have a lot to talk about. We could use some privacy. Maybe go down to the marina and grab a bite."

I couldn't take it anymore. I wanted to get away from the situation so badly, I was contemplating jumping off his terrace. The elevator and the stairs weren't fast enough. The only reason I didn't barge in and plunge to my death was because I didn't want Luna to be scarred for life.

I turned around and ran away, jerking open the door to the stairway. My legs moved quickly, much like they had when I was stealing. *Tap, tap, tap, tap.* The adrenaline felt different, though. More suffocating.

One floor, then another. Blood rushed to my head, and I could faintly hear the door open wider and Trent asking who it was. His echo carried all the way down. He sounded...*chill.* Like a man who'd been reunited with the mother of his child and was probably relieved to have her back in their lives.

Alone. I was all alone.

No mother. No father. No friends. No Trent.

I ran for a while, passing my car, which was parked at the promenade by the beach, and all the stores and all the people and all the things I used to love but couldn't look at anymore. This whole street was soaked with memories of Trent. The ocean, too. The first time he'd played with me, with my breasts, with my nipples, with my *heart*, after I was done surfing. All the wires in my brain sizzled. Would I ever be able to set foot in this place again? To surf? *To breathe?*

The only solace was that Jordan couldn't see me like this. He'd say I'd reaped what I'd sown. Remind me that I was nothing but a stupid slut who'd served as a plaything to a man who'd relentlessly searched for this one woman for years. I'd been a passing diversion, a fling.

The blisters on my feet were beginning to swell as darkness washed over the shore. I'd reached the other end of the town, stopping by the marina where the boats were docked. I had to take off my boots and limp the rest of the way. The wood was cool and soothing against my aching feet. I stopped by a small, white, and rusty houseboat floating next to the dock calmly, like it didn't have a care in the world, just like its owner.

I realized I hadn't called him before my arrival, again making the same mistake I had with Trent.

But Bane wasn't Trent. Bane was a friend. In fact, we'd never been serious lovers. Neither of us could destroy the other person.

I climbed aboard his boat and knocked on his door. He opened it, shirtless, a girl and a guy—both half naked—sitting on his bed. His blond hair was shaggy, and his eyes were red from smoking.

"I need you," I croaked, feeling the tears in my eyes again.

Bane nodded solemnly, not taking a breath before he instructed, "Craig, Shea, get your asses out of here."

I collapsed into Bane's arms. He held me together loosely, like the safety pins on my backpack, making me feel no less forlorn than I did when I got on his boat.

Then my only friend in the world clutched me close to his chest and whispered into my ear, "I told you so."

CHAPTER TWENTY-NINE
TRENT

Saying I didn't want Val there was the understatement of the fucking decade.

Problem was I had zero choice.

I got home at six, fully intending to change into some workout clothes and go downstairs to the gym to let off some steam after Edie had walked into her father's office with the flash drive holding all of my ammo, but I had a surprise waiting for me at the door.

Fucking Valenciana Vasquez, leaning against a wall, looking twenty shades of sex on red heels, and of course, it did nothing for me.

"Trent." She batted her eyelashes, a venom-glazed siren. "Long time no see."

I walked right past her, jamming my keys into the hole. "Hey, you heard no complaints from me." My jaw twitched once. "To what do I owe the pleasure?"

She braced herself against the wall, probably overwhelmed by my underwhelming reaction. If she had been expecting tears, shouts, and "we've been waiting for you" Hallmark card sentiments, she was deeply mistaken. Luna was mine. Mine to love, mine to raise, mine to fix. Val just presented a complication to me, and I was going to eliminate it, nip it in the bud before she could say Jack fucking Robinson.

"I'm here for my daughter, of course." She scoffed, slithering in my direction and sneaking through the door I'd opened.

"What in the good fuck do you think you're doing?" I asked when her shoulder brushed the doorframe. I blocked her way with my body, turning around and making sure she had no room to slide between my arms.

She blinked away her shock at my steel voice. When Valenciana had found out she was pregnant with Luna, she'd asked for five hundred grand to make the pregnancy go away. It had been borderline cute, how she'd thought she could blackmail me. My answer to her had been—*go ahead, sweetheart. Have my kid.* Money wasn't the issue—I could pay her off with little to no effect on my lifestyle. But having an abortion on my dime was out of the question. It would have been different if it had come from *her.* But since she'd given the choice to me, I had chosen not to choose. Simple.

So she'd had Luna. Then she'd walked away from us.

And now she'd come back.

If she thought she could do so without an explanation and declaration of intention, she had another think coming.

"I'm trying to get in so we can talk." She stomped her heel.

"Luna is going to be here any second now from dance class. She can't see you." Each of my words dripped ice, so I wasn't surprised to see her shiver.

"Who took her?"

Is she a dancer? What is she like? Does she have any other hobbies? So many questions she could have asked. Of course, that would require her to give a minimum of two shits about Luna.

"None of your business. You wanna talk about *my* daughter, we do it somewhere else. My office. A coffee shop. In another fucking state. No matter where it'll be, you won't get access to her until I figure out your angle. Now go."

"Trent…" Val glided her way to me, hell on heels, her palm on my chest. I threw it off, giving her a piercing look. She swallowed, batting her lashes. "I flew all the way from Georgia," she whispered.

I started laughing, about to give her a piece of my mind, when the elevator slid open and Luna and Camila walked out. Camila was holding Luna's backpack while my daughter bounced on her steps—something she'd started doing ever since Edie had come into our lives—and awarded me with a smile that melted quickly when she realized I wasn't alone.

"Oh my gosh, Luna! Look at you! You're so pretty! Do you know who I am?"

No. Fuck no. I stepped forward to scoop Luna up, but Val's big mouth was ahead of me. "I'm your mommy!" she exclaimed, flinging her arms theatrically. "I finally came to see you! I'm so excited to get to know you, sweetie!"

Luna's eyes bugged in disbelief, her face twisting to search my gaze. I kept my mouth shut. I wasn't exactly sure what was going to come out of it if I allowed myself to respond. Punching a woman was not something I'd ever contemplated doing. But hell if Val didn't make it difficult to not want to end her.

"All right, let's get inside and have a nice cup of tea." Camila was the first to move from her spot, her words tense, her eyes skating between Val and me. There was an edge to her tone that warned me that I couldn't tell Val to fuck off like I normally would. That I couldn't let a bomb drop on my kid and then go, *So, that was awkward, huh? Anyway, now that I've kicked your mom out, shall we see what's on television?*

We all went into my apartment, Val taking everything in, no doubt making an inventory and calculating how much money she could milk out of the situation.

Suddenly, she turned around and produced a stuffed seahorse from her designer bag, handing it to Luna. "I heard you like seahorses, so I thought I'd give this to you."

My heart missed a beat, the air stood still, and all I could feel was calamity seeping through every crack in the room, poisoning us like invisible gas.

Click, click, click, the pieces of the puzzle fell together.

Val didn't have any point of contact with anyone Luna and I knew. Her mother, who lived in Chicago, had given up on her relationship with Luna before it had even begun. She was too busy with an ex-boyfriend-turned-inmate to Skype with her grand-daughter. Val, therefore, had a snitch from my inner circle. Now I had to figure out who.

Luna's eyes sparkled with surprise and delight, and she grabbed the seahorse, clutching it close to her chest. Luna smiled at her, and if there was such thing as a soul—mine blew up and scattered all over the fucking floor. Because everything had just become a million times more complicated. I hated Val for being so reckless. For telling Luna who she was. I hated her and knew she'd done it for a reason. She wanted something from me, and it wasn't the kid full of hope and awe who stood in front of her, wearing a black leotard and an eager gaze.

"Hey, Luna? Daddy's gonna go talk to a friend on the phone. You stay with Camila and Val here, okay?" I jerked my thumb toward my bedroom, purposely uttering Valenciana's name. She'd done nothing to earn the title of Mom. I made eye contact with Camila to make sure she knew Val was not to be left alone with Luna at any point. She gave me a slight nod. I sneaked into my bedroom and called Vicious, who immediately said he'd contact Eli Cole, a family lawyer and Dean's dad, and that they would be on their way to me shortly. When I came out, I heard the front door slamming shut.

"Who was it?" I frowned.

"No one important." Val let loose a sugary smile, patting Luna's head as she explained to her something completely wrong and untrue about seahorses. Camila motioned with her head for me to follow her to the kitchen, her face twisted with anger. I looked between Val and Luna. I couldn't leave them alone, even a few feet away from me, in the living room. Val caught up with the problem quickly.

"I need to go freshen up in the bathroom." She straightened her spine, waltzing down the hallway like she owned the fucking place.

I mustered a small smile and offered it to my daughter. "Germs, can you do me a favor and go to your room for a few minutes? Daddy and Camila need to talk about something that concerns grown-up people."

Germs. I called her Germs.

When the coast was clear, Camila turned to me, fire in her eyes. "Edie was at the door." She exhaled sharply, rubbing her forehead, one hand on her waist.

"Not following," I said, mainly to buy time, because *what the fuck?*

"She looked upset to see Val. What was she doing here? What's going on?"

I looked up and offered her the answer she didn't want to hear. It made no fucking difference if Camila knew or not. It wasn't like she had access to Jordan or would ever tell him.

"Dear Lord, Trent, she is just a kid!"

I shook my head, tired of hearing the same old shit. "She's more of a woman than the bitch who walked into my house two seconds ago and told my kid she's her mother."

"Your so-called woman ran away from here in tears, looking every inch the teenager she is."

Another sucker punch to my stomach. They just kept on coming today. I wanted to grab my keys and run after Edie, but of course, I couldn't. Not with Val here. I didn't even care about the goddamn flash drive anymore. All I cared about was saving Edie and Luna's asses. If I could get mine to stay intact after this was all over—that was a nice bonus.

I heard the bathroom door creaking open and turned around with the intention of marching to the living room and ending this shit show. My doorbell rang again.

Edie.

I was about to get it, but Val beat me to it—again, as if she lived here—and when she swung the door open, the final piece of the puzzle fell.

Jordan Van Der Zee.

Camila and Luna left for McDonald's (you knew it was the apocalypse when you let your daughter have McDonald's at half past eight on a weekday) on cue, leaving me to deal with the clusterfuck that had walked into my life the same afternoon an eighteen-year-old had decided to smash my heart into micro-pieces. Asshole Van Der Zee strolled toward Val, pressing a possessive kiss to her temple and jerking her by the waist to his side. "Long time no see, beautiful."

"It's only been a week." Her plump red smile had that extra confident curve, telling me whatever Jordan had planned for me, she was part of it. I glanced between them, doing the math. Collecting the pieces of this fucked-up riddle and patching them into the full picture.

"You haven't been going to Zurich." I threw my head back, laughing bitterly. "SwissTech doesn't need your ass to pay them regular visits. We already renewed their contract weeks ago. We thought you were banging a European piece and writing off the expenses."

"You were wrong." Jordan sighed and sat on my couch with a grin, oh so fucking proud of himself. "Georgia is closer and so much more tempting with this lady by my side." He pulled Val down, and she fell onto his lap, giggling breathlessly like some fucking fifties' New York showgirl. "Now, be a good servant and get us some drinks so we can all have a talk." Jordan winked, looking more approachable and nicer than I'd ever seen him. I stood in front of them, one shoulder propped against the wall separating the kitchen and the living room, hawk-eyed and ready to dive for an attack.

"I'd advise against those kinds of jokes. If you keep them up, you might need to live off liquids anyway because I'll break every tooth in that smug mouth of yours."

"Eh, there we are. A thug, showing his true colors."

"Quite the contrary. I'm beginning to see my color was never your problem. Val was."

"Luna and you are my problem," Jordan corrected, his eyes slicing to mine, glittering with uncontained hatred. "You walked into my life and messed it all up without even realizing what you'd done, Rexroth. Why do you think I bought your piece-of-shit company, run by a bunch of pampered little assholes?"

"Because you're only good at buying successful corporations? All the ones you started from scratch went under in less than five years. I've read between the lines of your squeaky *Forbes* interviews," I quipped, unblinking.

"No. I did it to make sure you'll never be with Valenciana," he said.

"Explain to me the logic in that, Van Der Idiot. Smaller brain and stuff." I tapped my temple sarcastically.

Jordan smirked, leaning down for his briefcase. Val slid down from his knees to the sofa, plucking a pack of Marlboro Reds from her purse and lighting a cigarette. Val puffed a screen of smoke upward, and I walked over to her, snapping the cigarette in two.

"You've already abandoned your daughter. It is grossly unnecessary to make her a secondhand smoker, too."

She pouted, giving me her big Lolita eyes like they'd do something to me. Like they could touch what Edie had managed to somehow clutch and squeeze and fuck so raw I no longer felt like any of my inner organs were mine anymore.

"Party pooper." Val scowled.

"You have no idea. I'm about to shit all over your fucking life, sweetheart. Now, the seahorse. How did you know about it?"

Val unknotted her long legs and sat back, letting Jordan sift through his documents while humoring me at the same time. "Your little girlfriend was planning on buying it for her online. Jordan has full access to the search history on her phone and checks it daily. I beat her to it. Sorry, Trent. That's what you get for dating someone who still needs Daddy's allowance." *You're the one living off her daddy's money.*

"You're a fucking demon." I laughed, crazed.

"I could have been your demon," she whined, wild.

"You could never be anyone's demon. Soulless people cannot be owned or loved."

With that, I walked off to the kitchen, needing something… something to calm me the fuck down. I downed a bottle of water and came back to the living room. Jordan was arranging stacks of paper all over my coffee table. It looked like a plan. One I wasn't going to like.

"So let's make it short and sweet, shall we?" He rolled up the sleeves to his crisp button-down shirt, licking his fingers as he thumbed through the pages, acutely concentrating on them. "Five years ago, I had a company called SilverStar, Inc. It was located in—"

"Chicago," I finished for him.

Jordan's shoulders shook with a chuckle. "That's right, boy. And so, during one of my many trips to Chicago, I met Valenciana, and we started dating."

I was tempted to remind him the word he was looking for was "affair," but semantics weren't really top priority at that moment.

Jordan plucked one document out of a pile.

"Val caught my attention on one of my trips. How could she not? Look at her. We began to see each other every time I was in town. Which was a lot. I admit, I was smitten. Val, however, did not share the sentiment, as she continued her straying ways. I let her because let's admit it—she wasn't my only mistress, either."

He handed me the document, and I took it, examining it through a mist of red anger. It was a report conducted by a private investigator named Barry Guilfoyle. There were highlights of the times I'd been away from the apartment, from Luna, showing I was working long hours and going on frequent business trips, leaving her with Camila or with my parents.

"We were supposed to get stronger as time progressed, Val and me. I told her to have an abortion. It didn't matter who was the father. I didn't appreciate being fiscally chained to some stripper, either." Jordan drew a breath, handing me some more documents. "Val said you were the father. That you were too good a financial opportunity to pass up. I didn't offer her money, assuming that you would. I'd knocked up a couple of women in my day after marrying Lydia, and I bought my way through their abortions easily enough. But you chose not to pay, and by the time I calmed down and got back into the picture, Val was already five months pregnant. Too late for her to get rid of the kid."

To get rid of the kid.

I clenched my fists, my jaw, my fucking ass, in an effort not to murder him. He passed me a few low-resolution printed pictures. They showed Camila frowning at Luna. That was just Camila's stern expression sometimes. It didn't mean shit. Another picture of me pulling Luna's curls into a ponytail. She liked her ponytail tight, no bumps, so it looked like I was hurting her. But I wasn't. She was standing between my legs in a coffee shop, both her arms resting on my thighs, looking elsewhere. The pictures looked bad, but the situations were completely innocent. Still, why take any chances?

"You better watch your mouth," I warned, "or you'll be very fucking sorry."

Jordan laughed, sighing with contempt. "When we did a test and realized the baby was yours, I left. But I got back with Val... eventually. See, in the space between the time Luna was born and when she turned one year old, Val was trying to win you. Seduce you. Be with you. I get it. You're younger, hungrier, better looking. But you're not smarter, Trent. You're a bloody idiot who got lucky because his friends were too generous and let him have a piece of the pie. But the pie is not for you to eat."

I gritted my teeth, letting him finish, processing everything. The pictures. The reports. The case Jordan had been building against me for fucking years. My greatest fear—Val coming back to take Luna—was materializing in front of my face, with a cherry on top in the form of Jordan scheming against me. I knew exactly what Val's angle would be. We had done coke together the night I knocked her up.

She could say I had a drug problem in court.

She could even make it believable.

Our case had years in court written all over it.

I took a step in his direction, and he almost flinched. I tipped my chin up, looking down at him. "Why go through all this trouble?"

"Because I never lose, peasant. Especially not to another ex–poor boy like you."

Ex–poor boy. I should have known that Jordan was like me. The chip on the shoulder was there—it was always there—only difference was mine was skin deep. His—bone deep.

Every muscle in my body told me to pounce on him and rip him apart. My mind told me to wait it out and hit harder than with my fists.

"I won Val back, but not without a fight. While I kept her in Atlanta, she begged me to contact Luna. I, of course, told her it was out of the question. I purchased your company, wanting to be close to you, wanting to study you, to see what made you tick. Because the endgame…" Jordan got up, scooping the papers on the coffee table and tucking them under his arm. "The endgame was to end *you*."

The moment of epiphany made me feel like Samson on his last breath, when God had given him the strength to push the pillars, bringing the roof down. Samson had been killed in the process, but he'd taken the Philistines down. I knew I'd do the same if I had to.

Jordan bought into my company because he wanted to demolish me, personally and professionally, so that he'd have more control. And to punish me for something I hadn't even been aware of.

He'd promised Val a happily ever after and her kid back.

He'd wanted to frame me, ruin me, and take what's mine. The woman I didn't want and the girl I'd do everything for.

Jordan flicked the papers, causing them to rain down on the floor, and tugged at Val's limp arm to get her up from my couch. "And with Luna not wanting to talk, this is going to look very bad in court, Rexroth. You traumatized her with your lifestyle—she's too terrified to make a sound. With that in mind, I suggest you hand us your resignation first thing tomorrow morning, sell me your shares in the company, and meet us this weekend to discuss joint custody with Val. She wants in on Luna, and she expects you to pick up the bill for her accommodation. I think it's fair."

I smiled as the documents scattered all around us. What Val wanted was access to my money. Bonus points: living in a glitzy SoCal town close to her multibillionaire lover who was smart enough not to marry her ass. Jordan was a flaky bet. Prone to piss off at any moment. *Once a cheater, always a cheater,* after all. And oh, wouldn't she know.

Jordan stormed out, his shoulder brushing mine. "Keep the duplicates, Rexroth. My treat."

I was still standing there with my heart in my fucking throat and my soul clutched in my fist when Jordan and Val reached the door. She looked like a guilty, apologetic mess, and he looked like the devil. He turned around.

"And there he is," Jordan drawled. "The man who defiled my daughter."

The man who is fucking obsessed with her, more like.

"Trent Rexroth being mute. Hardly a surprise."

"You want words?" I took a step in his direction, grinning. "Here's something to tide you over: Thank you for giving me the play-by-play of your game. Keep your eyes open." I pushed both of them out of my apartment, my arm slung over the door. The last thing I said before slamming it in their bewildered faces was "*My turn.*"

CHAPTER THIRTY
EDIE

"I can't believe you're making me do this," I moaned, knocking Bane's shoulder with mine. Dark sunglasses covered the better part of my face, shielding my pumpkin-sized puffy eyes. I wore one of his surfing tank tops and short shorts because I hadn't had time to grab anything from my parents' mansion before my father had changed the locks and essentially kicked me out without giving me the chance to grab my stuff.

Bane and I stood on his mother's wide porch. The rustic material and elaborate, colorful garden were oddly reassuring. Someone who lived in such a warm, inviting place couldn't be the type to hurt me, right?

"It's been a long time coming. Especially now when Rexroth is busy playing house with his ex." Bane pushed his blond hair up into a bun, rapping the door loudly. I thought it was weird that he didn't walk in, but Bane was a master when it came to strange relationships. Considering he'd moved out of the house at eighteen and not gone to college, I figured he liked his space, and maybe his mother did, too.

"She's not his ex, and I have no evidence they're playing house together." I sniffed, rubbing my tired eyes beneath the shades. Seeing Val there had hurt like a thousand violent deaths, but I tried to tell myself that this was what was best for Luna. And Trent... If he wanted to get back with her, I couldn't blame him. I knew nothing about relationships, nothing about being a parent, and next to zero about how to keep a family united.

The door swung open, and the person on the other end knocked my breath out of my lungs.

Bane stepped in, oblivious to the fact that the rug, once again, had been pulled out from under my feet.

"Gidget, this is my mom, Sonya. Sonya, this is Gidget, also known as Edie Van Der Zee."

Sonya.

The redheaded woman Trent had been having sex with when I'd walked into his office. To get back at me for allegedly having sex with Bane. *Her son.* I didn't know whether I should feel horrified or annoyed at this. Sonya obviously shared my feelings because she took a step back from the door and clutched the fabric of her baby-blue blouse, momentarily rendered speechless.

"Oh," she said, the word escaping from her mouth barely audible. I believed Trent when he'd said he was no longer seeing her, but it didn't make it any less awkward. I wondered if she knew about him and me. If she resented me for it. If she'd even want to help me.

"What are you waiting for, Gidget? The fucking pope? Come on in," Bane grunted, making his way through the tiled hallway to the kitchen at the end of it and throwing the fridge open. He took out two cans of beer, like we weren't eighteen and underage, and sauntered over to the open-plan living room. I stayed on the threshold, unable to do so much as take my shades off.

"Edie," Sonya whispered urgently, opening the door wider. "It's okay. You can trust me. I've worked as a child psychologist for fifteen years now. Forget what you saw that day. This will not affect you or your brother."

My brother. That's right. She was the reason why I'd seen him that Sunday.

Gingerly, I took a step in. Bane was already in the living room, cracking the beers open, the Black Keys' "Lonely Boy" blasting from the speakers. Sonya and I walked like two stiff figures toward the couch, and I tried to cough away the ball of shame and jealousy building in my throat.

"Wash it with a beer." Bane flung his long legs over an ottoman, dropping to a shabby, something-from-*Friends* purple couch. I glanced at Sonya, who gave me a polite smile.

"You've had a long week, I hear."

I downed the can in a couple of long gulps and threw my head onto one of the pillows, closing my eyes for a moment. *Thank you.*

Sonya laced her fingers in front of me, her legs crossed, giving me her undivided attention. She was dressed to kill, and my feelings toward her were at war. I wanted to dislike her, but how could I when she was hell-bent on helping me and being so goddamn nice?

"Enjoyed that beer?" She grinned. I nodded, cradling the empty can instead of placing it on the coffee table. My father would kill me for less than staining his precious Italian oak.

"Did you know that in Europe it is legal to drink from the age of eighteen? I always preferred the Russian way better." Her smile was so big it almost felt like a wink.

Roman "Bane" Protsenko had an interesting mother. She'd run away from Russia with him, giving him freedom, and he, in exchange, lived his life to the fullest.

And she was happy for him. Content.

How odd.

"Now, tell me all about your brother and your father's threats regarding him. I want you to start from the beginning. From when your father placed him in the first group home." Sonya grabbed a glass of what smelled like vodka from the coffee table and took a sip.

And I did.

I poured my heart out, telling her about how Theo was never loved, not really, by either of our parents. How Jordan had bribed his way out of being a parent, always taking the shortcut, always placing Theodore in institutions and hopping from city to city every holiday so we wouldn't have to visit Theo.

I didn't know what was more horrific—reciting the years in which Theo was neglected, saying it out loud and realizing how bad it sounded, or seeing their faces as I confided in them. Sonya looked like she was about to cry, and even Bane turned down the music at some point and stared at me like his world had turned a shade darker.

When I was done, Sonya cleared her throat, looking down at her thighs. "Roman, please step out of the room."

If Bane was shocked, he didn't show it, taking his beer and sauntering over toward the door. "I'll be on the porch, smoking my ass off after that depressing story."

When the door closed behind him, Sonya met my eyes. "Trent didn't offer to help you?"

"I…" I tapped my lips, thinking about it for a moment. How much did she know? How much did *I* want her to know? Screw it. It wasn't about my summer affair with an older man. This was about Theo. "We got involved for a while, and he helped me with paying for Theo's facility, but nothing more than that. And I doubt he'd wanna help me now. We're…no longer in touch."

Sonya uncrossed her legs, took another sip of her vodka, and pressed it to her cheek. Her eyes were glazed over, and for a moment, they held the same look as they'd had when Trent had entered her. *Drunk.* I shuddered into Bane's shirt.

"Why?" she asked softly.

I blinked. "Why what?"

"Why did you end it?"

"Why do you assume I'm the one who ended it?" I wanted to get up and do something, anything, but the need to find out if she knew something I didn't ignited and burst into flames in me.

Sonya put the glass on the table, looking up at me with a sad smile. "Because he never would."

"How do you know?" I hated myself for asking. It shouldn't have mattered to me. He needed to focus on his family.

Sonya looked up at me. "Because, Edie, he is in love with you."

CHAPTER THIRTY-ONE
TRENT

Luna came first, and I had to remind myself of that.

The first thing to do was to secure my daughter's future. *With me.*

Still, the need to confront Edie was almost feral. I wanted to slam my fist above her head and yell at her for giving Jordan the flash drive. I wanted to scream and shout and curse and fuck her despite all of this shit. To make her see how not over we were, how we were only just beginning, how I was losing my mind over her. I wanted to show her how I loved the fuck out of her body and hated that we were wrong. Deeply, crazily, absurdly wrong for each other.

Which meant I had to take a step back.

The moment after Jordan and Val left, I was in the car, slicing through the streets looking for the one woman who *could* help me, who wouldn't betray me. I called Dean on my way to her.

"I need you to go to Edie Van Der Zee and get some of my shit from her."

"Why don't you do it yourself?"

"Because she handed my ass to her dad. Because she fucked me over. Because if I see her lying, cheating face in person, I would shit on everything I care about. In a nutshell." I cleared my throat, my eyes on the road. People were walking and laughing and living their lives, not giving a damn that mine was collapsing.

No one was taking my daughter. No one.

"I take it you'll elaborate later." I heard Dean trying to calm a crying Lev down. "What do I need to do?"

I told him, adding, "And whatever you do, don't tell her about what happened with Jordan and Val. Her loyalty lies with one person—her brother—and she'll do whatever's best for him. I'm still not sure if it's what's best for me. Got it?"

"Got it," he said.

I arrived at the office of the woman who was there for me, who'd help me take down Jordan.

"Oh, and Trent?" Dean asked from the other line. "Luna will always be yours. You better goddamn believe we'll make sure of that."

Very few things were certain in this life.

One day, you were going to die. Every year, you'd pay taxes. If someone hated you before you'd even opened your mouth, watch out for them—they were out for your blood. Before I'd even had the chance to shake his hand, Jordan Van Der Zee had had it out for me.

It turned out Val hadn't needed a new identity; she'd had Jordan. He'd housed her. Given her his credit cards—under his name. Cash galore. He paid for her lifestyle and her every little whim to keep her happy. And he'd promised her that one day, when the timing was right, he would strike and give her the life she'd always dreamed of. The kind of luxury only Todos Santos and the South of France had to offer.

Val was content with waiting because she had nothing to lose. She'd never really cared for Luna or for me. She cared about materialistic things—the same materialistic things Edie hated so much—and Val knew that no matter how much Jordan loved her, he was going to replace her with an upgraded version one day, just like he had with Lydia. Coming back here would secure her financial support for the next fourteen years—*four-fucking-teen*—plenty of time to get her shit together and find another idiot who was stupid enough to give her his credit card. She had that shit all figured out.

Or so she thought.

As for me, I finally understood why Jordan hated me so much—I'd touched what was his and chained my destiny to her. Jordan didn't love Val, though. He thought he did, but it didn't matter. She was his. He was not the losing kind.

I made him lose.

He hated that.

Val had come back for Luna because she wanted to enjoy both worlds. Living with Jordan in Todos Santos and getting child support from me so that when—and yes, it was when, not if—he dumped her, she'd have something to fall back on. Luna was no longer a baby. She was relatively independent. Val could dress her up and parade her around like a pretty accessory.

Jordan and Val thought they had this shit on lockdown. I could see it from the way they strode out of my apartment like they had me in their pockets. They were sorely mistaken, and I wondered how they'd even gotten to the conclusion I was a pushover. The facts spoke more loudly than I ever did.

Val had spent the last years in hiding from me because she knew my wrath.

And Jordan held four times as many stocks as I did in Fiscal Heights Holdings and still couldn't move an inch without me breathing down his neck.

That was why I went prepared to the office the next day.

Amanda's main job hadn't been to find Val. What she had given me in spades—what I securely kept on my flash drive—was a lot of dirty, dirty information about Van Der Zee.

Which was why I felt completely at ease sitting on his chair, my signature legs-on-desk position with my hands behind my head, waiting for him first thing in the morning.

He walked into his office at eight a.m. like nothing had

happened. Like it wasn't his mission in life to try to destroy me. Like his other partners didn't now know he was a lying, cunning piece of trash. Jordan stopped on the threshold, staring at me vacantly. His unpleasant surprise—me—stared back at him with enough hatred to blind him.

Reaching for the breast pocket of his blazer, probably to call security, he stopped when he heard me laughing as I lit a J.

"What in the world do you think you're doing?" he asked through gritted teeth, taking a step forward. I tapped my chin, pretending to think it through.

"Making myself feel at home, seeing as this office *will* be my second home soon."

"Smoking here is illegal," he pointed out, choosing to ignore my blunt statement.

"Funny you should mention that, Jordan, since illegal seems to be your favorite flavor." I got up from his chair, strolling over to him with the wickedest smile in my arsenal.

"What are you talking about, Rexroth?" His voice sharpened with panic, coated by annoyance.

Progress, I thought, *but not enough.* I wanted to pull it out of him. The terror. The inability to fucking breathe it hurt so bad. Because that was what losing Luna would feel like.

When my pecs nearly brushed his, I stopped, towering a few inches above him. "You need to sit, Mr. Van Der Zee."

"Don't tell me what to do." He spat out the words but did as I said. This was the best kind of victory. The one where I got what I wanted watching my opponent dragging his feet. He was about to take a seat behind his desk when I *tsk*ed from my place in the center of the room.

"Forget about it, Jordi. Where you're going, not only do they not have executive chairs—but I hear the mattresses are really fucking bad." I tilted my head toward an ottoman by his oak bar. He stared at me. When he saw I wasn't kidding, he warily made his way there, grunting. Jordan was eager to find out what I knew. The answer was simple.

I knew everything.

Amanda had helped me build my case, slowly. Slowly enough to know I couldn't take him down while Edie and I were forming a relationship.

But then yesterday had changed everything. I'd sent my friends to Edie while I drove straight to Amanda. I'd turned the world upside down. I'd fought the waves. I hadn't drowned.

I would never drown. Not when I needed to keep my kid afloat.

I knotted my hands behind my back, pacing the room leisurely, the joint still clasped between my fingers. "You know what I never understood, Jordi? How come you were so goddamn successful when every company you incorporated before 1997 failed miserably and went under. It was like you were fiscal poison. Everything you touched turned into shit. The growing list of companies you've founded and that have filed for Chapter 11 was the first warning sign. We all saw it as a red flag, but your track record after 2003 was so solid, my friends decided to overlook it. Well"—I shrugged, taking a hit of my joint, exhaling the smoke on a smile—"I didn't."

At first, I'd thought all I was going to find out about Jordan was the usual shit—maybe a bit of tax evasion here, embezzlement there. Even his affairs didn't strike me as too interesting. After all, he wasn't even trying to hide them. But I'd found more. So, so much more.

Jordan's teeth gritted so hard I could hear them all the way across the room. His face remained tense, holding on to the last shreds of his dignity.

"I went to a private investigator and asked her to find me everything there was to find about the massive success story that was Jordan Van Der Zee. The first thing I found out was that you may have gone to Harvard on a scholarship, but that scholarship wasn't entirely kosher, was it? You had someone footing the bill for your education after the first year. The poor Dutch kid who couldn't even afford butter and bread—your words, not mine. I wondered who could help you with such large sums of money and found the name. A shady McConman who lived in the British Virgin Islands named Kaine Caulfield. Caulfield is *such* a peculiar name. Very *Catcher in the Rye*. Some would even say…fictional. I decided to dig deeper, especially considering you shouldn't have known someone who'd lived in the British Virgin Islands. Unless…" I put the joint between my lips and fished a document from my back pocket, throwing it in his face with the rollie still in my mouth. "Money laundering."

"This is preposterous," he muttered, intending to stand up, but I pushed him back down to his seat with the tip of my shoe.

"Sit," I commanded. "So, drugs, huh?"

"I don't know what you're talking about." He flung his arms in the air, visibly shaking. He was losing it, and fuck if it wasn't the best show in town.

Laughing, I shook my head. "I mean, I guess it could explain how you even got that far in your first company. Or how you put down some investment money when you opened your own firm three years after graduating."

"This is hearsay, and if you continue this line of conversation, I will have to contact my lawyer…" Jordan started, standing up on his feet.

I pushed him back down again, not even sparing him a glance and walking over to his bar. "Finally we can agree on something. You should definitely call your lawyer. But not yet. You'll ruin the surprise."

I poured myself three fingers of scotch and downed them in front of his floor-to-ceiling window, turning on my heel to look at him again. I felt oddly content with fucking up his life. The only person whose feelings I worried about was Edie, who was about to part ways with her father, but hey, she didn't need him anyway, and I was going to do her a favor by locking him up.

I was going to give her Theo.

"You know, I think I *am* going to be the one to take your office. It's plenty spacious. Luna will have a place to play when she visits me every Tuesday," I mused, brushing my fingers along the giant canvas painting on the wall. A Dutch painter. Another Van Der Whatever. Waves crashing on the shore.

Edie.

"You're leaving the company, Rexroth," he said tiredly, but he didn't mean it. Not really. I could see it in his eyes. The defeat. It had a color and a smell and a fucking taste. It was everywhere on his features, everywhere in the room.

"Save me the bullshit. You and I both know that time is money." I polished off his liquor and dropped the remainder of the joint into the expensive glass. "So—drugs. They put you through school. Good for you. When my PI came to me with this information, I was surprised to say the least—a man like you, who fell in love so fucking hard with the glitz and glamour, dealing with crack-heads and drug dealers? Nah. You're fancier than that, Jordi. That's why you struck a deal with MNE Pharmaceuticals. They provide you with prescription drugs. Have been for twenty years now. Oxy. Ambien. Vicodin. Xanax. Valium. Codeine. I can continue, but you get the picture. You got them. You sold them through hundreds of salespeople you have carefully targeted and trained. You laundered the money through offshore companies, and that's how you managed to invest in new companies and become the mogul you are today. But fucking up strangers' lives wasn't enough, was it, Jordan?"

His face was so white I thought he was going to faint. I didn't help him when his legs failed him and he crashed to the floor. My shoes next to his face, the only thing he saw from his position.

"I dug even *deeper*," I continued.

"Stop, stop," he choked, spluttering saliva all over like a fucking pussy. I chose the exact same time to wipe his desk of the documents I'd prepared on it in advance, making it rain statements and pictures of him meeting with the CEO of MNE and checking big trucks full of boxes containing drugs.

"I was wondering about that pretty wife of yours." My voice was velvet, almost soft. "I mean, Edie got her beauty from somewhere, and it sure as fuck wasn't from you. My PI told me that your better half barely leaves the house anymore, which is sad, really, but also suspicious. And oh so fucking convenient."

He got up on his knees—shit, on his fucking knees—and crawled toward me. This had escalated so quickly, I couldn't keep a straight face. Then again, I couldn't exactly laugh at him, either. This wasn't a joke.

"No. No. No. You don't have any evidence," he kept chanting, clutching my legs. I took a step back, repulsed by his eerie behavior.

"I clearly do." I pushed one picture of him next to a truck at the pier in his direction with the tip of my derby shoe. "You're not the only one who knows how to use a goddamn printer."

"Lydia didn't… She never…"

"You fed her drugs. You messed with her prescriptions, didn't you?" I asked dryly. He shook his head. *Liar.* I saw him, under me, and for the first time, it was without the screen of hatred. I saw the boy who wanted to get far and didn't know how. Then I saw the greed. The gluttony. Everything that had ruined Edie's life. I saw it and I knew, without a shadow of a doubt, that regardless of what we were—or weren't—I needed to protect her from her father and his destructive lover, but even more importantly, I wanted them out of the picture. For good.

"Her *tea*," I hissed. "Fuck, Jordi, you got some sick mind."

"I can't go to jail. I can't." He choked on his tears. "I don't…"

"You can't? Well, here's a spoiler for you—the cops are waiting downstairs. Shit. Did I say cops? I meant FBI. Nope, wait, I think it's both. But before I let you leave, you will sign three documents—one handing us Fiscal Heights Holdings in its entirety, one in which you give up custody rights over Theo, and finally, a third one handing over and destroying all your material about me regarding Luna. Your little friend, Val, I'll take care of separately. Wash your fucking face, asshole. There's a lot of work ahead of you. Now, go."

I saw him ushered to the waiting cars. To the men in the sunglasses. To the person who had read him his rights.

In perfect harmony, Jordan's head was ducked into the police car, his hands cuffed behind his back, when Val poured herself out of a cab behind them. She barely had time to straighten her scarlet come-fuck-me dress and fix her film-noir smile when I approached her.

"What's going on?" she half-stuttered, half-begged, clutching at my sleeve. She looked up to me, and I saw Luna in her face. I wish I hadn't. It would have made things so much easier. But essentially, Val was just a child. She proved it over and over again by trying to find a rich guy to babysit her.

And it was funny how people viewed Edie as the kid because of her age when she'd been nothing but a lioness throughout her short life.

"Your boyfriend just got arrested." I shook her—and the spell of her Luna eyes—away from me.

"For what?" She followed me on her impossibly noisy heels.

"You name it." I started walking back into the Oracle building. She tried to keep up with my pace, stumbling her way behind me.

"What for?"

"To sign all the papers so I can get full custody of Luna."

"Why would I give her to you?" She tried to laugh. Failed.

I stopped, turning around to face her. "Hey, remember when we first met? You were coked out of your ass, and shortly after the whole pregnancy revelation, I had to throw you into rehab so you could get better and not fill my kid with enough drugs to grow a second head.

And that was before I knew your side piece is the lord of drugs. Care to piss in a cup for me, Valenciana, dear?"

Her face drained of blood, and I could see how it seeped, slowly but surely. The fear. Val was using. Jordan provided drugs to her. She swallowed hard. I stepped aside, motioning with my hand for her to enter the elevator.

"Ladies first."

She walked in, knowing exactly what was going to happen once we got to my office.

CHAPTER THIRTY-TWO
TRENT

"I love it when we get fucking vicious." Dean lit a joint, sprawled on a settee in front of Vicious's Olympic-size pool, throwing the spent match in the latter's direction. "No pun intended, asshole."

"Ha-fucking-ha," Vicious said, popping a grape into his mouth, lying on a lounger like a mad, entitled king. "But I have to say, the look on Val's face when she signed those papers? Priceless. I'd feel sorry for her if it wasn't for the fact that she hadn't even asked about Luna. Bet she ran off to the nearest bar to try to score some rich old businessman before the happy hour was up."

Vicious thumbed through the documents we'd examined earlier that week with Eli Cole, Dean's lawyer dad. The last couple of days had been hectic, with each of us running around like a headless chicken trying to block every single evil plan Jordan Van Der Zee had concocted for me. I had my friends to help me, and they were there, hound dogs out for blood. "Your ex-girlfriend saved your ass. Thank fuck she is no longer a minor and can testify the shit out of her dad's wrongdoings."

My stomach dropped at his last sentence, and I rolled my lower lip between my fingers, playing it off. I sat on the edge of the low table, trying to look like my heart hadn't burned into ashes at mere mention of her. When I'd sent Dean, Vicious, and Jaime after her, the rules had been clear—no telling her about Jordan and Val. I didn't want her sympathy, and I didn't want her to knock on my fucking door with crocodile tears.

Even though I wanted to knock on her door all the goddamn time.

Luna was with my parents. It was way past midnight—she was safe and sound and *mine*—and still, the hunger was there. The hole in the pit of my stomach sucked all my feelings and spat them back out into something numb.

"Edie talked?" I asked.

Dean laughed. "Talked? She sang like a fucking canary. She gave us so much information about how abusive Jordan was toward his son and her. Yeah, Edie padded us real good with all the info we needed. Why do you think Amanda gave you a bulletproof case? Edie told us about the abuse, the neglect, the bruising grips. Then she mentioned something about her dad constantly making her mother tea, and the addict in me got inspired and put two and two together. He drugged her mother. She just didn't fucking realize it."

The tea. All the info I got had been through Amanda. But a lot of what she'd given me had been patched from the cloths my friends and Edie had produced.

"Edie also hooked us up with the woman helping her with her brother's case—your little friend, Sonya." Dean's lips curved into a knowing smile. We were all sitting in front of the pool, but our bodies were tilted to one another. A huge stone lifted from my heart, and I began to breathe again, coughing out the sweet, rancid smoke inside my lungs.

"How the fuck did Edie have Sonya's contact info?" I gritted my teeth.

"Sonya is her best friend's mother," Vicious supplied, opening his arms in a check-out-this-shit-show gesture.

My jaw locked. "Bane?"

"Five points to the man with the sixteen-inch dick." Dean clapped.

"That motherfucker." Jaime laughed. "You should have seen the stare-down between him and Vicious. Vicious straight up asked him if he was his made-in-China version."

The four of us shared a low chuckle before Vicious arched an eyebrow. "Hey, asshole?" he called to me from his lounger.

I looked up from my joint. "Yeah?"

"Do you miss her?"

Vicious was not the kind of asshole to pillow talk—not with his wife and sure as hell not with his friends—so I knew he had a motive. The lie danced on my tongue. No matter how big and tall and old and rich you were, when asked about the girl who'd broken your heart into a thousand pieces, you'd always be the thirteen-year-old kid who still didn't know what to do with his hard dick and out-of-control hormones.

I shrugged.

"Answer with words, Mute," he pressed.

All eyes were on me. I looked away to the pool, squinting. "She's in my fucking blood," I admitted.

Vicious got up, shoved his hand into his pocket, and threw something small in my direction. I caught it, opening my palm and staring at it in disbelief.

I looked back up. He shook his head.

"She never gave this to Jordan, Trent. She couldn't do it."

Dean leaned toward me from his lounger, nudging his shoulder against mine. "Did you hear that, fuckface? You finally got someone to love your cold ass. You need to put that shit on lockdown because she is still young and naive enough to like you."

I clutched the flash drive in my fist. I swore it smelled like her.

Later that night, I sat in my car and stared at it, thinking it could be so easy. I could ignore it. I could move forward with my life. We wouldn't have to deal with how I'd locked her father up in jail and the judgmental stares and the uncomfortable questions and the fucking gossip.

We were already apart, and we were surviving just fine.

The flash drive dug into the skin of my palm until I bled. Then, and only then, I started the car and drove away.

CHAPTER THIRTY-THREE
EDIE

The worst parts were the nights.

When I couldn't feel his body next to mine as I lay on Bane's sofa. The memory of him was a weapon against me. His lips brushing the back of my neck like a lion about to dig into his mate and fuck her raw. His hands running along my arms like he was undressing me from all my hang-ups, worries, and dark thoughts. His warm, slow breaths against my mouth. His pulse beating against mine. Was life worth living without these moments?

Every time I asked myself this question, I pushed the thought away and turned to the other side of the couch, either fighting the yellow itchy fabric of the back of the sofa or squinting away from the light of the TV in Bane's cabin, which was directly in front of me. Bane had been great about giving me a place to stay without asking when I was going to move or to chip in on any costs for groceries. He did not, however, stop for a second his wild, rough life. Not that I'd expected him to, but with Mom in rehab and my father in jail, I really had nowhere to go. Mom's lawyer had offered to rent me a room in a hotel, but that was just more money I couldn't afford— and who in the hell wanted to be alone in my situation? I needed a distraction. Human contact.

Bane screwed other people in his room like he was trying to break some kind of record.

They were loud and lewd, and there wasn't a door separating his bedroom from the tiny living area.

But every time I thought about packing a bag and going to a hotel, I remembered the thoughts about the unknown with Theo. And the known and devastating truth about. I couldn't deal with either thought, and so, I changed my mind.

This was another night on the sofa.

Tick, tock. Tick, tock.

I wished Bane had gotten rid of that clock after he'd gotten this boat. It seemed to have served as a reminder it'd been days since I'd seen both Trent and Theo.

And Luna. God, I missed Luna more than I'd expected to. The little sounds she made when she was amused or eager. They'd been my trophies for making her smile.

In the distance, I heard fishermen walking, chatting, and spitting, their heavy steps making the wood beneath their rubber shoes creak. It must've been nearly dawn. They always came before the sun was out. Funny, the things you learned about a new place to make it your home. Noises, sounds, habits, people, smells…

The boat creaked.

That was the thing about living on a boat. Everything threw your world off-balance. Bane loved it. Living on the edge of everything. Me, I craved stability. I wanted to feel like I was rooted into the ground, not blowing in the wind.

Something dropped outside on the deck. Something…light. I craned my neck, peering toward the small window by the door. It was dirty and made of cheap plastic. But I could see something. Someone. Someone who shouldn't have been there.

Carefully, I got up from the sofa and tiptoed to the makeshift kitchen. An open jar of peanut butter was on the counter and a half-licked sharp knife on the edge of the sink.

I grabbed it, for once thankful Bane had the tendency to use a steak knife to make anything, even peanut butter and jelly sandwiches.

I passed by Bane's open room, wondering if I should wake him up. Probably not. It was probably one of his drunk friends, passing out on the deck or pissing into the bucket he kept there for when he went fishing. Slipping into my Dr. Martens, I opened the door a few inches and peeked outside through the slit.

Nothing.

No one.

I looked down. There was a pile of seashells waiting in front of the door. I opened it wider and walked out. The shells were the same kind. Yellow prickly cockle. Not too rare, but your chances of picking a handful of seashells and finding the exact same type were slim. Seashells were like people. They differed in size, color, and shape, but all were beautiful all the same. I squatted down, taking one in my hand. It was still cold and fresh from the ocean. I squinted my eyes, staring ahead at the pink, purple, and blue of the sunrise, looking for the person who'd left them, when my eyes rested on another pile by the stairway leading to the deck.

More shells.

Walking over to where they were, my heart began to pound more furiously. A cluster of jewel box shells, rare and gorgeous, was waiting for me. Cold. Fresh. *How?*

I picked one and pocketed it along with the prickly cockle. Then moved forward, descending to the pier, where another pile waited.

Rose Murex. I pocketed one. Moved forward.

Periwinkle. Jesus, how? *How?* Pocket.

I jogged from the pier to the promenade, eager to find out the meaning of all this.

Lion's paw.

Banded tulip.

Turrid.

Pointed Venus, and I was so far from the marina, I had to look up and see where I'd stopped. There were no more shells to collect, and I was standing in the middle of the promenade, panting, still wearing an oversized shirt I'd borrowed from Bane, my hair a matted mess. I looked around me. All the shops were closed. What did it mean? What in the hell was happening here?

Pointed Venus.

Where was it pointing? I looked straight in the direction of the sharp edge of the shell. It was an alleyway. An alleyway I remembered. An alleyway where I'd left one of my sweetest, roughest, most heart-defining memories.

It was where Trent had shoved me against the wall for the first time, threatening me, taunting me, calling me out on my bullshit.

On shaking legs, I crossed the road. My whole body was humming a song I didn't know. I felt so alive I thought I was going to scream. The hope it filled me with was dangerous. It threatened to crush me to pieces if it was wrong. I walked into the bluish dawn readily, knowing it could give me all the light I needed.

"Trent?" His name sounded like a wish. What was I doing, hoping to see him there?

But I heard nothing. I took another step, pressing my back against the same wall, at the same spot we'd met for the first time, closing my eyes and taking a deep breath.

"Please," I said.

"Please, what?" His voice came out of nowhere. I didn't open my eyes. Maybe it was just my imagination. Maybe I'd gone crazy. And perhaps I didn't care anymore. I couldn't risk opening my eyes and not seeing him there, so I kept them closed.

"Please forgive me."

"For what?"

"For trying to ruin you. For trying to ruin myself, *us.* For not trusting myself enough to do the right thing about my father and Theo for so long. For being a coward. But most of all, I am sorry for not telling you how I felt. Because maybe then you'd have taken a step back and none of that would have happened."

"What are you feeling, Edie?" He cupped my cheek in his big, warm palm, and that was how I knew it was real. That *he* was real. My eyes snapped open, and he was there, in front of me, in the flesh. The man who filled my heart with music with his silence.

"I…" My mouth parted, but I couldn't finish the sentence. His lips slammed into mine in a desperate kiss that made my head spin and sucked the air from my lungs. His lips sucked mine, comforting me with their sweet warmth, and I gripped his flexed forearms, pulling him closer.

"You never gave Jordan the flash drive," Trent said.

I wanted to cry. Every night, I'd lain in bed praying he'd somehow figure it out without me telling him. I didn't want him to have to choose between Val and me.

"How could I?" I moaned into his lips. "How could I when you're my ocean."

We drowned in another kiss. A different kiss. A kiss of affirmation. That this was real. And no matter how twisted and wrong and bad it looked—and sometimes felt—it was also ours.

"I don't want to come between you and the mother of your child," I whimpered into his mouth so pathetically, I had to claw my fingers deeper into the skin of his arm to keep him close. Shockingly, he gave me what I wanted, gluing his body to mine, giving me everything he could.

"The mother of my child came between her relationship with Luna, not you. You were the one who taught Luna to smile. You were the one who spent time with her. Who fucking took her by the hand when she was bullied. You're more of a mother to my daughter than Val would ever be. I don't know what you saw the day when Val came to my apartment, but whatever it was, you got the wrong idea. She never gave a shit about her kid. She came here to claim money and power. And she is going to crawl back to where she came from."

"I'm so sorry." I touched his face, pulling away, staring at him.

"I'm not," he said. "I'm also not sorry for sending your father to jail. Edie, he did some terrible things that you need to know about."

I nodded. "I believe you." And I did. I'd already heard some of them. No matter what Trent would tell me about my father, I knew he would be telling the truth. Because Jordan Van Der Zee had absolutely no limits.

Trent kissed my nose softly, his forehead dropping to mine. "I love you," he said, cupping my neck from both sides and shaking his head in exasperation, like this was a mistake. Like he shouldn't be loving me but had no other choice. My heart swelled. "I'm so fucking in love with you, Edie Van Der Zee, I don't know where I end and where you begin anymore. I love you despite knowing that it is crazy. That our situations are disastrous. I love you knowing that you should have at least a few more experiences before you find *the* love. I love you even though we're not at the same place in life, have nothing in common, and started off so fucking bad. And still, I love you."

"I love you." I sniffed, holding back my tears, pressing my forehead deeper to his. "I love how fierce you are when it comes to the people you care about. I love that you're so aware of your flaws. I love that you fight them. I even love it when you succumb to them. I love every single part of you. The good and the bad. And I will never love anyone else the way I do you because it's not about my age. It's about my heart. It belongs to you. Trent Rexroth, you're my ocean. You make me wet."

He grinned, pulling me into a tight hug. "I would have come for you, Van Der Zee, even if you had given him the flash drive. Even if you threw me in the lion's den. And I promise to never stop making you wet, my Little Tide. Promise to always keep you drenched."

EPILOGUE
EDIE

The door slams, and I know exactly who it is.

The only person in the house to treat doors like they have somehow wronged him and the universe. Crass movements, gentle heart.

"N-n-no! Never again!" Theo bellows, kicking his muddy shoes in the hallway. "I'm d-d-done playing football. I'm no g-g-good at it."

"What the hell are you talking about? You can tackle a fucking elephant to the floor if need be."

"Trent," I singsong from the kitchen, smiling to keep myself from scowling. No matter how much time passes, no matter that we live with thirteen-year-old Theo and five-year-old Luna, my boyfriend still can't seem to let go of the word (and act) *fuck*. In fact, he drops enough f-bombs to wipe away our whole continent. "Language."

"Yes, M-m-mom," Theo mocks me from the hallway, wearing his new confidence like a cape. I stand in the kitchen, looking over my shoulder at my mother, who is cutting vegetables on a board with an unsolicited grin. I'm glad she doesn't mind that Theo calls me that sometimes. Glad she knows it's just a joke.

"Your child is out of control," I note, dumping the diced steak into the hot frying pan.

"In my defense, you were the one to raise him for the majority of his life," she says with melancholic acceptance. She comes to our house every weekend to spend time with him and Luna. And every Thursday, Trent and I go out, and Camila watches the kids.

Every Thursday, we act our ages. Well, my age, anyway.

Every Thursday, we make out in cars, let abandoned city halls swallow us in darkness, go to the movies and restaurants and clubs where I don't have to worry about a fake ID because my boyfriend is influential enough to own this city.

We live in a house with tides and lows. Where the ocean is always stormy, but that's okay because we're great swimmers. We live in a house of seahorses, of survivors, of people who have tasted the other side of life. People who stood on the sidelines, begging to go unnoticed.

But we notice. We notice each other in this chaos called life.

We go down to Tobago Beach every weekend to surf and eat and laugh and not give a damn. Not about the world and not about the money.

Luna and Theo love each other. They bathe each other in mutual respect and attention, and it is heartbreaking and wonderful to watch. He finally gets to be the responsible older sibling, and she gets to have a fierce big brother. She has a room that is blue, with an aquarium of seahorses, and he's got a room that's green, with posters of Tom Brady Trent manages not to rip off the walls—but just barely.

And then there's us. Me. Trent. Our love.

Our love draws attention like a wildfire. We're a biracial couple with a huge age gap. We carry baggage in the form of two kids. It looks bad. Tragic, even. Not half as photogenic as Vicious's perfect little family or Jaime's gorgeous fair-haired nest or Dean's sweet, no age-gap, no-nonsense household.

We're different, and we wouldn't change it for the world.

Trent, Theo, and Luna saunter into the kitchen with huge grins on their faces. Luna is the first to jump on me with a hug. She still doesn't talk, but she does communicate using sign language. And it's a huge step forward.

"The boys kept you busy?" I ask, feeling her long, thin limbs enveloping me as I return a hug. She nods into my shoulder. When we disconnect, she signs me the words *Theo almost killed a swan throwing the ball.*

"That's…" I wrinkle my forehead. "Very bad."

"He was just eager." Trent ambles toward me, planting a kiss on my forehead, a bottle of water already in his hand. My mother gets the same treatment—only a kiss on the cheek—and Theo is trying to help Mom now.

"Not before you wash your hands, bud," I warn. He scoffs but walks over to the sink. The steak is sizzling in the pan, and the kitchen is warm with food and company and love. With family. With everything I didn't have at my parents' house.

Trent comes behind me and whispers into my neck, "A word."

"I'm cooking," I protest, but not really. Living with two kids with special needs, we've mastered the art of sneaking out for quickies. Though this is too much, even by our standards. I mean, they're all right here. I can't be that quiet. Not with him.

"I don't care," he growls like the HotHole he is. Ruthless. Cold. But always full of heart.

I cut my gaze from the food I am cooking to my mother and kids. Yes. *My kids.*

Trent does the same, frowning. "Get your mind out of the gutter, Edie. If it was a quick fuck I was after, these people behind us would have been eating McJunk down the road, safely locked outside this house."

I laugh because I can't help it. I've already come to terms with the fact my boyfriend is a grade A jerk. Most of the time, I'm not even mad about it. It is actually pretty charming, in a screwed-up way.

"I can't leave Mom with both kids," I say under my breath, a trickle of panic seeping into my heart. Not that I don't trust my mother, but she's come a long way in a very short period of time, and I don't want her to feel overwhelmed by taking care of two kids.

"Yeah, you're right." His hand brushes my ass so deliberately it is almost comical, as he moves to the stove and picks a piece of juicy meat, crushing it between his white teeth and chewing.

Just as he says it, Emilia and Rosie walk into my kitchen, holding brown bags with fresh food peeking from their edges.

"Hey, everyone!" Emilia greets, while Rosie opts for a "You guys, turn on the air-con before I melt on your floor. Aren't these new tiles? Yeah, turn that thing on. There are too many people in this room."

"What are you doing here?" My eyes are wide. In the past year, Emilia, Melody, and Rosie have become great friends of mine. And although Melody is the older wolf in the pack—the one I turn to when Luna drives me mad and Theo is acting crazy—the two LeBlanc sisters are the two female BFFs I never thought I would have.

"We're giving you a day off. You deserve it." Emilia nudges me away with her butt, winking playfully. I don't argue with that, even though I don't feel like I should take a break. I love my life. Every morning, I take Theo and Luna to school then go to the beach and teach people how to surf. In the afternoons, before I pick them up, I have lunch with my hot boyfriend, and then we have sex before we pick up the kids. Then he cooks, and rubs my feet in front of Netflix after dinner. I don't deserve a vacation. I'm living it.

"But I…"

"Don't argue, Tide." Trent grabs my wrist, tugging me into his hard body. Even now, after a year of living together, I melt a little at that gesture. Like that morning in the alleyway never changed us. Like I am still a love-struck puppy with a bad case of unreciprocated love.

He leads me outside, the pan still sizzling behind me, but I can already hear Rosie lowering the fire on the stove and Emilia cracking open a bottle of wine.

"What's happening?" I ask Trent when we go out to the porch—ocean view—on the promenade.

"I'm not sure, but I think I'm losing my balls in the process." He grimaces.

I laugh. "What? Why?"

"Because"—he opens the door and red light pours in, and I am standing in front of nature in its rarest beauty—"the sunset has never looked so fucking amazing, and if we could have one perfect moment, I want it to be this one."

"That's why you asked Rosie and Emilia to come here?" I quirk an eyebrow.

"Nope." He turns to face me, brushing his thumb over my cheek. His eyes are light, his soul is dark, and everything else about what he gives me is full of colors. "I called them here in case you say yes."

"Yes?"

"Yes to my crazy-ass idea." He kneels down on one knee, in front of the sunset, with cyclists and joggers and couples passing by us, and produces something from his pocket. He is still wearing his workout gear from taking Luna and Theo to the park, and that just makes him look even sexier. What's insane about this—other than the fact we've never talked about it, not even once—is that I'm not nervous in any way. Just excited. We already feel like a married couple, and I say that in the best, least boring way possible. He is stability and love. Security and confidence.

I'm his tide, and he's my anchor. Or maybe the sand itself.

"Edie Van Der Zee, I want to dip my toes in the waves you make every single day for the rest of my miserable life. I want to fuck you—just you, only you, no one else—and a lot. Every. Single. Day. I want to live with you. I want to parade that fucked-up thing we have that keeps people raising eyebrows and thinking I'm a cradle-snatching douchebag because fuck 'em, they'll never have what we have. Will you marry me? I don't ask for a lot. Not for kids, not for dinner, not for anything to be done in the house. I don't ask you for anything other than what you're willing to give me."

Luna peeks from the door, smiling. I turn my body to her,

smiling. I expect her to sign me something. Something like "aw, gross" or "Daddy is being silly again". But she doesn't.

Instead, she arches one eyebrow, opens her lips, and lets the words fall out, awarding her father with the best present he could ever have.

"Say yes."

TRENT

Up until Edie, December was my favorite month of the year.

Not because of Christmas. Fuck Christmas. Because of the cold. It was the only month when it felt for a second that SoCal wasn't going to burst into flames next time someone lit a match. Years ago, when Fiscal Heights Holdings opened a branch in Chicago, I was on that shit like a rash at a community college party. I loved the winter. Loved. Past tense.

I hate the winter nowadays.

I still enjoy feeling like the sun is not trying to fucking kill me, but I don't like seeing Edie running barefoot across the promenade, a surfboard tucked under her arm, laughing like a crazy kid between the fat pearls of raindrops. Sometimes I run after her and tackle her to the sand for breathless kisses, trying to convince her to calm the fuck down and pass on her morning surf session. Most times I know it's futile.

The ocean is her drug.

She is mine.

To accommodate this shit, I move things around. And it's funny, how I always thought I'd die alone, and suddenly, I have all these people around me. Theo and his weird love for Tom Brady, Luna and her noisy, mostly content silence, and my soon-to-be wife.

First thing I did after throwing Jordan Van Der Zee into

jail—he's a white-collar bastard who gets lots of visitation rights and perks, but no one wants to see him: not his ex-wife, not his kids, and certainly not Val, God knows where she is—was to buy the surf club on Tobago Beach. I wanted Edie to have flexible working hours, and now she's her own boss. The second thing was to summon my three friends and partners and tell them I was going to cut back on the hours, majorly.

"I have a family now. A big-ass, in-your-face family with a crap ton of needs and a tight schedule," I explained. Dean smiled.

Vicious said, "Another one bites the dust."

Jaime nodded. "We've got your back."

And they do. They have my back all the time. So much so that they weren't even horrified when I told them I was asking my nineteen-year-old girlfriend to marry me. It's absurd. You think I don't fucking know that? Think again. We should wait until she hits her twenties.

We should keep it on the down-low.

We shouldn't display this. We shouldn't draw attention. We shouldn't make declarations.

And we don't. Fucking. Care.

"Mr. Rexroth, your...ah...Edie is here to see you," Rina informs me through the intercom. I toy with the idea of correcting her—fiancée, that's who Edie is. Shortly after she said yes in front of the most beautiful sunset to ever be seen in SoCal, a cab took us to the airport for a Hawaiian weekend. She surfed a lot. We fucked a lot. The engagement ring was too heavy for her to give me a hand job. You live, you learn. It's now in the safe in our bedroom, collecting dust.

I push the red button on the switchboard while smoothing my tie. "Send her in."

She walks in, unapologetically young. Her body covered in baby-blue short overalls and a yellow tank top. Dr. Martens and a smart-ass smirk. She doesn't have an engagement ring on her finger, and it doesn't make her any less mine. She is too natural for this stone, anyway. She's got a seashell hanging around her neck, a new one—identical to the two she made for Luna and Theo.

"I dropped in to say hi." She waggles her brows, holding a Panda Express bag.

I lean back in my chair and cross my legs over my desk. "I think you came here to fuck because I couldn't come home this afternoon."

"Oh, and that, too." She shrugs, laughing. She dumps the oily food onto my table. I ignore it completely.

"Are you trying to bribe me with food?"

"Actually," she says, walking over to behind my desk and parking her ass on my erection—because I always have an erection when she is around—knotting her arms around my neck, "I was thinking you could look at this wedding catalog with me. It's so weird to plan a wedding. I don't know where to start. Other than Millie and Rosie, all my friends are male and teenagers."

"Don't remind me," I groan. I made peace with Bane, but that doesn't mean I don't keep an eye on the bastard. I place my hands on her waist and pull her in for a dirty, messy kiss that will soon turn into office sex, and we both know it. "I'll help, but when I asked you to marry me, I didn't mean this month. Or this year. I just want to put it out there for the world to know and to see—we're getting fucking married. End of story."

"Yes, but *I* want to marry you soon." She brushes her nose against mine.

"Why? Thirty-four is not actually that old, Tide. I'm not gonna die on you in a year or two."

She swats my chest and laughs. "I just mean I want to be Mrs. Rexroth. I want Theodore to be a Rexroth. I'm ready to change our last name to something we'll both be proud of."

I used to love December, but now I love September.

Because it is in September when a seahorse is kissing a tide, creating a gorgeous fucking wave, and my fiancée places my hand against her stomach. "I think I'm ready for a dynasty."

"I think you're crazy," I reply, but not really. She can have it all. And she knows it.

"Why not both?" She smiles.

This is where it's at. The thing I've been looking for. In those eyes. In those lips. Our story is not perfect. My daughter is still not speaking. I am still the Mute. Theo isn't cured, and Edie is still the product of a fucking asshole.

But imperfection is where we thrive. In the dark alleyways of society where we first met. I take her face in my hands and kiss her again, our teeth clashing together. *Imperfect.*

"Bend over and bite your forearm for me, Edie."

And she does. "I love it when you hurt me."

"I love you when I do and when I don't," I reply, caressing her ass cheek through the fabric of her overalls.

"Strong words, Mr. Rexroth."

"Well, Mrs. Soon-to-Be Rexroth, if you want to be strong—then be strong."

SINNERS OF SAINT CHARACTER INSPIRATION

Baron "Vicious" Spencer—Sean O'Pry

Emilia "Millie" LeBlanc—Emilia Clarke (with pink hair)

Jaime Followhill—Austin Butler

Melody Greene—Juliet Doherty

Trent Rexroth—Jesse Williams

Edie Van Der Zee—Dove Cameron

Rosie LeBlanc—Alexandra Daddario

Dean Cole—Chris Pine

Roman "Bane" Protsenko—Brock O'Hurn

Jesse Carter—Shailene Woodley

BONUS SCENE 1
TRENT

TRENT FINDING OUT HE AND EDIE WILL SHARE AN OFFICE

"Give the man a break!" Blondie shook off her father's deathly grip, her long legs making their way to Vicious, Dean, Jaime, and me. Her silken skin was soaked with sun, the bronze of her skin making her freckles and bright blue eyes pop out. I had the decency not to let my glare slide farther south to the rest of her body. She was a child. At least, I should think of her as one.

"He said he was sorry. Why would he deliberately screw up? Come on. He's got a family to feed!" Her little nostrils flared, cold fire blazing through her eyes.

Dean and Jaime stared at her like she was an adorable little puppy, toothless and powerless. Vicious, however, stared her down like he couldn't wait to shove her into a meat grinder.

"I love this." Dean was the first to recover, slapping Vicious' back good-naturedly with a chuckle. "Bossed around by a teenager. *Cute.*"

I could tell Vicious was losing interest in the whole event. Edie Van Der Zee did not concern him one bit. Just like the rest of the population who wasn't named Emilia LeBlanc-Spencer. He waved Russell away with a snarl, allowing him to see another day. Then Vicious looked around, searching for his next prey. "Secretary!"

he barked, snapping his fingers and conjuring a flustered, newly recruited thirty-something woman, who scrambled toward him with her iPad clutched to her chest. He had long ago given up on the idea of memorizing their names. What was the point, when they kept quitting after less than a week? "Bring me my black ivory coffee," he demanded sullenly.

"Ugh," I heard one of the college student interns sigh behind me dreamily while sorting through filing cabinets. "He has total main character energy."

"Hannibal was a main character, too..." Edie muttered under her breath, only to be heard if you were paying attention to her. We had a smartass on our hands. Great. Problem was, her ass was more than just smart—it was mouthwatering, too.

Great job not noticing, pervert.

"Is this bring-your-kid-to-work day?" I bared my teeth, eager to speed the process of whatever this was along. "Because I don't remember getting the email."

"Edie will be working here for a while," Jordan announced, tugging his rigid daughter back to his side. Her small wince when he touched her did not escape me, and if I found out the asshole was hurting her, neither would he. I had a strict no-hurting-women policy.

"Says who?" I drawled.

"Says me."

"I haven't agreed to that. None of us have," I pointed out.

"Then it's a good thing I didn't ask." Jordan's lemur fingers constricted around Edie's arm, and anger unfurled in the pit of my stomach. My skin scorched where he touched her, like I could feel her desperation and pain. I started moving toward them, mainly to show Jordan he needed to back the hell off and take his hand off his daughter's arm.

"With all due respect to white, upper-class nepotism and awarding your underqualified daughter with a job most deserving candidates would kill for, every major HR decision goes through all of the partners, correct?" I turned to look at Dean, Jaime, and Vicious. The three nodded solemnly. It didn't matter if I had told Jordan he needed to wear a fruit bowl as a hat for the remainder of the day. They'd still agree. We always had each other's backs.

"For God's sake, Rexroth! She is going to be an assistant, not an account manager!" Jordan's fingers now dug violently into the gentle skin on his daughter's arm, and my anger morphed into a stone-cold need to murder the man. I didn't know if I felt protective of her as a man seeing a woman in distress or as a father to a daughter myself, but what I did know was that I absolutely did not need this fucking distraction in my life. Caring for others was not on my agenda. I had my hands full as it was.

"She is going to be on this floor"—I glanced at my watch— "have access to our things. I don't care if her job is to peel bananas in the kitchen. This goes to a board meeting tomorrow morning. End of discussion."

Everybody in the office stared at me in shock. I couldn't blame them. I rarely spoke. Aimless chatter did not interest me. Small talk downright disgusted me. I only talked when I had something important to say, and as it stood, I only had words for my family, friends, and daughter.

"You're really going to fight me over this." Jordan rubbed his cheek with his knuckles, shock marring his face. I dipped my head down to look him straight in the eye. A wry smile tugged at the corners of my mouth, my voice dropping into a venomous whisper. "I would fight you to death over anything, Jordan, including the service provider for the coffee machine, if need be."

"Fine." Jordan bared his teeth. "We'll take it to the boardroom."

Jordan finally—*finally*—let go of her arm, making me heave a sigh of relief. He scurried off to Dean, Jaime, and Vicious, no doubt about to plead his case as to why they should hire his experience-less, barely legal child.

My eyes traveled to his daughter, who stood beside him, tall and defiant, chin held up high. She was perfect in every way that I could count. From her thick, fluffy eyebrows to the slope of her button nose, to the way her top-heavy rosy lips looked like her mouth was stuck in a permanent kiss. She was young, *too* young, the kind of young that made you feel guilty just for looking.

"I don't like you," I said, more to myself than to her. Her scent trickled into my system, and I could barely keep my eyes from rolling to the back of my fucking head. She smelled like exotic, sandy beaches, brine, and coconut oil. Like summer and adventure and the raw beauty of nature.

"I never asked you to." She shrugged carelessly.

"You won't be working here."

"Good. You'll be doing me a favor. My father is the one forcing me to work here. He's pissed I turned down five Ivy League colleges. Remind me, Mr. Rexroth—which top-tier university did you attend for your degree?"

Ah, so she'd read my *Forbes* interview. I went to a shitty state college. *By choice.* I'd received countless offers from Ivy League schools, offering full rides and perks. I'd rejected them all, opting to stick around next to my parents.

I smiled, the kind of patient, fatherly smile I offered Luna whenever she colored out of the lines, which wasn't very often, because she was exceptionally talented. "Edie." My lips were almost at her ear, my breath grazing the shell of it, and we were close, so close her heat seeped into my body, like sunshine penetrating through the skin. "If you know what's best for you, you will turn around and leave right now."

She tilted her head up, catching my gaze again, and smiled back, her expression resolute. "I think I'm going to find my desk now. I'd wish you a good day, Mr. Rexroth, but I think that ship has sailed. You're a miserable man. Oh, and one for the road." She buried her hand into her purse and fished something out, pressing it against my chest. Her touch made every cell in my body fucking riot. I was no virgin. Far from it. But a simple touch had never made my heart accelerate like it did when Edie Van Der Zee was so close to it. A sign I should stay as far away from her as humanly possible.

Edie turned around and walked away, leaving me with my hand on my chest to protect whatever she'd slammed against it. It took me a full ten seconds to recover and look down at my hand, unfurling my fingers to see what it was she left behind.

A Nature Valley bar.

I'd avoided temptation my entire life, only to have it hurl itself into my life in a skintight pencil skirt. Those sad, perceptive eyes were going to haunt me.

And, in time, drown me, too.

BONUS SCENE 2
TRENT

DURING VICIOUS'S BARBECUE

"I think it's time to make some popcorn, kids. These two are going to give us the best show this town has to offer." Vicious guided Vaughn and Knight out of the room by their little shoulders, turning around and making his way down the corridor and back outside.

Edie and I took a breath, sweaty and shaking with desire. Our lips were swollen. I couldn't believe I'd fucking kissed someone, much less that I'd kissed my daughter's nanny. My enemy's daughter.

You idiot.

Worst still, the look on Edie's face was unmistakable. Under the hazy, lust-drunk expression lay something else, deeper—a connection. A line had been crossed. We'd shared a moment, an emotional one, and I could tell it had changed something in her. I couldn't fucking take those eyes. They were full of trust and expectation.

"I'll help you with your top." I turned her around so her back was to me and began fastening her corset-like shirt that had loosened when we'd made out. Her tits spilled out of it, her nipples taut and hard as diamonds, making my cock strain against my zipper. I caught the strings that held her top together and weaved them in a crisscross pattern. She sucked in a breath. "That was…hmm, something."

"It was nothing," I retorted, hating myself for saying that, but saying it anyway. I'd just witnessed my daughter being bullied by Daria and nearly detonated the entire world. Loving someone was a weakness, and loving Edie specifically had the potential to ruin me. A few years ago, I probably would have taken that risk. But not today. I had a daughter to take care of. She came first.

"Keep telling yourself that if you want. We both know it's not true." She put on an airy tone, but I could hear the strain in her voice. I tugged the strings of her top toward me hard in one movement, making her back plaster against my pecs and abs as I put my mouth to the back of her ear, cupping her jaw from behind. "It's not me I'm telling this to, Little Tide. My cock is free of charge, but my heart is priceless. Not for the taking." I tried to keep our hookup light, casual.

Winning hearts and minds, Trent. As per fucking usual.

Edie's shoulder blades tensed against my pecs, and she drew a sharp breath. Goddammit, why couldn't she see this was a bad idea? Beyond getting each other's rocks off, we were not compatible in any way. Even if I put aside the fact that she was going for my fucking neck, I was too old, too damaged for her.

"Is that all this is?" Edie finally piped up. "You giving me your cock 'free of charge'?"

I tipped my head backwards, closing my eyes, before dropping a kiss on the crown of her head as I tied the laces of her top, securing it on her torso.

"There is nothing I could offer you," I said regrettably. "Not any of the things you deserve. The important ones." I had wealth, power, and reputation. The ingredients most women her age were drawn to. But Edie wasn't most women. She needed love and care. Someone to hold her hand while she wielded her sword at the villains she was fighting. And I couldn't be that person for her. I had my own princess to save—Luna.

"I'm not saying I want you to give me the world. I'm not even saying I want to become a part of yours." She swiveled to catch my gaze, pressing her palm to my chest. She put enough distance between us to sail a boat. And I didn't know why, but it felt like a punishment. "But I refuse to be objectified. I know I'm more than just a hookup to you, Trent, so stop acting like I'm disposable."

I caught her waist in my hands, pulling her to me again to steal another kiss. Our groins clashed, her heat meeting my cock through the barrier of our clothes. It wasn't the only thing I wanted to steal of hers. I wanted all of her smiles, laughs, and secrets. I wanted every blowjob and orgasm. Fuck, I was a greedy bastard when it came to her. My mouth came crushing down on hers, my tongue finding its way to the farthest corners of her mouth, stroking, massaging, claiming her as our bodies fused together again. We molded into one another instantly, like an octopus enveloping a starfish. Glued everywhere. And still, it wasn't enough.

"You're not disposable," I growled into her mouth, meaning it. "I'd make you a permanent feature if it wasn't for our circumstances. Never doubt your worth, Edie Van Der Zee. Because to me, you are everything." I sucked her lower lip into my mouth, flicking my tongue over it, nibbling on her sweetness. She made happy, greedy sounds that trickled their way to the pit of my stomach, hitting roots, making something liquid and warm spread there.

"Feel free to put a price tag on me," she retorted, grinning into our kiss, deepening it still, her arms enfolding me. "A hundred K sound good?"

"Your annual salary is sixty K." I removed my mouth from hers begrudgingly.

"Hmm." She extended her neck, giving me access to the sensitive skin of her throat as I found the place where her pulse throbbed, licking and sucking it. "That's the price I charge for bosses who *don't* put their dick inside me. Girl math."

"Boy death, if any such boss other than me exists." I forced myself to withdraw from her, giving her ass a gentle pat to let her know our make-out session was over.

She tilted one shoulder up, nestling her chin on top of it demurely. "Don't tell me you're jealous?"

I used my thumb and index finger to tilt her chin up. "Sweetheart, as long as it's you and me, it is *only* you and me."

We dragged ourselves out of Vicious and Emilia's house and out to the backyard. Barely. It was pure torture to rearrange my cock in my pants, considering ninety percent of my blood was currently nestled inside it. I almost chuckled to myself at how adolescent it all felt. Being driven to insanity by an actual *teenager*.

When we reached our friends, I immediately approached Dean and Jaime, who were now squirting ketchup and ranch onto the kids' paper plates, sticky fingers reaching to touch their faces.

"Took you long enough." Jaime dodged a dimpled toddler hand that tried to squeeze out his eyeball. "Don't tell me that you forgot your way around one of your best friends' houses."

"I had business to take care of." I reached down to kiss Luna's head. "Had to...tidy up Vaughn's room." *Really? Did I just give him a my-dog-ate-my-homework excuse?*

"Masterful gambit, sir." Dean brought his root beer bottle to his forehead in mock salute.

I flicked the back of his neck, shaking my head. "Shut up, idiot."

ACKNOWLEDGMENTS

Writing is a lonely job, which is why it is always important to have your tribe. I feel like I'm a part of something, a group that is always there to hold my hand (and I need a lot of hand-holding when I write, trust me). I would like to personally thank the following people:

To my editing team, who is there for me every step of the way. Tamara Mataya, you're a fantastically intelligent and witty human being. Bex Harper, you know how to bring the emotion out of everything. Paige Smith, you have such an eye for detail. You would probably make a great detective if the editing gig gets too boring for you at some point.

Special thanks to my beta readers, Ella Fox, Ava Harrison, Amy Halter, Danielle McDonald, Charleigh Rose, and Paige Jennifer. You are so, so good at what you do. Never leave me, okay? Ever.

To my agent, Kimberly Brower, for all the hard work you put in so my books are everywhere. To Letitia Hasser of RBA Design, you're one talented chick. Thank you for always getting it right. To Stacey Blake of Champagne Formatting, you make my books so pretty from the inside.

To my street team, Avivit, Lin, Kristina, Vane, Sabrina, Summer, Jennifer, Tijuana, Sher, Betty, Oriana, Sheena, Ilor, Jennifer, Becca, Julia, Josephine, Jacquie, Amanda, Erika, Sonal,

Ofa, and Vanessa, God, you're so amazing. You put a smile on my face every single day.

To the Sassy Sparrows group, thank you so much for everything. You're the best reading group an author could ever have. You got me addicted, hooked, and completely obsessed with this group!

To the bloggers who push my books so, *so* hard! You make my job worthwhile. I want you to know I see you. You're appreciated. You're loved. You're respected. Always.

To my family and friends for putting up with the long hours I spend in my office. Seriously, you guys are the best.

Finally, to my readers, thank you for taking the time and reading this book. You make my dream come true every time you decide to take a chance on me, and for that, I am forever grateful. Please consider leaving an honest review before you move on to the next book adventure.

Love (so, so much),

L.J. Shen xoxo

ABOUT THE AUTHOR

L.J. Shen is a *USA Today*, *Wall Street Journal*, *Washington Post*, and #1 Amazon Kindle Store bestselling author of contemporary romance books. She writes angsty books, unredeemable anti-heroes who are in Elon Musk's tax bracket, and sassy heroines who bring them to their knees (for more reasons than one). HEAs and groveling are guaranteed. She lives in Florida with her husband, her three sons, and a disturbingly active imagination.

Website: authorljshen.com
Facebook: authorljshen
Instagram: @authorljshen
TikTok: @authorljshen
Pinterest: @authorljshen